LEAGUE OF ANGELS

THOMAS TAN

This book is gratefully dedicated to
Stefanie Ann, whose love and support
made it possible for me to fight the good fight,
to run the race, and to keep the faith.

†

For it is not against human enemies that we have to struggle, but against the Sovereignties and the Powers who originate the darkness in this world, the spiritual army of evil in the heavens
– Ephesians 6:12

Chapter 1

Bernini's columns rose like ancient guards encircling the people on that day, their gigantic arms stretching out to draw in every tribe and nation, embracing the crowds like a mother drawing her children to her bosom. The sun was high but the last breath of winter was still blowing through the winds. An icy chill swept over the square, but the weather didn't seem to dampen the mood. You could feel the energy in the crowd rising with every decibel, their shadows wrapping the old cobblestones that groaned beneath the tired feet of pilgrims for centuries. This was Vatican City. And they had come to see the pope.

Forty, maybe even thirty years ago, this was not an unusual sight. Every Sunday at noon, people flocked to the open piazza before the massive basilica, milling around for a sight of an old man standing behind a tiny window high above the apostolic palace. He was just a speck of white above the sea of faces below. Yet his voice carried a strength and power that touched the hearts and minds of people everywhere.

For some time, this was the city's most popular attraction. To see the pope of Rome address the cheering crowds below, exhorting them to be courageous, to hold fast to their faith in a world that was rapidly denying them that right. They came in their numbers. They listened. And they prayed with him, each one trying to catch his attention, to show him their support.

That day, the crowds were still there. The pope was still there, though not the same one. And they were still trying to catch his attention, to make sure the old bishop saw them, heard them and knew what they thought of him...and his God.

But some things were different. It wasn't just the cold winds blowing down from the Aventine hills. There was a volatile energy in the square below. The voices and chants rumbled with hostility and the banners and placards signalled a darker time. Was it just his imagination, or was the gnashing and grinding from the square below getting louder, almost bellowing like some feral beast hungry for blood?

The papal secretary reached over nervously and tugged at the pope's sleeve. "Holy Father, please. I'd feel a lot better if you moved away from the window."

The pope sighed and remained where he was. "What news of the local churches," he asked. "How are they holding up?"

Down below, the restless crowd was looking more like a pack of wolves with every passing minute. Separating the protesters from the steps of St. Peter's was a perimeter fence designed to keep the mob out.

Without warning, a rock thrown by a screaming teenager struck a Swiss Guard in the head and opened a nasty gash across his temple. A crimson trail gushed over his tunic. He staggered into the arms of his comrades who raised their riot shields, only to greet another volley of angry projectiles.

The pope watched with grief, his knuckles white with anger. The papal secretary, Bishop James Spalding, a tall American cleric in his fifties, stiffened and opened a dossier fat with documents.

"The reports from our contacts are bleak, Your Holiness. The enemy has won majority seats in the recent German elections. They've begun seizing monasteries and seminaries. Catholic Spain and Portugal have declared war on public worship and have closed all Christian schools and churches until further notice. North America has decreed all religious symbols illegal in public, and has banned their use in classrooms and work places. England has long turned her back on faith and piety. France is a cauldron of anti-clericalism, and reports are constantly coming in of persecutions against priests and religious."

In the piazza below, things were coming to a boil. Emboldened by the modest Vatican security, some in the crowd advanced on the perimeter fence. A shower of Molotov cocktails burst into flames as they struck the metal barriers, leading the captain of the guards to order a few shots of tear gas. The menace withdrew quickly, cackling in their retreat. But everyday this dance of aggression would go through its paces like a tide of mockery.

"How many more this week?" questioned the aged pontiff.

"Seven. Two secular priests, a Benedictine, and a Jesuit. The rest were Sisters of Divine Mercy. Lumen agents also found Bishop Bartholomew in their company, he was hearing their confessions..."

"And?" inquired the pope with some impatience.

2

"They tortured him Your Holiness, for information about the Underground Church. But he refused to reveal any names or places, and he wouldn't renounce his loyalty to you."

The papal face stiffened with pain. Spalding noticed this and hesitated.

"What is it?" asked the Holy Father.

"We were told they broke his legs. And all his ribs," the bishop revealed.

The pope slammed his fist down on the windowsill. "But they'll never break his soul," he said defiantly.

Ever since the Lumen Corporation campaigned against institutional religion in Europe, hostility and aggression had grown against Christianity in particular, and especially against the Catholic Church in the person of the Roman Pontiff.

"And the rest, what of their safety?"

"I'm sorry Holiness, we have no news of their conditions," Spalding apologized. "They were shipped off under tight security."

"Where?"

"To that gulag they call *The Retreat* for re-education."

The pope turned and looked at his secretary and the bishop noticed the tears welling up in his kindly eyes. There was a moment of silence between the two; the older one standing by the opened window like some ancient rock weathering the storm, while the younger one struggled to keep his own heart from breaking with every piece of news he was giving the Holy Father.

"What do you see below, Giacomo?" asked the pope, who often had a habit of Italianizing the names of people he trusted.

Spalding approached the window and looked outside. "Puppets, misguided souls, led astray with lies," he replied. "I don't deny there are some truly dangerous people among them."

"And yet the real evil is the hand that pulls the strings," the pope answered. "Lumen Corp is a hydra of evil disguised as politicians, activists and business leaders. Vanquish one and another sprouts in its place. They've seduced crowds everywhere into believing that God is the enemy of human progress and fulfillment. They've distorted the image of the creator in his creatures, and they'll unleash a long descent into chaos for every human soul."

Trying to console the Pontiff, the American secretary lowered his voice and said kindly, "There's hope in Africa and Asia, Holy Father. Some leaders are challenging the social and political ideas of the

Corporation. Many in the East are not yet entirely under their spell. Our sources tell us there is growing resistance among the local governors and ministers."

"Yes but even there, our enemies are making inroads among the mighty and influential. Those politicians who ally themselves with the Holy See - men of goodwill - even they are feeling the grip of evil that's spreading like a cancer over the earth. Their cry to shake off the dark superstitions of God and religion as the press calls it is winning converts by the masses. This then is the new gospel; that only man can save man, and only the worldwide unity of a brave new economy and social ethos can redeem humanity from the curse of denying its own glorious destiny. It is Man who is now worshipped as the Alpha and the Omega, the beginning and the end."

The pope dropped his tired frame onto the cushioned seat of his chair, as if the weight of his office was too much to bear. He was not a man given to despair, but if nothing powerful was done to halt the tide, the path to perdition was clear.

The old man sighed and added, "It won't be long before this demonic pact enslaves more souls in their destructive lies."

"But we're fighting back, Holiness. The Gates of Hell will not prevail over the Church. God will not forsake his own," insisted the loyal secretary.

"That he won't my son, that he won't. But we must do more to fight back, much more if we want to stem this tide of darkness," replied the pope.

The phone rang and Spalding moved to answer it. A Vatican official on the other end announced the arrival of a visitor, and a smile escaped the bishop's usually cool demeanor. He replaced the heavy receiver on the papal phone and turned to face the successor of St. Peter with satisfaction.

"I think God has answered our prayers, he's here."

Chapter 2

The Clementine Hall was an impressive room dressed in glorious frescoes and renaissance art. Built in the 17th century by Pope Clement XIV in honor of his saintly predecessor Clement I, who was the third successor to ascend the throne of St. Peter, these walls have stood witness to countless centuries of intrigue and mystery. Their painted heroes and villains stand like immortal spectators to the fickle drama of human struggle - uplifted, torn and redeemed by an endless cast of saints and sinners upon the stage of history.

Mostly it was used to receive Vatican guests through the centuries. But now and then a pope would die and his body would lie in state beneath the frescoed ceilings, mourned by members of his personal entourage and saluted by various Cardinals of the Roman curia before being moved to the main apse of St. Peter's Basilica for public viewing. For the moment, the pope was very much alive, although there were many who believed that the best pope was a dead pope. The threats were always taken seriously, but the Holy See was confident that the Supreme Pontiff wasn't in any immediate danger, at least not yet.

Still, two imposing Swiss Guards stood nearby with vigilance, their eyes resting without exception on the foreign guest seated at the far end of the room. Between the three of them, the immense hall seemed to echo with the silence of eternity, except for the soft rustling of wooden beads in the hands of this stranger from the East.

The guards noticed that the old gentleman had kept his dark woolen gloves on. He was Chinese, in his late seventies, and looking far more ancient than time itself. There was something beyond the years he bore that stretched into infinity like a ladder ascending to heaven.

The heavy doors of the Clementine Hall swung opened and Spalding stepped into the room, preceded by two Vatican clerics in black cassocks. The Swiss Guards snapped to attention and lifted their halberds in salute as the pope followed closely on the heels of his secretary, filling the room with the quiet presence of his charisma, despite the stooped shoulders and painful limp in his arthritic legs.

"Holy Father, thank God you're safe!"

The visitor reached out to kiss the papal ring. But as he genuflected, the pope caught him in a warm embrace.

"Giuseppe, no ceremonies. We're both too practical to bow our old bones to protocol," said the pope, laughing.

Reluctantly, Joseph Li rose from his knees. He held on to the arms of the Vicar of Christ and smiled like a child standing before his father, though it was clear that he wasn't much younger than the pontiff himself.

"And pray tell, how was your trip to Rome? I trust it couldn't have been comfortable," said the pope.

Spalding motioned for the rest of the papal aides to leave the room and gave orders for the guards to stand watch outside. The pope was not to be disturbed.

"No one pays attention to an old crippled man, Your Holiness," replied Joseph. "And besides, once I reached the eternal city, His Excellency arranged for me to enter the Vatican through the secret passage in the Leonine Wall."

"I didn't realize that the passage was still open," said the pope, raising an eyebrow at Spalding.

The bishop smiled and confessed, "We began repairs to that part of the wall some six months back. Just in case."

Prudence had always been the bishop's great virtue. He couldn't take any chances with the pope's safety.

As providence would have it, the original wall had hidden an escape route designed to ferry medieval popes out of the Vatican in times of danger. Now this same route had been resurrected in modern times to smuggle people and information into the Vatican, to assist a pope imprisoned within by the darkness looming outside. The irony was not lost to them.

"Well, what matters is that you're here," the pope chuckled as he embraced his guest.

"I'm overjoyed to see you safe as well," said Joseph. "We heard so many things over the past weeks, we didn't know what to believe. When we saw the riots and burnings on television, we feared the worst. Even now, I can't believe my eyes. The crowds have gone insane…"

"Yes but the Swiss Guards still do an excellent job of keeping me alive, or should I say they try their best no doubt to ensure my safety, for only God can keep any of us truly safe in these dark times," replied the pope.

Indeed, the guards were exceptional. They were the only safeguard preserving the territorial lines between the Vatican and the puppet Italian state. Every single day brought new opportunities for them to demonstrate their courage and loyalty to the Holy Father, just as their military forebears had done defending Clement VII against the insane brutality of Spanish and Germanic forces in 1527.

Then, a small regiment of two hundred Swiss Guards were all that stood between the pope and a legion of twenty-two thousand warriors unleashed from the pits of hell. Still, the tiny papal army drew their swords and swung their spears in the service of St. Peter, and colored the steps of the basilica red with the blood of their own sacrifice. Over one hundred and forty-seven of the guards were slaughtered that day, but the remaining heroes; battered, bleeding and wounded, managed to escort the pope safely to Castel Sant'Angelo. It wasn't the first time that Rome would be sacked by her enemies in history. And it wouldn't be the last. Joseph knew this to be true even now. All along the route from the airport, he had seen the city of Rome besieged by a hatred for the Christian religion.

In the past few years, churches had been repossessed by the ruling government and turned over to new spiritual leaders. They were mostly apostles who proclaimed nothing, taught nothing, believed nothing and preached nothing except the gospel of man. Humanity had become the measure of everything.

Replacing every cross with the symbol of Lumen Corp, they offered mankind an olive branch of redemption from the old ways. With cold efficiency, the enemies of God had torn the figure of Christ from every crucifix, and upon the Church's desecrated altars the Corporation enthroned the golden calf of modern humanism, so that although religion wasn't outlawed, it was ultimately stripped of all divinity.

Walking the last few hundred meters to the Vatican, Joseph couldn't help noticing the anti-clerical slogans as well as the stark absence of any cassocked priest due to a ban on religious clothing in force. Any priest or nun hapless enough to be caught wearing a collar or habit in public risked being beaten and dumped into the back of a waiting police van.

Above all, Joseph noticed the Corporation logos emblazoned on every building and street corner. It was clear that they owned everything in this town - the police, the schools, the businesses, the places of worship, and of course, the media. Every level of society bore witness to the mark of the beast of the Apocalypse.

"Still, Lumen Corp won't do anything too insidious. They won't be so blatant as to break international law by invading the Holy See," the pope scoffed. "It's not in their best interests to be so transparent in their persecution. Evil works best under the illusion of good, and Lucifer has not given up his old disguise as an angel of light."

"That I am certain, Your Holiness. But how much longer will they stay their hand? Each day I see their shadows engulfing entire nations. Each day, the arrogance of evil grows from strength to strength. It won't be long before they move from arresting priests to arresting popes," said the old Chinese man.

The pope took Joseph gently by the arm and gestured for Spalding to lead the way.

"Listen to me my brother. For now, I think the Corporation will appear in public to sympathize with the Holy See. I don't think they'll reveal themselves too readily just yet. Nevertheless, pray for me that I may not flee for fear of the wolves."

Spalding opened a side door and ushered the pope and his guest down a corridor that led away from the Clementine Hall. Their steps echoed softly down the marbled hallway as the evening light filtered through the grated windows.

The Supreme Pontiff continued. "These agents of darkness have been working hard to usher in the reign of the Antichrist, and they've taken great pains to dress themselves up as champions of logic and peace, of real justice and progress, indeed as the heroes of a new and more humane revolution. They're far too sophisticated to manhandle the pope. Instead, they'll do all in their power to ridicule and preach the irrelevance of my office, so that the apathy of a world drunk on moral relativism will be the dagger that sinks its blade into the heart of St. Peter."

At the end of the corridor, the bishop unlocked another entrance that plunged deeper into the apostolic palace. He held the door open for the two men to walk through, and continued leading them down a labyrinth of rooms and secret archives.

"On the surface," interjected Spalding. "The Corporation appears to respect the diplomatic rights of the Vatican to exist as an independent sovereign state."

"But in reality?" asked Joseph.

"In reality they're making things very difficult for the Holy See by actively organizing these protests and demonstrations. And since they own the local utility companies, they severely ration the electricity, gas and water that we need to survive. They don't pull the plug on us, but they make it just enough for us to be uncomfortable."

"That is most unfortunate," lamented Joseph. "On the way here, the riots and hostilities, I noticed that the Italian gendarmes did nothing to dissuade the mob from attacking the Swiss Guards."

"Did you notice the Lumen agents in the crowds?" asked Spalding, barely hiding his contempt. "Like weeds among the wheat, choking every good conscience and sowing seeds of violence within the rabble. I've been watching their handiworks for so long, I can smell the stench of their signatures in every protest."

As they rounded a corner flanked by a statue of St. Anthony of Padua, the 13th century miracle worker known as the "Hammer of Heretics", Joseph noticed they appeared to be walking through an endless library of artistic treasures, some celebrating the lives of the saints while others immortalized the often, capricious rulers of Imperial Rome. Spalding walked a little ahead of the group but paced himself enough to allow the two old men to catch up.

"This vial of darkness has poisoned every major city in Europe and the Americas," the bishop continued. "Aside from parts of Africa and a few countries in the Far East, no one has been spared this potion of evil. The new Italian government not only fails to restrain the disorders in Rome, it's fueling this rage for destruction by celebrating irreligion with public holidays and festivities. In fact, Rome is simply the latest prize to be poached by the Lumen political party."

"And once again, the dragon bares its teeth upon the Church as it did during the persecution of Caesar," said the pope, glancing at a marble bust of Nero.

The old Roman Emperor was a vulgar lunatic who watched Rome burn to cinders as he played the violin from his balcony. And after the morning sun rose on the charred remains of the imperial city, he blamed the Christians for the fire he himself had started, and then opened the jaws of hell to crush them.

✝

Outside the apostolic palace, dusk was approaching fast. As the

9

last slivers of light quivered over the horizon, the Swiss Guards began to get ready for the night ahead. Swords, shields and halberds were fine for tourists in the past, but reality called for automatic weapons, night vision goggles and Kevlar equipment. Guard dogs like German Shepherds patrolled the perimeter fences, sniffing out intruders who managed to slip through the gauntlet of defense.

The pope was initially horrified to consider armed resistance, but the Commandant of the Swiss Guards had convinced him that it was necessary. If not for the marauding crowds, then at least for the safety of his own men.

In the fading light, one could see that the mob was slipping away into the darkness. The numbers of people were smaller. But in their place, several bonfires were lit in the square. Here and there, papal sentries had noticed fleeting shadows in the windows of the surrounding buildings. But even with their telescopic lenses, they couldn't make out any human shapes.

In the square below, a paper effigy of the pope was erected to applause. Several young people danced around the grotesque figure like drunken nymphs in some pagan sacrifice. A burly man in a dirty jacket strapped the doll tightly to a wooden stake while others poured gasoline on the figure. A middle-aged woman dressed in the legal robes of a judge stood before the effigy and read out a fictitious list of crimes against humanity. The pope was guilty in this unholy inquisition, and he would burn for it. As soon as the naked flames tasted the flesh of this gross parody, a roar of approval exploded through the ranks until the fires reduced the burning doll to smoldering ashes.

The Swiss Guards continued to monitor the scene. But as night descended on Rome, the sergeants ordered their men to stay alert, while many adjusted their own weapons for quick access.

†

Joseph wrapped the wooden beads of his rosary around his gloved hand. The dampness of his palm was beginning to soak through the wool. The pope noticed the discomfort but said nothing to embarrass him.

"Tell me more about the faithful in your church, Giuseppe. You've led them courageously all these years, hiding them, strengthening them and keeping them alive in the faith. I know their loyalty to Christ and my office is without blame."

Somewhat relieved that the mystery of his hands wasn't drawing any undue attention, Joseph shared copiously of the struggles in his community. Before the darkness swept in, it was common practice for Catholic bishops to meet the pope every five years to give an account of their stewardship before the Vicar of Christ. The Ad Limina visits as it was called, not only gave the bishops of the world a chance to share their pastoral concerns with the Bishop of Rome, but it also gave them an opportunity to renew and deepen their ecclesial unity with the Successor of St. Peter.

Of course, such visible unity could not be tolerated for long. The Lumen Corporation had a detailed list of all the bishops and cardinals of the Roman Catholic Church. Those who could be bought with power and politics were installed as demigods of the new kingdom. Others were converted by the prophets of pain and torture. But the remaining rebels who stubbornly clung to the Barque of Peter were given more violent incentives to surrender their vocations. And since the majority of the faithful bishops today were either dead, rotting in prison, or living underground in constant fear of assassinations, it was left to clandestine leaders like Joseph Li to keep the path to Rome alive. The oriental man was a bishop *in pectore*, consecrated by the pope himself, his episcopal identity a secret from all except his closest collaborators. To the world at large, he was just a bag of bones tottering on the edge of life. To those in the know, he was a successor of the apostles and a visible bridge to Rome.

Behind the hushed walls of the Vatican, Spalding and the pope listened carefully to the elderly Christian as he reported on the Resistance in the Underground Church. They heard that the community was growing in numbers as more and more souls starved of goodness sought out the light, but also that betrayals and arrests of the faithful had been increasing. There was always the threat of spies. In their efforts to spark a revolution, the community had not always been diligent in testing the hearts of their newly professed, and had suffered for their naivety with the birth of new martyrs. It was a sorrowful lesson for the church.

But there was a darker threat perched gravely on the threshold. Indeed, the enemy was already at the gates. There were shocking rumors at first. No one knew what to believe, but now the noxious odor of the damned seemed to burst forth from the dungeons of hell to singe the world with the stink of Armageddon. Reports of

11

demonic possessions kept coming in, bizarre stories of ritual sacrifices plagued the urban landscape, and mutilated bodies of the homeless littered the dumps as grisly testaments to monstrous attacks. The city itself was under siege, rocked by increased sightings of supernatural creatures leaving a trail of death and violence in their wake. Yet as soon as the smoke of Satan cleared, the incidents were covered up by the Corporation and reduced to little more than urban legends.

"I know they suffer much," said the Holy Father. "But tell them this from the pope. Do not be afraid, do not fear those who would bring death to their bodies but who cannot destroy their souls."

Joseph looked at the pope in earnest, and he could see the fire in his eyes. For all his wrinkles, there was a youthful energy about this man on the papal throne. He seemed to wear an optimism that was surprising to this present danger. Without question, there was something supernatural about his quiet sense of hope.

"In her darkest hours, the Church has always triumphed over her enemies through the blood of her martyrs. The cross will be our weapon of choice, and it will vanquish the powers of hell…"

The old pontiff stamped his wooden cane upon the floor for emphasis. "As surely as the dawn follows the night," he added, "the justice of God will come upon those who do evil."

As they approached the end of the corridor, Spalding led the company down a flight of stairs to a chamber guarded by a small detachment of Swiss Guards. Reverently, Joseph supported the pope as they climbed down the marbled steps together.

"With all due respects, Holy Father, the Underground Church has no lack of martyrs. Even now, there are courageous members in our community who give no thought to their own safety to keep the faith alive. But this spiritual war has reached new horrors. The assaults of Satan against the Church are not carried out by human agents alone, it seems the entire army of darkness is about to consume us," said Joseph.

"Indeed, Your Holiness knows about our growing encounters with the creatures of hell, monsters we can barely describe. And against such attacks, what do we have in the way of defense? We're as vulnerable as sheep for the slaughter."

"Not true Giuseppe, not true," answered the pope. He nodded to the guards and they pushed open the heavy oak doors to the room. Joseph walked into the cool interior of what appeared to be a sizeable chapel, warmly lit by a symphony of soft lights dancing off the gilded altar and religious art on the walls.

Spotting the sanctuary lamp burning beside the tabernacle, he genuflected before the altar, keenly aware that the pontiff and his secretary were also bending their knees before the sacramental presence of their God.

After a few minutes of prayer, Joseph rose to his feet and looked around. As his eyes adapted to the modest lighting, he could see where he had been mistaken. The walls were not really clothed with religious art at all. Instead, they were dressed from ceiling to floor with the precious relics of the saints. For a moment, he forgot the pain in his hands and marveled at the immense collection of sacred objects in one room. The old man had seen relics in churches of course, but nothing like this. This was a veritable temple housing the remains of Christian heroes.

"When news reached us that the Roman authorities were confiscating the churches for their Lumen overlords, we feared the desecration of these holy relics. We did our best to save as many as we could, but unfortunately we also lost quite a few to sacrilege. What you see here were rescued by quick thinking Christians at the time and smuggled to us for safekeeping. How much longer we can preserve these treasures, we do not know," said Spalding.

The bishop reached behind a pillar and turned up the lighting on the walls. The effect was stunning.

Gasping with awe, Joseph gazed around the chapel as if in a dream. In one corner he spied the relics of the crucifixion; pieces of the true cross carefully conserved among the nails and thorns. In another area, he easily recognized the tattered tunic of St. Frances of Assisi and the chains of St. Paul. The spearhead of St. Longinus glistened to the left of him, and the wall to his right sang with the memories of martyrs he had cherished from his youth.

But it was the pope who drew his attention to something he hadn't noticed.

"This chapel was dedicated to St. George the warrior," said the Holy Father. He beckoned for Joseph to follow him.

"It's a sign of the end times that Satan should send his legions to prepare the way for the Antichrist, but you're wrong in saying we have no defense against evil such as this. Then as now, our most powerful weapons have been prayer and the leadership of men such as yourself who fight the good fight, who witness with your courage and gather new warriors against this evil."

Joseph drew near the sanctuary and stood beside the pope. He saw that the altar was decorated with various panels celebrating the life of the saintly knight. And over the scene of St. George slaying the dragon, Bishop Spalding unlocked a hidden door and removed a longish box from within. He presented the wooden case to the Holy Father and respectfully stepped aside.

The pope turned to Joseph. "Open it," he said.

Taking the case with both hands, Joseph could sense a tingling vibration of energy that hinted at the power within. His eyes widened in surprise as he read the inscriptions on the box: *The Blade of St. George, the Dragon Slayer.*

Holding his breath, he opened the lid and saw the ancient sword of a Roman Tribune resting on a bed of purple silk. Unable to resist, he ran his fingers lightly over the blade. It seemed to come alive at his touch.

"This is incredible," said Joseph.

"You look surprised," chided the pope playfully. "Did you think he was merely a legend?"

"No…" stammered Joseph. "It's just that…well…the story of him fighting the dragon, that was just a popular myth, was it not?"

"It depends on how you see the dragon," replied the pope with a smile. "Evil takes many forms."

Joseph looked at the sword in his hands and raised his eyes to the Holy Father. He wasn't sure what the pope was getting at.

"The world we live in is shared with others, Giuseppe, it is our duty to defend it from the powers trying to enslave us. I know how much you've sacrificed to keep your flock together, and I know your valiant efforts to raise warriors for the Church. I'm counting on you to lead that struggle, to support those among you who will fight back, who will not rest until the name of God is restored to the hearts of men."

"We'll do our best, Holy Father, although each day brings its own struggles," answered Joseph.

"That's good news. It means you're alive, since only the dead stop struggling," said Spalding with a smile.

"I have no doubt that God will bless your efforts in His name. Do not be afraid of the odds against you. Accept this gift for your people," replied the pope as he patted the sword of St. George.

"Bring it back to your community and let it be for them a symbol of their fight against darkness. Bring them my prayers, bring them my hope, and bring them my love. Remind them that this is a war, and evil will succeed if good men do nothing."

Joseph felt his heart fill with emotion. He knew how much a gift like this would mean to his own people living in the killing fields of spiritual genocide. For the Successor of St. Peter to entrust this sacred blade to his besieged community, the pope clearly wanted to assure the suffering Church of his personal closeness to them.

Deeply stirred by the papal gesture, Joseph dropped to his knees as the pope raised his hands to heaven and prayed...

"Let us ask God to send us warriors of light, his angels and archangels to carry his standard, to push back this tide of darkness so that his truth and goodness may once again reign in our world," said the pontiff.

Tracing the sign of the cross over the leader of the Underground Church, the pope intoned the ancient blessing of the apostles and prophets.

"May the Lord bless you and keep you. May the Lord make his face shine upon you and be gracious unto you. May the Lord lift up his countenance upon you and give you peace. In the name of the Father, the Son and the Holy Spirit."

Joseph whispered with tears in his eyes, "Amen."

Chapter 3

The brooding elevator music only tightened the knots in his stomach. He had just passed the eightieth floor but the speed of ascent made him feel uneasy. He rubbed the tired stubble on his face and reminded himself to breathe. Clutching his doctor's bag, he looked out of the glass panels. The streets below were pulling away from him like a city lost to the shadows. How much longer would this town cannibalize itself?

The floors whizzed by in a blur. The numbers jumped to a rhythm that alternated with the flickering lights in the cabin. With every level, the faulty lights pulsated like a heartbeat throbbing in the steel arteries of some metal beast. The effect was rather hypnotic. He felt a little like Jonah in the belly of the whale; called to a mission he didn't want, sent to a people he despised, and about to be vomited onto the rancid shores of iniquity.

Before he could dwell on that thought, the metal doors opened with a slight hum that disrupted his reverie. He stepped out onto the ninetieth floor and looked for directions to the penthouse suite. It wasn't hard to find; there was only one apartment that stretched out across the entire level.

As he walked towards the front door, he could hear the screeching of a man's voice puncturing the hallway like the brutal howls of a dying animal. He placed his hand along the wall and felt vibrations crashing into his palm.

He closed his eyes and tried to absorb the energy.

For a moment everything slowed to a halt. Then slowly he saw inside the apartment, as if the concrete veil standing between him and his patient was suddenly torn down for a few brief seconds. It wasn't long but it was enough to send a chill down his spine. He removed his hand, took a deep breath and pressed the tiny buzzer on the wall. The sound of a heavy lock clicked into release, and then the big wooden door swiveled inwards.

At first, he wasn't sure what greeted him at the entrance. Standing there with a lighted fag dangling out of its mouth was an androgynous looking creature draped in black lace and wearing a crown of white frills. As far as he could tell, this grinning magpie with the painted face was stoned to the hilt and barely awake. It slouched to a corner as a tall lean man in a dark suit stepped forward. "You're the doctor she sent for?" he asked.

Raphael nodded. He hadn't given them his real name and they didn't ask him for it. He was known in private circles as the man with the cure, but most people simply called him *The Doctor*. He dug into his pocket and produced the password they sent him.

The man took the code and checked it against a list of names. His hands were large, pale and translucent, like the skins of some frogs. His face was drained of color and his lips were thinly stretched, making him look a little amphibious himself. He seemed almost fragile, but there was something intensely cruel about his eyes. Every time he looked up, Raphael felt like someone ran a serrated blade across his jugular.

Satisfied that all was in order, the gatekeeper tucked away the list. He was convinced the middle-aged man with the graying stubble was expected.

"Follow me but stay close," he said.

"I'll be right behind you," Raphael replied.

The black suit didn't wait. He turned around and dissolved into the crowd. Raphael picked up his bag and hurried after him.

The apartment was dark, musty and decked out like a carnival. Huge portraits of rock icons adorn the walls while a large painting of unicorns galloped across the ceiling. There were no attempts to be subtle. Between the strobe lights and rotating mirrors, the place was just a pimped out bunker for outrageous parties. There was even a pink fountain in the middle of the room and a giant chandelier hanging down to the floor.

The smell of sweat mixed with burning weed was intoxicating. The music was loud and trance-like, and the living room was writhing with semi-naked bodies coiled around each other.

Raphael felt like he was wading through a thick mist. With every step he took, he spied a familiar face in the crowd. He knew who they were - the sons and daughters of the new aristocracy - partying with their usual abandon, lost in the pull of debauchery that mixed the famous and notorious in one melting pot of hedonism.

For a moment, he felt the room spinning. He reached inside his pocket and closed his hand on the small wooden crucifix he brought along. Whether it was just his imagination or pure coincidence, he recovered his balance and began to steady himself. The evening was just beginning, and he had much to do.

✝

Max Sparrow was lying on a bed of royal silk, his head gently propped up against a feather down pillow. The music was loud enough to wake the dead, but all he could hear was the sound of his own heart beeping faintly on the monitor next to his bed.

His pajamas couldn't hide the open sores that dug into his bones and kept him wide-awake despite the morphine. Neither could his fortunes keep him from wheezing like the punctured bellows of a broken down accordion. He was dying and he knew it.

He tried to speak, to give vent to the despair that was swelling in his heart, but only gurgling noises rose from his throat like a blackness escaping from the pit.

"Shhhh," chided his sister as she rested her hand lightly on his brow. She wiped away the cold drops of perspiration from his forehead and caressed his face. For a moment, he felt his desperation give way to a calm that he had not known in the last twenty-four hours.

"Don't talk, just rest," Chelsea whispered as she held her brother close. "I've called for the doctor and he'll be here soon. When he gets here he'll take away the pain, and you won't feel so terrible anymore, Max. It'll be all right, I promise."

At this, loud chuckles scattered across the room.

"He's not a child you know, he's frickin' Max Sparrow! You don't have to coddle him," said a man trying to stifle his laughter by sucking on a bloated cigar. His other hand was busy balancing a scotch.

Zadok Martaban had many talents, chief of which was seducing some of the biggest names in showbiz to sign with his agency. He was a peddler of celebrity greatness, bartering in fame and fortune like a slave trader gushing over his stable of gladiators in ancient Rome. Trading in souls was the same thing as trading in stocks; it was all good business if you knew how to play the game. And Martaban was a genius at it. For that reason, he was the Corporation's man in show business.

"Why don't you just leave him alone?" cried Chelsea. "And for

God's sakes, stop smoking. You're standing next to the oxygen tank!"

"Ooooh…" Zadok teased the woman as he waved the lighted stub in her face. "Playing the loving sister are we? When did you start caring about Max?"

"I've always cared about Max, you shit. You're the one who always kept us apart," said Chelsea. "You didn't even tell me he was this sick until a week ago."

"And whose fault was that? Running around Greece and Milan, living it up in Barcelona…no cell phone, no emails, just a whole summer soaking up the booze, sex and beach parties. You didn't want to be disturbed, remember? Private time, vacation and all that…well I just have to ask…is it true the sausages in Italy are much tastier?"

The woman exploded with curses, which made Zadok laugh even louder.

"Oh yes, I've heard the stories. Life is hell for a top model like you. You're a living martyr, aren't you?" said the fat man, pouring himself another scotch.

"I hate you," Chelsea muttered without looking up.

"Of course you do. I'm the guy who made him a living legend. I showed him the greatness inside himself when everyone else said he was just pissing in the wind. Including you! Like it or not, I'm the only real family he has. Why you're here is a mystery to me," Zadok added as an insult to Chelsea.

Max glanced over at his long-time manager. He knew that Martaban was right. His whole career had been phenomenal and he owed most of it to this man. The concerts, publicity, parties and scandals, even the drugs, it was all part of the plan. And yeah, it was all good! For the last decade, he was a celebrated rock star who had the world marching to his beat. The crowds adored him and the press couldn't get enough of him. Nothing was too bizarre or extreme for "Mad Max". No limits, no restraints, no petty excuses. Just the wild confidence of a genius who knew how to feed the world his own brand of crazy. And have them begging for more.

The Corporation helped of course. They owned the music labels and they taught him that to shine in the heavens, he had to break free of the religious hogwash he swallowed as a young man. The day he turned his back on his conscience was the day he felt free to burst into life.

19

But Chelsea…

She didn't understand that it was all just a show, a great big performance. He was giving his fans what they wanted and they loved him for it. But she kept saying that the shows were killing him. That's why Lumen Corp had to send her away.

They kept her strutting on the catwalks of high fashion while her face sold millions on billboards and magazines. She even had a few successful movies and music albums to her name and was quickly becoming a pop icon in her own right. After awhile, she stopped complaining and started living the good life too. It was all part of the magic. And now that the time had come to cash in, there was only one way to seal the Max Sparrow legacy. It was to crash and burn with the best of them. He was going to light the sacrificial pyre of his legendary fame with the fires of his own holocaust.

All he had to do for a grand finale was to die in living color…with sex, drugs and rock and roll blazing in the background, even as the burning embers of his strength flickered in the throes of death. No regrets, no apologies, no deathbed conversions, just the perfect note of rebellion to end this song. Only then, he would be immortalized forever in the annals of rock history.

It's better to burn out than to fade away. At least that was what everyone said. Sparrow shuddered like a leaf.

"Max…are you ok?" asked Chelsea, a little startled when her brother suddenly lurched forward and grabbed her hand.

"Make it go away," pleaded the sick man. His eyes darted around the room, chasing something only he could see.

"Make what go away?" asked Chelsea. "There's nothing here."

She got up to adjust the pillows but Max started to writhe under the sheets like a man possessed.

"The poor sod, he's losing it!" said Zadok.

Chelsea glared at him like she wanted to scratch out his eyes, but he just swirled the contents of his glass and chuckled.

"I'm sorry, it's just the spirits talking," he apologized.

He inched closer to the bed and stood over his client like a racehorse owner about to cash in on his prized stud. Lumen Corp had promised him a big payout if he could ride his talents to the finishing line, and he could see that this broken horse was nearly there.

"Listen to me, Max. I know you're scared shitless. Hell, I'd be scared too if I was waiting for the grim reaper to drop in on my ass.

20

But that's just it my boy, you're not waiting for the boogeyman because you know he doesn't exist. There's no one to judge you."

Zadok pursed his lips for a sip but the scotch in his hand flew across the room and decimated the TV console. The manager jumped back in shock. Max was flinging his arms like a drowning man, slapping everything within his reach like a windmill spun out of control.

"There!!!" he cried, snapping a trembling finger at a table lamp in the corner. "The shadow, make it go away!"

"Calm down baby, there's nothing there," Chelsea responded with some irritation. She tried to keep her brother still. "You're safe. No one's going to hurt you."

Zadok was still fairly breathless from being startled. "Bloody hell, you nearly gave me a heart attack," complained the fat man. "Pull yourself together! Your fans are counting on you, I'm counting on you!"

By now, the party outside the bedroom was in full swing and the music hammered against the door like a battering ram hungry for a target.

"You hear that? That's the sound of success my boy, that's the sound of your immortality. Are you trying to throw it all away?" asked Zadok, chewing on his cigar.

Max began rolling his eyes like a man losing his mind.

"Look at me!" the manager yelled. "You're the biggest name in rock and roll. For years you lived the dream without once buying that crap about life after death. Sin was just a dirty word invented by those who peddled guilt. You told me that God was nothing more than a dog spelt backwards and now you're freaking out because you saw what…shadows? What are you going to see next? Fairies?"

In the corner of the room, the shadows melted away like a dream. And Sparrow began to doubt his own sanity. Groaning feverishly, he clawed at his face. Tears streamed down his sunken cheeks while he whimpered.

"What if I was wrong, what if you were all wrong?" Max mumbled hysterically.

"Are you going to start this nonsense again? What did I tell you?" asked Zadok.

The manager pulled out his pen and clicked it several times before Max's face. "You signed the contract remember?"

"Leave him alone", said Chelsea. "It's the morphine. He's been seeing things all day."

"I *know* it's the morphine," said Zadok. "But that's not the point! Hallucinations or not, he needs to understand that he has a responsibility to his fans and to himself!"

He plucked the smoking cigar from his lips and rudely squashed it against the bedpost, snuffing out the protesting embers on the gorgeous teak.

"Hey!" cried Chelsea indignantly.

Zadok ignored her protest and focused on his client. "You wanted to be the best, remember? And you asked the Corporation to help you do that, to recognize the greatness within yourself…"

He pulled up a chair and plunked himself down next to the bed. The wooden legs creaked in agony.

"Well guess what? Today you're the best there is."

Max was exhausted. He took a deep breath and struggled to speak, "My fans. The public. They didn't always think so…"

"You can see that they do now, and it's all thanks to you. You taught them not to be afraid, not to give in to arcane notions about right or wrong. If it feels right, it is right! The only real hell is wasting your talents and letting someone else enjoy the pleasures you worked so hard for."

Zadok turned around and made a sweeping gesture with his arm.

"And this here," he said, referring to the countless music awards that lined the walls. "This here's the real paradise, this is the real judgment call. You'll always be a hero to them, Max!"

Despite the fact that Zadok sounded as sincere as a bunch of ancient Greeks bearing gifts, there was a seductive quality to what he said, as if every word was dipped in honey and fed directly into the pleasure cortex of Max's brain. And once the Trojan was introduced, the effect was quickly noticeable. A strange calm came over the dying man, his anxieties dissipated with every syllable and his mind danced like it was soaked in the brimming euphoria of a potent drug. The former rock star started to laugh even though his insides churned like broken glass.

Bewildered, he looked over at Chelsea for answers but she didn't say anything. She didn't know *what* to say. It was as if a spell had descended on the siblings and cauterized their doubts.

Max twisted his sallow face into a ghastly grin, "I *am* the best, aren't I?"

The words came out like an odious vapor. He choked and

coughed a little, his body racked with nervous convulsions that brought more tears to his eyes.

"You know it buddy!" encouraged Zadok. "That's why I signed you up, took you away from that dump you called a gig and pushed you into the big time. In return you agreed to work your ass off, rock the world and use your music to help them break free of all that superstitious crap. And you know what?"

Zadok got up and walked over to the windows. He pulled back the heavy drapes and gazed out over the city. The setting sun blazed like an angry ball of fire on the horizon but the room remained trapped in cold shadows. It was as if the girth of this man eclipsed all the light in the world.

"Your music made us believe we could be free," said the portly manager, "All those times on the road - the concerts, the shows - you were bloody Moses leading us out of Egypt. And I have to give it to you…"

Zadok turned around and clapped his hands slowly.

"You actually did it, buddy. You saved so many lives, yanked them out of the dark ages into the light of reason."

"I supposed I did," Max giggled with delirium.

By this time, he found himself strangely elated without really knowing why. His tongue was loosened and he could speak without any struggle.

Zadok smirked and removed another cigar from his pocket. He snipped off the tip and lit the other end slowly, letting the fire jump from the match to embrace the Cuban tobacco. Puffing like a locomotive, he sighed with satisfaction.

"Ahhh…that's why the Corporation is throwing this party for you right now, not just in the next room but all over the world. People are celebrating your legend tonight, the moment when it all comes together. You've become much more than a star, Max. You've become a symbol of our freedom. And you know what happens with symbols; they live forever. It doesn't get any bigger than this."

Chelsea started to feel sick to the stomach. She tried to fan away the smoke in the room, but mostly, she was nauseated by the pungent grind of Martaban's voice. And yet, she couldn't find any real strength to resist him. Everything he said sounded so reasonable. The Corporation did take care of everything. Her own success as a model and a singer was proof of that. She was one of the most bankable faces in the business.

Even then, it all seemed so surreal. In fact, she had no recollection of when her star began to rise, or when she actually joined the ranks of the bold and beautiful in Lumen Corp. For as long as she could remember, she had always been in the "family" - as the girls liked to call it. Everything else before that was a blur.

Stroking his moustache, Zadok turned around and nodded towards the wooden door.

"Listen to them," he said.

By now, the party in the living room was an explosive orgy and you could feel the tremors slamming through the walls.

"This is it! They're honoring your legacy. No one has lived this life more freely, more genuinely than you. You're the reason young people today are free from all that papal bull."

He paused to suck on his cigar before blowing a cloud of smoke at his client.

"Do you want to turn your back on them now? Do you want to send them back into the arms of those sick bastards who'd like nothing better than to run their holy fingers all over little boys? Is that how you want to be remembered?"

Max pulled himself into a sitting position on the bed. He gritted his teeth and shook his head.

"So what do you say?" asked Zadok at the top of his voice. He leaned close to the dying man like a coach pitching the final goal to his star player.

"What do you say to fairies in the afterlife?" he howled.

Max ripped the plastic tubes from his arms and swept the medication vials off the side table. He picked up a bedpan and threw it against the wall mirror, shattering his image into tiny pieces that scattered across the floor.

"C'mon Max, no hesitations. It's time to make your mark on history," he bellowed. "Do you believe in God?"

From a corner of the room, Chelsea watched her intoxicated brother thrust his middle finger into the air.

"That's my boy!" said Zadok with thunderous approval. He laughed maniacally and smacked his hands together like a toy monkey wound up too tight.

The noise of the party got louder. Max slumped back into his pillows exhausted, the weight of his illness had returned with a crushing blow. Still, he couldn't help giggling like a schoolgirl drunk on gossip.

He tried to smile but the garish grin on his face only drew his lips into a macabre death mask.

Chelsea knew it wouldn't be long now.

Chapter 4

There was a loud knock on the door. The agent with the pale skin pushed it opened and floated in. Raphael followed slightly behind. In the background, a vortex of naked bodies, chaos and deafening music swirled in the blackness.

Martaban looked up at the stranger and noticed the medical bag in his hands.

"Ah here comes the medicine man to take away the pain, make it all go away," said Zadok. "But as you can see, doc, the patient is feeling all better."

Raphael entered the room and cautiously stepped over the broken shards of glass on the floor. The agent shut the door.

"What happened?" he asked.

"Oh nothing you should be worried about, just a little excitement," Zadok snickered. "You might've noticed there's a party going on."

"Yes, your friend here gave me the grand tour," Raphael replied.

He glanced at the Lumen agent who stood by the door like some pagan deity guarding a pyramid tomb.

The doctor noticed Chelsea across the room.

"Miss Shields?"

She nodded.

"I understand you requested for me?"

Chelsea gazed at the man before her. He looked to be in his early fifties. He was tall, tan and a little weathered, but the lines and wrinkles around his eyes couldn't hide their piercing brightness. Despite his grizzled stubble and graying hair, there was a roguish handsomeness to his face.

"Randy told me you could help," she mumbled.

"Schofield?" interrupted Zadok. "The kid who follows you around?"

"The chauffeur who drives me around," she corrected.

"Same difference, except your limo isn't the only thing about you he wants to drive. I've seen the way he looks at you."

"That's actually funny, coming from someone who can't find his own pecker under all that lard," she replied.

Zadok held his gut and laughed like a choked bagpipe, but his eyes were burning like hot coals.

Chelsea noticed it and inched closer to Raphael.

"Randy told me you were the best, that you could work miracles. How come I've never heard of you?" she asked.

"Let's just say I only make house calls. The medical community doesn't like it that I don't play by the rules. And besides, you've tried everyone else in this town, what do you have to lose?"

"For Randy's sake, you'd better be able to help my brother. Otherwise, I'm telling these goons to rearrange his face. It'll be an improvement, trust me."

Raphael smiled. He liked her spunk.

"Well, Randy didn't give me too many details but..."

"Look," Chelsea interrupted. "I just want a doctor here in case...I don't know...I guess I just don't want Max to suffer anymore than he already has."

"Miss Shields, you made the right decision in calling me," Raphael assured her. "I can help to take away your brother's pain, make his final moments easier. Who knows, maybe I can even heal him."

She wanted desperately to believe that. Her eyes shimmered with hope. But her heart struggled to make the leap of faith. She was simply too out of touch.

"And I assure you doc, if you so much as waste our time, you'll have plenty of opportunities to heal yourself," threatened Zadok.

The pallid agent standing by the door picked up a piece of shattered glass and ran his fingers lightly over its cutting edge.

"Gentlemen please, I'm merely here to help Mr. Sparrow in his last moments," said Raphael. "No need for theatrics, I'm a physician, not a witch doctor. Save your threats for someone else."

"Oh wow, a doctor and a comedian," said Zadok with sarcasm.

He motioned to the Lumen agent who took a menacing step towards Raphael. Chelsea slipped between the two men and raised her voice.

"Please! Give us some privacy. The least I can do right now is try and give him some comfort from the pain, make it easier for him to let go."

Zadok shrugged his shoulders as if to say he couldn't care less.

"Please leave the room," Chelsea screeched. "Both of you."

"As you wish, princess," said the manager. He tried to stifle a grin as he made his way out of the room. His pale shadow followed him, dropping the splintered glass on his way out. The sound it made as it crashed to the floor, cut into Max like an open knife. The King of Rock doubled over in agony.

"Outstanding," said Zadok as he paused by the opened doorway. "Years of research, billions of dollars and no one has been able to do shit about this disease, but you're going to try and save him in one visit? I love a man with ambition. Good luck with that."

He winked at Raphael, turned and slammed the door.

✝

"Thank God," said Chelsea. "I thought he'd never leave."

Raphael locked the door and moved his medical bag to the side table by Max's bed.

"Do you believe in God, Miss Shields?" asked the doctor, smiling.

"Of course not," replied Chelsea.

"Well, you're in luck 'cos he believes in you."

"Where did you say you were from again?" asked Chelsea, a little suspicious.

"I didn't," answered Raphael. He pulled out a stethoscope and some sterile gauze from his bag and proceeded to examine the patient. Max was having trouble breathing and he was slipping fast. His eyelids were heavy with sleep.

"But I promise you, I am a doctor. And I've spent more time looking into the eyes of death than you can imagine. Although right now, it's life that your brother needs to see again."

He slipped on a pair of surgical gloves and gently drew back the silk pajamas from Max's upper body. The skin beneath was a tattered blanket of welts and putrid sores. The doctor wiped away the pus that was congealing and placed his hand lightly on the blistered surface. It seemed like he wanted to absorb some of the pain that cried out for redemption.

"And you can give it to him?" Chelsea enquired.

"I can offer it to him but he must want it. And you too, must want it for him," replied Raphael. "And that takes courage and faith."

He put on the stethoscope and guided it over Max's chest, listening for signs of hope. The harsh murmurs confirmed advanced pneumonia. But there was something else he was looking for, something much more elusive.

"When medical science is not enough, we need to rely on the science of faith. Do you have the courage to believe for your brother?" the doctor asked Chelsea.

"You're asking me if I have the courage to believe you can heal him?"

"I'm asking if you have the courage to help him turn towards the light and leave the darkness behind, to know he can do it, that he *must* do it, and that it's not too late?" urged Raphael.

"I suppose. If it means he can jump out of bed and be okay again, I can try. But what do you mean, I'm not sure I'm getting you," she said.

Raphael folded away his stethoscope and peeled off his surgical gloves. He looked down at Max with a sadness that surprised her. The patient was not fully conscious at that point. What little life he tapped from Zadok earlier was now conspicuously absent. In fact, he had slipped into a burning fever that boiled with the dregs of delirium.

"I won't lie to you Miss Shields, his body is too far-gone. It's almost a tomb encasing his spirit right now. But if we don't rescue his soul, he's going to burn in this deathtrap for eternity."

"Wait a minute," said Chelsea as she took a step back. "Who the hell are you?"

"I already told you," said Raphael, "I'm a doctor."

He reached for his bag and tucked away his equipment. When his hand reappeared, it was holding a narrow strip of purple cloth emblazoned with a tiny cross on each end.

Baffled, Chelsea watched the man reverently kiss the linen cloth and drape it over his shoulders. It hung over his white jacket like a prayer woven onto his soul.

"What I haven't told you is that I'm also a priest," said the man calmly.

His words struck her like a brick in the face. Everything she knew about priests, everything she was taught to believe about these sewer rats living in the Underground Church caught her in a vice of panic. Chelsea staggered and felt her blood go cold with fear.

"Don't come any closer," she cried. "I'm calling security!"

She paused briefly, unsure of what to do next. Her eyes darted to the exit and she made a dash for the door. But before she could reach it, the doctor stood before her, barring her escape. He held onto her arms.

"Wait, listen to me," said Raphael.

Before he could utter another word, Chelsea broke through his hold like a wild mare. He tried to subdue her but she was stronger than he expected. Without warning, a searing pain tore into his brow and he felt warm blood trickle past his eye.

He grabbed both her wrists and chucked her against the wall, but he was careful to avoid her claws. Her nails were blood red and desperate to open another wound. He tightened his grip. She thrashed like a snake crushed underfoot.

"You will stop this!" he bellowed. "Or I'll slap you so hard, the only thing you'll model from now on is a hockey mask."

"Do your worse!" Chelsea shouted in disgust.

"I mean it, I'll hit *you* if you don't calm down."

Chelsea could see that the priest was nervous too. His hands were cold and beads of sweat rolled down his face. She tried to break free but he held firm.

"Listen to me," he pleaded. "We've only got a couple of minutes before they come through that door again. You can help me save your brother or you can damn him to hell for eternity."

"Let go!" she screeched. "You're hurting me."

Raphael loosened his grip and at once, Chelsea jerked her hands away. She rubbed the soreness from her wrists and stared at him in defiance.

"Do I look like some old crone with a rosary in her hand? You priests have been spreading that lie forever, just so you could enslave us in your bogus religions. How dare you come here to preach this filth? I won't let you do this to Max, I won't let you take away his freedom."

She stumbled over to her brother's side, taking care to keep her distance from the doctor in the priestly stole.

"I suggest you leave before I report you," said Chelsea, reaching for the intercom by the bed.

"Now!" she barked. "And take your false God with you."

"And how will you survive your nightmares?" asked Raphael.

She froze, her eyes widened in surprise. "What're you talking about?"

"That thing you saw in the middle of the night, was it just a dream? It's been haunting you for some weeks now, always the same shadow, blacker than night. No face, no features, just the pungent

30

smell of burning flesh. It's been following you around every night, watching you when you shower, when you sleep. You kept telling yourself it was just your imagination…"

"Stop it," she shouted nervously. "Who told you that?"

"Last night, it came into your bed," the doctor continued. "You tried to scream but you couldn't move a muscle. It stayed beside you and ran its fingers over your body but you were so paralyzed with fear. You felt it suffocating you. You knew this was no dream. So you did something you never thought you would…"

Raphael paused and searched her face. "You cried out to God to save you, didn't you?"

Chelsea was pale with confusion and fright. Her eyes welled up with emotion.

"Don't you remember?" Raphael pressed on. "In your panic you clung to the God of your youth. You invoked the name of Jesus, the name that strikes fear into the bowels of hell. And the evil ran from you like a horse struck by lightning. Now that God wants to save your brother from a worse fate, you would stop him?"

"I said stop it! I swear, if you're trying to trick me," she threatened.

"Am I? You know I speak the truth. Your bed stinks of sulfur and the scorch marks are still on your sheets."

Chelsea felt her knees buckle. She could almost smell the burning odor of fear that still clung to her skin. Despite her resolve, she slid to the floor in a puddle of tears, her tall lanky frame twisted in uncertainty and turmoil.

Her mind was racing and her heart felt like it would burst. Everything this man had said was true. But *how could he have known?* The last few weeks had truly been a nightmare. She was depressed, suicidal and on heavy medication. But that thing in the house, she had convinced herself it was just her psychosis. It had to be. What other explanation was there? She was doubtful of everything except the growing conviction that she was losing her mind.

"Leave me alone," she sobbed uncontrollably. "I don't know who you are or what you want, but get away from me."

"Look at your brother, Chelsea," Raphael called out to her gently. "He doesn't have much time, help me save him."

Her eyes drifted over to Max who lay dying in a bed of sores. The sorry sight of the rock star festering in his pajamas suddenly looked darker than the night, as if some unseen presence was eating away at his life.

"What do you want me to do?" she asked in consternation.

"Lend him the strength of your faith," said the doctor. "What little you can believe, believe for him. He has been hemorrhaging spiritually for decades, he needs a transfusion of faith right now, and the best person to help him is his own blood."

"Please don't ask me to do this. I can't," she whimpered.

"You've done this before. You've prayed to God when you needed help. Now pray to God for your brother."

"I can't!!!" Chelsea shouted back.

"You can't believe or you won't believe?"

Chelsea turned her face away.

"Then for crying out loud, don't be an obstacle to grace," Raphael retorted. "Step aside and let me help him."

"Fine!" she snapped, her pride stung by the rebuke. "Just do what you have to and leave!"

The doctor moved quickly to check on Max. The shadows in the room grew longer as the sun clung in vain to the horizon. The skies outside the windows were drenched in deep scarlet, and beneath the storm clouds, ragged fingers of light clawed desperately to keep the darkness from cloaking the earth. Dusk was approaching. He knew he had to act fast.

"What's his baptismal name?" asked Raphael.

"James," answered Chelsea. "Maximilian James."

Raphael lifted Max's eyelids and saw that his eyeballs had rolled all the way back, revealing only the whites. He removed a small bottle from his medical bag and squeezed a few drops of holy water into each ear, massaging the lobes as he did so.

"*De profundis clamavi ad te Domini,*" he whispered into the man's ear, "Maximilian James, wake up."

Immediately, the patient's eyes uncoiled to their normal positions. A loud sigh gushed out of the sick man like stale air escaping from a sealed casket. Trying hard to sit up, Max clutched wildly at the priest for support. He felt like he had been pulled out of a tar pit and the sticky blackness was still clinging to his lungs.

"What happened?" he groaned. "Where am I?"

"You're standing at the gates of hell, my son. And I'm here to help you turn back," said Raphael.

Max looked up and noticed the blood stains on the medical jacket. There was a vicious wound over the man's eye and he was wearing a purple stole around his neck. The rock star frowned in confusion and struggled to connect the dots.

"He's a priest, Max," offered Chelsea. "He's here to help."

The words barely escaped her lips when her brother flew into a rage.

"Get this freak away from me," he shouted and twisted around for the intercom.

Before his fingers could reach the call button, Raphael grabbed a music award and jammed it into the plastic casing, completely shredding the circuitry. The entire panel exploded in a shower of sparks. He tossed aside the metal trophy and left the remaining wires dangling like the gutted entrails of a dead animal.

Cursing, Max made a fist and swung weakly at the stranger, missing him by a mile.

"We don't have time for this," said Raphael.

He clamped his hands around the patient's face and intoned, "God, creator and defender of the human race, look down on this your servant, whom you formed in your own image and now call to be a partaker of your glory."

The lights in the room began to flicker. Max squirmed and tried to shove Raphael away but the doctor simply held on and prayed.

"Kyrie Eleison, Christe Eleison, Kyrie Eleison," chanted Raphael. "Have pity O Lord on your servant, remove the veil of darkness and show him the depths of his misery."

A loud cry exploded from Max. He unleashed a string of blasphemies and struggled to break free, shouting for his sister to assist him. Instead, Chelsea stood frozen to her corner like a deer caught in the headlights, her own primal fears unraveling with every word that the priest was chanting, as if something dark inside of her was also being forced to the surface. In the fading light, the mild tussle between the two men seemed like an epic struggle between day and night.

As Raphael continued with the prayers, Chelsea felt her pulse quicken and the air around her grew cold. Frightened and wanting to break the spell, she tore her eyes away and noticed something strange on the bedroom walls. They were crawling with what appeared to be a colony of tiny insects.

Mesmerized, she reached out and plucked one from the wall. There was something odd about the fly. It was hideous and deformed - the bug had two heads but only one wing and seemed to be secreting a pungent slime onto her hand. She shook it off and saw that the wall next to Max was quickly disappearing under a swarm of tiny wings. Alarmed, she grabbed a magazine and swatted as many as she could. But as soon as she cleared a segment, new and more bizarre creatures appeared in their place.

She looked up and saw that Raphael had let go of her brother. But Max was no longer worried about the priest at that point; he was busy trying to brush the scary looking bugs from his soiled pajamas. The plague had moved onto his bed.

"What's happening?" asked Chelsea, petrified.

Immediately, there came a noise like the scraping of little feet against wood. The scratching became louder and louder. At the same time, the drapes by the window shook violently, as if something was gnawing furiously at the fabric. Chelsea felt as if her heart was being wrenched from her chest. All of a sudden, an army of black rats poured out from under Max's bed and rushed towards the poor girl. She leapt onto a sofa and balked at the tide of rodents now infesting every corner of the floor. It was like a giant sewage pipe had burst opened and vomited its vermin into the apartment.

The stench was unbearable and the rats were everywhere. They hissed and tumbled over the carpet in a feeding frenzy, biting anything they could sink their teeth into, including each other.

Chelsea screamed at Raphael, "What are you doing, what's going on?"

"I'm showing him what his true legacy looks like," said the doctor. "He sold his soul to live in filth. Now he's about to die in filth and the owners are coming to collect."

At once, the bedroom ceiling burst into flames. A ring of fire opened up above the bed like a portal to hell. The smell of burnt flesh was overwhelming.

Max was terrified. He grabbed Raphael by the collar and yelled at him, "You're the one who's doing this! Stop it now or I swear…"

"You'll swear by what? The devil?" asked Raphael. "This is real. Hell is real! And God is giving you a peek at what awaits you."

Max looked up and saw the flames above his head. Plunged into this hellhole were human shapes blown about like ashes in the wind, blackened by clouds of fire and shrieking in pain and despair.

"No! They said God doesn't exist. The devil doesn't exist," Max squawked in panic. "They promised!"

He threw aside the covers and tried to flee his infested bed, but

Raphael grabbed him and thrust him back into the sheets.

"They lied," the doctor roared. "Open your eyes and see your destiny!"

Max shook his head furiously and buried his face in his hands. He was clearly under some spell. This had to be some trick, some illusion forced upon him by the bloody priest. He was not going down this way.

"It's not too late, you can still repent, still save yourself," said Raphael.

A ball of spit hit the doctor squarely in the face as Max laughed defiantly. Raphael wiped the slime from his cheek and took a step back. He wasn't worried about being splattered, but something nasty was creeping up the bed. And if Max Sparrow wouldn't listen to a servant of God, it was time to let the devil do the talking.

"Max!!!" Chelsea shouted, pointing vigorously in his direction.

Sparrow turned his head and spotted movement by the bed. It was darting between the shadows like a mist. He couldn't tell what it was, except that it was translucent and fleeting. Before he could react, something jumped out and latched onto his chest.

"Get it off, get it off!" Max cried out as the creature dug its talons into his flesh.

Chelsea couldn't see anything except for a set of claws shimmering like a mirage. She wanted to reach over and help her brother, but the ocean of rats kept her stranded on the sofa. There was a horrifying shriek. She looked up and saw Max lifted off his bed like a rag doll and slammed back into the sheets.

"Help him!" she bawled.

Raphael removed the small crucifix from his jacket. He traced the sign of the cross over the creature and said, "In the name of our Lord Jesus Christ, and by the power of his blood, his cross and his resurrection, I bind you spirit of evil, and command you to show yourself."

The serpent hissed and bared its fangs. For the first time, Chelsea and Max could see the monster in its entirety. It flickered, screeched and tried to hide itself like a chameleon, cloaking its coils in shadows.

"Oh Christ, we adore you and we praise you, because by your holy cross you have redeemed the world. Unmask the enemy of mankind, let all his deceptions be made known, and all his evil plans be defeated," said Raphael.

The beast squirmed like a suffering leech in a barrel of salt and fought to remain invisible.

Once again, Raphael raised the crucifix in benediction. "Behold the wood of the cross, on which hung the Savior of the world!"

A second blessing forced the creature into the light, and it was clear that the monster hated to be seen. But there it was, in full sight of the terrified siblings and snarling with all the fury of hell.

"God is real, Maximilian, and he wants to help you. But you must call on him now!" said the priest with urgency.

"Anything Father, please," cried Max in anguish. "Tell me what to do"

The giant reptile turned and hissed at Raphael. Its eyes were huge marbles of murky black, swimming with intense hatred for the priest in the medical coat. And yet, the creature seemed choked by restraint, unable to harm the cleric. Instead, it lashed out with an odious roar and clamped its jaws around the patient's throat, refusing to lose its prey.

Max felt the agony of a thousand daggers buried in his neck. He squealed like a stuck pig and cried desperately for help.

"Gahhh…no…it's killing me!"

"No more delays, Max, confess your sins," said Raphael. "Tell God you're sorry for rejecting him."

"Do it, Max!!!" pleaded Chelsea.

The dying rock star caught his own reflection in a shard of broken mirror on the floor. The startling sight of his wretched state drained the blood from his face. Even his putrid sores reeked with the stench of sin. Something told him this was no illusion. No drug ever conjured a vision like this. He knew this was for real.

The serpent tightened its grip. Max could feel the veins in his throat popping with stress. A few more seconds and he wouldn't be able to talk, much less confess anything.

"My God, I'm sorry. Help me!" cried the broken penitent, struggling to free himself from the jaws of hell.

Amazingly, no one outside the room heard anything or was even aware of the drama. A pall of secrecy had mysteriously descended and hidden them from Zadok and the rest.

"Hang on," said Raphael. He held up the crucifix and recited in Latin, "*Crux sacra sit mihi lux! Nunquam Draco sit mihi dux!*"

There was a rumbling noise that shook the room. A loud din came from the rats as they rose in aggression. The river of vermin turned their noses toward the priest and charged.

"O Sovereign Lord, my strong deliverer, who shields my head in the day of battle. Do not grant the wicked their desires, O Lord; do not let their plans succeed."

The floor shuddered like it was rent by an earthquake. Chelsea could see that Raphael was still moving his lips but she couldn't hear anything. The entire space had suddenly been thrust into a vacuum of silence, as if something had suddenly sucked all the sound from the room.

Then just as suddenly, the crackling rumble returned and Chelsea was thrown from the sofa. As she hit the floor, a blinding bolt of light shot out from the crucifix and struck every corner of the room. The searing brightness caused the woman to cover her face. She felt power wash over her like a wave of intense heat. The insects peeled off the walls like taffy and dripped mercilessly onto the burning floor. The rats exploded with horrifying squeals and disintegrated in the brilliant flash.

Raphael continued to pray and raise the crucifix over the serpentine form. The hideous monster on Max's chest shrieked like a banshee. All six of its eyes burned with ferocious venom as it tried to slash the servant of God with its talons. But the light of the cross cut like a guillotine and the creature was forced to keep its distance. It was filled with complete and invincible hatred for the priest. At the same time, it was completely impotent to harm the cleric.

All of a sudden, the flaming vortex above the bed imploded with violence. The portal opened its mouth like a yawning beast and devoured the reptilian menace, spewing forth fire and ash before vanishing in a ball of blue flame. This was followed by a deafening noise like a clap of thunder. And then without any explanation...

Chelsea opened her eyes and was stunned to see that everything was back to normal. The furniture was in place, the walls were intact, and the only sound that could be heard was the rapid beeping of the machines. It was like nothing had happened.

She looked across at her brother and saw that he was shaking like a leaf.

"Was all that real?" asked Chelsea, her heart still jumping wildly.

"I'm not a magician Miss Shields, I don't do tricks," answered Raphael.

He turned to his patient and said, "Confess everything, my son. Reconcile with heaven. There isn't much time and hell wants you bad."

Max sobbed uncontrollably. "I'm sorry," he sniveled. "Please forgive me."

Sparrow had been baptized Catholic, but like most people whose faith was more cultural than real, it didn't take much to fall off the edge. The story was always the same. Karl Marx was right; religion was the opium of the masses. It was responsible for sectarian wars, violence and injustice. The old Gods had to go. The world was preaching a new gospel, and the Corporation was its mighty herald. No moral authority, no Church, no doctrine or revelation could presume to challenge the ultimate authority of individual conscience. Each person was his own God and his own salvation. In time, whole generations became skeptical of the supernatural. Secularism flooded into churches, temples and mosques, and new creeds were founded to worship at the altars of relativism.

For Man to live, God had to die. But for Max Sparrow, it seemed that God was going to have the last word.

Tears streamed down the patient's face. Raphael leaned his ear close to the dying man and heard his confession. The words were choked with emotion and pain. A lifetime of regrets, an eternity of consequences, and a moment of grace that came none too soon.

Chelsea was still shaking with fright. She picked up the crucifix left on the bed and gazed at it in wonder. Her heart was filled with dread and confusion. She had no idea if Lumen Corp was really evil, but she knew that after today, her whole world had been turned upside down. She could never go back to the way things were. If God existed, where did that put her on the scales?

She looked at her brother and saw something different in his eyes. She couldn't tell what it was, but he looked like how she remembered him as a kid - dreamy and innocent.

The priest recited the formula for absolution, "God, the Father of mercies, through the death and the resurrection of his Son has reconciled the world to himself and sent the Holy Spirit among us for the forgiveness of sins. Through the ministry of the Church may God give you pardon and peace…"

He traced the sign of the cross over Max and continued, "I absolve you from your sins in the name of the Father, and of the Son, and of the Holy Spirit."

The penitent sighed softly and closed his eyes. A tiny smile crept over his lips and framed his tired face like a wreath of flowers. He was exhausted, bruised and wounded, but Max looked surprisingly peaceful considering what he had just gone through.

Then without warning, the cardiac machine went flat line. Chelsea jumped at the shrill cry of the monitor. Her heart dived in shock as the noise of the alarm pierced the room like a scream for help.

Raphael called out Max's name but the patient was deathly still. He tried to feel for a pulse but there was nothing - no respiration, no signs of life - only the silence of eternal rest. The priest turned back to look at Chelsea.

She returned his gaze with tears in her eyes. "Is he gone?" she asked.

"Yes," said Raphael. "But he's safe. You made sure of that when you called me."

The heart-rate monitor rang harshly in the quiet of the room, tracing a straight line across the screen. It was painful for Chelsea to bear this terrible toll of death.

"Shut it down," she begged.

Raphael nodded with sympathy. He reached up to turn off the machine. But before he could flip the switch, it exploded with a brutal bang and spat debris and wires at the priest. Stunned, he tried to shield his face from the shattered glass and fell back against the wall. The ceiling fan spun out of control and catapulted into the furniture, shredding the wood and fabric like a loose turbine. The lights in the room sizzled and blew out of their sockets.

Raphael grabbed Chelsea and wrestled her to the floor. "Get down!" he said.

Chapter 5

Outside, the party in the living room was about to get interrupted. The pulsating lights over the dance floor popped like overheated kernels and showered everyone in sparks. The crowd whistled and clapped, thinking it was all part of the entertainment. There was a loud whine from the sound system when the giant speakers crashed to the floor. Laughter continued as the tumbling boxes raced across the room, mowing down everyone in its path and pulverizing a young couple against the wall.

The crowd was too stoned to react with fear, but Zadok knew that something was wrong. Before he could drop the naked teenager from his lap, the giant chandelier tore free from the ceiling and scattered its parts like a carpet bomb on the guests. Pieces of crystal ripped through flesh and bone and buried themselves in eye sockets. There was screaming and panic everywhere. In the kitchen, the cooking grills exploded and incinerated several people nearby. Carving knives flew from their holders and cut deep into an orgy of socialites, spilling blood and pandemonium throughout the house.

Back in Max's bedroom, the electronic equipment had come alive, seemingly tossed about by unseen hands. Chelsea was freaked out.

"What's going on? Why is this happening?" she cried.

"Stay down!" Raphael ordered. "Satan doesn't like it when he loses a prized catch. The old goat is just throwing a tantrum, but we've got to get you out of here."

The doctor stood up and threw off his stole and jacket. Chelsea noticed he was wearing a tightly packed garment around his torso. It resembled an armored vest but looked way too thin to stop any bullets.

"What're you doing?" she asked.

Raphael rapped at the windows with his knuckles and replied, "We're going to have to jump."

"Are you insane? Do you have a parachute?"

"I'm wearing one," Raphael said casually. "It's an experimental prototype. But don't worry, I was told it's top of the line. I got it from the military."

Chelsea was horrified. "You want us to jump out of a building with a chute that's not properly tested? Are you nuts?"

"Probably. But it's too late for a refund. We have to go. Now!"

A second later, the bolted lock was ripped apart by gunfire. The door flew opened as agents stormed in with automatic weapons.

Zadok followed closely behind. He saw the purple stole lying on the bed and noticed the crucifix still clasped in Chelsea's hand.

"What the hell are you doing with that?" he shouted at Chelsea, who hid nervously behind the doctor.

The manager took a quick look at the lifeless body on the bed and knew right away what had happened.

"You lousy son of a bitch," he cursed at Raphael. Grabbing a pistol from an agent, he pointed it at the priest.

"Wait, it's not what you think," said Raphael, trying to buy some time. He removed a small device from his pocket and attached it to the glass window behind his back.

"You've got a lot of guts coming here," Zadok barked. "I'm going to cut off your balls and feed them to my dogs!"

Raphael smirked and replied, "Let's hope they like them with a bit of shrapnel."

He grabbed the woman and dropped to the floor.

†

Ninety floors down, young Randy Schofield was leaning against a limo in his neatly pressed chauffeur's uniform. Finishing his first pack of smokes did nothing to calm his nerves. Instead, he pulled out a new stash and lit another one.

The streets were quiet, except for a smattering of tuxedos and evening gowns across the road. Another swanky building was hosting another private party. This city was full of rich wallets and even richer appetites. He had chauffeured some of them in the past - big wigs and fat cats with their mistresses and wives in tow. They pretty much owned the whole town. At least, that's what Lumen Corp wanted them to believe.

Life was a carnival of fast cars, designer drugs and crazy sex. Round after round, the whirlpool of pleasures kept them spinning in a carousel of sin. The ride often got so dizzy that no one ever got off, much less notice that Armageddon was erupting right under their cocaine-powdered noses.

"Frickin' zombies, every one of them," thought Randy, shaking his head.

He brought the cigarette to his lips and heard a crackling explosion. The noise made him duck on reflex. Glass and debris rained down on the streets below and pelted the tuxedo party across the road. They scattered like pigeons in a panic.

Randy looked up and saw a gaping hole where the penthouse window used to be. Clearly the explosive charge had worked, but where was the priest? He squinted and saw two figures fall from the tower. The doctor had grabbed Chelsea and they were both plummeting to the ground.

"Shit!" cried the chauffeur. "Time to call in the Cavalry."

Above the crowds, Raphael tumbled like a rag in the wash cycle. He held on to Chelsea in a bear hug and reached desperately for the red tab on his front vest. The ground was rushing up to greet them. He pulled the ripcord and a giant canopy shot out like a glider and snatched them back into the air. But the chute swung them dangerously into the path of death. A hail of bullets whizzed by and slashed into the nylon panels. Before he could get a grip, a burning pain cut across his leg.

No bones were shattered; it was just a graze. But Zadok and his agents were emptying their guns in his direction, and sooner or later, the villains were going to get lucky. Raphael clutched the harness controls and struggled to steer the chute to safety. He knew it was a matter of minutes before the Corporation caught up. But if he could get to the car in time, they might just make it.

Chelsea was too scared even to scream. Her body had gone limp with terror. At this speed, the icy winds tore at their faces and they would hit the ground too fast. It was going to be close. And undoubtedly painful!

"Holy Mother of God, help us," cried Raphael. The pair slammed into the branches of a tree and hit the floor hard. The fall knocked the wind out of them.

Randy saw all this from the safety of his limo. He had the phone glued to his ear and was muttering away with anxiety.

"C'mon, pick up, pick up!" he kept chanting.

High above, Zadok Martaban stood by the shattered window of the suite, a smoking gun in one hand and a phone in the other. He had reported the incident to his masters at the Corporation, but there was no telling how they would react. As he listened to the sullen voice on the other end, every drop of blood drained from his face.

Quickly he turned to the Lumen agent by his side. "Unleash the dogs!" he ordered.

Straight away, the tall man with the pale skin chanted an eerie prayer and leapt out the window with nothing but the clothes on his back. A few seconds later, he slammed into the pavement below with a resounding thud, shattering the concrete slabs. The dust had barely settled when the creepy man stood tall without a scratch to his person. Instead of blood and brains, there was a fiery pentagram at his feet. As the dark servant increased the sound of his incantations, bright yellow runes began to swirl around his body like ghostly shapes taking form.

Raphael saw the scene unfold a few hundred yards away. He knew something nasty was coming.

Scrambling to his feet, he tried to get Chelsea to the waiting car. As he dragged the frightened girl off the pavement, he heard the vicious growl of an angry dog behind him. The doctor turned and saw a terrifying creature snorting fire from its snout. It was completely hairless, covered in sores, and flaunting a crushing jaw. Its eyes were fueled by a bloodlust that alarmed him.

Terror stricken, Chelsea watched in disbelief as more canine forms emerged from the mystic runes. They rallied around the first animal like a hunt organizing itself. Thick globs of mucus oozed from their fangs and a chilling sound like the cry of lost souls echoed in their howls. It was clear the pack of hounds were impatient for the kill.

The Lumen agent calmly pointed at the doctor and whispered a command. Instantly, the dogs leapt into action.

Chapter 6

The broken silhouette of the church rose into the night like an ancient castle born from the earth. There was very little moonlight, but it was enough to see that this was once an impressive structure. The tall wooden doors were brittle with age and the stone columns holding up the façade had long succumbed to weeds and graffiti. Inside the sanctuary, its desecrated altar lay buried beneath decades of dust. The empty pews no longer echo with the voices of faith, but were rotting with the silence of a murdered creed.

Once upon a time, this had been a vibrant parish. It was the only church for miles around. And the folks who lived and worked these farms knew little of the turmoil that was brimming in the big cities. But in time, even small country parishes began to fall under the eye of the Corporation. New laws and policies were enacted to strangle country parishes like a gauntlet designed to crush every sign of faith.

Caught in this vile persecution, the priests responded with harsh words from the pulpits. Sermons were preached to wake the consciences of the dead. And like vultures waiting in the shadows, the Corporation retaliated. Criminal charges were filed against the clergy, charges of sexual abuse abounded, and conspiracies against the State were alleged. Even bomb-making materials were conveniently discovered in some presbyteries. Some of the allegations were true. Most however were complete lies.

Yet almost overnight, entire churches were emptied of their priests. Special police units arrived in the hours of darkness and dragged the astonished men from their beds. Most were arrested and incarcerated in re-education facilities. Some mysteriously disappeared. And without the priests, the life source of the Church - the Eucharist - disappeared along with them.

The message was clear. Resistance was futile.

Like many others across the country, this church was now just a decrepit old building jutting from the shadows and forgotten by time. Within its grimy walls, nothing of beauty remained from its hallowed past. The stained glass windows were long gone. All that remained was a broken altar table, some rotten pews and a damaged tabernacle box that now hosted an owl and her chicks instead of the Lord of Hosts. The only thing of beauty was a colossal statue rising over the sanctuary. It stood like a tombstone marking the death of a religion that society had long discounted as a relic of the past.

Even so, it was easy to see the majesty that once adorned this imposing sculpture. At the dedication ceremony, the good people of this parish had installed this statue of the Archangel, and they had prayed that their patron saint would guard and deliver them from all evil. Clad in his battle armor and armed with an impressive spear that bore down on the dragon at his feet, it was a powerful reminder of divine protection.

But today, the Church of St. Michael was boarded up and condemned. And the only protection the angel seemed to provide was for the animals that had taken shelter under his wings.

To all appearances, the house of God was dead, its memory decomposing with the surrounding walls. But inside this mausoleum, life was still coming through the floorboards. The pulse was weak but unmistakable.

Unknown to many, there was a little chapel under the main church. On this particular night, it was crowded with a small band of faithful. The warm glow of lighted candles contrasted greatly with the morbid darkness of the sanctuary above. Hidden in the basement, a group of Christians were quietly celebrating Holy Mass. Most of the congregation was made up of women and children, their faces rapt with attention and reverence. The few men who were present sat in their pews with the pained expressions of survivors who had seen too much of the horrors of war.

An Underground bishop presided over the service. He crouched over the pulpit like an old lion that had survived more than a few skirmishes with the wolves. His back was no longer straight, his voice barely a whisper. Yet in the eyes of the tiny flock, he was a giant among men, one of the few still alive who refused to bow to the tyranny of oppression, and who spent his days instead eluding his captors and ministering to his flock under the cover of night.

But here in this chapel there was no need for clever disguises. He was where he belonged, with his people at the altar of sacrifice. This was who he was ordained to be - a bishop and a successor of the apostles.

A tall miter sat on his head like a holy crown of office. Wrapped around his torso was a chasuble of exquisite beauty, which signified the royal virtue of divine love. And on his finger sparkled the symbol of his authority as bishop - his Episcopal ring.

He was a good shepherd faithful to Rome. Unfortunately, there were not many of them left. The hunt was quickly depleting the Church of ministers loyal to the Holy See. Reports of treachery were coming in more often and the vice was getting tighter. For even among angels, there were spies and traitors. But this didn't stop the old bishop from mounting the pulpit like a prophet. In the battle for souls, there was no room for cowardice.

The crowd listened attentively as the bishop spoke about peace. He knew there was little of it left in the world. But even in the heart of the Church, it was clear that the smoke of Satan had crept in. Did they understand that the absence of peace was a warning that the devil was already at the door?

There was only one way to counter evil. The remedy was always the same: conversion, repentance, prayer, and penance. The chaos of darkness and the assaults of hell were only symptomatic of the greater disease that had taken root in the hearts of men. Through their rejection of the moral life and the reality of God, the sons and daughters of Adam had opened their own souls to the seduction of evil. With such a sick tree in the world, it was only a matter of time before its fruits poisoned all of creation as they fell to the ground.

Confession, said the bishop, was still the most powerful means to break the chains of darkness. Many abstained from this great cure or ridiculed the mysteries it contained. But for a person who had taken poison, he could either ignore the antidote or avail himself of it. Either way, death was already in motion.

Yet not all was lost. The bishop cautioned against despair. Did not Christ promise that the Gates of Hell would never prevail against the Church that he founded?

"So stand firm," said the old shepherd, holding aloft his crosier like a battle flag. "Do not be afraid. The enemy wants to wipe away every sign of God from your hearts but they won't succeed. We won't let them. This is not an old world dying, but a new one being born."

"I invite you to renew your commitment to Christ, to stand up for your faith," continued the prelate. "Even now the Lord raises new warriors among us."

When he said this, some of the younger men in the congregation straightened their backs and perked up. In every generation, there were those who were eager to die for their faith. Unfortunately, too few were willing to live for it. The bishop understood the recklessness of youth and told his flock that the best defense was living the faith courageously; in the universities and schools, in offices and hospitals, in cafes and pubs, in wherever a good Christian found himself, and not in courting martyrdom in the dragon's lair. For most of them, this was where the battle lines of faith must be recaptured, in the arena of reason and public life. This was no less important than fighting the hordes of hell. In the end, the city of God would triumph over the city of man. And from the ashes of the suffering Church, a new dawn would emerge.

Clutching his crosier, the bishop ended his homily and blessed the small congregation. Returning to the altar, he began the prayers for the Eucharistic liturgy, where the bread and wine would soon be consecrated and transformed into the body, blood, soul and divinity of Jesus Christ.

It was a core Catholic belief, and most of the congregation crowded around the altar to be as close to the miracle as possible. Some prayed for the strength to survive the oncoming storm. Others begged for the grace to stand and fight. But one man in particular knelt in the shadows of the last pew - unmoving, mysterious, and unnoticed. No one had seen him come in except for a little girl of six. Hiding her face behind a plush rabbit, she stared at the lone figure kneeling in the back.

He looked up and noticed the beautiful girl with dark curls and winked at her. That made her smile. She had seen him before. He had joined the community some weeks earlier, but many still did not know him well. The man had a hard face but he wasn't intimidating. Despite the scar running down his eyebrow, she wasn't the least bit afraid of him.

Blushing, she wriggled her fingers shyly. He wriggled his fingers back. Thrilled with the attention, she crawled off her pew and wandered slowly down the aisle like an adventurer exploring a new find. Her mother was too engrossed in prayer to notice the child leaving her side. It wasn't very bright in the chapel. Instead of light bulbs, candles were used to minimize exposure to the surface, but the flickering wicks also ensured that most of the pews were plunged into darkness. Only the sanctuary was sufficiently lit for the Mass to proceed.

Hugging her toy, the girl strolled to the back of the chapel and stopped at the last pew. The man in the hooded jacket looked up in amusement. She smiled and held out her soft woolen bunny with the missing button for an eye. For a second, the stranger seemed unsure of what to do. In spite of himself, he reached out and patted the doll with his calloused hands. The child broke into a smile. She ran gleefully back to her pew with her bunny in tow and her cheeks flushed with pleasure.

Meanwhile the liturgy had progressed. The congregation stood and knelt in successive waves of prayer until finally, with the consecration of bread and wine, the bishop held the pristine white host above the chalice and intoned, "Behold, the Lamb of God who takes away the sins of the world. Happy are those who are called to receive Him."

The faithful confessed their unworthiness and begged the Lord for healing. And then it was time to receive Holy Communion. A line began to form as people left their pews and shuffled slowly to the altar to receive the bread of life. At the risk of detection by the Lumen authorities, there was great care taken to be silent. But the mood was always one of deep reverence for the sublime mysteries of the faith.

Looking very much like an ancient king, the bishop stood on the threshold of the sanctuary, assisted by a young acolyte dressed in white. He held the golden vessel called a ciborium in his left hand and gave out the consecrated hosts with his right. The hungry flock, starved of spiritual nourishment for months because of the lack of priests approached their shepherd gratefully.

The stranger however remained kneeling in the back. His face showed no emotions as he watched the faithful genuflect and rise to receive the sacred host on their tongues. Even in the shadows, it was easy to see that he was a big man. He waited patiently for the communion line to grow thin. Finally, he reached for his jacket and drew the hood over his head. Keeping his face lowered, he got up from the darkness and joined the queue, trailing quietly behind the others until it came time for him to kneel before the prelate.

"The Body of Christ," said the bishop, holding aloft the consecrated bread. The man dropped his right knee to the floor and bowed his head without hesitation. As he rose to his feet, a gunshot rang out in the chapel. The bishop dropped the host and staggered back in surprise.

"Amen," said the man.

He raised the smoking barrel and fired another round. The impact of the bullet threw the bishop against the altar table and sent the old man sprawling to the ground. As he collapsed, the ciborium rolled out of his hands and scattered its sacred contents all over the wooden floor.

At first, the crowd was too stunned to react, until the cries of the children roused the adults into panic. Terrified, the flock scrambled in all directions, worried that the gunman would soon turn his madness on the congregation.

In the chaos, two men lunged at the stranger and tried to wrestle the weapon from his hand, but he tossed them aside like rag dolls. That same moment, metal canisters rolled out from the shadows and detonated in a series of blinding flashes. The ceiling ripped opened as armed men in balaclavas rappelled through the cavity and pointed their weapons at the scattered sheep.

There was absolute mayhem in the chapel. People fell over each other in alarm. Warning shots were fired over the heads of the congregation, and those who attempted to flee were dragged, beaten and tied together like livestock. Others who tried to resist were tasered into submission. It was all very brutal and quick. In less than five minutes, confusion had succumbed to an orderly arrest. The prisoners were tied with plastic handcuffs and thrown onto the floor like bags of sand. Only the children, frozen in fear, remained free to cling to each other.

As the raiding party watched over their captives, an officer detached himself from the assault team and approached the stranger. His face was hidden behind a black ski mask.

"Tangos ready for transport," he said. Then glancing at the fallen target, he asked the man in the hooded jacket, "Is he dead?"

The stranger walked over to where his victim was lying in a pool of carnage. The bishop was still breathing. Clutching his pectoral cross, the prelate tried to pull himself up by clinging to the altar cloth. Instead, he toppled the chalice and the consecrated wine splashed onto his red vestments and mingled with his own blood.

The stranger pointed his gun at the dying man and blew his brains out. "He is now," replied the killer, pulling back the hood from his face. "Search the chapel for any kind of intel that can give us a lead on the Resistance."

"You heard the captain," said the lieutenant to his men. "Move your asses!"

The squad burst into action and tore up the chapel. The officer slung his rifle over his shoulder and stepped over the bishop's body. He bent over the carnage and stripped the pectoral cross and jeweled ring from the dead man. Turning the loot over in his hands, he pulled off his balaclava and squinted at the plunder.

"Amethyst and gold," he said laughing. "Wasted on a dead cockroach."

"Put it back," said the captain.

"Why? He's not going to need this, is he?" said the officer with a wry smile.

But before he could pocket the spoils, the taller man seized the lieutenant by the collar and dragged him to his feet.

"Get back to your position and secure the transfer," the captain grunted. "We're soldiers, not common thieves."

"Oh I assure you, there's nothing common about these babies," the junior officer replied with sarcasm. He slapped the captain's hand away and proceeded to stash the loot in his vest. Then adjusting his weapon, he smirked and walked away.

The tension was explosive. The lieutenant was new to the team, but both he and the captain were old style gladiators chained at the wrist. One was a decorated veteran of several military campaigns. The other was a cold-blooded mercenary direct from Lumen headquarters. Forced to work together, they hated each other with a vengeance. But with growing reports of underground activity across the country, resources had to be combined. The result was the unhappy fusion of Army elites with Lumen Corp's own Praetorian Guards, created specially to seek out and destroy the Resistance.

As a rule, every assault team was required to have Praetorian members on their squad. It was an arrangement the captain wasn't happy with. The precise discipline of the Special Forces warriors he commanded clashed with the marauding barbarism of the Lumen vandals. Thankfully the numbers of Praetorians were small, but there was no question as to who was signing the cheque. The military was kept under the heel of the Corporation.

Still, the captain wasn't going to let a loose cannon endanger the mission. As the lieutenant walked back to his position, a few of the prisoners looked up at the unmasked officer. His blonde hair was a buzz cut and his green eyes were splinters of cold jade. He gazed down at the Christians in open contempt.

"What're you looking at?" he barked at the acolyte who was serving the Mass earlier. The young man said nothing but averted his eyes.

"I asked you a question!" shouted the lieutenant. He swung his rifle around and smashed the carbon butt into the boy's face, breaking his teeth. "And when I ask you a question, you answer!"

He grabbed the bleeding youth by his hair and yanked him to his feet.

"Leave him alone," cried a woman in the group. In response, the officer shoved the boy back down onto the floor. He reached for the woman and rammed the muzzle of his rifle between her eyes.

"Say again?"

"That's enough lieutenant!" shouted the captain. "You know the procedure, get these people ready for transport. I want everyone out of here in five."

"I say we leave no witnesses," the lieutenant yelled back. He cocked his weapon and took aim at the screaming crowd.

"Stand down, that's not part of the mission directive," ordered the captain. "The primary target has been neutralized. No one else dies tonight, is that clear?"

Ignoring the injunction, the lieutenant tightened his grip on the trigger until he felt cold steel pushed up against the back of his skull, followed by a distinctive clicking noise.

"You can stand down or you can join the bishop on the floor. Your choice," said the voice behind him.

Reluctantly, the lieutenant lowered his rifle and chuckled, "Whatever you say, El Capitan, you're the mission leader."

"That's right," answered the captain. "If you need a reminder, I'll be happy to send a message to your brain."

He nudged the barrel against the lieutenant's head.

"Give me your rifle," he said.

The lieutenant quietly handed over his weapon.

"The rest of you, wrap it up and let's go!" said the captain.

He holstered his handgun and cradled the Praetorian rifle as his own. Immediately the squad hauled the Underground Christians to their feet and began marching them out the door.

"Surely you're not serious?" the lieutenant protested.

"These sewer rats are like the plague. If even one of them escapes, they'll find some way to let the rest know. And then poof, they'll vanish. They'll hide in their little burrows for months, probably for years, and you won't be able to find them so easily again."

When the captain didn't respond, the lieutenant grabbed a shotgun from a passing soldier and chambered a round into the rifle.

"We can't afford to leave witnesses and you know it," he grumbled.

The threat of imminent slaughter alarmed the prisoners. They began to struggle against their captors and had to be subdued by force.

"I'm not going to say this again," said the captain. "Our orders are to bring the rest in for interrogation. So either you get with the program or get out of my way."

To press his point, he raised his rifle slightly in the direction of the Praetorian officer.

"Yes sir!" the lieutenant replied scornfully. "You're the boss."

He spat on the floor and rejoined the squad. There was little doubt that he held his superior officer in contempt. In return, the scowl on the captain's face only deepened.

With only one way in and out of the chapel, it didn't help that the doorway was designed to be narrow and concealed. The roof had been torn up during the assault but they couldn't evacuate the throng that way. The squad rustled up the crowd and forced them through the exit one at a time. Raising a hand, the captain signaled for his men to pick up the pace.

As the team pushed the prisoners forward, he noticed a pair of dark eyes looking up at him. She was lost in a sea of frightened faces and carried along by the crush of human bodies. Separated from her mother, she stumbled along like a newborn lamb trying to find its way. When she got near the captain, she reached out and brushed the tip of his hand with her fingers. The lieutenant barked and shoved her back in line. In the tussle, her toy bunny slipped from her hands and fell to the floor. It got kicked around and trampled by the crowd until it slid against a pew by the wall.

The child started to whimper. She called for her mother but the woman was too far back to reach her. Pushing desperately against the human tide, the little girl inched her way back until she saw an opening in the line. Going down on her hands and knees, she crawled past the cordon and decided to make a quick dash for her doll.

As she got up and scampered towards the pew, the lieutenant caught sight of the runaway girl and raised his shotgun. The captain noticed the drama and quickly pointed his rifle at the officer.

"Put the gun down!"

"She's trying to escape," said the lieutenant.

"Put it down!" yelled the irate captain.

When the girl reached her bunny, she picked it off the floor and hugged it to her chest. The woolen rabbit disintegrated as the blast tore into the stuffing and sent the child flying into the pews. Her petite body slammed into the benches like a missile and crumbled in a heap of torn flesh. Blood was splattered everywhere, even on the captain's face.

The screams of her mother pierced the chapel in a tragic howl, but the child was unable to respond. Her beautiful dark curls were matted with death and her limbs were twisted like a pretzel soaked in carnage. The savage butchery was too much to bear. It was impossible for these Christians to turn the other cheek. Erupting with anger and violence, they threw themselves at the soldiers, sparing no effort to bite, punch and kick their way to freedom. The assault team fell back briefly and fired warning shots to contain the crowd, but if the prisoners could not be subdued safely, it was clear that a massacre was inevitable.

"Like I said, we can't afford any witnesses," replied the lieutenant.

In response, the captain squeezed the trigger on his rifle and emptied the entire clip at the Praetorian officer, shredding the lieutenant like a cheese grater. The M4 Carbine screamed with 750 rounds of death per minute, but all the captain could hear was the voice of vengeance in his ears.

And then everything went black.

When he opened his eyes again, his cell phone was ringing like a fire alarm. The noise pummeled his brain without mercy. Clutching his head in agony, he leaned back on his chair and tried to remember where he was.

It was a dingy pub off the edge of town that simmered with more garbage than the city sewer. However, the place was mostly empty that night. There were a few drunks at the counter slumped over their drinks, but apart from the bartender and waitress, he was the only one still sober enough to think.

He groaned in anguish and looked at the empty glass before him. Feeling a little disoriented, he tried to pour himself a drink but the bottle was dry. He stared blankly at the mirror reflection across the bar and saw the man who killed the bishop staring back at him. The face was the same, just older and more grizzled with pain. The flashbacks were getting more frequent. As much as he tried to forget, the images kept haunting him like a ghost that would not be exorcised. His face was still drenched in cold sweat.

"Hey buddy, you wanna answer that?" asked the bartender. The phone was still ringing off the hook.

Fighting a hangover, the irritated man waved an apology and calmly took the call. The voice that came through however sounded frantic.

"Slow down, I can't hear what you're saying," replied the man.

As he listened to the caller, a steely resolve came over his face. He furrowed his brow and shifted uncomfortably in his trench coat, which he wore like a long tunic. It had a collar that was buttoned up high to cover his neck, but it was opened at the waist for greater mobility.

"Where's your location?" he asked the caller.

When he got up to leave, the lower end of his garment flapped gently behind him like a small cape. Strangely enough, no one could see anything beyond the blackness of the fabric. There was something unusual about the cloth. It seemed to absorb all the light in the room, giving the impression that the stranger's body was constantly wrapped in a cloud of shifting shadows. If he wanted to, he could conceal an arsenal under that coat and no one would notice.

He walked to the bar and fished out a few dollars from his pockets.

"Hang on, I'm on my way," he said into the phone.

Slapping the money on the counter, he ran out the door and jumped into an old dented car named Scarface. He may not be a captain anymore but he was still a soldier, and whether he liked it or not, there was still a war to be fought. The angry machine roared to life and raced off into the night.

The chubby waitress picked up her pencil and stirred the remains of the crumpled notes on the counter.

"Thanks for the lousy tip, you stinking bum," she muttered in disdain.

Chapter 7

"Punch it!" shouted Raphael.

Randy jammed his foot on the gas pedal and rode the limo like a rodeo. Chelsea bounced around wildly in the backseat. She reached out and grabbed Raphael for support but landed on his ribs. The doctor grimaced in pain. He snatched the seatbelts and strapped her in.

"Slow down," cried Chelsea.

"Slow down and we end up as doggie-snacks," said Randy. Checking his rear-view mirror, he saw that the pack was closing in fast.

"I'm not ending up as a snack for nobody!" he shouted.

The car careened around a corner and dived straight into oncoming traffic.

"Oops…" Randy cried out.

"Look out!" yelled the rest. The chauffeur swerved madly to avoid a truck and took out a fire hydrant instead.

A quick peek in the rearview mirror confirmed that the hellhounds were hot on their heels. The creatures were jumping over traffic like a romp through the park. Some were even running up the sides of buildings and scuttling over concrete walls. Clearly gravity was not going to be a problem for these creatures.

"I'm sure the S.P.C.A. won't mind if I do this!"

Randy spun the wheel and rammed the car against one of the hounds that caught up alongside. The monster turned its head and chomped off the side-view mirror like a biscuit. When the chauffeur tried the same trick again, the hound threw itself against the car and sent the two-ton vehicle skidding.

"Jesus," exclaimed Randy as he tried to regain control.

Chelsea saw that the pack was gaining on them.

"They're right behind us, do something," she screamed.

"Great idea, what do you suggest I do?" Randy retorted.

As the car turned a corner and screeched into an alley, Satan's hound leapt from a fire escape and landed on the front bonnet, smashing the metal hood like tin foil. The impact crushed the engine and flipped the machine into the air, causing the entire vehicle to overturn and crash loudly into a bunch of trashcans.

The lights in several apartments came on abruptly and angry faces popped out of their windows cursing. But when the residents saw a pack of frightful beasts encircling the wreck, they quickly ducked their heads back in and locked the windows.

High above them, a dark shadow raced across the rooftop. The silhouette jumped and sped along the building with speed and agility, his coat flapping behind him like a pair of wings. But back in the alley, Raphael groaned as he tried to extricate himself from the car wreck.

"You okay?" he asked Chelsea, who was tangled up in her seatbelt.

"Get me out of here!" she squawked.

From the driver's seat, Randy poked his head into the back and grumbled, "I frickin' hate dogs!"

As he twisted around for the door, the entire steel panel suddenly got ripped off and flung aside.

"Holy crap!" Randy shouted as he pulled back his hand.

Crouched in the opened doorway was a monstrous head, its fiery eyes burning with hate and its massive jaws attached to a skull of rotting flesh. Behind the creature, the rest of the pack was gathering for the kill.

"*Vade retro Satana!*" Raphael shouted, tracing the sign of the cross.

This only made the beast more furious. It plunged into the vehicle and roared at the screaming occupants. Thankfully, the hellhound was too big to reach all the way in. As it tried to separate Randy from his legs, the chauffeur panicked and started to kick desperately. With seconds to spare, Raphael pulled the young man into the back seat just as the creature plunged in for the kill.

Suddenly the car shook with a loud thud. Something big and heavy had landed on it. Everyone, including the demon dog, felt the impact. As the hound jumped back to investigate, its head exploded like a ripe melon. Chunks of red goop splattered everywhere.

"Ugh!" Randy cried out with disgust as he wiped the gore from his face.

Raphael and Chelsea scrambled out of the vehicle while the headless dog collapsed in a puddle of slime.

When Randy finally crawled out of the car, he saw a pair of

combat boots standing on top of the wreck. They belonged to a man wearing a black trench coat and holding a weapon that could only be described as devastating.

"Michael!" the chauffeur cried out with relief.

"Fall back," the man responded.

He jumped down from the wreck and threw a magnetic disc at the vehicle. It caught the axle and switched on. Keeping his weapon poised at the beasts, Michael grabbed Randy and yanked him away from the car. He fired a few shots at the demon pack but the growling mastiffs dodged the bullets easily.

The hounds had recovered from the surprised attack, and were eager to pay back with generous carnage. Howling with fury, they opened their jaws and stretched their fangs like vicious daggers that suddenly grew in length.

"Oh shit," said Randy in disbelief. "Tell me you saw that!"

"Less talking and more running!" Michael ordered. He blasted the magnetic disc and the entire car exploded in a wall of flames. The fire shot twelve feet into the air and barricaded them from the hellhounds, but you could still see the silhouettes of the dogs behind the inferno.

"Move it!" Michael shouted.

Raphael grabbed Chelsea and staggered away from the blaze. The wound in his leg was still bleeding from the bullet graze.

"Wheezer, come on!" he called out to the chauffeur.

Randy scrambled after them like a lost puppy and tripped over himself, falling painfully to the ground. As he turned back to look at the inferno, a monstrous head emerged from the flames. Then two, then three, and finally four canine bodies stepped out of the firestorm snarling and unhurt.

"Jesus," shouted Randy in fright. He clambered to his feet and looked at Michael. The old soldier had thrown aside his dark coat and was staring down the demon hounds like the God of War.

His whole body was an armory of lethal weapons. Two small MP5s clung to his back, a Magnum 500 was slotted under his shoulder and his legs were pinned with Berettas and ammo clips. Along with other deadly gadgets, a retractable spiked chain attached to a large crucifix also hung from his gun belt. Most surprising of all, a circular white collar peeked out from under his black tactical vest. The man was a priest. But this was no gentle pastor. This was the angel of death.

Michael tossed a pair of metal capsules to Randy. "You know what to do," he said.

Without warning, the hellhounds charged into the fray. When the priest raised his weapon, the lead dog slammed into him like a sledgehammer and pinned him to the ground. The attack was fast and furious. The creature went straight for his jugular but was thwarted by the force of gunmetal shoved against its throat. The rapid fire of the bullets ripped the canine apart. There was blood and gore everywhere. Michael rolled away from the carcass and jumped to his feet.

Chelsea screamed as two more hellhounds cornered her and the doctor. She felt her knees buckle in terror, there was nothing separating them from the snapping jaws. The creatures licked their chops and converged on the pair, their instincts excited by the smell of fear. As the dogs approached, Raphael stared boldly into their eyes and saw a vision of the Lumen agent stirring the bellies of the beasts. He couldn't hear the words of dark magic powering the spell, but he could see the man utter the command to "Finish them!"

In that moment, a small device bounced off the pavement and blasted a cloud of white smoke at the snarling hounds. Randy flicked the switch on the second capsule and once again flung it at the creatures. A spray of incense ejected from the pod and smoked the dogs without mercy.

"Sniff on this, you stupid mutts," cried the chauffeur.

The vapors overwhelmed the shrieking dogs. The pack started howling and thrashing in panic. Their skins began to peel away in the burning cloud, spilling gooey chunks of rotting flesh to the ground. Unable to endure the powerful effects of the incense, the hellhounds melted away like wax figures in the furnace of God's wrath.

"Holy smokes, they worked!" said Randy, somewhat surprised at the effectiveness of the capsules.

Seeing his chance, he picked up a rusty pipe and smashed the whimpering dogs with all his might. There was no resistance. He took their heads off like a machete through a pumpkin patch, leaving their demon bodies to collapse like empty shells.

As the vanquished dogs hit the dirt, Chelsea clutched her throat and fell to the ground, as if gasping for air. Randy dropped the pipe and rushed to her side. She was gagging in tears.

"Calm down, just breathe normally," said the chauffeur. "It's only incense, it can't hurt you."

He tried to lift her up but she weighed a ton. Her limbs were stiff and contorted, and she looked like she was having a seizure.

"What's happening to her?" Randy asked Raphael.

The doctor checked her vital signs. But when he touched her face, he immediately saw a vision of something hiding in her soul – something buried and dark, something hitching a ride.

†

The last hellhound was ripping up pieces of the burning wreck and hurling them at Michael with frightening precision. The priest ducked and rolled as the twisted metal crashed all around him and burst into flames.

Reloading, he returned fire but the bullets missed their mark. The creature was hard to pin down. It weaved between the shadows and darted around with great speed, almost as if the canine had a cloaking ability.

This hound was faster, bigger and more cunning than the rest. The sorcery powering the spell was getting stronger, and Michael knew he had to end the combat fast. But before the priest could get a visual, a ferocious growl drew his attention to the ledge overhead. He swung his rifle at the sound but the canine form leapt from the wall and tore the weapon from his hands. It crushed the gun like a toothpick in its formidable jaws.

Michael whipped around and pulled out the MP5s from his back. He blasted away at the demon hound but the marauder faced the gunfire like a shifting mist, dodging the bullets with ease. The war veteran emptied both clips on the specter and hit only brick and mortar.

"Enough of this!" said the priest in annoyance. He threw down the guns and unhooked the crucifix from his belt. Pulling out the spiked chain, he stretched it like a lasso.

"Come and face me," Michael taunted like a matador. He pushed the metal corpus on the crucifix and a gleaming blade snapped out like a Bowie knife.

Emboldened by the challenge, the hound brazenly charged from the shadows. As it pounced on the priest, the man twisted his body to avoid the razor-sharp teeth, causing the creature to lunge past him. He snagged the beast with the metal chain and pulled the noose tight, sinking hundreds of jagged spikes into the demon flesh.

59

The fearsome dog smashed into the ground and thrashed like an angry marlin caught on a reel. It roared and struggled to break free of the metal leash, its eyes burning with molten lava and hate.

"Take this to your master," grunted Michael. He plunged the crucifix into the demon hound and gutted it like a fish.

Four miles back, the Lumen agent stumbled in shock, as if struck by an invisible blow. He dropped to his knees in agony and coughed up blood. At the same time, the glowing pentagram at his feet vanished like a mirage. The spell was broken.

Amidst the destruction, a fragile calm returned to the alley, threatened only by the possibilities of worse things emerging from the night. The danger was real. But Chelsea had recovered from the seizures, and had calmed down enough for Raphael to leave her with Randy. The doctor hurried over to his brother priest.

Michael stood tall in the middle of the kill zone, his cross blade dripping with blood. Lying all around him were the torn and mutilated bodies of the hellhounds.

"You better bind them quick," said Michael. He retracted the blade into the crucifix and restored the weapon to his gun belt. It hung there like an ancient sword ready to be drawn again.

Raphael stepped into the circle of carnage and raised his eyes to heaven.

"By the precious blood of Jesus Christ, I bind you spirits of evil," he prayed. "And command you in the name of God to descend to the pits of hell. Depart from this earth and return from whence you came. Remain in the abyss, that you may no longer harm any creature of God. I command you in the name of the Risen Christ."

Randy watched the ritual with curiosity. He had seen the priests do this before, but never with monsters such as these. It was important to lock away the spirits that were vanquished or cast out, as evil could never die. It could only be overcome. If nothing more were done, these creatures would be free to regenerate and return. The best way to stop that from happening was to bind them with the blood of Christ.

Raphael stretched out his hand and traced a cross over the fallen beasts. For a moment nothing happened. Then all of a sudden the hellhounds burst into flames. Their rotten remains imploded with violence and unleashed misty runes into the air. The luminous trail of spells rose into the night sky and funneled like a tornado returning to their source.

Elsewhere in the city, the Lumen agent looked up at the sky and saw the runes swooping down towards him. The plague he had sent out was coming back. Once again, they swirled around his body like a glowing thread of ancient letters. And once more, the letters transformed into phantom shapes that growled with the malice of hell.

However this time, only the massive heads of the hounds remained visibly strung together like a necklace of death. The grinding jaws edged ever closer like chainsaws around the man. The agent panicked and tried to slap away the vaporous fangs, only to find his hands cutting through the apparitions.

"No, stay back! I command you," cried the frightened man. He tore open his shirt to expose an amulet in the shape of a scarab.

"By the power of Anubis, yield to me!" he shouted, invoking the jackal-headed deity of the dead.

In answer to his pleas, the hellhounds tore into the man with utter cruelty, sending him on to the Egyptian god in pieces. Little was left of the human host apart from the scarab on a chain. It clattered noisily to the ground before the whole spectacle disappeared all together, leaving a bundle of entrails on the floor. The last thing heard was the savage howling of the beasts.

Overlooking the carnage from the penthouse above, Zadok stared at the gory remains with bated breath. His sweaty hands gripped the cell phone with worry. The Corporation had lost both Max and Chelsea in one day. And right under their very noses - *his* very nose to be precise.

He knew this was unacceptable to the management. Someone would have to pay. Dearly.

Chapter 8

Forty thousand feet in the air, a spanking new private jet cruised comfortably on its maiden flight. The huge airplane was nothing short of a luxury yacht in the sky, boasting the best in avionics, luxury and high-class entertainment.

Onboard the flying island, a party was in session to announce Lumen Corp's induction into the United Nations. It was neither a sovereign state nor a humanitarian body. Nevertheless it was granted permanent status to participate in worldwide conferences and agendas. No one could deny that this international organization was quickly becoming an unrivaled power in global politics and industry, and no one was naïve enough to ignore this rise in prominence on the world stage. The courtship from nations had long begun, but now the romance was getting serious. And it was time for the suitors to raise their stakes.

A celebration was in order. Mirth and champagne flowed richly from the coffers of greed. Many of the guests came with their own security detail. There were giants of industries and stardom, premiers and prime ministers, presidents and kings. And the man responsible for bringing them all together was Marshall Chambers - Lumen Corp's Senior Vice-president for Operations and International Affairs.

Chambers was a tall, lean and dignified looking man. He seemed to be cut from a diplomatic cloth that was tailored for success and leadership. As he smiled, flattered and worked the cabin, it was clear that the world's mighty leaders were as impressed with him as he was deferential to them. In a word, he was irresistible to the rich and powerful. And they were intoxicated with admiration.

"Your Majesties and Excellencies," began Chambers. "Ladies and gentlemen…"

"On this day, we gather to celebrate the future of mankind. We stand here united over conflict and confusion, with unity of purpose to overcome our differences. On this day, we come to proclaim an end to useless arguments and discord, discrimination and prejudice, and we raise our hearts to a better tomorrow."

The cabin resounded with applause and approval. Chambers motioned for the distinguished crowd to quiet down. He had only just begun, and there was much more thread to spin before the audience was fully in his grasp.

"We are no longer a shackled people, enslaved to every false promise and petty quarrel, quarrels that have kept us bound with injustice and strangled our futures for far too long. Today we raise our voices and say to those who would keep us imprisoned in mediocrity - enough!"

The Senior VP of Lumen Corp spoke with great appeal to his captive audience.

"Enough with the lies and deceptions, the narrow-mindedness and cruel dogmas, enough with the sham of superstitious creeds that have done mankind no service but to separate brother from brother, sister from sister. For the sake of humanity, now is the time to set aside childish things."

The leaders of many nations gathered around this man and looked on in admiration, their faces rapt with attention as they drank in the milk and honey of his words. Chambers puffed out his chest and raised his hands dramatically like a messiah pointing to a new promised land.

"Now is the time to celebrate our common journey towards light and greatness, to choose the noble path, to reawaken that eternal truth, passed from generation to generation that all men are created equal and free, and deserve a chance to live their dreams of happiness, fulfillment and peace, regardless of beliefs. The future is ours. Let us reclaim it from tyranny and darkness, from poverty and war, from fear and mistrust. I pledge to you the untiring commitment of Lumen Corp to help the world come together as one people united in vision, prosperity, greatness and peace."

A tall beautiful hostess approached Chambers with a glass of Champagne. He took the drink in his hand, raised it like a beacon of hope and said, "To you my friends and to the future of mankind...Salute!"

"Salute," echoed the adoring crowd as they downed their drinks with gusto. A harem of gorgeous waiting staff descended on the guests with more bottles of bubbly. The mood was exuberant if not festive.

As Chambers lowered his glass, a senior aide approached the VP and whispered something to him. He nodded slightly and turned to face his guests with a broad smile on his face - the kind that seemed to put everyone at ease.

"My friends, please forgive this intolerable disruption, but I'm afraid I shall have to miss the joy of your company for a few minutes," Chambers apologized. "The quest for world peace doesn't take any holidays, and it seems there's an urgent matter I must attend to. No rest for the wicked as they say."

He rolled his eyes and pointed to himself. The crowd laughed appreciatively.

"I shall however return shortly," assured the Lumen host with tantalizing charm. "In the meantime, please eat, drink and make merry. For today we face a new dawn of hope and triumph. Let nothing keep us from the celebrations."

The live band broke out in a jazz number while the lights dimmed to a sultry glow. Chambers smiled his way through a sea of dignitaries and shook hands with the movers and shakers, taking great care to make each one feel like the most important guest in the room. As he left the palatial ambience of the cabin behind, two Lumen agents rose from their seats like a pair of twins and escorted their boss up the luxurious length of the plane to his office at the front.

Accompanying Chambers was the senior Lumen aide from before, a stoutly built man of fifty with designer spectacles and a pronounced forehead that looked bulbous against his receding hairline. He said nothing but merely trailed his boss like a ghost. When they came to a luxurious steel door decorated with gold leaf panels, the agents took their places outside the office while the bulletproofed door slid opened to welcome the VP and his corporate shadow into the inner sanctum.

The office was a den of rich mahogany, with furniture that was clearly antique and seemed more at home in a royal palace than in a flying office somewhere over the Atlantic. The walls were adorned with priceless artworks and cultural treasures, while an ominous desk loomed from the back of the cabin like a sacrificial altar from the bloody reigns of Aztec kings.

Chambers walked over to the sumptuous armchair and sat himself behind the desk, allowing the soft Italian leather to embrace his body. He stretched out his open palm and the Lumen aide placed a small satellite phone into his hand.

"Martaban, how goes the chase?" asked the VP coolly.

In contrast, the voice on the other end sounded jittery.

"The line is secure," Chambers assured him. "You may speak freely."

The tone of the Lumen boss was calm and melodious, almost like he was discussing the weather.

"And the girl, did you lose her too?"

There was a long pause. The smirking assistant standing nearby guessed that Zadok was explaining himself with some trepidation.

"That's unfortunate," replied Chambers. "But not entirely unexpected. Still, the Board of Directors won't be pleased we lost our investments."

A flurry of apologies poured out from the phone. Martaban's pleas for mercy coughed and sputtered like an ill-fated engine.

"No, don't apologize. Of course it wasn't entirely your fault," answered Chambers with a patronizing sigh. "There was no way you could've known they would try something so brazen. Obviously you were not prepared, despite the number of agents you had at your disposal."

The sarcasm was too thick for Zadok to miss. But Chambers continued to amuse himself like a cat toying with a wounded mouse. He picked up a vicious looking knife lying on his desk and held the blade up to his eye. It was a Phurba, a Tibetan ritual dagger sometimes used to drive away evil spirits.

Strangely enough, this had an unusual effect on Zadok who was thousands of miles away. Although he couldn't possibly have known about the dagger, the manager suddenly became more nervous. Desperate to appease his employer, he promised to recover the losses.

"Yes I'm sure we'll find them soon enough," replied Chambers. "In the meantime, I have a new assignment for you."

He flipped the dagger in his hand, caught the blade by its pointed tip and glanced at the pommel. It was cast with three faces of a deity expressing joy, peace, and anger - faces that were sometimes reputed to come alive during Buddhist rituals to combat evil.

"Why don't you come to my office at Lumen Corp first thing tomorrow and we can talk about it then?" continued the Senior VP.

Zadok promised to turn up.

"And Martaban..." Chambers paused for effect. "Don't be late."

There was a slight choking noise on the other end, as if Zadok was busy trying to clear his throat. Before the portly manager could reply, Chambers hung up and tossed the phone back to his aide.

"Make sure he turns up, I have a surprise for him."

"Yes sir. And what do we do about these meddling priests? They've been raiding our stables for months."

"Don't worry, Norman, let them win their little battles. The war is only just beginning."

"I understand sir, but their exploits have been spreading like legend in the Underground Church. It's giving a new resolve to the Resistance. As of now, we have limited intel on who they are, or even how many there are. I fear the Board will be displeased at our lack of progress."

"Honestly Norman, do you really want to question me?" asked Chambers.

The senior aide bowed his head and apologized.

"No sir, but there's something different about these new priests. They don't seem to fear much and they're taking bigger risks each time, striking closer to our operations. It's getting harder to keep these battles from the public eye. "

The Lumen boss looked annoyed. He held the triangular blade of the Phurba in his hand and said, "Did you know that these daggers were originally crafted to hunt demons?"

Norman shifted uncomfortably. He wasn't sure if the question was rhetorical, in which case it would be unwise for him to answer.

Chambers got up from behind his desk and paced the room.

"Oh yes, Tibetan lamas used to make these things out of fallen meteors. They believed that only a knife forged from the heavens could slay a fallen spirit."

He tossed the dagger repeatedly into the air like a baton.

"These were powerful weapons indeed. The only problem was, the demons that were destroyed by these weapons often cursed the blade with their own evil. And in time, the Phurba grew a sinister will of its own, making it more a weapon of darkness than a weapon of light."

The anxious assistant stood deathly still while his boss circled him like a big cat, closing the distance with every step.

"Over time, those who served the darkness coveted the daggers for their fell powers while the servants of light wanted to keep them from the wrong hands…"

Chambers suddenly grabbed Norman by the hair.

"So you see," he said, pressing the wicked blade to his neck.

"There's no good on earth that cannot be corrupted and destroyed. If these rodents want to run in our shadows, they'll soon find themselves in the heart of evil. And no amount of good faith can save them from the legions of hell."

The hapless aide grimaced as the cold steel pushed against his throat. He tried nervously to agree but the pointed blade kept him from nodding his head.

"I assure you," said Chambers. "Once the bait is taken we'll find them soon enough. If we can't corrupt them, we'll destroy them."

When he said this, the bizarre carvings on the pommel suddenly opened their eyes, as if rudely awakened. The iron features folded into a scowl and hissed with anger. Norman could feel their unholy breaths caressing his skin. He stiffened as the demon faces edged closer to his own, each baring rows of jagged teeth that snapped at his flesh.

"Please sir," the Lumen aide pleaded.

With barely an inch to spare, Chambers suddenly turned around and plunged the dagger into a bowl of fruits. He stabbed a large apple and raised it like a trophy, watching the blood ooze from the punctured fruit and trickle down to each of the gaping mouths. At once, the fiendish tongues on the pommel lapped hungrily at the scarlet trails, eager for a taste of dark magic.

As soon as Chambers released his grip, Norman collapsed in a puddle of sweat, rubbing the broken skin where the dagger had left its mark.

"Now that you're a believer again," said the Lumen VP, smiling. "Shall we let the hunt begin?"

Chapter 9

The dusty elevator cranked into motion like some ancient creature coming to life, its metal sinews groaning in agony as the old transport car made its way down. The only illumination was provided by a single light bulb dangling from the roof. The shaft itself was mostly shrouded in shadows, making it hard to see beyond the rusty grills of the iron cage. Inside, a passenger grabbed hold of the gridiron to keep his balance.

As the carriage rumbled to a stop, the man pulled at the gate and it slid opened with some protests. He stepped off the elevator and removed a flashlight from his pocket. Switching it on, he cut the blackness with a beam of light and peered into the shadows. Adjusting his spectacles, he approached the dented fuse box and found what he was looking for. He pulled the lever and the whole tunnel was bathed with florescent light.

The ground was damp and the air was cold. That didn't seem to bother Gabriel Toshigawa one bit. He had been down here before and it always made him feel safe and at peace. The tunnel walls that enclosed him felt like a hermitage of stone and concrete to the young Japanese. He would come here whenever he needed to think and to pray. And without fail, his thoughts would recall the catacombs of Rome.

Those were harrowing times of great suffering when Christians would descend to the tombs of their spiritual ancestors to pray, surrounded as they were by the witness of countless martyrs buried all around them, only to emerge from the subterranean tunnels with their faith strengthened by the memory of those who fought the good fight before them.

There was no lack of dangers then or opportunities for martyrdom. And the same was true even now. The blood of martyrs had always been the seed of faith, and Gabriel understood this very well. The Toshigawa clan bore witness to that.

One of the light fixtures in the tunnel flickered erratically but Gabriel walked on unperturbed. He was in his mid-thirties but seemed more youthful than his age. His hair was a crew cut and he wore his denims and sweatshirt like a student popping out for a pizza. No one would've guessed that this modest looking man with the vintage glasses had a day job as a principle curator with the oldest museum in the city. He was lean and well built, but looked no older than a college senior. It didn't help that his haircut and spectacles made him appear almost nerdy. If anything, his undistinguished looks meant he often slipped under the radar of most people. It worked out better that way.

When it seemed like the tunnel would snake on forever, Gabriel suddenly turned a corner and stopped before a large metal door. He put his weight on the stubborn latch and pulled on the iron hinges. The door swung open and let in a burst of moonlight. It was bright and beautiful.

As he stood in the doorway, a dented old muscle car pulled up on the gravel and parked a few meters away. The passengers emerged from the vehicle and walked towards Gabriel. One of them was limping. The driver was a tall muscular figure in black.

"If you're selling Girl Scout cookies, I already bought a whole bunch this morning," said Gabriel.

"Ha-ha, that's so funny you're killing me. No really, you are," said Randy. "Now can we come inside before something else tries to eat us?"

"What? Not even a giggle?" asked Gabriel, pretending to look hurt. "Where's your sense of humor?"

"I lost it ages ago, along with my virginity," Randy replied.

Gabriel smiled. He liked the kid and the kid liked him. Between the two of them, they could've kept this up all night.

"You didn't tell me you were bringing a girl. I would've combed my hair," said Gabriel, rubbing the fuzz on his head.

"I didn't want you to get too excited," said Randy.

He took Chelsea by the hand and led her into the tunnel. The young woman was shivering even though the weather was balmy. She said nothing to Gabriel but kept her eyes down the whole time, avoiding his gaze. The curator noticed this and made a mental note to check on her later.

He looked up and saw Raphael hobbling towards him. Michael was close behind.

"You two look terrible. And you smell like my gym socks," Gabriel observed.

"Can we save the comedy for later?" the doctor groaned as he squeezed past Gabriel into the tunnel.

"Terrific, more stitches," said Gabriel, shaking his head. He noticed the bleeding wound on Raphael's leg. "We should join all your scars together to see if they form the shape of an ass."

"It's the price for souls, my friend," replied Raphael.

"Which you seem eager to cough up," remarked the younger man.

Raphael ignored the comment and tried to change the subject.

"Listen, there's something you should know," said the doctor. "The girl that just went in, she's the kid sister of Max Sparrow."

"As in Mad Max, the rock star?"

Raphael nodded. "I heard his confession and got him to renounce the blood oath he made. He's safe now. But the girl's a different matter. She's on the Corporation list as well. And I think she's infected, I felt a presence."

"What kind of presence?" Gabriel asked.

"Let's just say it's not the Holy Spirit," Raphael replied.

Gabriel raised his eyebrows and glanced over at Michael who was quietly standing by.

"Don't look at me. You're the exorcist," said the warrior priest. "If there's anything there, you cast it out."

He pulled back his trench coat and rested his hands on the holstered pistols. "If it comes out fighting, I'll take it down," said Michael.

Gabriel cocked an eyebrow and smiled. "Ok then, let's go say hello."

He got the men to come in and pulled the iron door shut. It clanged like a church bell echoing down the tunnel. Outside, a blanket of clouds had slowly crept across the skies. There was a flutter of wings. A raven squawked like a harbinger of death. Slowly, the moon with its gentle light had become obscured by shadows. And a cold chill blew across the dismal land.

†

The large room was dimly lit and rather eclectic to say the least. The walls were covered in earthy colors and sections of it were plastered with complex charts detailing mythical creatures and rituals. There were no visible windows. Thick heavy drapes hung from some corners like temple curtains guarding the holy of holies. The ceiling was naked and marked with ventilation pipes and electrical wiring, suggesting that this was originally a storage space rather than an office.

There were a couple of work desks, metal cabinets and loose furniture lounging about, but for the most part the place was filled with an assortment of historical artifacts stacked together like bargains at a flea corner. On one side, shelves of ancient parchments lined the wall like an archivist's wet dream. Across the room, broken pieces of ancient ceramic, metal and stone lay preserved in various containers that overflowed with messy abandon.

And yet despite the clutter, there seemed to be a genius to the organized chaos. Much of what was stored here had some kind of religious significance, making the place look like a private shrine to humanity's quest for the divine, as if whoever collected these things was keeping an audit of all things spiritual.

A life-sized portrait of Zhong Kui, the ghost-busting exorcist from Chinese folklore glared from the far end of the room like a guardian deity on duty. There was the noisy sound of metal bolts unlocking when suddenly, the entire framed picture swiveled outwards like a door to reveal an empty passage hidden behind.

Gabriel was the first to step through the portal. He waited until everyone had crossed the threshold before pushing the metal door shut. The huge portrait swung back like a veil to hide the entrance.

"What the hell is that?" Randy cried out.

He was startled by the larger than life image of the ghost catcher gaping down at him.

"Don't stare, you'll go blind," Gabriel said.

Instantly, Randy looked away as if stung by a bee.

Michael walked past the chauffeur and quipped, "You believe everything he tells you?"

Randy made a face. "Not everything," he grumbled. He led Chelsea to a sofa by the table.

Gabriel flipped a switch and flooded the room with light.

"Christ!" exclaimed Randy as he bumped into a terrifying deity.

The statue rocked unevenly as the young man backed away in panic. Immediately, Chelsea caught the wobbly carving before it fell to the floor.

"You really are a bonehead, aren't you?" she asked in annoyance.

"Oh he's usually braver than that," Gabriel snickered. "He's just not used to a beautiful woman in the house. It makes him jumpy."

71

The young Japanese stretched out his hand and introduced himself, "I'm Gabriel. Welcome to my pad. You're safe here."

"What is this place?" asked Chelsea. "It looks like a shitty museum."

"Well actually the shitty museum is right above you," said Gabriel, pointing to the ceiling. "This used to be a basement where we kept some of our more curious artifacts; items we weren't sure how to catalogue. And the tunnel you just came from? It's how they transported the bigger pieces, or when the museum wanted to bring in a private collection."

Chelsea wasn't that interested to hear about the history of the place, but there was no stopping Gabriel. He was on a roll.

"This place hadn't been used in over fifty years," he continued. "I stumbled upon it one day. It was dusty and full of rats. I don't think the current director even knew of its existence. It was just a forgotten part of the old foundation. So I took it over for my research office."

The woman shivered slightly and wrapped her arms around herself. She looked up as soft creaking noises sounded from above. Occasionally, a guttural moan echoed down from the ventilation pipes and the noise of tiny feet could be heard scuttling over the ceiling.

"Don't worry, it's just an old place. Apart from me, no one ever comes down here. If they did, they'll get hopelessly lost. These corridors are like a maze. It was originally a bunker for the military but all the blueprints were either lost or destroyed during the war. So apart from these few halls we're using for the museum, no one even knows how many tunnels are down here."

"And you work for the museum?" Chelsea asked.

"Curator - anthropology of religion - it's my specialty," Gabriel announced proudly. "Which explains all the knick knacks you see here. *When the mask falls and the core of our being is revealed, it soon becomes obvious that we are religious by nature, that religion is the secret dowry of our being.* A great theologian named Johann Metz once said that."

"So all these different religions are speaking the same truth? Each one claiming to be the right one, each claiming to speak for God. How can anyone believe all this nonsense?" said Chelsea in disgust.

"I didn't say all religions were the same or that they're all true. Only that man is religious by nature, and only by fulfilling his yearning for God can he ever be authentically man."

Chelsea rolled her eyes. "This is bullshit," she scoffed.

"Well whether you believe it or not, the spirit world is real. In fact, I understand from Raphael that you encountered some of this 'bullshit' earlier this evening and it tried to bite your head off," Gabriel retorted.

Raphael, who was putting the final touches to the bandage on his leg, decided to speak up.

"Chelsea, listen to me. Those creatures were real today. You saw what happened to your brother," he said.

The doctor pulled up a chair and sat across from her. "I know you're scared but you can't go on denying God in your life."

"God was never in my life!" Chelsea screamed. "And he never will be!"

She snapped her head back and bared her teeth like an animal. Her body spun around like a speeding top as she jumped up on the sofa.

"Chelsea!" Raphael cried out. He hurried forward and caught the girl before she could injure herself.

"Help me keep her still," he said to his companions.

Before anyone else could act, Randy threw himself on the distraught model and received a crushing blow to the groin. He flew backwards and crumbled in a heap of pain. The next moment, Chelsea was wide-eyed and lucid. She blinked as if coming out of a trance and fell back on the cushions.

"What happened?" she asked in confusion.

"You kicked me in the nuts, that's what happened!" Randy grimaced.

Raphael knelt beside the girl and reached for her hand.

"Chelsea, I need you to stay calm and listen to me," said the doctor. "I think you may have picked up something nasty from your time with Lumen Corp."

The woman balked. "What the hell are you talking about?"

She snatched her hand back, frightened and bewildered. Her mind had suddenly grown dark. She was dazed and confused, and her vision narrowed into a fuzzy tunnel that snaked through the room like a bad dream.

"You're carrying a spirit that maybe you don't know about," said Raphael. "It's hidden itself until now. But something spooked it and it manifested. We're not sure what, but we need to know how it got into you in the first place."

"You're saying I'm possessed? That's crazy!" Chelsea answered.

She couldn't believe her ears.

Even though there was no denying the nightmare that clawed its way out of hell earlier this evening, how could she be possessed? She had felt perfectly fine until now. Straight away, she got defensive and lashed out at the doctor.

"This is sick, you're all in this together. What did you do to me?" she screamed.

Twisting around, she grabbed a small reliquary and hurled it at the men. It smashed into a bookcase and fell apart like a broken piñata on the floor.

"Watch it!" shouted Gabriel, horrified that she was quickly reaching for another of his priceless artifacts. "Calm down, no one did anything to you."

She responded by throwing a terracotta urn at his head. The curator ducked with the skills of a martial artist and the absolute horror of a man losing another treasure.

"Damn it, woman!" he cried in frustration. "Will you stop that and listen?"

Chelsea angrily flipped over the coffee table and pushed past Raphael. She didn't know where she was going, only that she wanted desperately to flee. The terror in her mind drove her like a screeching ghoul. Randy stood up just in time to get elbowed in the face. He fell back down, muttering obscenities.

"Chelsea wait," said Raphael, scrambling to stop her.

With surprising agility, the woman ran past the cabinets and dashed for the hidden door.

Michael had been lurking in the background and he stepped forward and blocked her way. Chelsea reeled in shock as the human wall suddenly popped up in front of her. Before she could react, the priest slammed a gloved fist into her face. She wobbled and slumped to the floor like a broken marionette.

Gabriel, Raphael and Randy all looked at each other, a little stunned and bemused.

"What's the problem?" asked Michael. "It wasn't that hard."

He picked up the girl and threw her over his shoulder like a sack of flour.

Randy was incredulous. "I can't believe you'd punch a frightened defenseless girl," he gasped.

"Don't be silly," Michael replied. "I would never punch you."

He carried the unconscious girl to the couch and laid her down.

Turning to Raphael he said dispassionately, "Try again. And this time, make it count."

The doctor took off his jacket and wrapped it around the woman. "Get me some water," he said to his companions.

Randy rushed to fill a paper cup. As he approached with the water, Michael snatched the drink from him and threw it on Chelsea's face.

Raphael looked up in annoyance. "I was planning to give her a drink when she woke up," he said.

"Oh, I thought you were trying to wake her," said Michael awkwardly. "If it's any consolation, she's awake now."

Chelsea sputtered and opened her eyes. She rubbed her jaw in outrage, furious to be kept against her will. Refusing to surrender, she tensed her muscles and looked ready to spring for another run.

"Your brother signed a pact with the devil," Raphael said unexpectedly.

The shocking words hit Chelsea harder than the punch she took from Michael. Her heart skipped a few beats.

"What?" she uttered in disbelief.

"Max didn't take it seriously at the time. The contract with Lumen Corp included a spiritual deed to renounce God and religion. There was a secret clause to exchange his eternal soul for fame and fortune. It was all carefully worded to hide its real purpose. By the time your brother found out, he was too deeply entrenched in sin to believe or care."

"How do you know that?" demanded Chelsea.

"I'm not about to break the seal of confession. Suffice to say that he told me some things before he died. His soul was up for repossession. You saw that. You saw how Satan sent his minions to collect your brother. Up until tonight, Max never believed any of it. It was all a big joke to him."

Chelsea twisted her face and closed her eyes. Those frightful moments in the penthouse came flooding back like a tide. She could feel the creeping terror of the rats invading her psyche while her skin crawled with the memory of those insects. A powerful wave of anxiety washed over her as she tried to resist the images of the leaping hounds.

"Lumen Corp is out to harvest souls for hell. The same could happen to you if you keep resisting the grace that God is offering you," Raphael warned her.

When Chelsea opened her eyes again, she was barely able to contain her tears. The fear and confusion flowed freely, but there was also an aching relief that was spreading in her heart, as if the weight of having to deny what was true was slowly being lifted.

The woman looked up at Raphael. She said nothing but her eyes pleaded for help.

"Don't be afraid," the doctor whispered. "We'll do everything we can to deliver you from this darkness."

"But you're going to have to do your part," added Gabriel. "You're going to have to cooperate with grace. We can't force you to be free of the shadows in your life. You must want to be free. That's a choice only you can make."

"What can I do? I remember signing a contract too," Chelsea cried in frustration. "If what you say is true, I'm not even in control of myself. I don't know what to believe, I don't know what to think, I don't even know if I'm me anymore."

Raphael felt sorry for her. A lot had happened in just a few hours, and her whole world had come crashing down. Everything she had known, everything she had been taught had turned out to be a diabolical lie. But the doctor could see that she wasn't going to let anyone get the better of her. There was a vigor and stubbornness behind her tears that was fighting to find an anchor of faith. And he was going to help her survive the despair that was hungry for her soul.

The doctor reached out and wiped the tears from her cheeks. The warm touch of his hand felt like a gentle balm on her open wounds. It gave her comfort and restored some courage to her heart.

"We're not helpless spectators but the protagonists of our own histories. We have the gift of free will. God may have created us without us, but he won't save us without us. He calls us to cooperate with his providence, and providence has brought you to me. We can win this Chelsea, but I need you to trust me," said Raphael.

Chelsea took a deep breath and nodded quietly. She drew her hair back and asked for a drink.

"I'll get you some water," said Randy, perking up.

"I mean a real drink," answered Chelsea. "Scotch, if you've got any."

Randy stopped in mid-stride and looked over at the dark figure leaning against the shelves.

Michael pulled out a whiskey flask from his trench coat and

tossed it to her.

"Knock yourself out," he said.

Chelsea caught the carafe and looked at him in annoyance. The bruise on her chin was still aching.

Randy offered her a paper cup but she ignored him and took a swig from the metal flask. She was still scared and anxious about her episode, but the thought that a demon spirit was taking up residence in her body made her more furious than terrified. And she was determined to evict him.

"The first thing we need to do is find out how long this has been going on," said Raphael.

"What do you mean?" asked Chelsea.

"What happened earlier, have you ever felt that way before tonight? Like someone else was controlling your thoughts and actions?" enquired Raphael.

Chelsea shook her head adamantly.

"I'd know if something was wrong. The only thing that was troubling me were the nightmares," she remarked. "And that thing that came into my bedroom some weeks back."

Raphael nodded.

"You *still* haven't told me how you knew about that," Chelsea reminded him.

"That's not important," replied Raphael. "Did you see someone to take care of your problem, someone like a witch, medium or psychic maybe?"

Chelsea frowned and looked at him with disgust. "I think you missed out Santa Claus and the Easter Bunny in that line up."

"Chelsea, this is no joke. Please, try and remember," Raphael insisted.

"A friend from the agency arranged for a healer to visit me. But that was all she was, a healer."

"And what did this healer do?" questioned Gabriel. The Japanese man drew closer and leaned forward with attention.

"She placed her hands on me and said I was under a spell," said Chelsea. "Then she walked around the apartment chanting. She said it was a cleansing ritual."

"What else?" Gabriel asked.

Chelsea began to shiver as a chill ran down her spine. Everything had seemed innocuous at the time, even silly. But as she recalled the visit, a deep foreboding began to overwhelm her.

"She said someone had put a curse on me. As far as I was concerned, that was crap. I had no patience for superstition and I wanted to show her the door. But then she said she could prove it. She asked for an egg and started to roll the damn thing all over my body."

As soon as she said that, Chelsea was stunned at her own words. She paused for a few seconds, realizing that she had no previous memory of this.

"I'd completely forgotten about it until now," she said in surprise. Her voice quivered as she tried to go on. "When she broke the egg open, there was something small and black inside."

Startled by the sudden recall, Chelsea cupped her hand over her mouth, as if hearing her own story for the first time.

"I don't know what it was," she continued with difficulty. "But it fell to the floor and scurried off."

Gabriel sighed.

"That probably made it worse," he groaned. "Every single time people turn to quacks and faith healers instead of turning to God, they aggravate the oppression they're already suffering from. Evil cannot cast out evil, and whatever relief they experience is only temporary."

"I didn't ask for this," Chelsea lamented. "That crazy woman probably gave it to me. Maybe she was possessed in the first place."

"You don't catch the devil like you catch the flu, he's not contagious that way," said Gabriel. "But sometimes, people open a doorway for darkness to enter when they dabble in the occult, or when they stubbornly persist in serious sins."

Chelsea was a little miffed. "What're you saying?" she demanded to know.

"The devil cannot touch a life that's living in grace unless God allows it. He can only launch his invasion through the help of his allies – pride, lust, greed, gluttony, envy, sloth and anger – the concupiscence that stirs each soul with the unbridled passions of his fallen nature. Basically, everything that leads you away from a moral life can become a conduit for evil to slip in."

The woman was now quite upset. She knew her life had been a dizzying cauldron of sex, drugs and parties but no one had ever accused her of sleeping with the devil.

"Who the hell are you to judge me?" she shouted defensively.

Raphael lost his patience and stood up.

"Father Gabriel is right," he said curtly. "And he's not trying to judge you. He's an exorcist who's trying to help you!"

"Father who? Christ, is everyone here a frickin' priest?" she remarked.

"I'm not," Randy was swift to answer. He gave her his sexy smoldering look, which was quickly doused by the icy glare he received in return.

Gabriel motioned for the doctor to sit down. He then turned his attention back to the woman and tried to calm her.

"Miss Shields, I'm not saying you invited this. In all likelihood, it sounds like you've been ambushed. But the fact remains that you've stayed away from God and the sacraments for too long, and that makes you extremely vulnerable to a diabolical attack, which is what I think this is."

"Are you saying this was all planned, that someone intended to do this to me?"

"That's what I'm trying to discern," replied Gabriel. "What else did this healer say to you? Did she give you any charm or amulet to wear, or some cleansing ritual to perform?"

"I…I'm not sure," stuttered Chelsea. "She made me drink something, I don't remember what."

"Think," implored Raphael. "This is important, what did you drink?"

The doctor was anxious for her. As Chelsea struggled to remember, Michael suddenly interrupted gruffly.

"What happened to the creature that came out of the egg?" he asked. "Did anyone catch it?"

Chelsea trembled like a leaf. The walls of her suppressed memory came tumbling down and the flashbacks returned with frightful clarity.

"Yes she did catch it, it actually leapt into her hands," recalled the woman. "And she crushed it and mixed the remains in water. And she made me drink it. She said it was the only way to be free of my troubles. I don't know why I believed her, but I just wanted the nightmares to be over."

"Bingo," exclaimed Gabriel. "That's the entry point."

"So what do we do now?" asked Randy. He looked over at the gorgeous model and was genuinely concerned for her.

"Chelsea, with your permission, we would like to expel the unclean spirit through an exorcism," said Raphael. "Are you ready for that?"

Chelsea was anxious. She had no idea what was involved, but everything she had been told about this ancient ritual reeked of medieval torture and fallacy. Exorcism was the paradigm of superstition in the Church and despite all that happened, she wasn't sure if she was jumping out of the frying pan and into the fire. But what choice did she have?

Sensing her fear, Gabriel tried to reassure the young woman.

"Calm down Chelsea, an exorcism is nothing but a prayer," he said. "There are no magic formulas or bizarre rites. But it is indeed a powerful prayer of the Church that invokes the help of God to deliver you from evil. The devil has more to fear from this than you do."

"Will I be completely free after this?" asked Chelsea.

"That's up to God, but also up to you," answered Gabriel. "There are three important factors for liberation: the attitude of the victim, the action of the priest, and the permission of God. At the end of the day, liberation is a gift from God who can deliver anyone, anywhere, anytime without the need for an exorcist. But ordinarily, God will work through human vessels, especially in His Church, so that poor souls like ourselves may grow in holiness by responding to grace."

"I know, God will not save me without me," said Chelsea, recalling what Raphael had told her earlier.

"I'm glad you understand. The effectiveness of the ritual in large part depends on your cooperation," said Gabriel.

There was no ignoring the stakes involved. Chelsea took a deep breath and clenched her fist, knowing she was about to tackle the biggest battle of her life. She was tired of being a chained pony in the Lumen stable. Before tonight, she didn't even believe in the afterlife. Now, there was no way she would give up her soul without a fight. She knew she had to make a choice.

"Let's do this," she said.

"There's one more thing I should point out," Raphael added. "Like your brother, I think you should make your confession first. It can make all the difference between success and failure."

"You want me to do what?" asked Chelsea. "I don't even know where to start."

"Don't be afraid, I'll help you," said Raphael. "Believe me, the devil fears confession more than he does any exorcism."

Gabriel agreed.

"He's right. Exorcism can drive evil from a person's body, but confession can drive evil from a person's soul. Otherwise, it can be difficult to expel the demon. Unrepentant sins can give the enemy something to cling on to."

Chelsea sighed in resignation. She would never have suffered this humiliation previously, but under the circumstances, she had seen enough to know there were worse things than confessing your sins to a man, no matter how shameful you felt. Reluctantly, she agreed.

Raphael got up and led Chelsea to a small alcove to the right. It was a cozy corner tucked away with some armchairs and a potted plant. He sat her down gently and traced the sign of the cross over her, beginning the healing process for the Catholic Rite of Reconciliation.

Gabriel turned around and ushered Randy towards another room. Michael threw off his trench coat and followed them both. His weapons however were still strapped for action.

"All right gentlemen," Gabriel quipped, "Let's get ready to rumble."

Chapter 10

The room was spartan. It was formerly used to store Asian antiquities confiscated from the black market. But now, the only antique item in the room was an ancient cypress crucifix hanging on a wall. Gabriel had transformed it into a simple chapel without the usual tabernacle, candles, flowers or pews. It was easier to dismantle in case of a raid.

A big block of limestone sat beneath the wooden crucifix like a makeshift altar, and upon its rugged top was laid some framed pictures of Jesus and Mary. There was also a portrait of St. Dominic, founder of the Dominican Order in his distinctive black and white habit.

As Gabriel entered the room, he turned towards the crucifix and bowed. Randy and Michael did the same. In a world where society was systematically stripped of religious images, where Christian schools, hospitals and even churches were robbed of their spiritual patrimony, there was no refusing the homage due to God.

Gabriel headed straight for a small closet in the corner. Opening the doors, he pulled out a white tunic with a separate hood called a capuce. He also removed a long white scapula from another hanger and draped it over his arm.

"If she's confessing and cleaning house right now, you should be able to kick the squatter out with no problems, right?" asked Randy.

"There are no quick solutions," Gabriel explained. "The devil will do everything he can to hide himself, even faking expulsion. Like any medical treatment, it may take more than one session for the sick person to be completely cured.

"So there's no guarantee she'll be free even after this?" asked Randy, disappointed.

"Maybe, maybe not. You won't always find quick liberation in every case," replied Gabriel. "But you'll always find quick relief through an exorcism, I guarantee that."

"Jesus Christ," muttered Randy in annoyance. As soon as he said that, he felt a stinging slap to the back of his head.

"Why can't you stick to saying 'shit' like everyone else?"

complained Michael.

"Stick to shit – that's a nice image," replied Randy, rubbing his head.

"You think blasphemies are a joke? Demons cower at the name of Jesus and you blaspheme without fear."

Randy had no witty comeback. He knew Michael was serious and he didn't want to get smacked again.

"Be careful Wheezer," said Gabriel. "Every sacrilege you utter hardens your heart against God and chokes your soul. Do it often enough and you commit spiritual suicide."

"All right, next time I feel like cursing, I'll just scream: *MICHAEL HIT ME!*" said Randy with a chuckle. "How's that?"

"Perfect," said Michael, removing his gloves. "I'll be happy to oblige."

Right away, Randy stopped chuckling and scuttled off to arrange the chairs.

"You know the drill, Michael," said Gabriel. "If the demon gets violent, I need you to hold Chelsea down so she doesn't injure herself or any of us."

The young exorcist removed his spectacles and put it away. He could see well enough alone. The glasses were just a convenient prop to maintain his bookish persona in the museum.

"Ok…so what about me, what do I do?" asked Randy.

Gabriel pulled a small rosary from his pocket and tossed it to the chauffeur.

"Pray," he said.

Turning around, he laid the white tunic and accessories on the altar and began to vest for the ritual.

The Japanese priest was a member of the Dominican Order, officially called the Order of Preachers. Founded in the 13th century to combat heresy, the Order itself was barely alive when Gabriel first walked through the doors of its novitiate many years ago.

Despite having given birth to some of the most luminous stars in history, the sons and daughters of St. Dominic were hunted down and suppressed with Lumen efficiency until their houses, universities and priories resembled a barren wasteland. The Order itself was accused of preaching subversive ideas and outlawed. And like so many others before them, the surviving Dominicans simply vanished from view and reappeared as shining lights in the Underground movement.

Gabriel was one of those lights. A priest as well as a Dominican *friar* – from the Latin word *frater* - a term used to describe the member of a mendicant order. He picked up the long tunic and recited the prayers for donning the Order's habit.

"Clothe me, O Lord, with the garments of salvation. By your grace may I keep them pure and spotless, so that clothed in white, I may be worthy to walk with you in the kingdom of God. Amen."

He slipped on the tunic and did the same for the leather cincture and rosary, reminding himself of the prayers associated with those parts of his religious dress.

Then taking hold of the scapular, he wore it like a protective chain mail and invoked the Mother of God, "Show yourself a mother, He will hear your pleading whom your womb has sheltered, and whose hand brings healing. Amen."

Next, he slipped the Capuce over his head like a war helmet and made the following appeal, "Lord, you have set your sign upon my head that I should admit no lover but you. Amen."

Over his Dominican habit, he wore a short linen garment called a surplice that reached down to his knees. Finally, he removed a long purple stole from a drawer, kissed the embroidered cross at the nape of the vestment and draped it over his neck.

The vesting complete, he tossed the white hood back like a medieval knight flipping up his metal visor. His left hand patted the rosary hanging from his belt like a warrior making a reassuring feel for his sword. In the space of a few minutes, the Japanese curator was no longer there. In his place stood a Christian friar dressed in armor and ready to do battle with a dragon.

"One more thing," said Gabriel. "Can you pass me that book with the red cover by the cabinet?"

Randy grabbed the leather bound tome and exclaimed, "This old thing?"

The soft wrinkled cover bore the words - *Rituale Romanum* - in gold letterings. The spine was loose and the pages were yellow with age. Randy flipped through the tattered book with careless ease and noticed there were missing pages in the back.

"Be careful with that," warned Gabriel. "There aren't many copies left in the world."

"I'll take that," said Michael, lifting the book from Randy's hands. He passed it to Gabriel, who found the chapter he was looking for.

"That's not what I think it is, is it?" asked Randy.

"It's the Roman Ritual," answered Gabriel. "It contains all of the Church's liturgical services and rites that can be performed by a priest or a deacon - prayers, sacraments, blessings - everything useful for the spiritual life of the Church.

"Including..."

"Yes Wheezer, including the Rite of Exorcism," nodded Gabriel.

The young chauffeur was dumbfounded. He started wheezing like a punctured tire, which was how he got his nickname. His breath would always whistle when he got nervous.

He shuffled up to Gabriel and whispered, "Dude, in case you haven't noticed, the book is missing a bunch of pages."

"I know," said the exorcist.

"Then you know working with this is like doing brain surgery without the lights on," complained Randy. "You've got the skills and equipment but you're blindly feeling your way around."

"Well genius, unless you can find me a complete manual pronto, this will have to do," the friar replied.

It wasn't just that the Roman Ritual was out of print; it was hunted down like a weapon of mass destruction by the dark powers behind Lumen Corp. The solemn Rite of Exorcism was a bludgeoning terror to the demons. Unclean spirits knew the torture the prayers could inflict.

In the last decade, every reference on the Internet, every known copy of the Ritual, and every rumor of its existence was tracked, confiscated and destroyed with ingenious precision. But Satan's high priests knew they couldn't stop the Underground Church from reproducing the originals and distributing them across the nations. Hence if they couldn't disarm the world's exorcists, they would at least give them a blunt weapon to fight with. The truth had to be distorted. Weeds had to be introduced into the wheat field.

Forged copies of the Ritual eventually flooded the landscape like a virus of deceit. The prayers and rites were still there. But they were sanitized, impoverished and robbed of any real supernatural power to be effective. The Exorcism Rite was no longer a loaded gun. In time, the altered version was approved, endorsed and promoted by Bishops in the Church who were deep in Corporation pockets. Only an experienced exorcist could tell the difference between the real deal and the worded doppelganger.

Michael smacked Randy on the back and quipped, "Don't worry, your girlfriend's in good hands. Pray and trust in God, everything will be fine."

"That's right Romeo," Gabriel assured his young friend. "Your girlfriend's in good hands."

He removed some items from a small case and assembled the tools of his trade on the altar. There was a bottle of holy water and a small crucifix with the Benedictine medal and some blessed salt. The last item had long been used as a symbol of incorruption in the Christian tradition, and exorcised salt was known to scourge demons without mercy.

"Why are you so confident?" asked Randy.

Gabriel paused and looked at the crucifix.

"In truth, I fear all things from my weakness," he said solemnly. "But I trust blindly in his strength. He will not forsake his own."

Just then, the door opened and Raphael led Chelsea into the room. The doctor had changed into a white alb with a rope cincture around his waist, and he too wore a purple stole around his neck.

It was time to begin the ritual.

†

"All right Chelsea, I'd like you to take a seat and just relax," said Gabriel.

Randy had arranged for a chair to be placed in the middle of the chapel facing the altar. He stayed seated at the back of the room while Michael took his position just behind the possessed girl.

"What's going to happen?" asked Chelsea, nervously.

The two priests in their religious vestments intimidated her. She hadn't darkened the hallways of a church in over twenty years, yet here she was undergoing the Church's most infamous ceremony. The whole idea seemed completely insane. The fact that she was the only woman in this place also haunted her. The walls in the room suddenly felt like they were caving in. And her thoughts began to scramble under pressure.

"I'm going to pray the words of the Rite over you," said Gabriel. "Don't worry, it won't harm or disturb you in anyway. The only person who's going to feel any pain would be the unclean spirit. With the help of God, we're going to torture this evil until it has no choice but to leave you."

Chelsea tried to put on a brave front. She swept her hair back into a ponytail and wiped the dampness from her cheeks. She was a delicate beauty with serious, expressive eyes, but there was no hiding the iron will behind the pretty face. The sultry model with the gorgeous figure had conquered more than a few runways of pain and regrets. She was certainly worried and anxious, but she wasn't ready to play the helpless damsel just yet.

"Just make sure you hurt this damn thing," she answered grimly.

That was all the assurance Gabriel needed. Without wasting time, he picked up the holy water and sprinkled a few drops on Chelsea.

Stretching his hand over her head he began, "In the name of the Father, the Son and the Holy Spirit."

The air was thick with tension but Chelsea remained calm and collected. After a short prayer to St. Michael the Archangel, Gabriel skipped the Litany of the Saints and the opening psalms and jumped straight into the exorcism prayers.

His voice was low and constant, almost as if he was reading to himself. The imprecatory prayers asking God to save his daughter from the clutches of the evil one rolled off his tongue like an old hymn. Gabriel had clearly done this before.

He continued with the Rite, pausing sometimes to observe the patient, switching the order of prayers now and then, and dousing her with more holy water between intervals. With half a Ritual as a guide, Gabriel was improvising according to his experience.

After fifteen minutes, there was still no adverse reaction from Chelsea. The only change was a regular bout of burping from the young lady, as if she had suddenly developed a bizarre case of indigestion.

At this point, Randy was starting to feel optimistic. Maybe the Fathers were wrong. Maybe she wasn't possessed at all. She was too beautiful and strong to get mixed up with this stuff. It had to be a mistake.

"Guys, she's perfectly fine," said Randy. "There's nothing there."

"Not so fast," Gabriel replied. "There're different grades of possession. It's the nature of every demon to hide itself, to trick you into believing it's not there. Let's see if we can give it a little nudge."

The friar turned and whispered something to Raphael. The doctor reached out and placed his hands on Chelsea. Instantly, she twitched like a small current had gone through her. It lasted barely a second before she recovered and continued burping.

According to the official guidelines, it was advisable to have a medical doctor and a psychiatrist present at an exorcism. There was no room for endangering a victim's overall health. But Gabriel couldn't have asked for a better helper than his brother priest. Raphael wasn't just a physician, he was a powerful clairvoyant - someone who was endowed with a charismatic gift of knowledge and discernment, much like a psychic - except that his charisms were stronger and they came from God.

The doctor continued to pray over Chelsea. The woman was conscious but deeply reserved. She was quiet the whole time and simply stared at Raphael with a kind of detached amusement.

"What's the verdict?" asked Randy.

Raphael removed his hands and confirmed the diagnosis. "It's a demon all right, a fairly stubborn one too. It's hiding but I can feel the hatred and rage."

Randy felt the blood drain from his face. He looked over at Chelsea who seemed unnaturally calm. Her eyes were glazed over like frosted glass, almost like she wasn't even there.

"But what about the holy water?" he asked.

Gabriel removed a metal capsule from his pocket.

"Demons are not clones," he said. "They're as unique as each of us. Some will react to holy water. Others are strong enough to withstand the pain for some time. A few won't like it when you breathe on them, but all will try and hide their presence. We just need to find out what pisses this one off."

Opening the device, he loaded a small piece of resin into the chamber and snapped the cover shut.

"Fortunately, there's more than one way to flush out a rat," said the exorcist.

He clicked the capsule and a stream of incense burst over Chelsea. Almost straight away she was overcome with the same crisis that gripped her earlier. Her body stiffened like a log of wood and she started hyperventilating. The chair creaked under enormous strain as she became heavy with dread.

Suddenly, a terrifying howl burst from her throat and tore through the chapel like screeching nails. It sounded like the Gates of Hell were grating open to swallow the men. Chelsea writhed and twisted violently but Michael held her down.

Gabriel immediately resumed the exorcism prayer and traced the sign of the cross over the possessed girl. Another frightful howl leapt from her mouth. Like a brutal animal being whipped, the cry was a hateful, guttural mix of laughter and pain.

"Is that all you've got?" shrieked the demon. "You have no power over me!"

Gabriel calmly placed his hand on her head and draped the end of his purple stole over her shoulder. At once, her fingers retracted into talons and she gave a blood-curdling scream. The vestment that most signified the priestly office burned the unclean spirit like a branding iron on bare skin.

"You bastard, I'll make you pay for that," the demon screeched.

Raphael joined his hands together and followed the exorcism prayers, his lips moving quietly in petition to God. Occasionally, he would make the ritual responses to parts of the rite that he knew.

"Shut up, you stupid priest, you're tickling me," laughed the voice. "I'm going to eat your heart, you stinking sack of shit."

It was tempting to retort with anger, but the Ritual expressly forbade unnecessary dialogue with the demon but directed the exorcist to demand answers to only two questions. Gabriel was ready to start the interrogation.

"I command you, unclean spirit, whoever you are, along with all your minions now attacking this servant of God, by the mysteries of the incarnation, passion, resurrection, and ascension of our Lord Jesus Christ, by the descent of the Holy Spirit, by the coming of our Lord for judgment, that you tell me by some sign your name, and the day and hour of your departure…"

The boisterous demon suddenly clamped up and refused to utter a word. Chelsea's eyes rolled back until the whites were visible and she started foaming like a rabid dog.

Gabriel recognized the signs immediately. "Hold her," he said.

But before Michael could act, Chelsea jumped up, lifted the chair over her head like a feather and hurled it at Gabriel. The exorcist sidestepped the missile and it smashed into the limestone altar behind him.

Michael grabbed Chelsea and tried to secure her to the floor, but she turned around with incredible speed and punched him in the chest. The blow threw the seasoned warrior into the wall with such force that he fell to his knees coughing.

"By the blood of Jesus Christ I command you to be still," ordered Gabriel.

Chelsea spun around in a pirouette and continued to pivot on her toes. An angry profound growl reverberated from her lungs as she kept her face turned towards the ceiling, refusing to glance at the cross in the hand of the exorcist.

Raphael signaled for Randy to bring forth another chair. Michael gritted his teeth and resumed his position behind Chelsea. His solar plexus was throbbing with pain beneath his tactical vest.

"By the power of Christ, tell me your name!" said Gabriel.

"Nooooooo," cried the demon, dragging the word out like a rusty chain. Chelsea shook her head vigorously until her face was a bleeding blur.

"All right, let's do this the hard way," threatened Gabriel.

He jumped back into the ritual and the thrashing resumed right away. It was impossible to know how much pain the prayers were causing the demon, but each line, each word, each invocation seemed to hammer the spirit with excruciating blows.

Certain parts of the ritual would whip the demon into a frenzy of curses and screams, as if it was being boiled alive. At other parts, the spirit would plead with the exorcist...

"No more! Enough, you're killing me!"

"Then answer my questions," commanded Gabriel. "Or I shall make you suffer grievously for tormenting this child of God."

"Assassin! All priests are assassins," shouted the demon in anguish. "If not for the Nazarene, I would tear you apart right now!"

"Then look upon Him who is your king and judge, it is He who commands you," rebuked Gabriel, pushing the crucifix to its face. "Answer me! What is your name?"

In response, Chelsea opened her mouth and dislocated her jaw, her tongue rolling out like a long slippery eel. It was completely black and hung down to her chest. The fleshy organ twisted like a snake and split to resemble a serpent's fork tongue.

"Holy crap!" said Randy in panic. He almost fainted at the terrible sight.

Suddenly, the possessed girl bolted from her chair and flew right up. She clung to the ceiling like a soul caught between heaven and hell. A cold gust of wind swept into the room and the temperature quickly dropped below zero.

Gabriel was unperturbed. He continued to read from the ritual.

"God, Creator and defender of the human race, who made man in your own image, look down with pity on this your servant, Chelsea, now in the toils of the unclean spirit, now caught up in the fearsome threats of man's ancient enemy.... Repel, O Lord, the devil's power, break asunder his snares and traps, put the unholy tempter to flight…"

He grabbed a handful of blessed salt and flung it at the demon. Instantly, Chelsea plummeted from the ceiling and fell to the floor screaming. A thin veil of smoke sizzled from her clothes like burning embers.

Throughout the session, Randy felt as if he was witnessing a more intelligent, superior being engaging the fathers in combat. It was like watching David versus Goliath. And yet at the same time, this fallen spirit with all its preternatural powers seemed intimidated by these simple men of faith. There was clearly a greater power tormenting this minion of hell.

"Kneel before the cross of Christ," ordered Gabriel with the crucifix in his hand.

"No, no, no," the gruff voice kept repeating like a tortured chant. "I will not, I must not."

"Behold the wood of the cross, on which hung the savior of the world," said Gabriel, tracing the sign of the cross with his crucifix.

"Fool, he died on a tree and is no more," cried the voice of perdition. "Why do you persist in believing this fairy tale? We are more powerful."

From experience, Gabriel knew that the demon was trying to wear him out. Fighting an underworld titan required strength and stamina. If he allowed himself to become discouraged, the battle would be lost. The exorcist decided to call for reinforcements.

"St. George, slayer of dragons, come to our aid," prayed Gabriel. "Make this wretched creature kneel before Christ the King."

At the mention of St. George, the demon became alarmed. Chelsea's eyes rolled back to expose huge circles of black. The pupils became so enlarged that they seem to suck in all the light in the room.

"No, please," cried the unclean spirit. "Stay away."

Gabriel ignored the protests and continued invoking the warrior saint. The fear on Chelsea's face was palpable. The demon reacted as if an apparition had descended from the clouds. It began to whimper like a beaten dog when suddenly, a loud slapping noise drove the possessed woman to her knees.

"Now kiss the crucifix," ordered Gabriel.

"Never," cried the demon with contempt. It twisted the girl's head around but a greater power compelled the demon to move her face closer to the cross until her lips touched the crucifix with reverence. This caused the spirit untold suffering, and it lashed out at the exorcist. But an invisible hand deflected the claws and struck the demon with more painful blows.

Gabriel smiled to himself. The battle had definitely reached a turning point and he was determined to press on with the advantage.

"How many are you?"

"Just me," replied the infernal spirit. "I don't need others to deal with a worm like you."

"By the power of Christ, tell me your name and why you entered this woman," repeated the exorcist."

"My name is Deception," the demon answered with rage. "Satan sent me to report all I see, all I hear to your enemies, and to delay you while terror descends upon your house."

"What do you mean by report? Speak the truth clearly," rebuked Gabriel. "Or I shall ask St. George to give you a beating to remember for eternity!"

"I *am* speaking the truth. I don't want to, but *He* compels me!" said the demon, beholding the crucifix with fear and loathing.

But tortured as it was, the spirit could not resist boasting.

"Thanks to me, they know who you are, where you hide," gloated the demon. "This whore is nothing but a vessel for me to expose you. Your enemies knew you couldn't resist, that you would try to save her. And now, who will save you from those who seek your blood?"

Hearing this, Raphael was filled with dread. Chelsea had been used as a courier to bring the enemy into the walls of their camp, and he had unwittingly opened the gates to welcome them. He knew the girl was innocent, but now that the trap had been sprung, he wasn't sure if any of them would survive the night.

As if reading his thoughts, the demon answered Raphael in a mocking voice, "I love it when a plan comes together, don't you?"

"Silence!" commanded Gabriel. If the foul creature was telling the truth, he had precious little time to free the girl. The young exorcist was determined not to leave her in the clutches of hell.

"Hush, listen," the evil spirit pretended to be worried. "Did you hear that?"

It perked up its ears and lowered its voice. "Gasp, they're already at the gates. Time for you to die!" laughed the demon hysterically.

"Enough!" cried the exorcist. "Time for you to leave!"

Summoning all his faith, Gabriel resumed the assault like a

charging samurai.

"I cast you out, unclean spirit, along with every satanic power of the enemy, every specter from hell, and all your fell companions; in the name of our Lord Jesus Christ…"

Once again, the evil spirit tried to resist. But this time the punishment came hard and fast like a mandate from heaven. The die was cast. There was no delaying the moment of liberation. The prayers tore into the possessed girl like a fiery sword and began to cut the bonds of evil from her body, causing the demon to howl like never before.

"Say these words as a sign that you will leave," Gabriel insisted. "Hail Mary, full of grace."

"Grace full of hail," said the demon resisting. Raucous laughter exploded from the possessed.

"By the authority of Jesus Christ, I command you to say the words in the order I give you. *Hail Mary full of grace,*" Gabriel bellowed.

And the demon screeched with terrible anguish. In spite of itself, the evil spirit screamed and spat out the words, "*Hail Mary full of grace…*"

Within seconds, Chelsea started to retch with painful spasms. Apparently, something was crawling up her throat. A jolt of raw energy shot through her body and she quivered like someone plugged into a live socket.

Sensing that the end was near, Gabriel held the crucifix firmly against her forehead and pressed on.

"Begone! Stay far from this creature of God, for it is He who commands you, He who flung you headlong from the heights of heaven into the depths of hell…"

All of a sudden, Chelsea snapped her head forward and vomited a copious amount of slime. She coughed and gagged and collapsed on the floor with great violence.

"Please don't die, please don't die," said Randy, rushing forward with concern.

It was then that he noticed that Michael was no longer in the chapel with them. But what he saw next frightened him.

Swimming in the puddle of filth was a small black creature that looked like a miniature cat with six legs. It was attempting to flee the scene, but Gabriel reached down and poured the entire bottle of blessed salt on it. The tiny creature burst into flames. It gave off an agonizing shriek and then vanished in a puff of black smoke.

"Are you all right?" Gabriel asked Chelsea.

The woman looked around the room like she had just woken up from a bad dream. Apart from being a little disheveled, her features had gone back to normal. She looked exhausted. Randy helped her up and gently brushed away a lock of hair from her face. She stood unsteadily for a few seconds, blinking at the light in the chapel as if she was emerging from a dark tunnel and seeing the sun for the first time.

"Where am I?" she asked, somewhat confused.

During the whole exorcism, Chelsea had felt like a bystander watching the struggle for her soul unfold like an intense movie. She had no control over her body and the only pain she felt was a great temptation to despair. But she knew she could turn the fight by renouncing the enemy with faith and prayer, and for the first time in a long time, she prayed with all her might.

"Well done, Chelsea," said the doctor. He checked her vital signs and made sure she was okay.

"You did it. You fought the good fight," Raphael told her.

The woman was not entirely convinced. "Is he gone?" she asked cautiously.

The color had returned to her cheeks, along with the flexibility and strength of her limbs. But her mind was still reeling from the experience.

"Well how do you feel?" asked Gabriel.

She thought for a second and then sighed with relief. "I feel free," she said, smiling.

Without warning, the chapel door flew opened with a loud bang. Michael stood there with a duffel bag full of weapons.

"Break this up," he shouted. "Security has been breached. We have to go. Now!"

Chapter 11

Shortly before dawn, the area surrounding the museum came alive like a nest of hornets. Heavily armed soldiers descended on the grounds, each man wearing a black seamless mask that hid his identity as a mercenary of hell. One detachment was already inside the museum, combing through the exhibition halls. The other was crouched outside the compound like a hungry lion digging for a kill. The thick iron door shielding the entrance exploded and flew off its hinges. As the Praetorians prepared to enter, the Commander issued his men a clear order.

"Do whatever you have to, but bring me their heads!"

He gave the signal and the marauding horde poured into the tunnel.

Within the vast complex, another platoon uncovered the dusty entrance to the underground chamber. They dived down the staircase and fanned out with automatic rifles at the ready. Instead of a single compartment, they halted before a labyrinth of rooms and corridors, each of which could easily slow down their search and allow their targets time enough to slip through the gauntlet.

Back in the chapel, both Gabriel and Raphael had changed out of their vestments and were hurriedly getting their gear together. In particular, the friar made sure not to leave behind an heirloom of the Toshigawa family. With deep reverence, he removed the katana from its lacquered case, wrapped it in black velvet and slung it across his back.

Michael was studying a couple of small monitors hooked up to motion detectors and cameras that he had previously set up. Randy looked over his shoulders.

"These guys are packing a lot of heat," observed the wheezing chauffeur. "They've got enough ammo and body armor to invade a small country. Who the hell are they?"

"Praetorian Guards," grunted Michael with disgust. "Make no mistake, they're not here to arrest us. This is an execution squad."

"So what do we do? We're dug in like rats with nowhere to run."

"Take this map," said Gabriel. "It's a tunnel I discovered just a few weeks ago. It's very old and unstable, but it'll take you out the sewage system and into the open river. Father Raphael will lead the way but you've got to go now!"

"Wait, what about you guys?" asked Chelsea.

"We'll try and hold them off," said Gabriel. "Maybe we can buy you enough time to get out."

Michael whistled and tossed a Beretta into the air. Randy looked up and caught the automatic pistol. He nodded and tucked the gun into his belt.

"Take this," said Michael, passing a small MP5 to Raphael. "You'll need it."

"What do you want me to do with this, shoot them?" asked Raphael. "I'm a priest, not a killer."

"No one will die," said Michael. "I've switched the ammo rounds. Each pellet contains an electrical charge that's strong enough to knock them out, maybe even leave them with a nasty burn but that's it."

"You'll also need these," said Gabriel, passing out comlinks. "It'll help us stay in touch."

He pushed a button on his table and a tall metal cabinet slid open to reveal another hidden door.

"Now hurry, go!"

Randy grabbed Chelsea and headed for the exit but the girl broke her stride and turned back to look at Gabriel.

"Thanks for not giving up on me," she told the exorcist.

Gabriel nodded and smiled. "Get moving, there's not much time."

"And that includes you," said Michael, slapping Raphael on the shoulder.

The doctor was reluctant to leave. He walked over to his brother priests and clasped their hands. Under the circumstances, he feared he might not see them alive again. Looking into their faces, he gave them a final blessing.

"God be with you both," said Raphael with emotion.

"Et cum spritu tuo," replied the other two.

With a heavy heart, Raphael turned and led Chelsea and Randy through the exit. The secret door shut behind them like a sealed tomb.

"It's just you and me at the Alamo, bro," Gabriel sighed.

"Then let's even the odds a little, shall we?" Michael remarked.

✝

The Lumen troops moved through the bowels of the museum like wolves on the scent of blood. As the first detachment broke through a sealed door, the lights suddenly went out and plunged the guards in darkness. The soldiers immediately switched to night vision and proceeded to scour the rooms.

"Black King, this is Knight Two," reported the sergeant. "They know we're here."

"Good, go introduce yourselves," replied the voice on the comlink. "I want those heads on a pike."

The sergeant gave a signal and his squad continued prowling through the halls. But as the Praetorians rounded a corner, they tripped a motion sensor and a flurry of explosions detonated in their faces. The powerful blast tore a hole through their ranks and sent some of the guards flying. Without warning, a burst of gunfire erupted and brought a few men to the ground. The rest quickly dove for cover and scanned the shadows for movement.

"There!" shouted a soldier, spotting a ghostly shape.

"Light him up!"

A barrage of bullets pierced the darkness and tried to cut down the figure in black. The sound of battle ripped through the halls with deafening force. As the men pursued their quarry, two flash grenades flew out of the shadows and lit up the corridor. The explosion of white light took the troops by surprise. Grimacing like moles caught in the sun, they tore off the night vision goggles and struggled to regain their sight.

Michael knew he had to act fast. Catching the chaos in their ranks, he pointed his weapons and let loose. The barrels screamed with murderous zeal and splattered the soldiers with crippling volts.

Four men collapsed in a bundle of twitching flesh. Undaunted, the sergeant shouted for the rest to push forward. Almost instantly, the full weight of the Lumen assault bore down on the priest. The chamber shook as Praetorian rifles blasted away with lethal force.

Michael turned and fled down the corridor, making sure to stay in the shadows. When some of the guards got close enough, he whipped around and squeezed off his guns. Again, huge volts of

97

electricity crippled the soldiers and they toppled like bowling pins.

The sergeant was furious. He clamored for blood. Suddenly, the sharp pings of metal catches sprang noisily into the air. Michael recognized the sound and looked up. A pair of frag grenades whizzed by and dropped near his position. Quickly, he ducked behind a heavy cover and steeled himself. The blast shook the walls and nearly brought down the roof.

As the dust settled, the priest saw that the path forward was sealed off by fallen debris. The path back however was still blocked by Lumen guns. The situation was critical. With bleeding cuts to his hands and face, he reloaded his weapons and took a quick glance over the top. There were maybe four or five Praetorians left, including the sergeant.

Michael knew he had to keep moving or he was toast. The space around them was very confined, with metal cabinets on both sides. Spotting a water pipe overhead, he pulled out his handgun and banged a few live rounds at the sprinklers above the troops. A cascade of water showered down on the enemy and soaked the floor wet. Knowing what the priest was up to, the sergeant shouted for his men to back off. But not everyone was quick enough.

As Michael fired his MP5s, the electrical pellets smashed against the wet concrete floor and unleashed a current of pain that jumped from one soldier to the next. The sergeant was the only one who dodged the attack in time. Cursing, he watched his men fry in their boots and drop like flies.

✝

Back in the research room, all was dark except for the laser sightings dancing from the rifles of the Lumen hunters.

"They were definitely here, sir," reported a Praetorian Guard. He emerged from the side chapel with the cypress crucifix dangling from his hands.

"There's fresh muck on the floor and signs of a struggle," added the soldier. He handed the crucifix to his squad leader.

Eyeing the antique cross with suspicion, the officer smashed the ancient relic against the wall and threw the splintered wood on the floor.

"Search the area," he ordered. "I want them found."

The guards descended on the halls and leveled the shelves of artifacts to clear away any hiding places. They stood before the statue collection like a firing squad and blasted the pagan Gods into submission. When they were done, the soldiers split up in pairs to comb the darkened office, their boots crunching over the broken remains of the sculptures.

As it happened, two of them drew near to the giant portrait of Zhong Gui and didn't notice a dark figure perched atop the rafters until it was too late. Shurikens flew down with a vengeance and cut deep into the exposed parts of their Praetorian armor, severing nerves and muscle. Before the wounded men could make a sound, the silent figure fell upon them with sharpened blows that robbed the wind from their throats.

Gabriel rose up in the darkness, with the fallen soldiers at his feet. They were still breathing, but the bloody tips of the Japanese sai in his hands had done their job. The men would live, but they would be in a world of pain when they woke up.

The Toshigawa clan had trained him well. For centuries, his family had kept the faith alive and sometimes suffered greatly for it. To survive the constant threat of betrayals and arrests, the elders taught every generation to fight for their faith, and if necessary, to fight for their lives. Gabriel spent as much time in the dojo under the tutelage of Bushido warriors as he did in the Underground Church learning the faith of his ancestors. Indeed, scripture told of a time for everything, even for war. And now, the time had come to stand and fight.

The Japanese friar blended into the shadows like a phantom and reappeared with deadly strikes against two more Praetorians behind a shelf. Their rifles clattered to the ground as the steel blades ripped into their hands. Before they could even twitch, Gabriel slammed the handles of his daggers into their temples and knocked them out cold. In the process, the victims tumbled and brought the shelf crashing down around them. The noise quickly alerted the others and suddenly, the priest found himself dotted with red lights and staring down a posse of professional killers.

Four down, five more to go, thought Gabriel.

"Finish him!" screamed the officer.

As the triggers jerked back, Gabriel did the unexpected. He threw his daggers with lightning accuracy and struck two guards at the front. They fell like broken shells. While the rest opened fire, he dropped and rolled under the spray of bullets, drew the katana from his back and swung the angry blade at two more.

There was a flash of cold steel…and then chaos.

The first guard had his feet cut off at the ankles while the second lost a hand that was still attached to his rifle. Both men screamed in agony as they writhed on the floor, soaked in a pool of their own blood.

The officer jumped back, reloaded and blasted the rebel priest several times in the chest.

Gabriel felt as if a wild beast had sunk its teeth into his torso and ripped out his guts. The pain was excruciating. But he knew he had to get up, he had to act fast!

The Lumen officer took aim and focused his sights between the cleric's eyes. Before he could pull the trigger, the katana left the friar's hand like a javelin and skewered the Praetorian in the face. His rifle clunked noisily to the floor, followed by the dull thud of his dead body.

Exhausted, Gabriel lay on the floor trying to catch his breath. He had hoped to avoid taking any human lives, but this war was getting harder to fight without spilling any blood. If push came to shove, the warrior in him had no trouble stopping evil with righteous aggression. He knew that the Judeo-Christian law that "thou shall not kill" referred to the criminal act of murder, and not the lawful defense of good against evil. As far as he was concerned, this was a just war. He would deal with scruples later.

For now, he struggled to his feet and gripped his tortured chest. The metal slugs were barely stopped by the Kevlar. It was a good thing Michael forced the new prototype on him. Knowing Gabriel's penchant for close combat, the priest gave him the only body armor left. He might be a little less agile wearing this thing, but he was also a lot more alive. As he painfully stripped off the vest, the comlink in his ear sounded a warning.

"Do not head for the sewer," Michael ordered. "I repeat, do not head for the sewer. It's been compromised."

Raphael's voice came back through the static. "What? We're almost there."

"Do not proceed, stop where you are!"

"You've got to be kidding me," complained Randy. "I can see the exit from here."

"Turn back! Find a safe zone and hold your position," Michael insisted. "I'm on my way."

Gabriel yanked his blade from its victim and returned the sword to its scabbard.

"Crap, no one was supposed to know about this tunnel," the friar grumbled. "It's not even on any blueprints."

"Get over it," Michael barked over the comlink. "I need you there. Now!"

The soldier priest terminated the comms and looked at the tracking device in his hand. He had rifled it from the Praetorian sergeant who now lay bloody and bruised at his feet. The small display panel showed the enemy advancing on the location grids; the Lumen forces moving as green blips that were cutting off Raphael's escape. He estimated two minutes to contact.

"You won't survive the night. None of you will," said the voice on the floor.

The priest looked down at the wounded sergeant he had dropped earlier. The man was still conscious and grimacing in pain. Michael raised his weapon and fired a point blank shot. The body twitched violently from the electrical volts and fell back like a log.

✝

The air in the tunnel was dank and humid, and Randy was wheezing more than usual. But now, he also had to worry about an army of Lumen killers headed his way.

Raphael had led them to the rendezvous point. But the exit door was smoking around the edges, like something was trying to burn its way in.

"Why does all the scary stuff have to happen at night?" Randy grumbled.

"Give that to me," said Chelsea, snatching the gun from his belt.

"I can handle it," said the chauffeur, trying to retrieve the pistol.

There was a shattering noise and the iron door burst open like a dam unable to hold back the flood.

"Come on, this way," shouted Raphael as he led them back down the passageway.

The three fugitives ran like the wind, their hearts pounding in their chest. Ten meters in, they came back to a fork in the tunnel.

"Ok, we took this path earlier," said Raphael. "So the way back should be the tunnel on the left."

"No, it's the one on the right," argued Randy. He snatched the map from the priest and shone his flashlight on it.

Immediately, a barrage of bullets bounced off the walls. Randy dropped the flashlight and ducked low as a volley of tear gas flew into the passage and choked up their vision. In his panic, he grabbed Chelsea and blindly ran down one tunnel.

"Wait!" shouted Raphael. He started to run after the couple, but the gunfire and tear gas pushed him back and pinned him to a corner.

"I'm taking serious fire!" Raphael barked into his comms.

"Fall back," ordered Michael.

The dark silhouettes of the Praetorian soldiers poured through the burning smoke. Raphael could hardly breathe. He pointed his weapon and fired a hail of protest.

He couldn't see enough to hit anything accurately, but the sound of his barrel spitting death gave pause to the menacing troops.

"I lost the other two! We got separated. They went down the other way."

"Just stay alive!" Michael shouted back.

There was a shuddering blast that threw Raphael into the air. He flew backwards like a busted toy and smacked his head against the concrete wall, dropping unconscious in a pile of rubble.

Before the dust could settle, troopers wearing gas masks swooped in like vultures and encircled the fallen priest, their weapons ready for the kill. The triggers were taut with tension but no one fired a shot. The guards were given last minute orders to take the prisoners alive. Someone high up in Lumen Corp had changed his mind. There would be no executions tonight. That would be too easy. Death would come only when these men had paid for their sins. Not taking any chances, five guards remained to secure their prisoner. The rest of the Praetorian horde turned right and poured after Randy and Chelsea.

The young chauffeur had dragged the spunky girl headlong into the darkness, but he didn't get very far. The tunnel finished abruptly in a dead end. Now, all he could hear was the sound of combat boots running towards them.

"Fantastic, we're trapped," said Chelsea in frustration. The noise of their pursuers got closer. There was only one thing to do.

"Give me the gun," said Randy. "I'm not going down without a fight!"

He took the Beretta from Chelsea and pumped the weapon for action. They didn't have long to wait before the guards showed up.

The young man fired a few rounds and watched the tracers fly into the darkness. An aggressive cackle of machinegun fire echoed back and riddled the walls around them.

"Get down," cried Randy as he pulled Chelsea to safety.

The chauffeur took a diving roll to the other side and continued to engage the impossible odds. There was little else he could count on except the adrenaline shooting through his veins. Without any combat experience, he knew it was a matter of time before they were snatched, tagged and bound by the enemy. That moment however came sooner than expected.

Randy gripped the searing pain in his side and felt a sickening wetness creep through his clothes. The warm sticky sensation made him feel faint. He had taken a hit. The guards couldn't have been more than a few feet away. Frightened and confused, he looked up in time to see the metal butt of a Praetorian rifle smashing into his face. The blow was startling and vicious. His cheekbones crumbled like plaster and the cartilage in his nose snapped under the impact.

Randy tried to get up but his legs were dead with pain. He felt like he was drowning in a pool of darkness. The last thing he heard was Chelsea cursing in the background. And then suddenly...all was quiet.

Chapter 12

In a different part of the subterranean complex, Gabriel and Michael had crossed paths and were trying to breach the obstacles that had sprung up in their paths. The Lumen forces had sealed off their way to the sewer exit, and now a wall of fallen debris and concrete stood between the two priests and their rescue efforts. There was no way to reach Raphael and the rest.

"Wheezer, come in. Are you okay?" asked Gabriel, his earpiece buzzing with static. "Raphael, do you copy?"

There was no response from either. Gabriel feared the worse.

Michael squatted near the rubble and studied the damage. If the enemy rigged the tunnel to cave-in at this spot, there was no reason to think that the whole stretch wouldn't be mined with explosives. His special operations background made him suspicious. The tunnels might be too extensive for the guards to launch an effective dragnet. He knew that a better way would be for the mercenaries to just blow up parts of the bunker and hope that they bury their victims alive under the aging foundation.

He stood up and scoured the darkened surroundings with his flashlight until he found what he was looking for. There were two explosive packages primed on the rotten roof of the tunnel.

"Is there another way out?" he asked Gabriel.

"There's an old metal hatch two corridors south that leads above ground, but it's been rusted shut. I'm not even sure if you can blow it open."

"If you pack enough power, you can blow anything open," said Michael, pulling some plastique from his pack. "Come on, let's go!"

"What about Raphael and the rest?" asked Gabriel. "We can't just leave them here."

Before Michael could answer, the tiny lights on the detonators above started blinking.

"Move!" he shouted.

The two priests threw themselves into a gallop and pounded the earth with everything they had. A few seconds later, a giant fireball lit up the darkness and the tunnel began collapsing, its concrete pillars falling over like a scorching wall of deadly dominos.

Above ground, the chain reaction was spectacular. There were multiple explosions throughout the underground maze, shaking the very core of the foundation. Different parts of the museum began crumbling to the ground like some kind of destructive symphony. The noise of the devastation sent shockwaves through the air.

Raphael stared in disbelief at the scene unfolding before him. The demolition played out like a bad dream, with the entire complex collapsing in slow motion. Despite his concussion, he knew this was no dream. Chelsea and Randy stood beside him, paralyzed with horror. All three were handcuffed, bruised and supported by gun barrels pressed against their backs.

Guessing their thoughts, the Praetorian Commander stepped in and said, "Oh I wouldn't worry about your friends, I'm sure it'll take more than a few firecrackers to bury those two."

He glanced at the pair of Japanese sai in his hands. They had to be twisted off his dead guards with some effort. The blades were completely embedded in bone.

"From what I hear, they're like cockroaches. You try and squish the shit out of them, they fly in your face and try to bite your head off," laughed the Commander.

"But you have to admit," he paused, sweeping his arm at the panorama of destruction. "That's one hell of a showstopper, don't you think?"

He turned to Raphael and grinned, his face a wax mask of silicone terror. The man's features were coated in some kind of synthetic material, allowing him to look human but still creepy in a cadaverous way.

"Kaboom!!!" said the Praetorian leader, when the last of the museum structures fell with a shattering crash.

"I love blowing shit up. But that, that's a work of art! What do *you* think?" he laughed maniacally.

Raphael wanted to lash out in anger but he held his tongue. Trash-talking when they had guns to their backs and a psychotic agent baiting them would only make things worse. He prayed that Michael and Gabriel made it out in time, but there was no way to be sure. The doctor kept his cool and stole a quick glance at Randy. The young man was in bad shape. His bleeding side was dripping like a leaky faucet and he was barely able to stand.

"What're you going to do with us?" asked Chelsea.

Her voice was calm and resolute, almost as if each setback, each crazy event that unfolded through the night only made her stronger and more determined to survive whatever madness the fates had in store.

"Well this is your lucky night," the Commander chuckled in amusement. "Tonight I'm just a dogcatcher, it's my job to return the cute little poodle to her masters. They sure miss you a lot, and I know you're going to enjoy the welcome home party."

Chelsea felt a chill crawl down her spine. She was afraid. But she also had enough of hysterics, of languishing in a limbo of uncertainty. In spite of this horrific new reality, she felt as if a choking leash of darkness had been lifted and she could breathe again. She didn't have all the answers, but at least she knew she wasn't losing her mind. There was a God. And there were those who would stop at nothing to keep the whole world from seeing that truth. The certainty of what she had witnessed so far had begun to set her free, and she was not about to let the Corporation put her back into the cage. She was nobody's pet.

"I can't say the same for these two however. Nobody really wants any strays," said the Commander, nodding at her companions.

"We'll keep them in the pound for a few days, see if anyone's willing to show up and claim them. Otherwise, we'll have to put them to sleep. What're you going to do? Life's a bitch."

And the whole Praetorian cohort laughed in response.

"Look, I'll head back with you," said Chelsea. "Just let them go. Please."

"No can do, I can't break up the team. It's bad for morale," said the Commander.

He grabbed a tuft of Randy's hair and pulled his head back.

"Look at that face, he misses you already," teased the scary looking man.

Randy was pale and suffering greatly from his gunshot wounds. He jerked his head away from the evil clutches and collapsed in the dirt, weakened by the loss of blood.

"On second thoughts, that's one sick-looking puppy," said the Commander.

"Leave him alone!" cried Chelsea.

The whole time, Raphael kept his cool. Only his lips quivered slightly in prayer. The sun was coming up soon, but he felt like darkness had only sunk deeper over the earth. As a medical doctor, he recognized the symptoms of shock, and there was no doubt Randy was in severe danger. He didn't know if his friend was going to make it.

If he could persuade the Commander to leave Randy behind, there was a slim chance that Michael and Gabriel could get to the wounded man in time. But at this point, Raphael wasn't even sure if his brother priests had survived the demolition. Unconsciously, his verbal prayers began to get louder.

Suddenly the Praetorian leader pulled out his handgun and pistol-whipped the priest. Raphael took the furious blow to his face. He turned back and tasted blood trickling down his torn lip.

"If you start with that mumbo jumbo," threatened the Commander. "I swear I'll cut your tongue out right here. Do we understand each other, *priest?*"

He spat the last word out with disgust. But Raphael refused to be cowered.

"Do whatever you want with me, but the kid's dying," he replied. "He's no good to you. He doesn't know anything, and he'll only slow you down. Let him go, I'll tell you what you need to know."

"Ahh, Christian charity; sacrificing yourself for another. How noble. But from where I'm standing, you're not in a very good place to negotiate. Still…"

The Commander looked down at Randy, who was unconscious and bleeding on the ground.

"You've got a point. I think *I will* leave him behind. He can deliver a message for me; tell your friends where to find you. After all, I hate to break up the team."

✝

The rusty iron hatch blasted into the sky like a geyser and fell some distance away. Two smoky figures crawled out of the opening in the ground and threw themselves down the hill. A jet of fire shot out of the hole and nearly singed their escape.

Michael and Gabriel tumbled down the dusty incline until they broke their fall against some trees and rocks. Picking themselves up quickly, the two men dived back into the shadows and clambered up to the edge of a precipice. From there, they could see the remains of the museum laid waste on a field of carnage.

"Crap! There goes my research grant," said Gabriel.

Michael shushed his friend and pointed to the space before the underground tunnels. His beaten up muscle car, Scarface, was still parked in the shadows. There was no sign of the enemy or anyone else for that matter. The Lumen menace seemed to have just vanished into thin air. Pulling out a pair of binoculars, he scouted the area for life.

"Where the hell is everyone?" asked Gabriel.

"This is not good. The troops are gone, which means they got what they came for," said Michael.

"You mean Raphael and the rest?"

Michael jumped up and tapped Gabriel on the shoulder. "Come on, if the tracks are fresh we can still trail them. Get to the wheels!"

He started running down the slope towards Scarface. Gabriel steadied the katana on his back and raced after his friend.

"You do realize this could be a trap."

"You got a better idea?"

As they neared the vehicle, both men slowed down and entered the perimeter cautiously. They squatted behind the foliage and scanned their surroundings before stepping out into the clearing.

Michael raised his rifle and crept out in stealth. Gabriel followed behind, his hand grasping a Lumen weapon he had picked up in the tunnel. He was never comfortable with guns. But after the standoff earlier, he was happy to use whatever he could to stay alive.

A little distance off, Scarface rested under a canopy of trees like a mustang waiting patiently for its rider. As Michael approached, he noticed someone sitting in the front seat. Instinctively, he took aim. Gabriel crept up and saw the same thing but he recognized the silhouette.

"Randy," he whispered under his breath.

The chauffeur sat behind the steering wheel, waiting for them. The two priests rushed forward, their faces filled with dread.

"Dear God, no!" muttered Gabriel with angry tears in his eyes. He opened the car door and stood there transfixed for a moment, unsure of what to do next.

Randy's torso was brutally skewered to the car seat. One of Gabriel's sai was jammed through his chest like a giant tack holding him in place. There was blood everywhere. Attached to the blade was a sheet of paper that taunted them like a white flag. The message was clear. If they didn't surrender, the rest of their friends would share the same fate.

"Let's get him out," said Michael.

But Gabriel was unable to move, he couldn't bring himself to pull his own dagger from the punctured heart of his dead friend.

Quietly, Michael leaned over the body and yanked the dagger free. Warm blood oozed out in abundance. The man had only just died. The tall priest reached in and lifted the lifeless body out of the car. He laid it gently on the ground and stepped aside for his confrere. Bullet wounds aside, Randy had been mutilated. His face had been carved up with hateful malice.

"Look what they did to him," cried Gabriel. The friar had been like an older brother to the young chauffeur.

Both men knelt silently beside the deceased, each grappling with their own emotions. Then slowly, Gabriel reached down with his thumb and traced a cross over Randy's forehead.

"Eternal rest grant unto him, O Lord, let thy perpetual light shine upon him."

"May he rest in peace," replied Michael.

His voice was stoic but his eyes betrayed the fury he felt at this desecration. Every fiber of his personality wanted revenge, but he willed himself to stay calm. He was still a priest. Reluctantly, he gazed at the dagger in his hand. The note was still stuck to the blade. Ripping the bloodstained paper from the pointed shaft, Michael stood up and read the message.

The date was set for tomorrow. The time was three in the morning. The location was indicated by a series of coordinates, and the instructions were brief - come alone and come unarmed, surrender peacefully or the prisoner would die. Try anything stupid and their fellow priest would be butchered in a way that made Randy's slaughter look like a paper cut. There was no mention of Chelsea or any exchange of hostages.

Michael knew that Raphael wasn't going to be freed even if they turned themselves in. If anything, this was a dare. The Corporation was challenging them to attempt a rescue, knowing that they would be walking straight into the dragon's lair. It was obvious that Lumen Corp wanted more than just their heads on a platter. They wanted to humiliate the three priests and break the spirit of the Underground Church.

Over the last two years, the Christian population had come to refer to Michael, Gabriel and Raphael as 'The Archangels'. There was clearly a mystical allusion to their names, despite the fact that the priests themselves took great care to remain anonymous. Most in the Resistance had never even met the clerics, but their exploits became legend and the stories of their struggle brought fresh courage to the rebellion.

To Lumen Corp, this growing symbol of defiance was more dangerous than the antics of three pesky priests. Beyond eliminating these zealots, there was a dangerous legend to kill as well. And after tonight, the Corporation was finally in a position to drive a stake through this stubborn myth.

"Strike the shepherd and the flock will scatter," thought Michael.

For a split second, his mind went back to the old bishop he had killed in cold blood. It happened a lifetime ago but it felt like he had just pulled the trigger that morning. His heart was still heavy with guilt. He crushed the paper in his fist and gritted his teeth. This was a challenge they couldn't refuse. Come what may, they would have to enter the jaws of hell to save their friend, even at the cost of their own lives.

Gradually, Gabriel stood up and looked over at Michael, as if reading his mind.

"Nobody gets left behind, Mike. Nobody."

Chapter 13

The striking man in the immaculate suit floated into the room wearing a spooky grin on his face. It was hard to know if the smile was real or just an illusion. Depending on the angle of his features, the look of mirth would dance in and out like a cheap hologram.

"Miss Shields, so glad to have you back. You don't know how happy I am to see you," said Chambers. "Welcome home."

"This isn't my home," Chelsea replied indignantly. She sat on a leather sofa in the private study of Marshall Chambers. The room was filled with antique books and beautiful furniture. The exquisite mansion housing it was nestled above the bustling city like a modern day Olympus in full view of the mortals below.

Chelsea shifted uncomfortably in her seat. Raphael was nowhere to be seen. They had been separated and taken to different rooms for interrogation. And even though she was alone with the Lumen Vice-president, she knew that the place was crawling with security.

"I think we could both use a drink. Let's see, what was it you liked? Scotch with a twist of lime?"

Chelsea had only met Chambers once at a party. And like everyone else, she had been smitten by his charm and winning smile. But now, trapped in the darkening orbit of his power and authority, that same alluring smile sent icy chills to her heart. Suddenly, she felt the first pangs of panic.

"Get away from me," she grunted in real fear. "I'm warning you, stay away." She turned and grabbed a brass candelabrum off the table.

Chambers laughed aloud.

"Come now, is that any way to treat your family? After all we've done for you, this is the thanks we get?"

He shook his head with a patronizing sigh.

"It's always the same with you young people today. We give you the best things in life, but you're always complaining, always hungry, always wanting more...like some insolent brat who doesn't know how to be grateful. I'm seriously hurt."

"What I needed was the truth. And the Corporation kept that from me. You kept that from all of us!" said Chelsea.

"What is the truth? That hogwash those priests tried to feed you? Did they give you an autographed copy of their Basic Instructions Before Leaving Earth? Was it signed by God?"

Chambers smiled like a condescending sage, amused by the naïve posturing of a child.

"Or perhaps the truth was your amazing career, the huge fortune in your name, the popularity, the gorgeous suitors, the photo shoots, not to mention the endless parties. And everything else you ever wanted in your young life. That was *your* truth just twenty-four hours ago, so what makes you think the truth is any different now?"

Chelsea was nervous before this man, but she was also upset by his question. After what she had seen and experienced, she didn't want to be reminded of how close she had come to falling over the edge.

"Why are you doing this? Why does the Corporation want to destroy the Church?"

"Oh don't be mistaken, it's not just the Church that gets our attention. Bring on the temples and the synagogues, the mosques and what have you. Lumen Corp abhors the slightest hint of discrimination in our termination policies. I assure you, we're very inclusive that way. Everybody gets their fair shot at persecution, but especially the Christians. What can I say, it's hard not to have favorites."

"So Lumen Corp intends to take over the world, to kill organized religion? Who are you people?"

"To hell with organized religion," laughed Chambers. "Use your imagination, it is God who must die!"

For the first time since her capture, the beautiful brunette allowed herself a smirk.

"Even I know you can't kill God, he's omnipotent," she scoffed.

"How right you are. One night away from the nest and you've got yourself a brand new vocabulary. We may not be able to kill God per se, but we can murder all traces of his life within each human soul, and that Miss Shields is much more fun than taking on the big man himself. When the world is dead to God, humanity will destroy itself. It's inevitable."

"But why?" demanded Chelsea. "Why destroy humanity?"

"Why else? To remake man in our own image; the image of the

112

Prince of this world who deserves no less to be worshipped than that pitiful usurper on the cross."

"This is madness! You want to remake mankind in the image of Satan?" Chelsea was aghast.

Once again, the room rocked with laughter.

"Listen to you," chuckled the senior Lumen executive. "It wasn't so long ago that you believed the devil didn't exist. Or if he did, he was just a figment of your imagination."

"That's because the world told us that lie! You and your kind made us believe that."

"As if we could make you believe anything you didn't want to," said Chambers.

His grin became wider. The corners of his mouth stretched disturbingly.

"My dear girl, your generation put up a flashing sign above your empty souls that said - *Vacancy, don't be shy. Come on in.* You left the doors wide opened to begin with. Are you really that surprised that doubt, cynicism and disbelief have moved in?"

Chambers bent over the girl and stretched out his hand. "Come with me, I want to show you something."

Chelsea was afraid to take his hand, but she was more frightened at the prospect of refusing it. Gingerly she allowed his fingers to wrap around hers. Strangely enough, his touch seemed to calm her nerves like a sedative coursing through her veins.

Chambers opened a side door and led her into an ornate hall clothed in Corinthian marble. The floor was so black as to appear to plunge into an abyss. The walls however were blushing with Mediterranean hues. Gorgeous paintings and manuscripts hung from exquisite frames while sensuous lighting made the room glow softly like a grand boudoir of passion.

"As you can see, I'm a man who appreciates beautiful things. We have a lot in common, you and I," said the Lumen official, his voice all smooth and silky.

Chelsea looked around the private gallery and recognized some of the more iconic masterpieces and historical blueprints adorning the room. She didn't know very much about history or art, but she didn't doubt that the priceless paintings and scientific sketches were originals. How they came to reside in the private collection of the Corporation's Vice-president was a mystery not worth exploring. She knew enough to know that what Lumen Corp wanted, Lumen Corp obtained.

"Darwin, Caravaggio, Galileo," said Chambers, nodding appreciatively at the walls. "Even the grand master, Da Vinci himself. These great champions of the human spirit struggled their whole lives to create works of real beauty and truth. And yet they had to face lesser mortals who fought endlessly to oppose them, to denounce their creative genius with cowardly threats, criticism and censure. And believe me, no one is foremost in that crusade to imprison the freedom of the human mind than the Catholic Church."

The Vice-president inched closer to Chelsea and placed his hand softly on her cheek. "I hope to save you, my dear, from that terrible fate," he added, smiling.

Chelsea knew next to nothing about the Church apart from what she had been taught to believe. But with everything that's happened, the only people defending her from the forces of hell were clearly members of this same Church. And conversely, the only dangers to her soul and body came from the direction of her Lumen 'family'. In the face of this truth, she was determined not to drown in the seductive warmth of this man's charm.

"Spare me the drama," said Chelsea, sounding very bold all of a sudden. "What does any of this have to do with killing innocent people and raising hell on earth?"

"Miss Shields, you're not dense and yet your naivety depresses me."

"Then speak plainly," Chelsea rebuffed. "Anything more comes from the devil."

She was surprised at the words that left her mouth. Where did she learn that? It was as if some latent memory was suddenly resurrected from those dusty days of religious instructions she endured as a child.

Chambers reacted with genuine surprise. He cocked an eyebrow and burst out laughing.

"Touché! Then let us speak frankly," he said, ushering Chelsea towards a pair of noble armchairs that rested like thrones in the middle of the room.

Chambers seated himself on one and motioned for the young woman to take the other.

"Sit," he urged Chelsea. "Please."

But she felt safer keeping her distance and remain rooted to the floor. Chambers smiled and shrugged his shoulders.

"How shall I put this delicately?" he quipped, rubbing his chin thoughtfully.

"As I said, you're a gorgeous, talented young woman with enough star power to light up a whole galaxy. But you owe most of that to the support and encouragement of your family here in the Corporation. So the right thing to do, the smart thing to do, would be for you to continue your reign as one of the most desirable women in the world."

Chambers got up from his seat and approached Chelsea. He draped an arm softly over her shoulders and ushered her gently to her seat. "Please…"

This time she didn't resist.

"In return, I'll forget this little infraction. I understand it wasn't even your fault. You didn't plan to be kidnapped by religious zealots and held hostage, and I'm sorry that you were brainwashed by their fanaticism. All we want now is for you to return to your life of privilege and glory."

"Privilege and glory?" repeated Chelsea. "I'm nothing but a bitch with a diamond collar on a leash. You'll have to do better than that."

Her heart was beating wildly under her calm exterior.

Chambers removed a thin cigarette from an expensive case and balanced it on his lips. From out of nowhere, Norman the Lumen aide appeared and offered his boss a light. Chelsea was surprised to see the man emerge from some dark corner, especially since she didn't even see him come in. She shivered slightly. Everything about these people gave her the creeps.

"Your brother was a cultural icon, a rock legend. And you're one of the most beautiful women in the world. Lucky for you, I do so like beautiful things," said Chambers.

He sucked on his cigarette and stroked his chin.

"Between the two of you, you've got millions of young hearts wrapped around your precious little fingers. Listening to everything you say, dying to be like you, hopelessly lost in your charm."

He paused briefly to exhale more pungent smoke.

"Well at least you still do," he laughed. "Max's little digits are probably feeding maggots right now. But the fans, the sponsors, the magic and mystery that made you both larger than life – that lives on. And now that your brother is pushing up daisies, you're in a very unique position to inherit his legacy."

Chambers moved closer to make his pitch.

"Together, we can make you bigger than ever. There're many

people depending on you to go on as the Goddess of fashion and beauty. Indeed, the whole world is laid out at your feet. Your fans need you. Your sponsors are crazy for you. And most of all, we as your corporate family can help you succeed."

Once again, the smile returned like a slimy serpent coiled around her throat. She could feel her breath tightening under his gaze. Chelsea knew that the man before her was making no attempt to veil his threats. He wasn't even hiding his contempt for her and Max. Like everyone else in the Lumen universe, they were merely chess pieces in the grand scheme of things.

She mustered all her courage and returned his glare.

"In the last twenty-four hours, Lumen Corp sent creatures from hell that tried to eat me. I saw a demon try to take my brother and I found myself possessed by an unclean spirit. And now you're offering me a career advancement?"

Chambers burst out laughing. The cackling noise reverberated like a ghastly echo. He wiped the tears of amusement from his eyes and said, "I'm offering you a chance to make history my dear. A new world order is upon us. Believe me when I say we're nearing the end of this nauseating struggle with the prophets of doom and gloom. As we speak, the City of Man is already dismantling the City of God. Soon, there won't be a single church spire, minaret, or temple dome left standing. The question is, where will you be when it all comes tumbling down?"

Chelsea felt an oppressive fear wrap around her like a blanket. Her limbs became bound with dread and her pulse quickened as Chambers went on. She glanced furtively around the room and saw no escape.

"The terrible things you've seen – the hellhounds, demons and spirits – yes, they're as real as the stinging bruises on your pretty face. But you should know, the Gates of Hell are opening wider each day. Your *friendly* encounters are little more than tiny contractions in the womb of destiny, crying out with labor pains to deliver the Antichrist. You wanted the truth?"

Chambers suddenly got up from his seat and leaned over Chelsea, his twisted mouth hovering slightly over her own luscious lips.

"I'll tell you the truth."

Dropping his voice to a whisper, the powerful man breathed on her like an evil shaman and said…

"Our time has come. This is our century. When the master of this world reclaims the throne that is rightfully his, we who serve him will rule like Gods in a brand new world. The future is ours I assure you. But know this, the meek will not inherit the earth. We grant it only to the brave and the bold. You see, I too dream of a better world. I lie awake at night praying for mankind to fulfill its destiny, for us to shed our human skins and finally reveal ourselves as the Gods we were always meant to be."

Before Chelsea could grasp the intent of his words, he leaned in and kissed her on the lips. Instantly, icy shards of pain shot through her veins and she felt her blood empty of life. The feeling was more intense than anything she had ever felt. Just when she thought she would black out from the frozen terror, the Lumen VP broke off and sat back in his chair. The young model fell forward clutching her chest, gasping as the breaths trickled from her icy lungs like steam on a winter day.

Smirking, Chambers returned the cigarette to his lips and gazed idly at the girl trembling at his feet.

"So, will you stay with me and reign like a queen in this brave new world, or will you join the tide of extinction that's coming to all who oppose us? Choose carefully, you have only this one chance."

"I'm not afraid of you," shouted Chelsea, her eyes stinging with tears of rage.

It was more stubborn pride than courage but she was determined not to be intimidated. Her brief encounters with the priests had somehow galvanized her with a new resilience she had not known previously.

"Why not choose some other bitch in your collection and just have me crucified like the rest?"

Chelsea knew she wasn't the only prominent talent in the Lumen stable. She knew scores of equally gorgeous and talented celebrities who would kill to enjoy the fame and fortune that she was being offered. And she knew that the Corporation would not keep her alive purely for the sake of their investment.

"Because you already know that heaven and hell exist. You've seen the supernatural proofs," said Chambers, his voice rising like a musical note.

"You see, venial choices are made out of weaknesses and ignorance but rarely with the full consent and knowledge of the will. What I want is for you to make a public statement; a fully informed mortal decision that despite knowing the truth, rejects God and

117

breaks his hold on you."

The Lumen boss looked down and brushed a spot of ash from the sleeve of his expensive jacket. Norman who had stayed in the shadows suddenly came forward and yanked Chelsea to her feet. She flew off the ground like a stringed puppet and shook nervously at his touch.

"We need to make a statement and you're going to help us," Chambers explained. "Stories of your dramatic rescue and Max's conversion will likely give the Underground Church a hard on. I want you to show the Christian resistance that you want nothing more than to spit in the face of redemption. You're more than just a fashion model. You're a model for millions of young people who're trying to live the dream. So show the world what you stand for. Tell God and his sanctimonious rabble that it's better to reign in hell than to serve in heaven! Make that choice boldly in the full knowledge of all you've seen and heard. Condemn these criminals in public. Let the world know that the efforts of these imbeciles to frighten and convert you are futile."

Chambers approached and brought the burning cigarette close to her face.

"Most of all, I want you to know that if you refuse to do so…"

His voice trailed off in silence as Chelsea stared at him in a mixture of anger and terror.

"There are truly worse things to endure than death on a cross," Chambers suggested. The seductive smile remained frozen on his face like a porcelain mask.

"Let's take a walk!"

He got up and slipped his arm around Chelsea's back and gently herded her towards the back of the room. She didn't want to budge from her spot, but her legs pulled away on their own and she found herself swept along by his soft insistence.

"Did I tell you about my latest acquisition?" he asked abruptly. "Oh, *you must* see it. It's all the rage in nouveau art."

Chambers walked over to a part of the gallery that was softly lit by an overhead lamp. There was just enough darkness framing the area to draw one's attention to the lighted object hanging on the wall. Tucked away between two exquisite works of art was a large picture frame covered by a huge red curtain. It was comparatively bigger than most of the other exhibits in the room, almost like a life-sized painting as far as Chelsea could tell.

"I'm a little embarrassed to say this, but I'm something of an artist myself," he confessed, almost shyly.

"It's one thing to be an avid collector, but there's nothing like the thrill of creating something unique and special. As far as I know, it's the first of its kind. I have to warn you though, it's a little controversial but what's that they say - beauty is in the eye of the beholder?"

He grabbed the golden tassel holding the curtains in place. "No peeking now…"

Chambers tugged at the cord and the heavy drapes drifted back to expose a gruesome sight. Chelsea stumbled back in shock and nearly fainted. She wanted desperately to scream. But her throat was so constricted that all she could do was blanch in horror.

"I haven't decided what to call it yet. But be honest, tell me, what do you think? Is that a masterpiece or what?" asked Chambers proudly.

Stretched over the wooden frame was a canvass of human flesh - stitched, woven and sewn together like a ghastly fabric spun from the most excruciating torture imaginable. It was almost as if someone had taken a knife to the man on display and skillfully carved off his features and skin in one seamless act of malice.

"You have no idea how long it took me to do this," said the Lumen VP, grinning from ear to ear. "I had plenty of help of course, human tissue is such a pain to work with but the end results are just stunning, don't you think? The hardest part though was keeping him alive."

Chambers reached up and snapped his fingers before the grotesque face on the artwork.

"Isn't that right, Martaban?" he hollered. Painfully, the eyelids pulled back. A terrifying groan slipped out of the victim like the ghostly wail of some lost soul.

Chelsea was paralyzed with fright. Only then did she notice the tiny tubes sewn into the flattened folds of his living flesh, pumping artificial life into the desiccated shell of his mutilated body.

Zadok was still alive. Humanly speaking that wasn't even possible. The man was nothing less than a nightmare, a grotesque picture of hellish deformity, animated only by a concoction of powerful drugs and even more powerful magic. The sight was so horrific that Chelsea tried to turn away. But Norman caught her and forced her to gape at the monstrous spectacle.

"Tragic really," said Chambers. "He was such a disappointment as an employee. We gave him all the support and help he needed to do a good job, and he couldn't even keep from losing his clients. But the good news is, he's doing quite well in his new assignment. I like him far better as a piece of art than as a manager. So we'll let him hang around for a bit."

Chambers laughed and rubbed his hands gleefully like a pleased little boy.

"In fact, he looks so good that I'm tempted to add to the collection. I'm sure it'd be less painful for everyone the next time round," he said, looking at Chelsea.

The broken sounds of Zadok Martaban echoed back in agony.

"Ok, maybe not for everyone," said Chambers, chuckling. "Now where were we? Oh yes, destiny awaits."

Again, the same smile crept over his lips.

"So tell me, young lady, what's your decision?"

†

Somewhere else in the mansion, Raphael remained strapped to a cold metal chair in the middle of a room. He was stripped to his waist and covered in sweat. His face was swollen and bleeding. His nose looked like it might've been broken.

"I'm going to ask you again. Where are the safe houses?"

Raphael couldn't see the man behind the voice, but he could hear the cackle of at least two others who were taking turns with his torture. It was all he could do to keep his eyes from swelling shut. They were cut and purple with pain.

"Still not talking? I thought you preachers liked nothing better than to flap your jaws, mounting the pulpit and spitting fire and brimstone," said one of the others derisively.

Again the priest felt a brutal fist pummel his face.

"Or maybe it was just little boys and girls that he liked mounting," said another voice. The group laughed like a pack of hyenas.

The sound of a metal door creaked opened and heavy footsteps followed. Raphael squinted but he couldn't see who it was. The interrogators moved aside and made way for the newcomer. Although the pack said nothing, it was clear from their shuffles that an alpha male had entered their midst.

"That's not very nice, leave the poor man alone," said the new voice with sarcasm.

"Not all priests are perverts and degenerates. I'm sure the good Father here is a faithful, holy man of God. Aren't you, Father?" asked the man who just came in.

Raphael raised his battered face and peered at the vision before him. The image was fuzzy but he recognized the scorn and hatred.

"Oh come on, don't give me that look," chided the Praetorian Commander. "It's not as if we planted pedophiles and monsters in your Church. You did that on your own. Your progressive bishops welcomed anyone into the seminary during those years. Well, anyone who wasn't too orthodox or attached to doctrines anyway. Faithful men like you would've made the Church look too…how shall we say…*out of touch with the times?*"

The words were bitter, but Raphael knew that even demons sometimes spoke the truth. There was a period when good, virtuous men were turned away from seminaries because they were too Catholic or conservative for the liberal tastes of a politically correct Church hierarchy. Instead, the doors were flung opened to welcome anyone who could make the faith more popular and relevant to the times. In many places, fidelity to doctrinal beliefs was stripped along with the sacred altars in the churches. Both often lay broken and trampled under the marching orders of a new reformation.

The pope at the time had convened a council to better equip the Church to evangelize a world that he knew was creeping towards nihilism. Unfortunately, his enemies hijacked the intentions of the council and ripped a hole through the body of Christ that continued to bleed to this day. In less than two decades, the Holy Spirit was exchanged for the spirit of the world. And once the smoke of Satan entered the house of God, it took whole generations of suffering, havoc and martyrdoms to cleanse the Church from this filth.

"In fact, most of your bishops were incompetent bureaucrats. The rest were as corrupt as the stink they were letting in," laughed the Praetorian leader. "So what's harboring and abetting a couple more criminals in the old boy's club?"

The Commander grinned and slipped his hands into some leather gloves. "Oh I'm sorry, did I say a couple?" he added, flexing his fist. "I meant a legion."

The priest doubled over in agony as heavy knuckles slammed into his sides. A trickle of blood dribbled painfully from his lips. The cohort in the shadows erupted with insane laughter.

Raphael kept his cool and tried to breathe calmly despite his broken ribs. He had already endured an hour of beatings. He knew the taunting was just the icing on the cake. The enemy was rubbing salt in his wounds to break his spirit. Silently, he called out to God for strength.

"And when the scandals broke, all we had to do was fan the flames, and all the credibility and good your Church ever did went up in smoke. Sigh, I love the media. Journalists are so much better than mercenaries when it comes to killing the faith," said the Commander with a sardonic smile.

"What can I say, the miracle of the modern press. Good thing we own the newspapers eh?"

He lifted Raphael's chin with his gloved hand and sneered at the bruised and bloodied face.

"Enough with the chit chat, what say we start over? Where are the rest of your buddies hiding out?"

He smacked his hand against Raphael's cheek and blood splattered from the swollen gash. The exhausted priest grimaced in distress but said nothing in response.

"We can keep this up all night," replied the Commander.

Chapter 14

The drive out of town was quiet. The roads were starting to swell with the noise of traffic but the cabin itself was solemn with dread and worry. Both Michael and Gabriel had not said a word since they buried Randy in the woods near the museum.

The prayers were brief and simple. The grave was unmarked. There was no time for the proper rites. The haste with which they prepared the body for burial only heightened the reality that they were at war. And both men knew that before the weekend was over, there would be more casualties.

"Take a left at the lights," said Gabriel, breaking the silence. He pointed to an old duplex tucked between two grey apartment blocks. Michael nodded and continued to circle the blocks a few times while checking the streets for danger. Finally he turned into the alley and stopped near a simple signboard decorated with paper lanterns.

Gabriel got out of the car and approached the Japanese diner. He slid his fingers along a ledge and recovered a key for the back door. He unlocked it and stepped inside the cool interior. Michael came up in time to follow his friend into the establishment.

It was still very early in the morning. The tiny yakitori diner was usually opened only for dinner. Gabriel closed the door behind them and quietly approached the stairs on the ground floor.

"They're probably upstairs," whispered Gabriel. "Try not to make too much noise, they can get a little jumpy."

Michael froze in his tracks and seemed rather amused. Recognizing the look, Gabriel turned around and broke into a sheepish grin.

"Too late," snapped an older gentleman coming down the stairs. "I can hear the two of you shuffling downstairs like elephants. I had to calm your aunt, she thought there were rats in the kitchen. Big ones!"

"Oji," said Gabriel, bowing slightly.

"You boys look like road kill," said the man, observing the bruises and cuts on their faces. "A bit of scuffle with the old goat?"

"More than you think, uncle," said Gabriel.

Hiroshi Toshigawa stopped at the bottom of the stairs and frowned. Before he could respond, a chubby woman in her sixties jostled past him and reached eagerly for Gabriel.

"Obasan," greeted the young priest, smiling. She caught him in her arms and hugged him like a ten-year old child, almost lifting him off the ground.

"Enough already, let him go," complained Hiroshi. "Every time he comes over, you smother him. No wonder he hardly visits."

"And why shouldn't I?" growled his wife, Teresa. "He's the smartest, sweetest nephew we have."

Hiroshi rolled his eyes and grunted, knowing that Gabriel was their one and only nephew.

He turned to Michael and scowled. "I see you're still alive, Father."

"Ignore him Michael," grumbled Teresa. "His manners are not the only thing that's broken. It's good to see you both."

The old man snorted rudely at his wife and gave Michael a mischievous wink. The tall priest took the outstretched hand and smiled. He was usually not in a mood to be social but it was hard not to like these good people.

Hiroshi was a wiry old man with thick glasses and a dry sense of humor. His eyes were permanently set on squint, as if the sun was constantly shining on his face. He wore his hair short like Gabriel, but peppered with age and wisdom. In many ways, his modest, slightly paunchy figure was a far cry from the bold giant he really was.

Michael knew that Gabriel's uncle had suffered and done more for the faith than most people could understand or appreciate. And yet, the only reward he could expect was the safe refuge of anonymity and the shadow of the cross, besides the certainty that he was doing the will of God.

"You do realize that you're dripping all over my carpet?" exclaimed Hiroshi. Michael looked down and noticed that blood was trickling down his sleeve.

"I'll get the first aid," said Teresa, rushing to the kitchen. "And while Hiro patches you up, I'll make us something to eat. You both look like you could use a hot meal."

"Don't bother Auntie, we can't stay," interrupted Gabriel. "We just need to hide out for a few hours, get some supplies and then we have to go."

Teresa turned around in exasperation.

"Does this look like a motel or a transit lounge to you? This is our home and you're both family. Don't disrespect us by treating it like one. Now please, go sit down and I'll prepare something for you. I can tell from your faces that you're sick with worry."

Gabriel started to protest but Hiroshi interrupted him. "Listen to your aunt. You won't help anyone by being a stubborn mule," he said. "Whatever it is, we can talk later."

Grabbing a pair of scissors, he stripped away Michael's sleeve to reveal a nasty cut on his upper arm. A tiny piece of shrapnel was still sticking out of the wound like a metal fin.

"Let's remove that and get you stitched up," he said. Turning to his wife, he hollered for her to bring him a bottle of sake to numb the pain.

"It's all right, I brought my own," said Michael, pulling out the whiskey flask from his jacket.

"Who said it was for you? The sake is for me," said a serious looking Hiroshi. "I hate the sight of blood. This will hurt me more than it hurts you."

The priest laughed quietly and took a big gulp from his carafe. He was used to the scathing sense of humor in this house. He knew well that Hiroshi had suffered more brutality and picked up more scars from police interrogations than most people did from fights.

"I guess you're still in a lot of pain," assumed the older man.

"I've had worse."

"I'm not talking about this scratch," said Hiroshi. "Both God and his Church has long since forgiven you, when will you learn to forgive yourself?"

Michael said nothing. His previous role as an assassin for Lumen Corp was no secret to Gabriel's family. If anything, his notorious past had only made him a more lethal weapon against evil after his conversion. Numerous clashes with the army of darkness had only confirmed that. Still, there were casualties in every war, and his growing taste for hard liquor was starting to worry his friends.

Few in the resistance had thrown themselves into this holy crusade with greater violence than this former enemy of the Church, but it was also true that Michael had spent years dancing with the devil to a symphony of murder. It was too much to expect that he would escape the wretched music unharmed when the tango ended.

"You're a priest," said Hiroshi. "You should know better than to doubt God's forgiveness and mercy. Why do you persist in punishing yourself when the Lord has already absolved you? Remember, it's arrogant to exaggerate our guilt before the divine mercy."

Hiroshi knew that the priest was hiding a great deal of pain, and that much of his reckless forays into battle were fueled by a maddening desire for reparation. But he also knew that if kept unchecked, this damning guilt would swelter in the slime of personal pride and lead to self-destruction.

Even Michael himself recognized that. Yet night after night in the troubled corridors of his mind, the voice of evil would play on like a broken record, scourging his memories with guilt and despair. The shame and anguish were often so violent that a weaker man would have jammed a loaded gun into his own mouth to silence the chaos.

Fortunately, Michael was anything but weak, though in recent times, he was relying a lot more on the spirit in his canteen than the Holy Spirit to get him through the nights.

The wounded priest yanked the loose metal from his arm and blood began to flow freely. Grimacing with pain, he quaffed down another shot of whisky and grumbled at the old man, "We're wasting time, let's do this."

"Good, bury the pain, let it fester, what do I care?" said Hiroshi, putting pressure on the wound.

The priest winced in agony. "If you were a younger man, I'll kick your ass," Michael remarked.

"If I was a younger man, I'll give you a lot more to cry about than this girly cut on your arm," answered Hiroshi.

Gabriel smiled at the friendly tussle between the two men. He knew that of all people, Michael respected Hiroshi greatly, and his uncle in turn cared deeply for the ex-mercenary turned priest.

As the sounds and smells of the kitchen wafted into the dining area, Gabriel began to feel a twinge of nostalgia for the place. He had grown up in the loving care of his two relatives after losing his parents to a police dragnet that filled the gutters of Nagasaki with their blood.

The killers wore real uniforms and flashed real badges, but there was no doubt as to who was behind the ambush that toppled the Underground Church in his prefecture. His uncle and aunt barely escaped the gauntlet themselves.

In the ensuing nightmare, Hiroshi had taken the young boy and fled Japan with his wife for the relative safety of a new country. Over the years, they moved from place to place, crossing state lines and keeping a low profile, while staying connected to the Resistance. Until finally, they were able to put enough distance between themselves and the past to settle down in this small duplex they called home.

No place was completely safe of course. The growing influence of the Corporation was such that each day brought new rumors of crosses being torn from altars and churchmen being dragged away on conspiracy charges. Violence and persecutions were always lurking just outside the front door.

Despite the hazards, his guardians did everything possible to give their nephew a normal loving home. But Gabriel understood early on that prudence and discretion were crucial to their survival. And that ultimately, it was up to him and his generation to do more than just survive. They had to turn the tide.

He looked up when his aunt bustled into the dining room with several bowls of steaming hot noodles. The aroma tickled his nostrils with delight and filled him with a soothing comfort he had often known as a child living in this house.

All of a sudden he was ten again, sitting in the dining room doing his homework while his aunt prepared the family lunch. His eyes moistened as he watched his uncle put the finishing touches to Michael's arm, recalling how he sat in the same spot for years while Hiroshi treated the injuries he picked up from hours of martial arts training after school each day. His guardians loved him deeply like a son.

Then as now, Gabriel knew that he owed them both his mortal and spiritual life, not only because of their human devotion towards him, but for their heroic witness of the faith. Often, he saw them risk everything to help refugees escape the Lumen blitzkrieg that invaded the earth, frequently harboring entire families behind the hidden walls of their diner home.

As a young boy, he could hear the murmur of their prayers in the stillness of the night, their voices trembling like the pious whispers of ghosts from another age. That made a deep impression on the young man and gave birth to his vocation as a priest.

"All done," said Hiroshi, stepping back to admire his handiwork. "Do you want me to autograph that?"

"Not bad," replied Michael, looking over his stitches. "You sew good. Can you patch up the hole in my pants as well?"

In spite of himself, Hiroshi burst out laughing.

"All right, the two of you can continue your jousting later, the noodles are getting cold," complained Teresa. "Clean up and prepare the table."

She looked over at her nephew and motioned to him. "You too, Father."

Gabriel awoke from his reverie and approached the dining table. The cozy lighting, the smell of his aunt's cooking and his uncle's laughter made him feel like a young boy back in his childhood home.

Gazing fondly at his guardians, he suddenly realized how old and tired they looked. Now in their twilight years, peace had finally caught up to them. Life had gained some degree of calm and stability.

Both Hiroshi and his wife were no longer fully active in the Resistance. Their duplex home no longer harbored fugitives or hosted clandestine meetings, and the greatest danger to their health these days was slipping on the bathroom floor at their age.

It was a change of pace that Gabriel welcomed with relief. But outside this sanctuary, he knew that storm clouds were gathering across the land. The weather was going to get a lot worse before it could get better.

Although the two priests had avoided capture by the grace of God, the dogs of war were sniffing closely on their heels. Even now, there was always the chance that they might've been followed. Despite their precautions, it was possible that Praetorian Guards were now amassing just outside the door. Death could burst in at any moment and surprise them.

Suddenly, Gabriel's heart skipped a beat. He felt a lump rise in his throat.

"Are you all right, dear?" asked Teresa, looking concerned. Gabriel smiled and nodded.

He didn't want to upset his guardians. But secretly, the young priest wondered if he had done the right thing in coming here.

✝

The table was laid out like a royal banquet, the food was rich and opulent, and the waiting staff was impeccable in attending to the slightest needs of their host. Marshall Chambers sat on one end of the table like a king hosting a private luncheon. Joining him was the most desirable woman in the world.

"To new beginnings," said Chambers, lifting his glass for a toast. Chelsea smiled and took a sip of champagne from her own.

The mood was surreal. Just hours before, she was reeling from the Lumen portrait of the new humanity; stapled, stitched and framed against a terrible bed of living pain and suffering. Now, she was clothed in a gorgeous dress and sipping champagne with the man who threatened to paint his new masterpiece with her if she was stupid enough to refuse him.

"If we do not live as we think, we shall soon think as we live," said Chambers, recalling a phrase he once heard. He shook his head and continued. "Ironic isn't it? That most religious men should seek to justify themselves with philosophies that are no more real than the false Gods they worship."

"Strange, I thought it was mostly irreligious people who needed excuses to justify their lives," said Chelsea squarely.

"Really?" asked Chambers in mocked surprise. "Good thing I have billions of people who agree with my excuses then," he laughed.

Chelsea knew better than to respond. She smiled affectedly and returned the champagne to her lips. The sight of Zadok stretched out on the canvass had chilled her to the bone. That was the real image of humanity that the Corporation was striving to create; one of abject pain, anguish and despair. Despite her resolve to break free of her Lumen chains, her courage had failed her at the last minute.

Sitting there across from Chambers in a lap of luxury, she felt like she was trapped on a rollercoaster flying off the rails and straight into the jaws of hell. Try as she might, she couldn't slip off the harness holding her to the deathtrap. The only escape from this cursed ride seemed to end with her mortal life, but even that wouldn't come easy on Lumen terms.

"Chelsea...may I call you Chelsea?" asked Chambers, "I know you might be feeling a little pressured, but try and look like you're having a good time. I've seen criminals on death row look chirpier than you."

He tugged on his napkin and wiped traces of truffles and foie gras from his lips.

"Life is not over for you but only just beginning, so celebrate! It's not everyday that a beautiful woman like you passes from the shadow of death to a glorious destiny all in one afternoon. I promise you that the Corporation will ensure that your star outshines even the sun."

Chambers motioned for his servants to open another bottle of wine. The waiting staff reacted like flawless machines programmed to meet every whim of their master with perfection.

"You have so much to smile about," he said to Chelsea. "It's unbecoming that you should frown like some cheap copy of a virgin saint when we both know that you're neither."

Chambers took a big gulp from his freshly filled glass and sighed. "So please, don't stain this table of plenty with any sanctimonious scruples. It spoils my appetite."

He placed the wineglass down and looked at Chelsea with annoyance. The charming smile that had always graced his voice vanished from his cold, hard face.

"You're right," she answered nervously. "I'm sorry, I should be grateful. It's just that I've been through a lot in the last few hours and I'm tired."

She offered the Vice-president of Lumen Corp a timid smile.

Chambers was silent at first. Then slowly, his lips curled into an oily smirk. "It would be a shame to cancel this contract on a misunderstanding," he replied.

Before Chelsea could respond to the threat, there was a soft, almost hesitant rap on the parlor door. Chambers looked up and nodded to the Lumen agent stationed nearby. The man walked over and opened it.

Standing there in the hallway was a little girl who looked about six years old. Her auburn hair was long and curly. Her face was somewhat pale and sad. She wore a black cotton dress with lace trimmings and clutched an old Winnie the Pooh bear in one hand.

Chambers pushed aside his chair and opened his arms with delight. "Come here, my darling," he said, beckoning to her.

The child tottered forward like a wonky doll. Her gait was rather awkward, as if she was trying hard not to fall off a cliff. As the girl got closer, Chelsea noticed that she was wearing orthopedic braces on her little legs.

Her jerky motions pushed her into the arms of Chambers who lifted the girl onto a chair next to him. He patted her cheeks lightly and asked if she wanted something to drink. The child shook her head. There was hardly any light in her eyes. She merely stared at the fashion model like a curious cat spying something new.

"This is Chelsea," said Chambers, "Say hello to Chelsea, Magdalene…"

The girl refused. Chambers turned to his guest and apologized.

"You'll have to excuse her, she doesn't like strangers."

"She's very pretty," said Chelsea, wondering if the girl was his daughter. It was hard to imagine a man like Marshall Chambers fathering anything other than an abomination from hell.

"Yes," said Chambers, stroking the child's hair. "She's beautiful, isn't she? The perfect little girl; sugar and spice and all things nice."

He leaned over and kissed her on the forehead. A cold draft suddenly swept into the room from the open balcony. Chelsea shivered slightly. She felt uncomfortable watching the Lumen leader gush over the young girl. This was one of the most powerful, sinister men in the world, and he was fawning over a tiny package of pale skin, dark curls and metal braces. The image was confusing and creepy.

The child however seemed oblivious to his touch, lost as she was in a world of her own. Her eyes were dotted with sadness, her lips pale and thin. She hugged the bear and whispered a haunting melody into its fluffy ears.

At first glance, the girl looked innocent enough, humming quietly to her imaginary friend. But behind those pupils, there was a palpable darkness that made Chelsea shudder to imagine what painful secrets they might hide.

"Do you like children, Chelsea?" asked Chambers suddenly. "I love children, like little Magdalene here. Everything I do, I do to build a future for her."

He slipped a hand behind the child's neck and massaged her nape gently. In spite of her resolve to stay impassive, Chelsea cringed and felt as if Chambers had draped a slimy eel around her own shoulders. It was a reaction that was neither prudent nor subtle, but the Lumen VP said nothing to suggest that he was offended. In fact, he seemed to take a wicked delight in her growing discomfort.

"And the future my dear, is what's at stake," continued Chambers. He looked up at Chelsea and the smile reappeared like a ghostly specter.

"A brave new story is being written, and in this chapter you're the new Eve and I'm the new Adam. Together, we can bring forth a new humanity. Hell on earth can be paradise for those who're ready to take their places like Gods in the new Eden. All you have to do is work with me to pave the way. Play the pied piper so that legions of young people will roll out the red carpet for the prince of this world. When he comes, a new vista of human history will unfold. And believe me, there'll be glory and pleasure beyond your wildest dreams."

"I would really like that. But doesn't scripture say that God will triumph," said Chelsea. "That he has already won the war? I don't imagine he will sit back on his throne in heaven and do nothing."

"Pious lies, a bunch of fairytales concocted to enslave your imagination. God is as strong as the faith of those who believe in him. But like I said, this is our century. Look around you, nothing is sacred today. Man has turned his back on his creator. When the Nazarene returns, I assure you he will find no faith on earth."

"None at all?" asked Chelsea, raising a skeptical eyebrow. "Can the Corporation really succeed in killing God when so many others have tried and failed? I seem to recall reading somewhere that the Gates of Hell will never triumph over the Church."

Chelsea knew that her taunting was raising Chamber's ire. But even though her heart was cowering before the will of Lumen Corp, her spirit was still buckling for a fight. She was not yet ready to hand over her soul.

"Again with the fairytales," he laughed. "My dear girl, the Christian Churches are bleeding to death as we speak. Killing God and religion is much easier than it sounds. God wants to reign in the midst of every human activity, especially in the ordinary and mundane. He's terribly interested in humankind that way. So all we had to do was remove him from the world and lock him up in the churches."

A light came on behind Chelsea's eyes and she gasped. "And when you're done destroying all the churches, the last refuge of faith would be gone."

"You're quick to catch on. Keep religion out of politics, out of the social sphere, out of the schools and entertainment and in time, the world will no longer encounter the divine. God will be a bad joke jostling for a laugh with the tooth fairy. The rest as they say is patience. You can always count on humanity to give in to its worse instincts."

"But what about the pope, the Underground Christians, those priests who tried to help me? Surely they won't go quietly into the night?" said Chelsea.

Despite her determination to remain cool, her voice began to quiver with some desperation.

"This is hilarious. You've been given a chance to redeem yourself and you're *still* talking like a bible thumping lunatic. Did the exorcism drive away your brain? I see you still need some convincing to let go of these childish ideas," said Chambers, chuckling.

The room was taut with tension. The only sound came from the lilting lullaby of the young child. Her sad innocent voice only rendered the uncanny silence more pronounced. Chelsea wore her anxiety like a corset of fear. She could feel the strings tightening with every second.

Suddenly, without looking up from her soft toy, the pale little girl spoke. "Why don't we just kill her?"

The voice sounded gruff and unnatural for a child her age. Chelsea was stunned.

"Now, now, we're all family here," remarked Chambers. "But you know, Magdalene is right."

He looked at the fashion model and tapped his finger against his watch.

"Time is moving, madam. And if you want to survive, you mustn't run after ghosts and phantoms. After tonight, the Church will draw even closer to extinction. Isn't that right Norman?"

"Yes sir, arrangements have already been made."

Once again, she didn't see the Lumen aide come in. He seemed to materialize whenever his master summoned him. And for the moment, he hovered balefully near Chelsea like a raven perched on a branch.

"This is the beginning of the end for them," said Chambers. "Thanks to you, the legend of the 'Archangels' ends tonight. Starting tomorrow, we'll give them more martyrs than they can hang on their altars. We'll root out every residue of faith, every resistance in every sewer, home and dungeon. And when we're done, this country will be the first among nations to be completely purged of this infection."

"*This is crazy, I can't believe I'm hearing this,*" Chelsea thought to herself, her throat parched with distress.

"Believe it! It's the only thing you can have absolute faith in," replied Chambers.

Chelsea was aghast. Did he just read her thoughts or was she losing her mind? She couldn't be sure of anything anymore. Every minute in his presence was driving her deeper into madness and fear.

"When the Antichrist comes," added Chambers. "The weak will be separated from the strong, the loyal from the rebellious, and anyone who opposes our cause will burn in a cruel vengeance that will have no equal on this earth."

He opened the lid of a small golden case and pulled out a sleek looking cigar. Instantly, a servant appeared and hastily offered him a light. Chambers took a few puffs and then looked straight at Chelsea.

"I haven't really told you how Magdalene got those braces on her legs."

He paused and glanced at the little girl in the black dress. The child was still absorbed in her own world, her tiny hands gripping the bear like two unforgiving pincers.

Chelsea tried to stay calm but her face was flushed with apprehension. "I'm sure it's fascinating, like everything else you've been saying," she said, attempting to hold on to her sarcasm.

Her biting wit was the only weapon left to her, and she kept swinging it like a pike to keep her tormentor at bay. Unfortunately, her spiteful defense only baited the snake in Chambers to toy more viciously with her delicate mind. He found her amusing, like a stubborn mouse caught in the endless coils of his power, and yet willfully defiant of how easily he could grind her to dust.

"Oh trust me, you'll find it interesting enough," retorted Chambers. He was more than willing to dance with Chelsea in this dervish of taunts. "Don't be fooled by the pale skin and crooked legs, there's a tide of royal blood flowing in those veins. If you don't believe me, ask her."

He turned and quizzed the child in a condescending tone. "Are you a princess, Magdalene?"

The girl nodded mechanically. She looked like a porcelain doll hooked up to levers and strings. Chambers turned back to Chelsea and grinned like a puppet master working his magic. He was definitely enjoying the show.

"Well technically she's a bastard," he said smugly. "It's hard to claim any legitimacy when your mother, the beautiful queen of an oil rich nation, also happens to have a chronic weakness for good-looking young men. Imagine what the king had to say when he discovered the unwanted intrusion in his palace. I can tell you it wasn't pretty."

He took a long drag on his cigar.

"The rest as they say is hush-hush. The kingdom could do with one less scandal. And seeing as how their Majesties have been such loyal friends of Lumen Corp, we offered to make the new baby go away with the utmost discretion. No medical records, no newspapers, no witnesses."

"And the man who fathered this child," said Chelsea, looking at Magdalene. "What happened to him?"

"You'd be amazed at how easy it is to make someone disappear from the face of the earth, even for a prominent man like our foolish Romeo. All it took was a two dollar bullet to the back of the head and a little paperwork and voila, it's almost like he never existed."

Norman, who was standing behind Chelsea began to snigger. The noise irked her immensely, but also reminded her of the danger to her own life that was always hovering nearby.

"Indeed, no woman should have to carry a baby she doesn't want. You agree with that, don't you?"

The fashion icon widened her eyes like a deer caught in the headlights. Cold beads of sweat began to form on her forehead. She tried to divert the question from herself.

"I don't understand, it sounded like you arranged for an abortion," said Chelsea, a little confused. "But she's sitting right here."

Chambers turned around and did a double take, as if seeing Magdalene for the first time.

"Good lord, you're right! What're the chances of that?" he said exaggeratedly. "I don't know anyone who has ever survived an abortion with a Lumen doctor, and yet here she is, the miracle baby!"

He threw his hands up and pretended to be outraged.

"I mean at the very least, she should've been burnt like a piece of toast. These things normally come out of saline abortions looking like baby rats soaked in napalm," said Chambers, chuckling.

"But for Magdalene, would you believe it? No scars, no tissue burns, no harm to her body except for the crippled legs. She popped out strong as hell and pretty as spring, screaming her lungs out, despite twice the dosage. It was a real shock for the doctor doing the procedure, not to mention the mother."

He flicked the ash from his cigar and leaned back in his chair.

"Tragic huh?" griped Chambers, shaking his head like he still couldn't believe the child had survived.

"Now ordinarily, it's professional courtesy to finish the job. But I'm thinking, God must have special plans for this girl. And it would be a shame to let the old man have all the fun. So in the end I decided to keep this one for myself. After all, every king deserves to have a princess by his side, don't you think?"

Chelsea was too disturbed to respond. Her memories came flooding back like an open wound, bleeding her heart dry of every last drop of courage. She kept her face down, afraid to look up at the little girl across the table.

"Are you all right? You look like you've seen a ghost," Chambers enquired. He leaned forward and made a mocking show of concern, which only unnerved his victim all the more.

"Don't be so harsh on yourself. You were having the time of your life, and your career was just taking off. There wasn't any reason to keep the babies then," remonstrated Chambers.

At the mention of her failed pregnancy, Chelsea wanted to flee from the room. But when she tried to get up, she felt numerous ghostly hands press down on her. The weight was unbearable.

"Why so surprised? There's nothing you can tell me that I don't already know."

He snapped his fingers and a servant filled all their glasses with more champagne.

"But there is one thing I'm curious about," he said.

"What's it like for someone like you to look into the eyes of someone like her?"

Chelsea tried to avoid looking up but Norman grabbed her head from behind and violently twisted her face towards the strange little girl.

For a split second, she fell into Magdalene's eyes. And almost immediately, a powerful feeling of despair washed over her like a tidal wave. It was as if she sank to the bottom of a whirlpool that drowned out all the sounds in the world.

The only thing she could hear was Chambers droning in the background...

"Knowing that you killed your own child...while she survived her own mother's attempt to kill her!"

Chelsea gritted her teeth and struggled to block out his voice. Every cruel syllable felt like a sharp knife twisting itself into her spirit. She clenched her eyes shut in defiance, but her ears remained vulnerable to the words echoing in the darkness...

"You honestly think God would ever forgive you?"

The question stabbed her like an accusing finger. Despite having confessed her sins to Raphael, she had left out the sad detail of her abortion.

Did she dare hope for redemption? Was she even deserving of

life? It seemed like everything was going to depend on what would happen later that night.

Whatever the fates had in store, she prayed.

She prayed hard that God would send his angels to help her.

Chapter 15

The grounds had been deserted for years, the metal gates rusted shut. Except for a noisy raven cawing above an old street lamp, there were no other signs of life. Several blocks of an abandoned structure rose in the background like a great wall of graffiti, their concrete flesh tattooed with colorful words of blasphemy and hate. For over two decades, this was a public asylum for the criminally insane. Now it was just a rotting compound of derelict buildings festering on the edge of town.

A tall figure slipped into a complex and disappeared down a grubby corridor in one of the smaller wards. The man glided past the elevators, their iron pulleys no longer working, their cables tied up in great big knots of steel and grime. Turning a corner, his footsteps echoed down a valley of metal steps, descending into the belly of the sanatorium until the noise vanished altogether in the dark.

At the bottom of the stairs stood a filthy green door encrusted with dirt. The intruder stretched out his gloved hand and pushed the door ajar. It creaked open like the entrance to a tomb. The air was stale. The smell of cigarette smoke lingered in the room. But somewhere in the darkness, a pair of eyes locked in on the lone figure, following his every move with interest.

Michael slowly walked into the shadows, pushing aside his trench coat so that his holstered guns would remain free for action.

The room was littered with surgical tables and restraining belts, and broken equipment that looked like they were once used for electrotherapy treatments. It wasn't hard to imagine the terrible screams that must've filled this place of torment. The priest drew his handgun and cocked the weapon.

A single light bulb hung by a loose wire from the ceiling, casting a yellow glow on the rusty metal desk below. Smoldering on an ashtray on the table was a lit cigarette, its white smoke swelling up like a warning to Michael that he was not alone.

Before the priest could take another step, a shadow pounced at him from the dark.

Michael spun around and raised his gun but a powerful blow snagged his wrist and tore the weapon from his grasp. With lightning speed, the assailant drove a jagged knife at his target, but the priest reacted quickly with a bone-crushing move to disarm his opponent. The steel blade clattered noisily to the floor while the two combatants exploded in a flurry of punches and kicks that tore through the room like a tornado.

The battle was intense. Like an overexcited spectator, the yellow light bulb swung madly in all directions, casting shadows that danced like a vengeful mob calling for blood at a cage fight. At one point, the attacker rolled across the floor and recovered his knife. Michael braced himself for the assault.

As the blade rushed forward, the priest caught his opponent in a powerful lock and dropped him on the metal desk. Before the attacker could break free, the large crucifix leapt from Michael's belt and the vicious blade snapped out like a scythe aiming for the man's throat.

"Wait," gasped the panting voice on the table. "If you kill me now, I'm taking you off my Christmas list."

The priest caught the swinging light bulb and brought it over his prisoner. Blinking at the light, the man on the table scrounged up his face and broke into a grin.

"You stupid turkey, I could've gutted you," grumbled Michael. He recalled his blade and pulled the hapless man to his feet.

"You're slowing down, old man. Back in the day, you would've taken me down in two shakes of a lamb's tail."

"What the hell does that mean? You been crapping baby food and watching cartoons again?" asked Michael.

"Charming as always," replied Kazim Abdullah, better known to his friends simply as 'Kaz'. He bent down and retrieved the fallen gun.

"Hmmm, Beretta 92FS INOXs with extended mag, fully converted to auto," said the bearded man, turning the pistol over in his hand. "Not bad, I think my niece has one of these in metallic pink."

He tossed the weapon back to Michael. "Of course, if you're looking for a real gun, I could fix you up with something a little more manly," he laughed.

Michael looked at him grimly and returned the firearm to his holster. There was a brief uncomfortable silence.

"Okay...now you're just being rude," said Kaz, seeing that his clever repartee was lost on his priestly friend. "I worked really hard on that joke."

"I need guns," interrupted Michael, throwing a small cloth bag at the Palestinian man. "Something long distance but maximum collateral. Preferably remote."

Kaz opened the satchel and pulled out a thick wad of cash. He took a deep breath.

"Nothing like the smell of Lumen dough," he said with a smirk. "It always cracks me up that you hit their banks to pay for all this stuff. What happened to *thou shall not steal?*"

"Who's stealing?" Michael answered. "Wars are expensive and I'm just taking a loan. I intend to return every penny to them in lead. Here's what I need."

The priest handed over a list of requirements.

"This is a lot more heat than you normally request. Why do you need this kind of firepower? What're you planning?"

"Is there somewhere else we can talk?" asked Michael, looking around.

They might be alone in the basement of a deserted complex but in a world governed by the servants of sin, even dead buildings can be forced to tell tales.

"Anything for you, O' Reverend Father," quipped the grinning accomplice. "Follow me."

Kaz flicked on a small torch and led the way.

The two men left the room and meandered down the dark corridors. Michael trailed his old comrade at a steady pace, scanning the shadows behind them every now and then for movement. At one point, 'Kaz' Abdullah removed the grating on a wall and wriggled through an old ventilator shaft. Michael followed behind, squeezing his muscular frame through the tiny passage.

There was a sense of déjà vu, almost like both men were reliving one of the many campaigns from their warring past. Both had scars and nightmares to recall those years of treachery, when their leaders betrayed their service to evil. And both had been trying to redeem their memories ever since.

Without a doubt, the perils of war and the struggles for peace often forced violence on good men. Before Kaz was an arms dealer, he was an officer in the Palestinian Militia. And in those days of conflict, the ex-soldier of fortune often found himself crouching behind the trigger of death, staring down a barrel of bloodshed that spanned two decades and pilfered too many lives from the soil of his own country. For as long as he could remember, no one was spared the virus of insanity that brewed within the hearts of extremists, spreading an infection of terror and brutality that converted every diseased heart, prompting fanatics to cut every throat, kill every infidel, and slay every trace of humanity from their own souls.

In many places, it became impossible for different peoples to profess their religions freely without losing life and limb. Aided by the enemies of peace, the children of chaos gave themselves up to the father of lies and became his unwitting pawns in the destruction of all that was truly good and sacred. In the name of the Most High, they killed for the Prince of the underworld, and sealed their own fates with the blood of innocents.

Like so many of his generation, Kaz embraced the ideology of the time. Forged in the fires of hate and injustice, he knew the temptation for mindless revenge; that thirst for the blood of his enemies to quench the burning pain he felt inside.

Gripping the flag of martyrdom, he would've blazed a path to jahannam if not for the guiding hand of his father. The old Arab took the righteous anger of his son and turned it towards the light, showing him a better way to overcome his enemies.

In time, he learnt he could not fight evil with evil without being consumed by the hate and darkness himself. The only path to peace was reconciliation. And although revenge was sweet, it took real courage to turn away from bloodshed.

"True justice cannot be won by the sword, my son," said the old man. "But only by seeking to build bridges, by disarming hatred in the hearts of all, and by daring to sacrifice the bitterness of the past for the brightness of the future, even if that means forgiving our enemies."

It seemed like madness at the time. But his father, an old Imam who was not afraid to quote Christian mystics, insisted that the truth was worth defending…whether it came from the Bible or from the holy book of the Koran.

"Where there is no love, put in love, and you will find love," the old man had said.

But that was all before the smoke of Satan descended like a perfumed plague, blown about by the winds of the Corporation into every office, home and school. His father was adamant that their real enemies were not human, but the forces of evil that governed the hearts of men.

Little by little, the promise of political power and peace spread like infectious yeast until eventually, the leaders of the Arab nations became drunk on the wine of Lumen lies and seduction. While kings and presidents enjoyed the banquet of kisses and sweet caresses, the enemy stole the lands of their ancestors and enslaved the hearts of their peoples.

Everything once noble and proud about the Arab people vanished overnight. The name of Allah whom generations praised and adored became an archaic obstacle to peace and unity. Minarets that once echoed with the call to prayer now sang the doctrines of man, blaming organized religions for divisions and wars. All over the world, politics and culture throbbed with the pain of Lumen corruption, where nothing was grounded on sacred truths and no society could be found to uphold long-cherished principles of morality.

Those who bravely resisted, like his father, fought to keep their countrymen from descending into the depths of human arrogance, but the idolatry of the wicked seldom endure the voice of the righteous. The searing inferno that ravaged the local mosque rose like a bonfire of hate, turning the house of worship into a temple of ruins. By the time Kaz arrived as part of the security force dispatched to the scene, an explosive keg of violence had already been lit to bury the truth.

Sprawled across the burning floor was the old Imam, broken and torn among the savaged corpses of the village elders, their tongues muted forever by assassins, their bodies carefully arranged in the form of a cross. Whoever did this wanted the world to think that Christian fanatics were responsible, that this was the real legacy of all religious beliefs – intolerance and death.

But Kaz knew better. As a weapons specialist, he recognized the signature of the slayings. The bullet holes, the clean cuts across the jugulars, even the destruction of the mosque: it was clear that this was a Lumen operation. His father had warned him as much that the Corporation would not stomach any resistance. The stench of Praetorian violence clung to everything like an odor of blasphemy, fueling his anger and desire for vengeance.

That day, the young Abdullah mourned his father and made a vow that he would do everything in his power to make them pay.

"Watch your head," said Kaz, reaching up to deactivate the targeting system for a pair of high-powered machine-guns hidden behind some panels. "Don't want you to lose your noggin before you got a chance to brief me."

Michael followed his friend into a large room. He looked around and noticed that it was spartan except for a tall block of metal boxes pushed up against a wall. A thick steel door guarded each compartment with handle locks that suggested they were used as fridges for storing the dead.

"How do you like my office?" asked Kaz. "I decorated it myself."

The priest looked surprised. "I didn't know this place had a morgue."

"Are you kidding me? Did you see the equipment back there? There's enough juice in those machines to fry an elephant! Trust me, those boys in the white lab coats had no reason to cure anyone. Most of the patients here were political prisoners who ticked off the Corporation at one time or another."

Kaz held up a small remote and pointed it at the back wall. "Check this out," he said.

At the push of a button, half the wall slid opened to reveal a self-contained firing range within the underground bunker.

"You like?" purred the arms dealer. He unlocked one of the fridges and pulled out a metal slab holding a large body bag. "And for the pièce de résistance..."

He unzipped the gruesome black sack and removed a vicious looking weapon from the cadaver pouch.

"Cute," said Michael. "It must sound like a war zone in here every time you squeeze off a round."

Kaz flushed his cheek against the rifle and said, "You mean like this?"

He pulled the trigger and the target at the far end exploded in flames. The destruction was terrible. But the bark of the weapon was relatively modest considering the bite of the bullet.

"New and improved silencer in the barrel," said Kaz. "Plus this whole room is shut down with acoustical foam over insulation and armor plating in the walls. It's not totally high-tech but it works. Besides, the only things moving out there are crows and tumble weeds."

He chambered another round into the mighty rifle and said, "So, what demons are you taking on this time?"

"Maybe all of hell," replied Michael with a smirk.

Kaz wrinkled his brows in distress. He knew his friend was not one for exaggerations.

In a solemn voice, Michael recounted briefly all that had happened in the last twenty-four hours. Unknown to him, Gabriel was doing the same with his guardians at roughly the same time across town, filling them in on the gory details of the night before.

In each case, the story was the same, but the reactions of the listeners were quite different.

Hiroshi and his wife paid attention to their nephew, their faces understandably drawn with pain and concern, but there was little anxiety in their eyes. They seemed to receive the news with a prudence that was characteristic of people of faith. The only betrayal of their apprehension was the tension with which Teresa gripped the rosary beads in her hands.

In contrast, Kaz was beside himself with rage. The fire in his eyes blazed like an inferno as the tale of Lumen brutality fueled his own agonizing quest for vengeance. Cursing with venom, his lips trembled in fury as the memory of his late father bellowed for justice.

At one point, Michael wasn't sure if his angry friend was able to keep from tearing the room apart with gunfire. But when the Palestinian had calmed down a little, the priest looked at him and said, "I need to know something. Will you help me break them out?"

As the conversation went on, something unusual happened. Despite being miles apart, the hearts and minds of the two groups became one in the burning crucible of this terrible crisis. By a strange act of God, their dialogues grew into a common exchange that made it hard to tell where one person began and the other ended. It was almost like two separate events had become stitched together by some mysterious thread of providence.

"How do you know they're still alive?" asked Hiroshi. "I understand your loyalty to your friends, but what you're both planning to do is suicide."

"We have no choice, uncle," said Gabriel, "If we don't try, they'll be dead for sure, and I can't have that on my conscience."

Hiroshi took a deep breath and tried to maintain his composure. "Where will this meeting take place?" he asked.

"It's located downtown, but I want a detailed plan of the area," said Michael. "Parks, lanes, sewers…everything! We'll need satellite imaging for escape routes and gun positions."

Kaz fed the Lumen coordinates into his laptop. "It's the old cathedral in the middle of the city," he quipped in surprise.

"I know," answered Michael.

"Why the hell would they pick somewhere so public and crowded?"

The old gothic structure was in a prominent part of the metropolis, bordering the shopping district with its glitzy malls and fancy eateries. It wasn't the most practical place for a standoff, considering that the Corporation was always obsessive about wrapping their true natures under the cover of secrecy.

"They chose this venue for a reason. These monsters want nothing less than to humiliate the Church," grumbled Hiroshi.

For the first time since Gabriel broke the news, the old man was barely containing his emotions. "They're planning to perform a ritual killing," he said. "And you're the sacrifice!"

"I know," said Gabriel. "But it doesn't mean we have to play by their rules. We've got a few tricks up our sleeves."

The cathedral itself had been shut down years earlier and transformed into a sanctuary of sordid pleasures. Instead of prayers and church hymns, its hallowed cloisters now sang with the sirens of pubs and nudie bars, its chapel stripped of its high altar and re-consecrated as a gallery for the profane that the world so eloquently lauded as art.

"If they tried that with our mosques, I would rather tear down every stone than allow the house of God to be desecrated like that," said the Palestinian grimly. "How much time do we have?"

"Until the witching hour," said Michael, picking up the rifle that Kaz was using earlier.

"Three in the morning? That's a mockery of the Holy Trinity and our Lord's death on the cross," said Hiroshi in anger. "They want to sacrifice God's priests in a building that used to be the mother church of the city, in mockery of Christ's death on the cross at three in the afternoon!"

The macabre symbolism was not lost on the senior Toshigawa. If the forces of hell succeeded in their diabolical plans, the Resistance would suffer a grievous wound from which they might never recover their courage.

"I know, it's the unholy hour when demonic activity is strongest," said Gabriel. "But whether we like it or not, we have to do this. There's no other way."

"And you expect me to stand idly by and let my only nephew march to his death like a lamb to the slaughter?" asked the old man heatedly. "You would do this to your aunt and myself?"

Teresa tried to intervene as tensions rose. "Please…" she begged.

"I would do this for our Lord and his Church," said Gabriel, sounding annoyed. "I had hoped you'd understand. But I expected you to storm heaven and pray that God will send his holy angels to protect us."

As soon as the words left his mouth, he regretted using that tone with his uncle.

"Forgive me," said the young priest, his face torn by the anguish in his heart. He knew his decision was causing great pain to his guardians. For a moment, no one said anything. After what seemed like an eternity of silence, Hiroshi simply got up from his chair, walked over to his nephew, and hugged him.

Tears streamed down Teresa's cheeks.

"This isn't a rescue mission, this is madness," said Michael's old comrade.

"Call it what you like, it's what we have to do," answered the priest.

"Well if you're determined to go through with this crazy plan, then I'm sticking with you," said Kaz. "Someone has to watch your back."

"Security will be tight, I'm not sure how you're going to provide any support fire."

"You leave that to me," said Kaz. "I know some people who can move things around in this city. They hide among the cleaners, the janitors and nobodies. These people are practically ghosts. They're well trained and they're unseen. And best of all, they hate the Corporation as much as we do. I can count on them to move a tank into your living room and you wouldn't even know it's there."

He opened the metal doors of the fridges, pulled several instruments of death from the cadaver trays and assembled a terrifying spread of lethal weapons on the autopsy table.

"If they want a fight, we'll give it to them. I say we make Sodom and Gomorrah look like a theme park," he grunted.

Michael cocked the rifle in his hands and swung the barrel at the far end of the range.

"My thoughts exactly!" said the priest.

He pulled the trigger and the entire row of targets burst into flames.

Chapter 16

Gabriel was stripped to the waist in his room, his muscled torso flexing with each deadly stroke of the blade. Wielding the ancient sword in his hands, he sliced through the air with deadly precision. His footwork was meticulous, his strikes formidable. But even as he drove himself to perfect those powerful blows with the katana, his thoughts were really focused somewhere else.

The samurai blade flashed like a scalpel peeling back the skin of time, carving a path through his memories...

Growing up, Gabriel was told the story so many times it had become legend. Next to the Bible, it was the most sacred legacy in the Toshigawa household, passed from generation to generation like the blood in his veins. As the young friar continued to hone his fighting skills, his mind leapt back to 1597.

The way it was told to him, Toshigawa Kenshin was a young man in the service of the local Daimyo; an overlord whose power and authority was superseded only by the Shogun himself.

Despite his relative youth, Kenshin was already a renowned executioner in Nagasaki. His katana was his fame. And his skills were legendary. As a result, many high-ranking nobles would often pay him to test the cutting strength of their new swords. Sometimes he would run the blades against mutilated corpses. Other times, he would test their cold steel upon the living flesh of condemned criminals.

In just one stroke, he was reputed to be able to take a man's head off without spilling any blood. Not surprisingly, his unique talents won the gruesome admiration of many, although some records suggested he was far more feared than revered. People who offended the Daimyo often found themselves bowing their necks before this man. His voice was the last thing they heard, his blade the last thing they felt.

Kenshin never suffered any scruples on his part. Innocent or guilty, it was not his place to judge them. As samurai, he had pledged his sword to serve only his master's will. Everything else was a matter for the Gods.

But in the second month of that year, events were unfolding that would pit the loyalty of his oath against the honor of his heart. For many years now, the Catholic religion had been growing among the people, spreading like yeast across the country. Founded by groups of gaijin who wore black robes or brown hooded tunics, small Christian communities had begun to take root on Japanese soil.

In the beginning, the missions received great support from the Shogunate and Imperial government. The Japanese lords were not only keen to curb the influence of the local Buddhist monks, they were eager to establish trading agreements with Spain and Portugal.

The young Japanese Church suddenly found herself facing a new springtime of evangelization. Unfortunately, the corridors of power in the land of the rising sun were as fickle as the darkened courts of Europe.

Surrounded more by a cadre of whispering shadows than true counsel, the Daimyo was eventually persuaded that the Catholic faith was planted only to pave the way for foreign conquest and dominance. The best way to stop this threat of aggression, argued his warlords, was to destroy the Christians before they grew too strong.

Whatever doubts the Daimyo had about spilling the blood of hundreds of his own people, he also knew that in times of danger, circumstances dictated action. There was nothing left to do but to declare war on the new religion. Catholicism became banned in Japan. The edict was clear. Either renounce the faith or die.

As the dragon bared its teeth, the Church went underground in order to survive. But it didn't take long for the Daimyo's spies to flush out the leading members of the Christian community.

Kenshin received the news of their arrests with some sympathy. He wasn't a believer himself, but he was not entirely unfamiliar with their doctrines and their way of life. In the course of his duties he had met some converts, even executed a few who were unfortunate enough to incur the Daimyo's wrath.

In every case, the samurai discovered a people proud and dignified, much like himself. Even so, there was something more to their dignity that surpassed even the stoic code of Bushido. In all his time as an executioner, he had seen few people face tyranny and death with more hope and peace than these followers of the cross. It was one thing to resign yourself to the cruel hands of fate, but quite another to pray for your enemies and forgive them. The joy and serenity on the faces of the condemned made him extremely uncomfortable...and curious.

How can anyone face death with such radiance? Was it true courage or just madness? Or did they simply know something he didn't?

Either way, he had much bigger problems to worry about. Lying deathly pale at home was his youngest daughter, barely awake and slipping from his embrace with each passing day. The doctors had all but given up hope. Despite having served death to countless others, the sight of his own child creeping towards the underworld frightened him immensely.

For some days now, he felt as if the ground had opened up and swallowed him whole. As the child grew sicker, the usually composed warrior grew more desperate. He felt like his own strength was wilting away from the fever burning up his little girl. His limbs were tired and his bones ached with worry. At times, he could hardly lift his sword.

For the moment however, he had to put away all thoughts of rest. He was informed that the prisoners were already en route from Kyoto to Nagasaki, a six hundred mile trek that they were forced to make on foot. In a few days time, the butchery would begin, and then he would be called upon to draw his sword. Whether he liked it or not, he would have to gather his energies and focus his mind on the task to come.

But as fate would have it, he was spared from having to quench his blade with more Christian blood. The news soon arrived that these twenty-six traitors would be given special treatment according to their customs and beliefs. Since they had preferred to cling to their foreign faith than embrace the will of the Daimyo, these criminals would not enjoy the privilege of a quick beheading.

Instead, they would all be raised on crosses. Every single one of them – gaijin and Japanese, young and old – would be crucified in the flesh. They would be left to rot between heaven and hell like the diseased pigs that they were. Only a phalanx of angry spears, buried deep like harpoons into their bodies could properly silence the shame in their hearts. To no one's surprise, the town's leading executioner was given the task of organizing this slaughter.

Kenshin understood better than anyone else that this was no simple dalliance with death. This was high theatre. And Nagasaki was chosen to stage this macabre drama because it housed the biggest audience of converts. Indeed, the powers in Kyoto desired that this spectacle of human misery should ring like a death knell across the country, tolling for anyone who was foolish enough not to abandon their faith to save their lives. Japan must know that under the rising sun, there was no honor in being a Christian, and no escape for those who were.

Not long after, the caravan of the condemned came snaking through the plains, hugging the grieving land like a flock of sheep trotting to the butcher. A light rain had fallen from the skies, as if heaven herself was weeping for such a sorrowful sight. The quivering group of prisoners looked wretched, worn out and broken from the forced march, and quite visibly beaten and abused along the way.

As the tired company stumbled into town, shackled to each other, a jeering mob of the city's own vermin gathered to spit, curse and pelt the group with sticks and stones, and everything else they could pick off the ground.

Kenshin looked on with disgust. Whenever those who lived in darkness felt exposed by the light of virtue, they would bristle and snarl, bite and howl, and do everything within their power to silence the voice that called out their guilt. Then as now, it was sweet to point out the sins of others, if only to excuse our own demons.

Up until then, the witness of some Christians in Nagasaki had shown up the decadence of their neighbors in the courts, the slums, the sleazy brothels of dark alleyways and violent streets. Now that the Church was paraded in chains, it was time for the debauched to rise up and punish those whose living faith accused their paltry consciences to no end.

The group of soldiers who escorted the condemned shoved and struck the prisoners like cattle and did nothing to stop the heckling throng. When the captain of the guards finally halted the bruised and faltering company before the chief executioner, Kenshin had all but lost his patience with the unruly mob. Even the worse criminals deserved to be treated with some dignity, and these bystanders were no better than the unfortunate souls they had come to terrorize.

Shouting for his men to disperse the maddening crowd, Kenshin ordered that the captives be given some water and rest, which displeased the guards from Kyoto greatly. But no samurai among them would dare cross swords with the Toshigawa blade.

The assorted group of prisoners all seemed different in many ways. There were six Europeans among them, priests of the new religion. The rest were native Japanese. Kenshin noticed that three of the converts were just boys, not much older than his own sons. And yet, not a single one of them seemed afraid to die for their faith. The same tranquility, the same inner strength and hope, the same look in their eyes. Courage. Peace. Madness.

As he pondered those thoughts, he noticed a strange glow on the faces of the condemned. Was he dreaming again? The stress of his daughter's illness had taken a toll on his mind. But no, there it was. Beyond the sweaty features caked with mud and disgust, Kenshin saw something else, something he couldn't explain. It felt like a veil had been parted for a brief moment and he found himself on top of a high mountain, surrounded by a dazzling light and looking into the eyes of a man whose clothes were whiter than snow. The vision confused and frightened him.

Shutting his eyes tightly, he opened them again and found himself back on earth, staring into the face of a young Japanese Catholic who was being struck repeatedly by an irate guard. The victim offered no resistance to the vicious blows.

"Enough!" growled Kenshin, unlocking his blade from its scabbard. The sound of the sword threatening to leap out of its sheath paralyzed the guard instantly. He backed down like a small animal scurrying away from a tiger.

"Thank you, my lord," said the young prisoner, looking straight into the eyes of his executioner. His voice was soft and calm, and full of confidence. He wiped the blood from his face with the back of his hand, praising God in song. The rest of the prisoners started to join in softly, but their voices deep with faith.

Kenshin said nothing at first. He was a little surprised that these people would sing a hymn of praise after such a beating. But then again, he had come to expect such lunacy from Christians.

"What is your name?" asked the samurai sternly.

"Paulo Miki," replied the man, who had taken on a Christian name in baptism.

"You seem happy to die for your crimes, Paulo Miki."

"I am happy to live for my faith, sir," said the man politely. "Even if that means dying to this life."

The captain of the guards heard the response and burst out laughing. "How can you live for anything if you're already dead?" he bellowed.

The rest of his men cackled like hyenas.

Even Kenshin himself couldn't avoid a cynical smirk. The captain was right. The young man was obviously deluded, driven to insanity by the arduous journey and the prospect of death. He decided not to waste any more time on this fool. There was still much to prepare.

"Bring them to the holding cells," he ordered. The guards came alive and dragged the prisoners to their feet.

"My lord, wait," said the young man urgently.

But Kenshin had already turned away. There was no profit in listening to the feverish mumblings of a man soon to be executed. The spirits and phantoms surrounding such gruesome ends can often play tricks on the minds of the unwary. Perhaps he had done wrong in showing this man mercy. Perhaps the curious vision he saw earlier was nothing less than a warning to stay clear of these Christians and their dark magic. After all, this wretched man might easily put a spell on him. Too much useless curiosity could get him killed if he wasn't careful. He decided to ignore the voice.

"Don't be afraid sir! Your daughter, the youngest one, she will live," cried Paulo Miki. "I have prayed for you and your family."

Kenshin felt like a wall of bricks had suddenly sprung up in his path. He stopped and turned back to look at the prisoner, his heart pounding inside his chest.

By then, the young man had been dragged away by the screaming guards, lost among the flow of beaten flesh pulling in the other direction. If he wanted to, Kenshin could've stopped the guards. But he just stood there, cold and rigid like a man whose hopes were already stiff with rigor mortis.

That night, the fever rushed upon his little girl with such fury that it seemed like a vile animal was attacking her. The family was stricken with panic. The doctor was called in but none of his remedies seemed to provide any relief. After a torturous evening of wrestling with this malady, the physician threw up his hands in defeat and shook his head sadly. His lips were still but his eyes were brimming with apology.

Kenshin understood at once what the silence meant. As he prepared to send twenty-six criminals to their deaths the next day, death himself was coming to steal the apple of his eye.

Was this a punishment from the God of the foreigners? Has Paulo Miki and the rest of his ilk somehow turned heaven against him? He was not religious, but he knew there was more to the spirit world than was commonly accepted by the arrogance of men. The thought that this was somehow tied to the execution of the Christians made his blood boil with venom. If indeed they were responsible for this act of vengeance, he would truly send them to their God in pieces.

The break of dawn fell suddenly like a guillotine on the night. The household was awakened by the terrible sounds of pain that rocked the tiny body of the child. She began to convulse with violence, as if a great battle was rumbling inside her soul.

Kenshin rushed to find his daughter flailing in the arms of her mother. Taking the girl to himself, he called out to her like a man desperate to pull his child from quicksand. But it was obvious that she was sinking fast. His wife, Megumi, was beside herself with fear. The rest of his children stood behind the servants quaking with dread. No one knew what to do. White foamy saliva dribbled down the sides of her mouth as painful tears rolled past her cheeks.

"Otousan!" cried the child, screeching for her dad. Her voice was a grimace of terror and suffering, and it cut deep into the executioner's heart like no blade ever could.

Then as quickly as it began, the struggle was over.

Paulo Miki's claim that she would survive her illness flagellated his memory, mocking him in his pain. He couldn't hear the frightful wailing of his wife nor the cries and shouts of anyone else in the family. There was nothing at all, only a terrible silence punctuated by the thought that these Christians would dare scorn him with this terrible lie.

Kenshin clutched his daughter like she was the most precious jewel in the world, even though her spark was stolen and the icy coldness of death had begun to creep in like a thief. The agony in the household was unbearable. And just when it seemed like nothing could tear him away, there came a harsh knock on the door. A trio of voices called out from the courtyard, echoing his name. They sounded like ravens perched on a cemetery wall, crowing that it was time for him to leave for the execution.

Without saying a word, Kenshin placed his little girl in the arms of his devoted wife. Grasping his sword, he stood up and glanced briefly at the mother and child. His eyes were dry, but his soul felt like a boulder at the bottom of a freezing lake, lost forever in the choking weeds of despair. He wanted desperately to stay, to comfort his wife and children, to hold on tenderly to the pearl of his heart while the fading warmth still lingered in her limbs. But the ravens wouldn't leave him alone. They were squawking again in the background, shouting his name. Sighing deeply, he gritted his teeth and walked out the door.

It was still dark in the courtyard. The guards bowed deeply when he appeared but Kenshin did not stop to acknowledge them. He simply marched into the breaking dawn, his armed escorts swirling about him like dead leaves rustled up by the wind.

What happened next remained shrouded in mystery, even among the scribes of the Toshigawa clan. No one could agree on the actual details, only that something changed forever in the heart of the executioner.

The morning sped away quickly.

Kenshin buried his pain and threw himself into the task of directing the crucifixions. Despite being numb to the world, the samurai shouted, pushed and jostled his men to finish the job with cold efficiency. The guards scattered about their duties in haste, almost recoiling from the verbal whip of their master.

By midday, twenty-six people were beaten and strapped onto wooden crosses, stretched awkwardly with cords and raised atop a small hill in Nagasaki. Wilting in the afternoon sun, they hung like scarecrows planted to scare away any would-be Christians from the vineyard of the Church.

The delegation from Kyoto was pleased. They nodded appreciatively to the executioner. The stage was set, the play was now in motion, and the message was raised high for all to see.

As the local populace gathered around this macabre theatre of pain, it soon became obvious that the crucified players would not cooperate with the script. What began as a murmur, which the crowds mistook for cries of anguish, grew into a rumbling credo of faith that echoed like a mighty battle cry.

The guards and officials were flustered. This didn't sound at all like a vanquished people. This was a brazen refusal to be conquered.

To their amazement, one voice above all dominated the hill, defying the powerful will of the Daimyo. The Japanese Christian known as Paulo Miki began to preach his faith from the wooden pulpit of his cross. His face was an excruciating portrait of the tortures he endured, but his voice fell like thunder and his words flashed like lightning from his torn and bloody lips.

The guards couldn't believe their ears. Even in the face of death, this man would not curse his fate. There was no apology, no pathetic pleading for his miserable life, only words of praise and worship for his God. Even now, he was trying to convert the masses to his madness...

"Silence!" screamed a delegate from Kyoto, jumping to his feet. They would not suffer such insolence from a worm. Did these Christians not know that they were beaten, or were they simply too stupid to accept defeat?

"Make him stop!" shouted another.

Roused from their stupor, the guards leapt into action and started to beat the poor man with wooden poles. This only made the victim more determined to carry on.

Unable to restrain himself any longer, Kenshin pushed the guards aside and grabbed a spear from one of his men. He rushed to the fore and plunged the pike deep into the chest of Paulo Miki. Blood gushed forth and splattered him in the face, but the samurai was unstoppable. He twisted the weapon cruelly, driven only by his hate for the man who had mocked him in the depths of his despair.

"How dare you lie to me," he cried out in fury, ramming the spear right through. "Now prophesy if you will live, you fool!"

The cross shook with the impact of the thrust. Paulo Miki said nothing in return. The martyr simply cringed in agony, bowed his head and gave up his spirit.

As if released from their chains, the guards sprang up like a pack of wild animals and began to massacre the flock. One by one, the followers of Christ succumbed to a vicious onslaught of spears, drenching the soil red with the blood of their sacrifice.

With every fatal blow, the crowds roared in approval as the executions grew into a monstrous sport, matching brute against beast, thrust against thrust. The deadly rivalry sent the guards into a frenzy of cruelty. Each man tried to upstage the other to claim the ultimate deathblow.

Kenshin did not stay to watch. Wearing the blood of his victim on his face, he quietly slipped away. His anger spent, there was nothing left for him to do but to return home and bury his daughter. In the chaos and madness of the butchery, no one saw him leave. The lone figure floated down the hill in a limbo of misery.

Time passed slowly. Before the sun even touched the horizon, the broken man had reached the door of his house. He slid the wooden frame aside and stood there like a ghost unable to cross the threshold.

Aiko, his daughter, lay like a porcelain doll on the floor of the living room, surrounded by her grieving family. Her body had been washed and dressed in a white kimono, her black hair carefully arranged to frame her pale delicate features.

Kenshin was inconsolable. The sight of the tiny body robbed him of all his strength. He could hardly take another step. Struggling to hold back her tears, Megumi rose from her place and gently led her husband into the house.

At first, he followed her meekly. But when he got closer, the samurai threw down his sword and pulled the dead girl to himself, cradling her cold flesh against his own bloodstained cheeks. Despite his resolve, his sorrow burst like a dam, mixing his tears with the blood of the Christian he had killed earlier. He didn't care that the ashen face of his daughter was smeared red or that her pristine burial clothes were stained with blood. He held on like a man possessed, unwilling and unable to let her go.

And that's when it happened.

The dead girl suddenly sat up, opened her eyes and coughed violently, as if gasping for air. She seemed frantic and cried like a child breaking through the cobwebs of a nightmare, sending the servants scrambling in fright. Megumi and the boys were equally in shock. How could this be? The doctor had confirmed that she was no longer breathing.

Kenshin caught the girl and held her tight. Had Aiko really come back from the dead, or was this simply another cruel trick of the evil spirit? He wrapped his hands around her face and called out her name. Her skin felt warm and soft. Her voice was strong and her tears soaked his fingers like a river of life.

"My child," exclaimed Kenshin, quivering with emotion.

"Papa," the child cried back, looking at him with dark expressive eyes.

In that moment, a tsunami of love flooded the warrior's heart and swept away every trace of doubt and sorrow. This *was* his child. And against all human logic, she had truly risen from the dead.

Kenshin laughed and hugged the girl. The cries of his joy shattered the paralysis in the room, drawing his wife and sons into their happy embrace. Even the servants were grinning with excitement. What did it matter that no one could explain what had just happened? Aiko was dead for the better half of the day and now she was breathing again!

Freed from her silence, the child talked and talked, as if driven by some urgency to share her ordeal in the valley of death. She claimed that as soon as she died, two black and fearsome creatures had pounced upon her like animals. They caught hold of her and dragged her before a large abyss that groaned with the sounds of torture and despair. She would have been flung down this hole if a Japanese man had not suddenly appeared. He was dazzling and beautiful to look at. And his presence struck fear into the hearts of her captors. The fiery black figures dropped the girl in haste and quickly retreated into the shadows.

Taking her by the hand, her glorious companion routed the demons with a blazing cross that shone brightly from an open scar on his chest. She could see his wounded heart beating with light.

Shrieking horribly, the monsters turned and fled into the gaping hole, which closed up after them like a shrinking puddle until it was no more.

The young man then told her that she was safe. When she asked who he was, he said that his name was "Paulo". Then picking up the child in his arms, he told her that one day, she and her family would come to know "the Christ" who died to save them all. But for now, she had to be good and wake up. There was a blinding flash of light that made her blink. When she opened her eyes again, she was back in the arms of her father.

The story astounded everyone. Immediately, the boys pursued their sister with questions about her dream. Even the adults were unable to hold back their wonder. Only Kenshin was pensive.

He got up quietly and went into another room, taking his sword with him. Drawing back the sliding doors, he crossed the hall and approached a small garden at the back of the house. It was uncovered and opened to the sky. A gentle stream of moonlight poured into the backyard as the crickets echoed a song of praise. For a while, Kenshin simply stood on the wooden porch, listening.

Then slowly, he stepped out of the darkness and fell upon his knees. Choking back his emotions, the samurai prostrated himself and held out his sword in a gesture of fealty and surrender, as if offering his blade to the heavens in atonement.

From that moment on, the Toshigawa clan would always be at the service of Christ and his Church.

†

Gabriel looked at the sword in his hands. It was very old and the blade was marked by the violence of many conflicts. Still, the edge was razor-sharp and the steel glistened like a weapon forged in the timeless fires of ancient masters. He carefully returned the blade to its scabbard and stood up, drenched in the perspiration of his training.

"You've learnt to master that sword well," said the woman at the doorway. "Our ancestors would be proud."

Gabriel looked up at his aunt. "I always saw this as a family heirloom," he said. "I never intended to use it like this."

Teresa came in with a pot of tea, which she placed on a side table.

"That sword is a symbol of our fidelity to the Toshigawa oath, to defend the Church always," she said. "And that was exactly what you did today."

"By maiming and killing my way out of danger, by taking the lives of my enemies? What does that make me?"

"You know this is different, you're no more a murderer than I am. You're a warrior defending life against death. And sometimes, that means taking up the sword. We fight not against flesh and blood, but against principalities and powers, against spirits of the underworld."

"I know," said Gabriel. "But I am still a priest."

There was a look of weariness on his face. Years of training in the martial arts had not dampened his natural aversion for violence. The death of his parents had only made him more determined to avoid bloodshed. Nevertheless, Teresa reminded him that these were times of war. In the face of danger and death, a peace-loving sheepdog would have to risk everything to save his flock, even if it meant killing a few wolves.

Hearing that, Gabriel recalled that the medieval pun on the name of the Dominican Order was *Domini canes*, which meant the "Dogs of the Lord." He chuckled at the irony.

"So my dear nephew still has a few laughs left in him," teased the old lady. "And I thought I had to do cartwheels and cartoon impressions just to get a smile."

Gabriel rolled his eyes in jest. He remembered the antics his aunt would get up to in his childhood to save him from the depression of being an orphan. Now her motherly instinct was once again ready to catch him as she sensed his priestly heart falter.

"Sometimes, Father Gabriel forgets that he's an inspiration to all those who struggle to keep the faith in this time of darkness," she added. "Don't you think?"

Gabriel scoffed at the thought.

"I never set out to be an example. I never chose to be anyone's hero. I just wanted to make a difference, to fight for something I believe in. And even in that, I've failed a lot."

"Yes, we try our best and we still fail sometimes," said Teresa, smiling. "What matters is that we offer every moment to God. Even the difficult, messy ones that are filled with our own weaknesses and sins because good or bad, every moment belongs to God."

"I'm ashamed to confess that I desire a tidy universe, neat and uncomplicated," said her nephew. "That's how it is when your alter ego is the curator for a museum. Everything is tagged, catalogued and understood. Everything has its proper place. I like that, I can handle that..."

He turned the katana over in his hands.

"But this," he said, wrapping his fingers around the grip. "This isn't what I was ordained for."

He looked up at the clock on the wall, as if he was counting down to a deadline.

"Tell me what's really bothering you, my son," said Teresa gently. "Please..."

Gabriel didn't reply. Putting the sword aside, he got up and pulled a clean shirt over his torso.

"I know you're worried about your friends, we all are. But even though it frightens me to know that you and Michael will be walking into a trap, I know nothing will stop you two from trying to rescue them either."

"We have no choice auntie, we can't just abandon them."

"Nor do I want you to. We know you have to do this," said Teresa. "But please understand, this is also very hard on your uncle and myself."

"Don't you think I know that? It kills me to cause you such worry, but I'm also sick and tired of watching people I care about die. I wish the Lord would throw us a couple of lifelines instead of letting the enemy walk all over us. How long must we wait before Christ the King will deliver his own people from all these injustices?"

Teresa reached out and held Gabriel's hand. She knew that it cost him greatly to reveal his personal doubts. All his life he had tried to be brave in his vocation, to be fearless in his faith and hope despite the crushing weight of persecutions and hostilities. And not just for himself, but also for everyone who counted on him, who needed him to be there for them as a priest.

Above all, he always tried to be brave for his guardians. And now that he was going through his own dark night, she was determined to be there for him in his Gethsemane. Even the Son of God needed an angel to support him in his agony, what more this young priest whom she loved as her own flesh and blood?

"Did our Lord not deliver you from your enemies? The fact that you're here with us right now is a grace," she reminded her nephew. "And believe me when I say that through you and Michael, he'll also deliver your friends in their time of need. He hasn't abandoned us, child."

"Randy is dead, auntie," said Gabriel grimly. "The only deliverance I can give him now is to pray for him and offer Masses for his soul."

Teresa looked at Gabriel, her eyes brimming with sympathy. She wanted to console him, to lift his spirits, but she knew that the best thing to do was simply to listen.

"For years, we've been swimming against the tide. Whole generations have been told that religion is lame, that the Church cannot be trusted and that God is nothing but a superstition. Every single day, our Lumen enemies have been shaming Christians into submission, telling us through politics and the media that we're hypocrites, inferior and blind. They know that when we lose our pride, we lose ourselves. It's the same old rhetoric; wear us down and eventually they'll convince us that it's easier and safer for us to be cynical than to trust the Church."

"Gabriel, there'll always be Judases among us," answered Teresa. "Yet despite the betrayals of some of her members, the Church is the only real champion against evil. That's what Christ created her to do. And that's what you and the rest of God's faithful priests are doing; helping to save the world from Satan and his legions, whether the world wants it or not."

"Some champion! I don't even know what I'm doing sometimes," Gabriel responded.

"Maybe so. But just this morning, you delivered that girl from a demon. That's far greater than freeing her from a man-made prison. Rome appointed you exorcist because the pope saw something in you. There were others who were older and more experienced. But the Holy Father chose you because he believed you could make a difference. We all do. It's time you believe that yourself."

Gabriel sat slumped in a corner.

"I don't know if we can save them," he said. "I don't know if we'll make it back alive. Despite our faith, sometimes it seems like our lives are subjected to the ambiguities of fate. You might be a good person but you might not achieve what your heart longs for. There is no justice...."

The young priest buried his face in his hands for a moment, as if deep in prayer.

"Still, you're right, auntie," he sighed, raising his eyes slightly. "I believe. May God help my unbelief. I know his mercy surpasses my understanding and my doubts. I know that despite how everything looks, my hope in Christ will not be deceived."

"Do you remember this?" asked Teresa, removing a small wooden cross from around her neck. "You gave it to me as a present when you were twelve. You'd spent the entire weekend carving it, trying to inscribe something you read from a book about the Emperor Constantine, about how he survived a big fight and conquered his enemies even though the odds were totally against him, all because he relied on this symbol. You've always loved the adventures of knights and warriors, and you were so serious when you told me that this would keep me safe, that you wanted me to wear it always."

Teresa pressed the rough wooden cross into his palm.

"Well, I want you to wear this now," she said with a big grin. "And I want you to remember what that little boy discovered - that God's promises are forever."

Quietly, Gabriel took the cross in his hands and turned it over. Carved into the back were the Latin words - *In hoc signo vinces* - In this sign you shall conquer.

"Only one moment exists for you in all its beauty my child," said Teresa. "And that is the present. Live it completely in the love of God. Do your best and I promise you, God will do the rest."

Chapter 17

The full moon hung like a Chinese lantern against a black velvet sky, casting its radiant light upon a town that had long descended into darkness. Rising over the empty streets, the ancient cross atop the old steeple stood like a broken sentry watching its borders overrun by evil. Sadly, this was no longer a cathedral. And the city wasn't sorry to see the glories of the Church reduced to a parody of its former self. If the liberal elites had their way, the children of faith wouldn't be returning to their sacred home anytime soon.

Cast in stone over the rugged walls of the cloister was the word, *Chimes* - a satirical allusion to the sacred sounds that used to call the faithful to prayer everyday. Now the bells were silenced in their concrete cells, replaced by the vulgar screeching of hedonism and sin upon the grounds each night.

The strip clubs and pubs lining its cloisters had been ordered to close early on this occasion. The revelers and patrons hustled off by a warning of a bomb scare by religious fanatics on the premises. A four-block radius was locked down and contained by government agents, pushing every living witness out of the dead zone. Across the street rose two towers of concrete, metal and electrical wires - the skeletons of a commercial project that was still in construction. The media, usually abuzz with annoying persistence was conspicuously absent in this story. Ordered by their Lumen masters to retreat, the press corps whimpered back to their kennels like whipped dogs afraid to move unless they were given leave to do so.

It was a quarter to three in the morning when a black muscle car rumbled through the lonely streets towards the former house of worship. The scruffy vehicle chewed up the tarmac and screeched to a stop before the cathedral steps, its engine still idling with nervous energy.

Immediately, the dozen or so Praetorian Guards surrounding the steps took aim at the growling menace with the black tinted windows.

One man however pushed through the vanguard of armed troops and walked down the steps towards the car, a malicious grin plastered on the silicone veneer of his face.

"Time is ticking, gentlemen," said the Commander. "Shut it down."

Scarface protested and roared one final time before the engine fell silent. The doors swung open and the two priests calmly stepped out of the vehicle, both wrapped in Kevlar vests and black tactical suits.

"Search them," ordered the Commander.

The guards scrambled down like rats to strip the prisoners of their weapons.

"Handguns, ninja stars, and a samurai sword," said the Commander in surprise. "You're traveling light, aren't you?"

Spying the metal cross pinned to Michael's vest, the man slapped a hand to his forehead and laughed.

"Of course, how could I forget," he said. "You're counting on the Nazarene to help you."

As the Commander reached for the cross, Michael grabbed the man's wrist in defiance. At once, a chorus of automatic weapons converged on the two priests with deadly precision.

"I'd be careful if I were you," said the Praetorian leader. "My men are easily spooked. No telling what they might do."

Michael slowly released his grip. "The cross stays," he said.

"Keep it," the Commander replied with a smirk. "It won't save you."

Some of the guards then rustled up the duo and escorted them into the cavernous interior, leaving the majority guarding Scarface in case the prisoners attempted to escape. The Commander ordered a tracking device planted on the car before trailing his men into the cathedral.

✝

Inside, the old wooden pews had long been replaced by rows of dining tables and chairs, winding their way to a stage that occupied the space where the ancient altar used to be.

"Dominus Vobiscum," said Marshall Chambers, spreading out his arms to welcome the prisoners. He was seated on the Episcopal throne that belonged to the late bishop, surrounded by a retinue of guards who were armed to the teeth.

The Praetorian Commander climbed the stage and took his place on the right side of Chambers. On his left stood Chelsea Shields. Her face was tense and her eyes shone with anxiety when she saw the two priests. In spite of that, her heart began to beat with hope.

Gabriel scanned his surroundings and noticed a shroud of black cloth hanging above the stage, hovering over Chambers like a dark cloud. A second later, he spied the trooper hanging on to his katana. A different guard stood nearby with Michael's weapons tucked into his belt. The friar made a mental note of both their positions.

"Fascinating read," said Chambers, flipping through the Roman Ritual in his hands. It was one of the spoils taken from the raid on the museum.

"Liturgies, prayers, sacramental blessings, everything a priest needs to keep up his hocus pocus," he said with a grin. "And here it is, the Rite of Exorcism. Too bad it's all torn up and missing pages. Where do you get the rest of your mumbo jumbo?"

"The Roman Ritual isn't a book of magic formulas," retorted Gabriel. "It's a book of living prayer, alive in every Christian priest that calls on the Holy Name of God with faith and confidence. Destroy all the copies you want, it makes no difference to the Church. The prayers and rituals in those pages are merely expressions of our living faith. You'll find it easier to rip up paper than to tear out the faith in our hearts."

Chambers yawned. "If this is the quality of your preaching, I won't have to. You'll do me the favor of boring your congregations to death."

He threw the tortured pages at Gabriel. The book fluttered like an injured dove and crashed to the floor, resting its broken spine at the feet of the friar. Unimpressed, Michael threw out a booming demand of his own.

"Where's the priest? What have you done with him?" he roared.

"The priest? Oh you mean the good doctor," said Chambers calmly. "You'll have to excuse me. With all your secret identities, it gets a little confusing. Now let's see, where can we find a loyal, faithful, Catholic priest today?"

At this question, the Lumen forces in the room resounded with scorn and laughter.

Chambers rubbed his chin thoughtfully and looked at his men for advice. Rising from the bishop's throne, he paced the stage with his arms folded ponderously, his mind thinking aloud.

"Let's see, a priest acts *in persona Christi*, that is he acts in the person of Christ, offering his own sacrifice with that of the

164

Nazarene, especially in the memorial of Calvary or what you Catholics call the Mass. So that would mean…"

He stopped right behind Chelsea and looked over at the two priests. His face suddenly lit up like a light bulb.

"I've got it!" he said, snapping his fingers in triumph.

The ominous black shroud hanging overhead suddenly came sweeping down like a veil of death. Strapped to a large wooden cross on the wall was Raphael. His face was a swollen mess, his lacerated arms stretched from beam to beam by ropes and wires that cut into his flesh. Blood flowed freely from his tattered body as he hung like an icon of Christ.

"Gentlemen, I believe we've found your priest," said Chambers proudly.

Gabriel felt his blood go cold. Michael was pensive, but the veins in his temples bulged with fury. Even Chelsea was shocked at the brutality dispensed to the doctor after they were separated at the Lumen palace.

"Let him go," Michael said gruffly.

"Gladly," replied Chambers. "If you would tell me who your leaders are. I want a list of names and addresses. And I want to know the whereabouts of the one you call 'The Chinese'."

"We've no idea who you're talking about," replied Gabriel, his eyebrows twitching slightly as he said that.

"Come now, Father," complained Chambers. "A good priest shouldn't tell lies, shame on you for even trying. You know exactly who I'm talking about. If you won't give up the old man, we have no reason to prolong this little chat."

He gazed at the Praetorian Commander. The man with the silicone mask stepped forward and pushed a lever on the wall, lowering the giant cross until Raphael was suspended at eye level.

"I'll give you one last chance to cooperate," said Chambers. "I'm going to count to three. And then I'm going to give your friend here his last meal."

The Commander pulled out his pistol and jammed the barrel into Raphael's mouth. Without thinking, Gabriel took a step forward but a sea of rifles closed in on him, prompting Michael to reach out and hold back his confrere.

"You want to rescue him, yes? Maybe even give your life for him. But all you have to do is tell me where I can find the leaders of the Resistance, especially the old Chinese," said Chambers.

"And if we do, you'll let us all go free, won't you? Just like that," replied Michael.

Chambers smiled and wasted no time counting down his threat.

"One..." he droned, like an unfeeling machine.

Chelsea looked torn between her instincts to flee and her desire to fight. A part of her wanted to wrestle the gun away from the Commander, to try and save the priest from swallowing a bullet. But she knew it was madness to try.

"Two..." said the menacing voice. In spite of her fears, the woman took a bold step forward.

"Wait!" shouted Gabriel, trying to delay the inevitable.

There was a soft chuckle. The vicious Commander noticed that Michael had pulled off the metal cross on his vest and was holding it in his hands, as if in prayer.

"Like I said, that won't save you!" he sneered.

He cocked the gun in Raphael's mouth and tightened his grip on the trigger. With great difficulty, the tortured doctor raised his face to look at his friends one last time.

"Three..." said Chambers.

And a huge fireball ripped through the front gates of the building, sending a violent blast of fire and twisted metal into the hall. The explosion was so powerful that it blew out all the stained glass in the windows, raining a shower of broken saints on all who had been knocked off their feet. The heavy oak doors of the entrance lay burning in splinters on the floor.

Outside, Scarface was billowing in flames; engulfed by a tremendous fury of packed explosives that had gone off the moment Michael clicked the hidden detonator on the cross. Littered all around were Praetorian parts that greatly reduced the number of Lumen grunts on the ground.

When the startled Commander got back on his feet, Michael had already broken the neck of the guard in his reach, taken his Lumen rifle and was blasting a river of lead at the other Practorians. Gabriel had also retrieved his weapons from a dead guard and was slashing his way through the resistance.

In response, the Commander picked up his gun and pointed his wrath at Raphael, who was still tied down like a sacrificial lamb.

"Finish him!" ordered Chambers.

"No!" shouted Chelsea.

There was a deafening bang that tore through the hall with terror.

Gabriel turned around and saw the Praetorian Commander snatched into the air with a burning crack in his chest. Something high-powered had pierced the solid walls of the cathedral, found its target and blown a large hole in the man.

Within seconds, several more guards were ripped apart by the sudden hail of huge bullets drilling into the chapel, turning its stone walls into Swiss cheese. Thrown into turmoil, the guards stumbled over each other to escape the screeching death. It seemed as if the hand of God had suddenly reached down and shredded the Lumen troops into confetti.

Charging through the mayhem, Michael recovered his pistols and tried to get a fix on Chambers. Unfortunately, the man was nowhere to be seen. Several kilometers away, a Muslim warrior in an armored van was still keeping the *hand of God* busy, drenching the floor red with the blood of the ungodly.

The 'Warmongers' were three powerful sniper cannons adapted for urban warfare. Each weapon could blast through concrete walls and find their victims with pinpoint accuracy. Each was remotely controlled and guided by a targeting system built to triangulate human heat signatures through solid walls.

As Kaz monitored the action, his fingers ran lightly over the digital screen, locking the powerful cannons onto their living targets. Two of the guns peered down from the vacant offices of an unfinished building across the road, while the third delivered death from a small wooded hill overlooking the cloisters. Together, this trinity of smoking barrels was grinding the Lumen troops to dust.

Back inside the cathedral, Gabriel knew he had to get to Raphael and Chelsea fast. Both he and Michael were safe enough. Their wristwatches transmitted unique signals that allowed Kaz to identify them, but everybody else was fair game.

The Praetorians were down but not out. They couldn't neutralize the 60 caliber rounds pummeling their ranks, but they could still try and kill the two battling priests in the room. Despite the slaughter from without, the guards were not slowing down. Even as more troops got ripped apart, more seemed to be pouring in from the burning entrance, as if the gates of Hades had been flung wide opened.

Michael and Gabriel ducked behind the marble pillars as their opponents returned fire, blowing away chunks of their cover. At the same time, the hungry cannons were still devouring a great deal of

167

Praetorian flesh. A guard near Chelsea tried to use her as a shield. But before he could take her as hostage, the friar buried a few shurikens in his face. The man fell like a penitent at the foot of the cross.

"Cut him down!" shouted Gabriel, gesturing towards his friend on the cross.

Instinctively, Chelsea picked up a huge vase by the side and thrashed it on the wounded guard, knocking him out. She quickly bent down and retrieved the dagger from his belt.

By the time the friar dodged the bullets and made his way to her, she had already loosen much of the wires binding Raphael to the wooden beams. With one deft stroke from his katana, Gabriel freed his brother priest from the cross and caught him in his arms.

"Move it!" screamed Michael, ducking out from behind the pillar to offer covering fire. In all the chaos, no one noticed that the cannons had been silent for the last ten seconds.

Kaz's voice suddenly came crackling through the tiny receiver in Michael's ear: "They found the guns! I repeat. The 'Warmongers' are dead. Move to extraction now!"

Behind the stage were marble stairs leading down to the cathedral crypt where the late Archbishops were formally buried. The Corporation had left the old bones lying in their tombs, even as wanton sacrilege was forced on the cloisters and chapel above. It was done expressly to profane their sacred memories.

As Gabriel hoisted the battered body of his friend down the stairs, Michael finished the remaining guards and ran down after the friar, snatching Chelsea along the way and pulling her into the open gap with him. There were still troops pouring through the fiery entrance, flooding the chapel with masked assassins. But the priest knew that the stairs leading down to the crypt were fairly narrow, allowing only one person down at a time. It was the perfect place to defend their position - a hot gate that would funnel the numbers of their enemies into impotence.

Within seconds, tear gas filled the chapel and several explosions rocked the stage as Lumen grenades landed close to the fleeing priests.

"What're we doing down here? This is a dead end!" cried Chelsea. "And let go of me!" She tried to wrench her arm away from the ex-mercenary.

"Shut up and stay down!" Michael yelled, dropping her off next to Raphael.

Refusing to listen, Chelsea tried to get back up. But the wounded doctor restrained her.

"Please," said Raphael, his eyes almost pleading.

She looked down and collapsed like a frightened child. Both took shelter behind the elaborate tomb of a dead Cardinal.

Gabriel grabbed the Praetorian rifle from Michael and manned the bottom stairs, crouching to fire a few shots whenever Lumen shadows darkened the entrance.

"Hurry up," he said. "I can't hold them off for long."

Chelsea looked over at Michael who was quickly dismantling his two personal pistols. Confusion reigned over her face.

"Why are you doing that?" she quipped nervously. "Why are you taking your guns apart?"

Surely they could use more firepower, she thought.

"Because I need this," said Michael, relieved to see that his insurance was intact.

He knew that the Praetorians would merely confiscate his handguns; they wouldn't pay too much attention to a simple pair of pistols. But this other stuff would definitely alert them. The only way to avoid suspicion was to hide it somewhere safe, somewhere they would never think of looking.

He gently detached the tiny rolls of explosives from the empty gun chambers.

"Is that C-4?" asked Raphael, struggling to stand up. His body was bruised and broken but his spirit was indomitable. Plus he wasn't going to face death lying on his back.

"Better," answered Michael. "This is what blew up the car. A spot of this makes C-4 look like a party cracker."

Chelsea couldn't believe her ears.

"Wait a minute, you're not going to use that in here, are you?" she asked, her voice stricken with anxiety. She had been down into the crypt before during one of the many fashion parties held at this place not so long ago. She knew there was no way out except for the same hole they had just squeezed through.

In answer, Michael hurried to the doorway framing the entrance and plastered small pieces of the volatile putty at various points.

"This is crazy, he'll bury us all," protested Chelsea. Even Raphael was concerned about the plan.

"Michael, I think there's enough dead priests in here already," he said, glancing at the marble sarcophagi of the Archbishops lining the walls. "I don't plan on joining the list."

As far as the doctor could see, this place had all the makings of a sealed tomb.

"People, less talking please!" interrupted Gabriel over the noise of gunfire.

They were running out of time and ammunition. Without warning, a volley of Lumen grenades flew down the stairs and rolled into the crypt.

"Take cover!!!" shouted Michael.

Chelsea and Raphael crouched low behind the shelter of their tomb, wondering if the fortress of limestone and marble would hold. Michael and Gabriel had both thrown themselves behind similar structures, praying that the sanctuaries of the dead would shield the living from the claws of death.

A loud explosion of fire and debris rocked the crypt, as if the earth's core had suddenly regurgitated its fiery entrails into the tiny chamber. As the fire and brimstone subsided, Chelsea peeked over the marble slab and saw the narrow entrance transformed into a wall of solid rubble. At once her courage failed her. The plan had worked a little too well. They were trapped. The avalanche of debris cut off the Praetorian assault but it also sealed off their only escape. Now they were as buried as the bones in the crypt.

But not everyone was alarmed. Convinced that they were safe for the moment, Michael rose and pulled out a map from his sleeve. He studied the chart briefly and mumbled into his watch, listening carefully as the hidden communicator in his ear came alive with instructions.

The Japanese friar rushed over to make sure that Chelsea and Raphael were okay. Apart from frayed nerves and slight concussions, everyone seemed to be in one piece.

"What now, bright eyes?" asked Gabriel, ambling up to his comrade in arms.

Michael didn't answer. He simply moved from tomb to tomb, reading the Latin inscriptions until he found the one he was looking for.

"Give me some light," he said aloud.

Gabriel trotted close and pulled out a glow stick. He snapped the plastic tube and held it aloft, letting the chemical reaction bathe the tomb with luminance.

"What're you looking for now?" demanded Chelsea, who was still irate that she had followed these lunatic priests into a trap. "You're mad for bringing us down here."

"I swear if you don't shut up, I'll bury you in one of these myself," said Michael.

The situation was such that no one needed more tension.

"Chelsea, please calm down," said Raphael. "They know what they're doing."

He glanced over at Michael. "You do know what you're doing, right?"

The priest shot him a look of annoyance. Raphael decided to hold his tongue.

Within a short time, Michael had strategically placed the remaining explosives on the tomb. He had only one chance to make this work, and his demolition experience would have to shield them from being blown to kingdom come.

"You ready?" he asked Gabriel.

The friar glanced at the name of the entombed bishop, shrugged his shoulders and replied, "I never liked this guy anyway. Besides, I don't think he's going to protest. Let her rip."

Both priests hid safely behind a wall before Michael threw the switch. This time, the blast felt contained, as if the force of the violence imploded into the tomb rather than tore into the surrounding structures. The crypt shook with ferocity. Bits of plaster fell from the ceiling but otherwise, the underground chamber remained intact. A quick roll call confirmed that everyone was still alive.

As the dust cleared, the group emerged to see a gaping hole where the tomb used to be. It looked like the ground had yawned and swallowed up the heavy sarcophagus, leaving an abyss of darkness in its sleep.

Supported by Gabriel, Raphael stumbled forward and peered into the hole. He could see nothing inside but gloom. Taking little steps, Chelsea inched up beside them.

"What's down there?" she asked.

"Freedom," Michael replied. "Let's go!"

He was about to push the others into the waiting chasm when Raphael suddenly staggered back in pain.

"Wait!" said the doctor, gasping. He collapsed into the open arms of his comrades. "Something's not right. I sense a presence..."

Immediately, Gabriel grabbed his katana and asked, "Where?

Down there?"

Closing his eyes for a moment, Raphael tried to concentrate. He stretched out his fingers to grasp the invisible threads of danger lurking in the crypt.

"No," said the clairvoyant priest, jerking his hand back in dread. "Up here," he replied, his pupils dilating with adrenaline. The air suddenly seemed very cold. And then they heard it. It was soft at first, elusive like a wispy dream. Then slowly it became more audible until finally, squeals of amusement drifted out from the shadows in a disembodied voice.

Chelsea whipped around in panic, her eyes scanning the darkness for that familiar cackle.

"Leaving so soon?" asked the voice. "I'm disappointed, young lady. I thought we had an agreement."

Chambers stepped out into the light and grinned like the Cheshire cat. The whiteness of his teeth only deepened the blackness behind his eyes.

"The deal was you kept your destiny with me and I let you keep your soul," said the Lumen VP. "But now that you've breached your contract, there's hell to pay."

Gabriel moved forward and drew his sword, placing Chelsea behind the safety of his blade. The shrill cry of Japanese metal leaving its scabbard rang like a call for blood.

"Ohhh, I like the sound of that," Chambers purred with delight. "Let the games begin."

Michael's reflexes instantly kicked in. His rifle jumped up and he squeezed off, but nothing happened. The gun jammed.

Chambers stretched his lips and grinned. "Now it's my turn," he whispered.

Almost instantly, the shadows surrounding this man began to peel back. A young girl emerged from the darkness and clung to his side. Her tiny legs were encased in metal and her face seemed possessed by a ghostly light.

"Here Magdalene," said Chambers, handing a grisly artifact to the child. "Now go play with these nice gentlemen."

As the girl took the Phurba, the dagger immediately came alive. The hideous faces on the pommel started to spin at a rapid blur. When the demon heads finally stopped, their terrifying shrieks were so fearsome that Chelsea tripped over herself in shock.

Michael heard nothing. But he saw something else altogether.

Before him stood a little girl clinging on to her doll, her hair matted with blood and her body riddled with death. Her limbs were mangled and most of all, her eyes were bleeding with blame. This wasn't possible, this can't be, he told himself. This had to be an illusion. He held her body. He watched her die. Yet here she was, an apparition conjured from the past. He tried to wipe the accursed vision from his eyes, but the cold memory of guilt only pierced his heart and bludgeoned his soul with despair.

Everything around him suddenly turned black. Dizzy with vertigo, the priest tumbled to the ground. The darkness was cold and consuming, the voices of his companions had faded away. He could hear nothing but the desperate sound of his own heart beating. Trying to move, he found himself paralyzed. With every breath he took, he fell deeper and deeper into a bottomless pit, unable to fight the gravity of his sins.

No matter how much he struggled, he couldn't push back the tide. His courage dismantled, his heart threatened to burst. But just as all hope seemed extinguished, he felt a strong grip on his arm.

A moment later, his body smacked brutally onto the concrete floor. The force of impact woke him up.

Chapter 18

"Come on, get up!!!" shouted Gabriel, jerking Michael to his feet.

The priest got up unsteadily and realized that his friend had pulled him into the sewer beneath the crater. His vision was still blurred and he floundered like a drowning man.

"Snap out of it!" said Gabriel, slapping Michael across the face.

For a second, the soldier priest was stunned. The blow knocked the icy fingers of death from his mind.

"You okay?" Gabriel asked urgently.

Michael nodded. Shaking off the last dregs of chaos from his head, he pulled out a flashlight from his pocket and scrambled to catch up with the rest. But the priest was still nauseous from the trance. The stench in the tunnel was so overpowering, he had to hold his breath several times to keep from passing out.

Not far ahead, Raphael and Chelsea stumbled through the reeking passage, driven by the resolve to escape something far worse than the rotting sewage around them.

Gabriel brought up the rear. He was the only one who seemed unaffected by the odorous filth. As an exorcist, he had known few things on earth more foul than the scent of sin, and he waded through the sewage with impunity.

"This way," said Michael, overtaking the group.

Suddenly, the walls reverberated with terror. The howling dirge of a banshee closed in behind them. Chelsea started to panic.

"Ignore it," Raphael told the woman. "Just keep moving."

Rounding a corner, Michael paused and grunted into his transmitter. "I need directions," he said. "Where to now?"

His comlink came alive with instructions from Kaz, hurrying them on to the next checkpoint.

"I see it," said Michael, pointing his flashlight at the far end. He ran up to the rusty gate and kicked it. The shabby barrier flew off its hinges and clattered in the dark.

"Come on," he waved to the rest.

The group hurried to catch up. Whatever monstrous thing was

hunting them, it sounded like it was getting closer. As they squeezed through the narrow passage, Michael slipped to the left and pulled out a duffel bag hidden behind a sewage pipe.

"I see your buddy came through as usual," said Gabriel, keeping an eye on their flanks.

"He always does," Michael replied. The priest removed several packages from the bag and tossed them to his teammates.

"Now we're talking," said Gabriel, catching his parcel with relief.

He ripped open the package and urgently stocked up on the tools of his trade. In no time, he was strapped to the hilt with an arsenal of spiritual weapons that included relics, blessed salt, holy water and incense.

"What happened to you back there?" Chelsea asked Michael.

She had seen him take down a pack of hellhounds by himself. And yet, he was shaking like a leaf when confronted by the little girl.

Michael frowned and said nothing. Instead, he slapped a full magazine into a rifle and slung it across his back. Grabbing a grenade launcher, he ensured that all six chambers were stocked to the brim.

"We're going to need a lot more than that to stop what's coming," Gabriel cautioned. "I don't know what was unleashed up there, but I know it's going to be nasty."

"Did you see anything?" Michael asked the friar.

"You mean besides that creepy girl in black? As soon as that Phurba started freaking out, I grabbed you and ran. That thing in her hands is like a portal, only much more powerful. It feeds off the darkness of the one using it. I'm guessing she channeled something through."

"Demons," said Chelsea, expecting the worse.

"I guess we'll find out," Gabriel replied.

Undaunted, Michael dug into the duffel bag and pulled out his dagger with the crucifix attached. He retracted the giant blade and slipped the cross into his gun belt.

"I've got it covered," he said grimly.

Raphael however was more prudent.

"Guys, if we can, we run to fight another day," he reminded them. There was no sense in facing the enemy head-on under the circumstances. His ribs were still badly bruised and every inch of his body felt like it was on fire.

When he said this, a sudden quake ripped up the sewage floor, like something was trying to burrow its way up to the surface. The cracks were so violent that it threw everyone off their balance.

"What's happening?" shrieked Chelsea, trying to get back up.

Michael caught her as rapid convulsions shook the tunnel and split the ground beneath them. The narrow sewage canal erupted with tiny geysers of steam, prompting Gabriel to plunge his katana into a crevice and hold on. The stench of rotting flesh drifted from the open fissure like an infected wound.

With one hand wrapped around a pipe and the other catching a slippery ledge, Raphael found himself thrust into a vision. The vibrations on the wall slipped into his hands and tore a window into his mind, filling his eyes with a glimpse of the evil stalking them.

"Gabriel, below you!" the doctor cried out in alarm.

Instinctively, the friar pulled his blade from the crevice and jumped back as a red forearm smashed through the concrete floor and made a grab for him. A moment later, the rest of the burning body emerged from the crumbling foundation in a fiery mass of bone and tissue.

Michael immediately fired off a volley of shots with his high-powered rifle. But the bullets melted before they had a chance to make contact. The skin of this creature flickered like burning embers, with rivulets of fire coursing through its veins. Its eyes were frightfully ablaze with such anger that it seemed to set the whole world on fire.

Gabriel sheathed his sword and threw a handful of incense pellets at the creature. As the capsules burst into smoke, the beast howled with rage and dug its claws into the ground, ripping up a stretch of concrete that threw the friar into the air.

"Run!" Michael screamed at Chelsea and Raphael.

He turned his sights back on the apparition and fired off more rounds. Although he was praying rapidly, no one could hear what he said under his breath except for…"Libera nos a malo!"

At once, the creature reacted as if it had been slapped across the face. The bullets finally began to hammer through like a shower of nails puncturing the thick blistering skin, but they did nothing more than enraged the monster even more.

The red giant roared and swung at Michael, narrowly missing the startled priest. A huge section of the retainer wall came off like molten cheese, triggering a slight cave-in.

"I think you pissed him off," said Gabriel, climbing to his feet.

Hearing the friar's voice, the beast turned around and hellfire blazed out of its mouth. Gabriel managed to leap out of the way, but he wasn't quick enough to escape the monstrous red arm. It shot out and grabbed him by the neck, lifting him off his feet like a ragged doll.

Immediately, Gabriel jammed his boot against the chest of the creature, pushing some distance between his body and the burning orifice of jagged teeth. The friar was desperate to shut the rancid jaws, but he couldn't reach the katana on his back.

"Over here!" shouted Michael. He pulled out his crucifix dagger and tossed it to the Japanese friar.

Gabriel caught the weapon and released the killer blade from its catch. Aiming between the eyes, he slammed the consecrated steel into the cranium of the monster. The entity bawled in pain and flung the young man into the ground. The blow was so powerful that it broke the armor in his tactical vest. By a pure miracle, the katana on his back remained intact.

The friar groaned in pain. For a split second, Michael was sure his friend was done for. But Gabriel recovered quickly and spun out of the way.

Shrieking with fury, the creature yanked the crucifix from its head. It threatened to charge forward but a burst of metal shards exploded and sliced into its chest, forcing it to stumble back. But these were no ordinary shurikens. Each ring of killer blades held a medal of St. Benedict at its core - the very same medal that was heavily indulged with exorcism prayers.

Before the monster could retaliate, Michael hurled another batch of throwing stars at the beast. As the spinning darts cut into the flesh of the creature, the Latin prayers for deliverance triggered a violent reaction in the massive red troll. It writhed and screamed and fell to its knees, clutching its chest in agony. A different kind of fire could be seen blazing within its perforated wounds, and the pure flames of this chastisement were far more punishing than the fires of hell.

Michael smirked. This thing was vulnerable. If it could be hurt, it could be taken down.

✝

Chelsea stumbled through the darkened sewer, with Raphael leading the way in spite of his injuries. The good doctor had grabbed her and ferried her away from danger once Michael shouted for them to run.

"We can't just leave them back there," protested Chelsea. As much as she was frightened by the appearance of the flaming beast, she was genuinely worried for the priests.

"Believe me, they can handle themselves better if they knew we were safe," said Raphael. "We just need to keep moving."

Chelsea looked conflicted.

"Come on," Raphael cried impatiently. As soon as he said that, he felt a tremor down his spine. Something had followed them from the tunnel and Raphael knew it was evil.

A guttural noise like a belch erupted from the darkness, corrupting the stale air with the wicked odor of damnation. Both Raphael and Chelsea recoiled from the pungent attack, unsure of what hid in the shadows around them.

Pulling a flare from his pouch, Raphael ignited the stick and tossed it into the shadows. As it rolled into the darkness, it quickly fizzled out, as if the air around it was incapable of supporting any oxygen or life. A capacious roar of loud burps echoed in return, followed quickly by a very creepy and inhuman laugh.

Slowly, Chelsea began to notice a pair of grimy eyes staring at her from the shadows. They were mounted on a malicious grin of incisors and molars that stretched terribly like a black hole, eager to swallow everything in its path. Eventually, the ghastly thing emerged from the blackness and exposed itself. It was big, bloated, greasy and disgusting, and intensely suffocating in its vulgar appetite. There was no doubt it would consume them both if it could.

"Start praying," Raphael whispered to Chelsea, pulling her back slowly from the gloating evil before them.

"Our Father who art in heaven, hallowed be thy name," she began to stutter, her memory frantically trying to recall the words of her childhood.

At this, a terrifying noise rumbled from the bloated specter, trumpeting the hunger pangs of a demon fat with the taste of human souls. Quickly, Raphael invoked a prayer of protection and took two spherical devices from the pouch Michael had given him. He released the safety catches and dislodged the powdery contents onto the floor in a circle.

"What're you doing?" Chelsea asked nervously.

The doctor simply pushed her into the ring of white and grunted, "Whatever happens, stay inside the circle!"

Raphael crossed himself and pulled a crucifix from his pouch. The oily apparition rolled grudgingly into the light. It was a massive sludge of putrefying flesh, its seemingly bald head chuckling with malice while rotting food oozed out of its mouth like the contents of a meat grinder. Its heavy body was soft and pale, and its skin seemed to be sweating vomit from its pores.

Chelsea blanched and tried not to faint with horror. The sewage floor was plagued with an army of scum and pestilence fleeing this abominable presence. She looked down and saw that the rats and roaches scuttled all over in panic but veered away from the circle of salt that enclosed her.

She glanced up at Raphael and saw the look in his eyes. The doctor knew it was madness to battle this scion of evil in his condition. He could barely breathe without his ribs digging into his lungs. But there was little else they could do. He had to try and keep them both alive. Desperately, he prayed that backup would arrive in time.

✝

As the creature languished on its knees, Gabriel knew it was a matter of time before it picked itself up and tore them to pieces. From experience, he knew that demons were often reinforced from hell when they buckled under the pressures of an exorcism. Legions of evil spirits would sometimes rush into a possessed person when the host demon was weakened and about to be expelled.

He didn't know if this battle would be any different, but he wasn't going to take any chances. There were several explosions as Michael emptied the grenade launcher at the monster, but none did more damage than the slew of Benedictine medals earlier.

With Michael distracting the raging beast, Gabriel drew his sword and drove the blade into the burning flesh of the creature. The samurai steel hacked off an arm easily enough.

But the friar was in great agony. Having torn the ligaments in his back when the monster pummeled him to the ground, he gritted his teeth and bore the pain.

"This thing runs on rage and hellfire," he cried out to Michael. "Use the holy water!"

As he said that, the monstrous arm grew back and the furious creature climbed to its feet. Again, Gabriel threw a handful of shurikens at the savage beast. The fiery giant dodged the attack this time and went on a rampage, swatting the friar into a wall. Snapping its head around, the demon opened its jaws and roared.

Michael ducked as a jet of molten lava shot in his direction and ravaged the pipes behind him, melting the sewage ducts into a cauldron of boiling mess. He swiftly reloaded his launcher with several new canisters and took aim.

"Time to cool off," growled the priest as he pulled the trigger.

The creature bayed like a whipped dog and collapsed in agony, its neck and body peppered with metal syringes that pumped canisters of holy water into its flaming guts.

Bursting with wrath, it tried to rise from its broken state but tiny explosions of steam erupted all over its torso, tearing it into submission. In no time, the beast was rapidly turning grey and hardening, much like magma doused by the effects of cold water.

Michael and Gabriel knew this was their chance. The cartridges of holy water were quenching the furnace inside this thing. If they were going to stop this spawn of Satan, they had to do it now. The friar tore a strip of clothing from his sleeve and soaked it in a phial of clear oil that he pulled out of his vest. Then grabbing his katana, he wiped the blade with the sacred chrism that was consecrated for the divine anointing of priests and bishops.

"Hurry," said Michael, noticing that the monster was starting to recover.

Calmly, Gabriel stepped up to the hulking mass. The samurai sword flashed with a hungry edge and the head of a demon splashed into the sewer drain, its bulky shell of a body crumbling like a mountain.

To make sure this spiritual ogre was not coming back, the exorcist proceeded to bind the spirit with the blood of Christ. He had just finished the powerful prayer when a woman's voice echoed down the tunnel with terror.

"Chelsea..." said Michael, recognizing the scream.

Chapter 19

Again, Raphael invoked the power of the cross.

"We adore Thee, O Christ, and we bless Thee, because by Thy Holy Cross Thou has redeemed the World," he intoned, holding up the crucifix in his hands

The grossly corpulent spirit reacted with such horrific violence that Chelsea required all her self-control to avoid dashing out of the circle in fear. The creature tore its mouth from side to side, baring several rows of serrated teeth and a wicked tongue that looked like it would strangle the world.

She screamed. There was no doubt that this was a demon. Chelsea knew that in her heart. How they could exist in corporeal form she had no idea, but she knew that the only thing protecting her from those enormous teeth was the striking figure of the doctor standing between them.

Furious at not being able to break the circle of white grains protecting the girl, the festering globe of putrid flesh looked at Raphael and regurgitated, shooting a powerful stream of rotten food and grime in the direction of the man. The surge of vomit hosed the doctor to the ground and dislodged the crucifix from his hands. Again Chelsea wanted to breach the circle and run to his aid.

"Stay where you are!" said Raphael, gagging on the disgusting muck and slime.

He tried to get up but noticed that his body was covered with millions of maggots. Without warning, the doctor suddenly felt the cruelty of countless pins and knives being driven into him with terrible force.

In her eagerness to assist, Chelsea's foot slipped outside the circle. Immediately the demon looked at her and licked its swollen lips, cackling like an insane clown.

"Get back in!" shouted Raphael, twisting on the ground in distress.

The pain was so excruciating that the tortured man began to scream in spite of himself. Smelling blood, the grisly blob of evil lurched forward like a speeding boulder, unlocking its brutal chops to scoop up the injured doctor in its mouth and devour him.

Instead, the huge gaping jaws swallowed two canisters of holy water fired from a grenade launcher at close range. Michael switched to his auxiliary guns and blasted the creature with hundreds of consecrated rounds, forcing the rotund monster to roll back in panic.

"Help him!" Michael ordered.

Chelsea left the circle and sprinted to Raphael. She tried to brush away the maggots from his body but the plague only infected her, threatening to consume the girl as well.

"Hang on!" shouted Gabriel, skirting the corner.

He slid to a stop next to the afflicted pair and pulled out an incense capsule. Flicking the switch, he ignited the resin and sprayed the blessed smoke all over Chelsea and Raphael like a pesticide. The effect was immediate. The maggots disintegrated and fell away like crumbs, sparing the pair from being eaten alive.

"Stay here," said the friar. He drew his katana and prepared to join in the fray, but Raphael grabbed the exorcist and pulled him close.

"Wait, that thing is full of corruption and excess. We're dealing with one of the seven vices. It's a spirit of gluttony," said the doctor. "I'm sure of that."

"Terrific, just what we need," complained Gabriel.

He looked up and saw Michael dodging the rolling behemoth. The ex-soldier had thrown everything in his arsenal at the creature but it kept coming. This thing was adapting fast. And although the consecrated bullets and capsules of incense made an impact, they only kept the demon at bay for so long.

Michael scowled. "A little backup here," he shouted.

Gabriel rushed in and threw a pair of shurikens at the revolting form but the bloated creature absorbed the impact like a mound of gelatin and simply repelled the assault, ejecting the spinning blades back at the exorcist.

"Crap!" cursed Gabriel as he suffered a few cuts from the close shave. Being struck by the Benedictine medals only increased the creature's appetite for the blood of a priest.

"I'm guessing the holy water didn't work either," said Gabriel, landing close to his confrere.

"You think?" grumbled Michael, his voice tinged with sarcasm.

"So how do we take it down?"

"Good question, I was hoping you'd know," said the priest, adding a barrage of gunfire to his answer.

Physically, the huge ball of lard was growing bigger and stronger. The bullets pelted the creature with little effect, bouncing off the greasy façade. Squealing madly, the demon leered at the clerics and bowled through the chamber like a wrecking ball, smashing and gobbling everything in its path like a mouth of doom. Everyone quickly bolted out of the way.

"Stay alert, don't let that thing touch you," warned Michael, narrowly escaping the bulldozing mass of slime.

"Look out!" shouted Raphael as the giant orb of flesh missed the woman by a whisker and demolished a wall.

As Chelsea stumbled to safety, a light came on in her eyes. "The circle," she cried out excitedly, recalling how the menacing blob had left her alone when she was inside the ring of salt.

"She's right," admitted Raphael, surprised that he hadn't realize it sooner. "It's the blessed salt. It might be the only thing that can stop it."

Gabriel glanced at the amount of white residue on the floor. He knew that exorcised salt was a powerful agent against demonic corruption. Unfortunately, he wasn't packing any. The friar had given them to Raphael for his protection in case they got separated. And sure enough, the doctor had run into trouble and needed it. He desperately hoped they had some left over.

Michael fired his last shot as the demon lashed out with a long leathery tongue and wrestled the powerful rifle from his hands. The weapon barely disappeared down the rancid mouth before the gristly tongue shot out again and snagged the warrior in a death grip.

Luckily the priest had recovered his dagger from the battle earlier. He pulled the large crucifix from his gun belt. The cross blade lunged out like a monstrous tooth and bit into the bulbous tissue, sending the appalling tongue darting back into its snarling jaws.

"Hurry, give it to me," said Gabriel, motioning to the doctor.

Raphael grabbed the last metallic sphere from his pouch and tossed it to the exorcist. "That's all we have, make it count."

When the demon saw the shiny metal globe in the hands of the friar, it recoiled with astonishing dread. Something bizarre and frightening began to happen. The enormous entity stretched opened its mouth until its entire body seemed to disappear behind its own oral cavity, leaving nothing behind but a terrifying cave of teeth, mucus and tongue.

And then it began to suck the air out of that place.

Rats and roaches were the first to be pulled into the massive vortex of the creature's mouth. Even the huge pipes on the walls were torn off their catches and swallowed like snacks. Michael and the rest of his team clung to whatever they could, fighting to resist the powerful tow of the gaping black hole.

With one hand clutching an exposed wire mesh, the priest drew his sidearm with his free hand and tried to unload some carnage on the creature, praying all the time that God would lace the bullets with divine wrath and direct his aim. However, the suction was so strong that the pistol broke his grip and vanished into the cavernous jaws.

Chelsea slipped from her catch and tumbled down the sewage floor, rolling past Raphael who caught her as she flew past.

"Hold on," he cried, straining against the pull of death. His free arm was looped around her waist and was buckling with agony to keep the girl from plummeting into the swirling pool of teeth.

"Do it now!" Michael shouted to Gabriel.

The exorcist fumbled to activate the metal globe in his hand. The switch was jammed. Like a grenade, the orb was powered by a small charge designed to scatter its contents with maximum impact and range. But first, it needed to be triggered.

"Come on," Gabriel groaned with disbelief. Of all the times for a weapon to cock up, why did it have to be now?

He frantically pressed the trigger switch but the light just wouldn't come on. The only thing to do was to release the safety catch and manually empty the contents in the right direction. Before he could do that, the shiny metal ball flew out of his hand and dived into the waiting chasm. Straight away, his heart sank. He watched the drooling darkness yawn to swallow their last sliver of hope.

All of a sudden, there was a loud bang and the faulty sphere blew up in midair. Something potent had torn its metal shell to pieces. The exorcised salt rained down on the gluttonous demon. As soon as the blessed particles touched the putrid flesh, a heinous scream reverberated through the sewer, shaking everyone to their bones.

With the powerful suction interrupted, everyone fell to the ground. Michael rose from his corner and was astounded to see Kaz standing tall behind the smoking barrel of a modified shotgun.

The Muslim warrior began to punch holes in the hapless creature, weakened as it was by the spiritual effects of exorcised salt. With each cartridge he expelled, Kaz prayed fervently in his Arabic tongue, joining his heart to the voices of the three priests in the chamber who had broken out in a litany of Latin prayers.

The demon shrieked in horror, covering its ears. The Muslim and Christian world might still be buried in conflict in some places, its hatred and prejudices eagerly fanned by the sons of darkness, but here in the bowels of this former cathedral, God was one and the same. And he heard the prayers of the sons of light.

Wherever the hulking mass was ripped open by a shotgun blast, the salt would burn like hydrochloric acid on speed, puncturing the demon with a blizzard of leprous holes. In seconds, the creature looked and smelled like a rotting slab of cheese, caving in upon itself when its fallen nature could no longer bear the fervent prayers of the men, nor the powerful effects of the sacramental.

The fiendish monster wailed like a pregnant cat, its lamentation rising in fear as its outer shell deflated like a collapsible tent. All three priests raised their hands in synchronized fashion, tracing the sign of the cross over the miserable demon. There was a sudden burst of fire upon the squealing blob. A final ghostly moan quivered from its pudgy core and then the quaking mass was all but gone, leaving behind a puddle of smoking slime on the sewage floor.

"That's just disgusting," quipped Gabriel. He trotted over to the grimy remains and delivered the coup de grâce with a prayer to bind the spirit.

Michael turned to his friend. "What're you doing here?" he asked, still surprised.

"Saving your butt, what else?" replied Kaz.

He tapped the communicator in his ear and added, "I couldn't stand you guys screaming like a bunch of girls. I had to do something to shut you up."

Michael laughed. "Thank God you're a nosey son of a gun," he grunted, dusting the dirt from his vest.

"You're welcome," said Kaz. "Now come on, Lumen flies are gathering outside. We have to go now."

Clearly, the group had been delayed for too long. For all they knew, the Praetorians were already waiting in ambush up above. What's more, it seemed like the forces of good had taken some serious hits.

Gabriel hobbled over in pain. Now that the adrenaline had worn off, his back injury was starting to throb without mercy. He slipped an arm under Raphael and tried to help the doctor to his feet. Chelsea stared at the two priests with concern. It looked like they were both hurting pretty bad.

"You okay?" she asked.

"Yeah," they echoed together. It was obvious that they were both lying.

"Come on, we'll sort you out later," said Michael. "For now, let's get the hell out of here."

Kaz nodded his approval and turned on his heels. "Follow me, the exit is just up ahead."

As the group hurried off, Chelsea noticed something very peculiar. A strong perfume began to pursue and overwhelm them. The fragrance came from nowhere and filled the stinking sewer with the sweet scent of flowers. Yet as far as she could tell, there was no cause for this strange phenomenon.

"Do you smell that?" she whispered, almost afraid to give voice to her suspicions.

Raphael said nothing but he straightened up his shoulders, as if struck by the presence of something familiar. The rest were equally disturbed by the fragrance but they too held their tongues in check.

"Keep moving," Gabriel instructed. "And don't look back."

He had some experience with this sort of thing, and he knew it was better to ignore the ghostly scent.

"Almost there," he thought to himself. His back was hurting but he forced himself to soldier on.

The eerie smell of jasmine grew stronger but the group jogged along at a steady pace, closing the gap between night and day. In a few strides, they could see the break of dawn at the end of the tunnel. There was already a sliver of light coming through. They were nearly there. They couldn't stop now.

Out of the blue, Raphael had a startling vision. He stumbled and fell to the ground. Looking up, his face became ashen white.

"It's the girl," he groaned. "She's here."

At this, Michael spun around, his soul paralyzed with dread. He drew out his dagger and freed the naked blade from the crucifix. Although determined to face his own demons, he felt his heartbeat drop to a crawl. Sweat began to pour down his face and time itself seemed to tick away in agonizing drips.

In spite of their resolve to keep moving, the rest of the group turned around and gawked in the same direction. It was hard to see beyond the shadows but sure enough, there she was. Pale, alone and foreboding, the child stared unblinking from the far end of the tunnel. It seemed as if she could smell the stench of death from the breathing pores of the living.

Gabriel couldn't be sure, but the shadows around the girl appeared to be advancing like a garden of creeping vines, drawing endless lines of twisted black along the floor.

"Everyone, back up," he cautioned, pushing the team to retreat. But there was really nowhere else to go. They had already backed up into a dead end.

Michael gripped his dagger and prepared to make a stand.

To his surprise, a column of sunlight broke through the ceiling, scattering the shadows in the sewer. Astonished, Chelsea looked up and saw a retractable ladder dangling from the roof. Her face shone with relief when she realized what had happened.

With everyone else distracted by the encroaching danger, Kaz had slipped into the background. He had jumped up, grabbed the sewage ladder, clambered up, pushed opened the exit hatch and scrambled to freedom. As soon as he squeezed through the circular breach, he popped his head back down.

"What're you waiting for? Let's go!" he hollered.

Michael grabbed Chelsea and hoisted her up the narrow steel rungs. Then it was time for the other two priests to make the climb. Finally when everyone else had cleared the sewer, the soldier priest sheathed his dagger and made the leap for freedom.

The last thing he saw as he climbed out of the darkness frightened him more than the creatures he had just battled. The little girl had not moved an inch from her position. She simply stood there watching him. When Michael paused to glance back, she timidly hid her face behind the soft toy in her clutches.

And then slowly, she raised a pale hand and wriggled her fingers at him.

His heart nearly stopped beating.

†

Back in the crypt, charges were laid to clear the entrance. The explosions shattered the barrier and blew a hole through all the rubble. Praetorian Guards poured into the mausoleum and took their places around Marshall Chambers.

The Lumen VP shook his head in disgust. "Took you long enough," he griped.

There was not a whisper of protest from the troops. A small detachment of sergeants descended the stairs, followed by the sinister man in charge of them all.

"Commander," greeted Chambers. "Still alive I see."

The silicone face expressed no resentment to the taunt.

"Thanks to you, my Lord," said the Commander, bowing deeply.

There was a gigantic hole torn up in the middle of his chest. It was impossible for anyone to survive such a ballistic wound, and yet this man was not just alive, he was hardly inconvenienced by the fact that he was missing most of his upper body.

"How amusing, I can see right through you," laughed Chambers. "Which is more than what those meddling priests can say about our plans. Your men didn't fare too badly tonight."

There was a slight murmur among the ranks, which didn't go unnoticed.

"Come now, what is it?" encouraged the Lumen VP. "Don't be afraid to speak up."

There was restrained silence at first, then a nervous cough.

"Sir, if I may," said a Praetorian sergeant. "We lost a lot of good men in this mission tonight. It could've been avoided if we had been given more intel."

"You were on a need to know basis my friend," Chambers replied.

"That's what I mean. We were ambushed because we didn't know we were walking into a trap. There was definitely a need for us to know back there."

The Commander instantly drew his gun and shot the sergeant in the head. The soldier dropped to the floor like a ripe melon and spilled his brains on the boots of his fellow Praetorians.

"Looks like we lost another good man," replied Chambers. "Anyone else needs to know?"

A resounding 'No' came booming back from the troops.

"Good," answered Chambers heartily. He turned to the Commander and said, "Now make sure you don't lose the trail."

"Already on it, sir."

"Remember, don't crowd them. Give them enough room to move. I don't want them to suspect anything. Let them think they're safe, they'll lead us to the prize soon enough."

"Yes, my lord," said the Commander.

Distracted by the hole in his torso, he ripped away the shredded fabrics and glanced down at the state of his hollowed trunk.

"My lord...about this."

Chambers laughed and slipped his hand into the open cavity. Logically, there was nothing to keep this man from falling apart. Even the spine was shattered beyond repair. Yet, he was standing like a young stag in the spring of his youth. It was obvious to every Praetorian Guard that their leader was animated by dark magic, which made him less human and more terrifying than any officer they knew.

"Where is your faith, my friend?" chided Chambers. "I fixed you up before and I can do it again. It's nothing a little sorcery and science can't solve. You'll be as good as new, don't you believe that?"

The Commander had served long enough under Lumen princes to recognize that the question was nothing more than a veiled threat. Without hesitation, the man dropped to his knees in homage.

"I believe, my lord," he pledged loudly.

Immediately, the whole Praetorian assembly genuflected as one, echoing the confession of their gruesome leader.

"We believe and we pledge our obedience," they roared.

"Marvelous," said Chambers, smiling.

Chapter 20

It felt like they had been driving for hours, chewing up the tarmac outside the city limits with nothing but miles of relief under their wheels. The sun was already high in the sky, having left the first light of dawn behind. It was a miracle that they had gotten this far.

Every few miles, Kaz would check his onboard computer to see if they picked up a tail. So far so good, there was nothing behind them but rolling stretches of dirt road. The high towers of the metropolis were receding far into the distance like a bad dream.

But Michael knew that the absence of danger snapping at their heels didn't mean that they had thrown off their Lumen hounds. His tactical instincts told him that they might've gotten away too smoothly, and the thought made him nervous.

"Smoothly?" said Gabriel, his jaw slack with amazement. "We barely made it out alive. If not for the grace of God, we would've been ripped to pieces back there."

"He's right, I don't think they were holding back," added Raphael. Splotches of dried blood were still caked to his face like war paint. "Those demons would've finished us if they could."

"We need to dump this vehicle," Michael grunted, refusing to get into a debate.

"I'm way ahead of you, buddy," said Kaz.

The van pulled into a gas station by the side of the road. There was no one else around except for a single attendant lounging on the front porch of the small convenience store attached to the place. He was an older man with suspicious eyes and a mouth that seemed to be stitched into a frown.

Pulling down his glasses, the man looked up from his magazine with interest, but gave no signs of detaching his derriere from the small wicker chair. Chelsea noticed the wrinkled pages of a girly-mag in his hand.

"Whoa, whoa, whoa," said Gabriel anxiously. "Stay away from the public, remember?"

"It's okay," reassured Kaz. "He's cool."

As if to prove it, he lowered the vehicle's tinted window and made himself vulnerable to the curious gaze of the lone wolf in the grey overalls. There was a glint of recognition. The attendant, who happened to also own the station, spat a mouthful of chewed tobacco onto the floor and scowled.

"He's not exactly happy to see you, is he?" observed Chelsea.

Michael seemed to agree. He cocked the shotgun in his hands as a precaution. Kaz took the barrel and pushed it aside.

"I said he's okay," insisted the Palestinian.

Calmly, he guided the vehicle past the porch and nodded at the cranky owner. The old geezer snorted loudly and shot another squirt of brown goop on the floor. But to the gorgeous woman in the vehicle, he flashed his most inviting smile.

"Charming," said Chelsea, her face sour with disgust.

As they drove by, the owner got up, tucked away his porn and quietly walked into the gas station office. When he was sure that the van had slipped into the safety of the garage at the back, the man lowered the blinds over the store windows and flipped the large 'Open' sign to 'Closed'.

Meanwhile inside the dingy garage, a false panel wall collapsed to engulf the vehicle in the safety of a separate room. Once the fugitives were properly concealed, the panel wall shot back up like an alert sentry resuming his post.

The vehicle rumbled to a stop. Michael was the first to leave the armored ride. His feet barely touched the ground as he rushed to change out of his tactical clothes.

"We've got a couple of minutes to re-supply and move out," he said. "It won't be long before they pick up our trail, we have to keep moving."

In contrast, his two confreres peeled themselves from the vehicle with some effort. In particular, Raphael was breathing hard. His cracked ribs were hugging his lungs like a cheese grater, causing him excruciating pain whenever he moved.

"We'll need to immobilize your chest before you puncture your lungs," said Gabriel, trying to prop up the brutalized doctor.

"Negative, that's only going to make breathing impossible," remarked the victim. "Just get me some painkillers, it'll heal on its own."

"You sure about this?"

"Trust me, it'll work. *Ex opere operato*," Raphael simpered.

Gabriel could appreciate the painful humor coming from a medical doctor who was also a Catholic priest. The Latin phrase referred to the spiritual efficacy of a Sacrament regardless of the merits or disposition of the recipient. In this case, the medical effect of the painkiller was going to be effective regardless of the cooperation of the patient.

"What about you? You don't look so good yourself," observed Raphael.

"Who me? I feel fine," said the stubborn friar, trying not to betray his own agony.

Gabriel knew that morale was everything at this point. He wasn't going to douse the tiny spark of hope they had of escaping the Lumen threat. Grabbing the medical kit, he pulled out a syrette.

"Just until we get you some real help," said the Japanese friar. He stuck the syringe into Raphael and prayed that a small dose of the analgesic was enough to get his friend back to base.

It was true that apart from the Vatican, there were fewer and fewer sovereign countries that the Corporation didn't have a leash on in some way. But not everyone had bowed down to worship the beast. There were still people they could go to, people they could trust. Even so, they had to survive the journey first. And for that, they were going to need a new ride.

"What do you think?" asked Kaz, pulling the greasy tarpaulin off the spanking new wheels. It was a modern luxury sedan.

In any other city, this would stand out like a sore thumb. But here in the financial Mecca of the country, it was the perfect cover to drive around in. No one would notice another bloated car in a city stuffed with luxurious rides.

"Sweet," said Gabriel. "Let me guess…donated by the kind citizens of this great city?"

"Yup, all juiced up and ready to go."

"You just took it from some guy in a five thousand dollar suit, didn't you?" asked Gabriel.

"Well, somebody has to pay for this war," said Kaz. "So why not these clowns? They've been sucking the blood of the workingman for years. Every one of these parasites at City Hall has at least two dozen of these things parked in their garage, paid for by Lumen greed and corruption. They won't care if one's missing, which is why we've got a healthy black market for these rides."

"Viva capitalism," said Gabriel, shaking his head.

Meanwhile, Michael had changed into something less conspicuous. Sporting a crinkled jacket over his civvies, he approached the group and handed a small nylon bag to Gabriel.

"Listen up. There are fresh clothes in there so get changed. The weapons are already in the vehicle. If anyone needs to eat, we've got rations on the go. The packages are self-heating. Just tear off the lid and tuck in. The longer we stay here, the more danger we can expect. Make it quick, we need to hustle."

Gabriel pulled some of the contents from the bag and quipped, "New guns, new car and new clothes. And it's not even my birthday. Really, you shouldn't have. People might think we're dating."

Michael gave him a weary grin. It was the first time he showed any kind of humor since the conflict began, but the tension started to ease from his shoulders a little.

Gabriel knew that the best way to help his brother priest stay ahead in the game was to balance off his grimness with a little light-heartedness. In a combat situation, there was no questioning who was the leader of the pack. The less tense Michael was, the better their chances of making it back alive.

But Chelsea didn't agree. "I'm glad our present situation tickles you," she snapped. "We can all laugh about this when we die."

At once, the tightness around Michael's neck returned immediately, restoring a scowl to his face. Clearly the woman wasn't the only one who was miffed. The former assassin was all ready to share his own vexation with her when Gabriel interrupted.

"Everything will be all right, Chelsea, we just need to put some distance between us and them. Once we get back on the road, we'll be fine," explained the friar.

"Really?" said the brooding damsel, refusing to be coddled. "And where exactly are we going?"

"Somewhere safe."

"Safe?" she repeated harshly, as if the sound of the word offended her ears.

"Lumen Corp owns everything and everyone for miles around, our faces are probably all over the news by now. How safe can we be when presidents and kings don't even take a piss without checking with the Corporation? I'm not going to spend the rest of my life running like an animal, or hiding in sewers and tunnels, knowing that any moment they'll find us and they'll catch us. And I know what that man will do to me…"

Her voice trailed off, choked by the memory of Zadok Martaban framed in a portrait of pain.

"Christ!" she shouted, her nerves getting the better of her.

She tried to stifle her sobs, but the stress of her emotions only shook her like a twisted reed in the wind.

Feeling sorry for her, Raphael who had been languishing in the background suddenly struggled to speak. His voice was labored and intense.

"He won't hurt you Chelsea, we won't let him," said the doctor.

"And how do you know that, because God told you so?" she scoffed. "Or did your clairvoyant powers simply felt like it? Please I beg you, spare me your blind faith. I wouldn't be in this mess if you hadn't dragged me into this living hell to begin with."

She glared at Raphael with indignation, focusing all her tantrums at the poor man. The wounded doctor simply bowed his head and tried to weather the avalanche of spite.

"So you'd rather be a slave to Satan than to wake up and smell the sulfur, is that it?" asked Michael.

"Yes! No. I don't know…"

"And why don't you know?" admonished Michael. "I can tell you want answers but stop and think. You were up to your neck in sin when Raphael found you. Hell was already a part of your world, whether you liked it or not. The greatest lie today is that the devil doesn't exist, or if he does, he's a sickness in your head."

"Don't you think I know that? I know hell exists. I no longer believe because you told me, I've seen it with my own eyes! But this isn't my fight. I don't know anything about the Church, I'm not interested in your revolutions, and I sure as hell am not a Christian anymore. Don't you get it, I don't want to be a part of this!"

Brimming with impatience, Michael drew closer to Chelsea like an ominous cloud. Traces of anger flashed across his eyes. She could see the lines on his face fighting for restraint.

"You think just because you ignore the darkness in your life, the enemy will leave you alone? You're a bigger fool than I thought. There's no neutral ground here, there's no bliss in ignorance. You're in a war. We all are. And Satan doesn't take prisoners. It was a good thing Father Raphael found you when he did. You buried your conscience so deeply in sin, you were half-way down to perdition."

"Don't you judge me, you *don't know* anything about me," Chelsea retorted, extremely upset and agitated.

"I *know* you're scared. You've got a lot of your own stuff to work out before anyone can help you. But if you keep playing the victim, if you want to continue crying instead of fighting back, you're going to play right into their hands. They'll jack up your fears and work you like a puppet, they'll rape the hell out of your spirit. And no one, not even our friendly exorcist here is going to be able to save you from that kind of shit."

Furious at being talked down to, the feisty brunette tried to stomp off but Michael grabbed her by the wrist and pulled her back.

"Let me go!" Chelsea hissed like a viper.

"You want to go? The door's that way, you can crawl back to your glitzy nest and take your chances with whatever's coming for you," said Michael gruffly. "But if you want to live, I suggest you get in the frickin' car!"

"And I suggest you do it now," said Kaz, tapping his watch. "Take your quarrel on the road, we have to move."

Gabriel and Raphael donned their new jackets, dropping enough of the old look to avoid suspicion. Chelsea however was still rooted to the ground with angst, frozen like an ice queen.

"Whether you stand or fall, it's up to you," Michael rebuked her. "No one can force you to do the right thing, not even God."

She turned her head and caught Raphael's eye. The doctor looked like he was in a world of pain, but he lifted his face and nodded encouragingly to her.

"We have to go, Chelsea," muttered Gabriel, pulling out a dark top and jeans from the bag.

The irate woman said nothing. But she grabbed the clothes from the young friar and ducked into the car, slamming the door behind her. The silence was almost a relief.

Kaz shook his head wistfully and mumbled to the men, "Good luck."

"What about you?" asked Michael. "What's the plan?"

"I'm headed back into town."

"You can't be serious. It's ground zero back there," said Gabriel.

"Don't worry about it, Gabriel san. For the next few days, they'll be looking for the renegade priests who took off with their prize catch, not just *any* old rebel. No one gets under the skin of the Corporation more than the Catholic Church. Something tells me they'll want you guys bad. And believe me when I say this is my turf. I've made some arrangements. I'm safer back in own hood. They won't find me if I don't want them to."

"You sure?"

The arms dealer nodded with a roguish grin. "Besides, I've got my own war to fight in this city. Half the town is drenched in night, partying on without realizing that each time, the shadows grow a little darker, the nights last a little longer. Meanwhile the other half goes through their day like frickin' moles with no memory of daylight, cursing the sun for trying to warm their frozen hearts."

"And in the absence of God's light, someone needs to keep the 'Lumen sparks' from shining too brightly," continued Gabriel.

"You know it, brother," replied Kaz.

"Where's your transport, how're you getting out of here?" enquired Michael.

Kaz walked over to a large object and pulled the sheets off the mean machine. "I brought my own," he said, proudly displaying the beast of a motorcycle.

Michael looked down at the engineered bike and smiled. He knew that it was probably fitted with more weapons than they had with them in the car. He also knew that his friend had risked great personal danger to help them. For anyone either stupid or brave enough to challenge the Corporation, the shadows of death always trailed close behind.

"Well if we don't meet again in this world..." he said, extending his hand.

"...We'll meet in paradise," answered Kaz, finishing his sentence for him.

"As-Salamu Alaykum, my friend," he added, taking Michael's hand.

"And may God let his face shine upon you," answered the warrior priest.

Kaz turned to Gabriel and the Japanese friar gripped his sword and bowed gratefully.

"Arigato gozaimasu," he said. "We could never have made it without you."

Kaz laughed off the compliment and saddled his bike.

"Don't worry about it," he replied, throttling the beast into a rumbling roar. "It's always a pleasure to kick ass with *The Archangels*."

†

Outside the reinforced steel and concrete walls of the hidden safe house, not a soul was stirring. A couple of cars had zipped by uneventfully, dissuaded from pulling in by the large 'Closed' sign fronting the empty station. The old attendant was nowhere to be seen. The only mark of life came from a large black raven perched on a telephone pole, squawking periodically like a shrill alarm, calling out to a land already deep in the slumber of sin.

From high above its perch, the bird witnessed a car pull out from the station and rev down the road. A few seconds later, a lone rider on a modified Ducati sped away in the opposite direction.

The station owner peered through the blinds in his office, watching both vehicles disappear into the distance. But there was something else that was drawing his attention. The raven across the road was getting noisier and flapping its wings like it was being boiled alive.

He had noticed the large bird earlier in the day. It was not unusual for ravens to nest in this part of town. Apart from the racket they made, there was nothing really bizarre about these flying pests. Grumbling, he ignored the rumpus and went back to counting his money. There were few things he enjoyed more in life, and stroking a heavy wad of new greenbacks was definitely one of them.

The man hated the Lumen Corporation, but he didn't care too much for the religious nuts either. As long as the Palestinian kept greasing his palm with the big bucks, there was no reason not to put his back behind the Resistance. Like it or not, safe houses were expensive to maintain, and his loyalty was even more so. People ought to get rich for taking these kinds of risks, so why not him?

"Damn it!" he cursed.

The screeching had made him lose count of his bankroll. He should do something about that stupid bird. He threw the wad of cash on the table and soaked his grouchiness in a steaming cup of black coffee.

But before he could take a sip, something curious happened. The squawking stopped completely and a thick silence descended on the station. The old man put down his coffee and watched in consternation as the liquid drained away on its own, leaving the porcelain cup dry as an open tomb.

Then slowly, he began to hear it again. The terrible clamor

resumed, only this time it was much louder. Cawing and screeching, the noise built up until it sounded like the explosive whine of a jet turbine blowing away all normality.

The owner cautiously reached for the window and pulled the blinds apart. The raven was still there, hugging the pole like a creepy shadow, but this time it was not alone. A great flock of black feathers had surrounded the place, prompting an unmistakable stench of evil in the air.

Within seconds, a thousand angry beaks and talons had besieged the gas station. In all his years working this route, the craggy attendant had never seen an infestation that nearly blocked out the sun. He quickly dropped the blinds and sat back in dismay.

This was bad, real bad. He knew ravens don't gather in these numbers. This was something else, something diabolical and strange. And to make matters worse, he was left all alone to deal with it.

"Damn it," he cursed and spat on the floor.

Chapter 21

The sound of her wooden beads rustled softly in her hands, carried along gently by the cadence of Pater Nosters and Ave Marias that floated up to heaven. The rosary had always been her favorite prayer from young, giving her comfort whenever her heart seemed burdened by waves of worry and fear.

She was contemplating the divine mysteries woven into this prayer, meditating on the gospel scenes associated with the life of Christ. To the uninitiated, the rosary was nothing more than a monotonous, repetitive chain of silly mantras, often times ridiculed and condemned as superstitious and vain. But Teresa knew better. She was neither too naïve nor too sophisticated to recognize that this string of humble prayers had the power to shackle the forces of evil.

Her maternal heart sighed deeply as only a woman could at a time like this. Even though there was no word from Gabriel, she was convinced they had survived the night. Call it a mother's intuition, but her spiritual son was still alive. She could sense it in her soul, which had been prostrated before God since her nephew left their home to rendezvous with Michael the evening before. The sun had long risen in the sky, but she knew that the night had not yet ended. And she was determined to arm her boys with the protection of her prayers.

There was a gentle, almost apologetic knock on the door. Hiroshi stood in the doorway, carrying a beautiful bento box and a bowl of miso soup on a tray.

"Come, you must keep up your strength. I made your favorite tempura. Stop awhile and eat," insisted the old gentleman. "God knows you need a break."

Teresa did not seem to notice her husband at first. Her eyes were still transfixed on the crucifix standing upon the small family altar before her. The entire structure, no bigger than the size of a small television set, was collapsible and fitted perfectly into the hidden recess of the wall. It was not an exaggerated precaution. Hiroshi had designed a swivel platform to quickly hide the religious icons from view when necessary. In these dangerous times, piety without prudence was a sure ticket to painful oblivion. And the old man would never forgive himself if something happened to his wife.

"Please dear, take something. You haven't eaten anything since yesterday," said Hiroshi, pleading with concern.

Teresa reluctantly put down her beads and turned gratefully to her husband. She had no appetite, but the lines of worry on the face of this man who had been her soul mate for more than half her life, convinced her to leave aside her stubbornness.

"I'm sorry love, I'm such a burden to you sometimes," said Teresa.

"How can you say that, you silly woman," he huffed, pretending to be outraged. "You're my joy and my ladder to heaven."

"Is that why you step all over me?" she said with a playful glint in her eye.

"I knew you were going to say that."

"Am I that predictable?"

"Adorably so!"

He leaned over and kissed her loudly on the cheek, making a rude puckering noise. In spite of herself, she giggled like a little girl. For over fifty years, through every crisis and sadness, the weight of her heart had always been lifted by the strength of this man's great goodness and love.

"All right, tuck in before it gets cold," said Hiroshi.

Tenderly, he knelt beside her and laid out the dishes on the tatami mat, taking care to serve her with attention. In return, she accepted the luscious meal with gratitude, slurping up the handmade noodles and the crispy morsels of fried vegetables and seafood.

"Oishi," she remarked, nodding appreciatively.

The old man broke into a sheepish grin, ecstatic to hear his wife enjoying herself so. For the first time all morning he sat back with some relief, even though his eyes betrayed the lack of sleep and anxiety that tormented him through the night.

Teresa knew that her husband had fought valiantly to hide his own worries from her. But a lifetime of being together had made him transparent as a child in her presence.

"Don't worry Hiro, I'm sure they're all right," she said.

Hiroshi looked down and shrugged his shoulders. "How do we know that?" he sighed to himself. "Sometimes it makes me mad. It isn't just our boy. It's Michael as well. Why do they feel they have to save everybody?"

"Would you rather they leave their friends to die?"

"Of course not, I don't want that at all," said Hiroshi. "But when there's little hope of success and you're going to end up losing your life, what's the point of running into the jaws of death when you know it's suicidal?"

"We don't know that," said Teresa, trying to calm her husband down.

"But we do. And so should Gabriel! I taught him always to be careful, to not gamble away his life, to run and fight another day when things get too hairy. After what the boy has been through with his parents, you'd think he'd listen just once."

"He's not a boy anymore," Teresa reminded her husband. "He's a man. And he's a priest and a soldier for Christ. And yes, you've trained him well. You have to trust him now to find his own way."

Hiroshi shook his head in frustration.

"And what way is that, getting himself killed? How is that going to help anyone? If you ask me, he's just stubborn like his father," he grumbled.

Teresa knew the agony behind those words. Gabriel meant everything to Hiroshi, not just because the old man loved him with all his heart, but also because he promised his late brother to care for his only surviving son. And now against his uncle's better judgment, Gabriel had flung himself into a deathtrap, in complete disobedience to his guardian.

The elderly woman looked at her husband and saw the hurt etched across his face. Hiroshi would not reveal the brokenness of his spirit, but his brows were creased with concern and his shoulders slumped in sorrow. She reached out and took one of his hands in her own.

"It's always easier when it's somebody else's child, isn't it?"

Hiroshi said nothing. He ran his hand over his face and tried to rub the tiredness from his eyes, groaning at the very thought that his nephew might not have survived the night.

"Do you recall what he once said?" she asked.

"Who?"

"Gabriel! He must've been about sixteen or seventeen at the time. He was upset that we scolded him for trying to be a witness in school. He got into a fight with his classmates for talking openly about God, and you told him off. I never forgot the look in his eyes.

201

He said he wanted to live his life fully, that if he always tried to save himself, he wouldn't be living, he would just be avoiding death. And that, he said, was as good as being dead."

"Yeah I remember," said Hiroshi, snorting. "Dumb kid, always had to be a hero."

"But that's just what the world needs today," remarked Teresa. "Everyone's politically correct, nobody wants to be called a fanatic. As a result, a whole generation of dead souls have grown up, unable to call sin by its name, unable to tell right from wrong."

"If you asked them, they'll tell you it's all relative," said Hiroshi. "There're no moral absolutes anymore. Which is why so many people can do all the wrong things and tell themselves it's right."

"Then you know why your nephew must do what he can. There's a flood of wickedness and people are being swept away. If we don't cling to the light and stand our ground, there won't be anything left to fight for."

Calmly, Teresa put aside her lunch. Much of her meal had remained uneaten in the bento box. She reclaimed her rosary from the altar and wrapped her fingers around the tiny beads. They were very old, a keepsake from her side of the family, worn and polished over the years with familiarity and prayer.

"The enemy has infected the world these last decades with so much filth that the light of God is all but extinguished. How much more a priest of God, consecrated to serve his people and to battle evil, should not forsake his post, even if that path leads him to be crucified. We have enough cowards among Christians, among priests who are afraid to speak the truth, who worship the golden calf of popular culture than the Lamb of God. Do we not need heroes now more than ever?"

When Hiroshi didn't reply, she continued.

"Do you remember over thirty years ago when the popes warned of a new intolerance in society, one that attacked religious freedom in the name of non-discrimination?"

"I remember we couldn't display crucifixes in our schools, and Catholic hospitals were required to perform abortions," her husband replied. "Even our orphanages were ordered to place our children for adoption by people who viciously attacked Christian teachings on love and marriage. On the whole, the Church was being forced by law to change her beliefs on everything."

"To put it plainly, we were muzzled," said Teresa. "The Church couldn't live out her mission, we couldn't confess our faith in public anymore. In the name of non-discrimination, the law persecuted Christians and robbed us of any means to defend our faith, forcing us to accept beliefs and agendas that were clearly unfair to us."

"True, there's freedom and tolerance for everyone except those who believe in the eternity of God's word," said Hiroshi. "But let's be honest, not all of the attacks came from outside, much of it came from inside the Church as well."

The old man abruptly stood up and paced the room, his arms folded tightly across his chest. Teresa knew what her husband was thinking. She saw his cheek tremble ever so slightly, as if the images swirling in his mind caused him great distress.

"There're so few priests and bishops who keep the apostolic faith today, who're loyal to Holy Mother Church. Many have betrayed our Lord for thirty pieces of Lumen silver," he snorted.

"And then, there are those who give themselves totally over to evil; the wolves and perverts who prowl among our flock, masquerading as shepherds when their souls have been completely eaten up by sin. I often asked myself how they managed to get through the seminaries without anyone noticing? Were their formators stupid or blind? Or were they equally guilty of sleeping with the enemy?"

Something caught Hiroshi's attention and he stopped pacing. His voice trailed off and his thoughts flitted back into the distant past, chasing a memory of anger and suffering. As a young boy, he had heard the stories often enough. But when he became old enough to join the Resistance, reality came crashing through his door late one night, shattering whatever doubts left in his mind.

He remembered the incident well.

It was way past midnight. He watched his father stumble in from the darkened streets, clasping a wounded man in his arms. Blood dripped all over the carpet as the elderly stranger collapsed in their living room, unable to hang on much longer.

Hiroshi was still in shock when his father yelled for a medical kit. Roused from his stupor, the teenager leapt into action and tried to stabilize the victim. But there was no stopping this hemorrhage. Blood continued to gush from his body. The end was near, the stranger knew as much. Even though there was no priest in the house, the man began to unload his wounded heart with all the fervor of a confession.

In that moment, the young Toshigawa learned that the stranger himself was an elderly priest whom his father had saved from the hands of unknown assassins. Faced with the prospect of eternal judgment, the old cleric revealed that his vocation was born out of rivalry, fueled by the strong anti-communist stance of the Catholic Church beginning in the late 1940s, which pitted the successors of St. Peter against the successors of Stalin for the dignity of the human person.

For the next four decades, the Kremlin and the popes were locked in a struggle for religious freedom and moral supremacy. And despite its red army, secret police and brutal executions, the powerful Soviet Sickle was slowly losing ground to the Keys of the Fisherman, which had already unlocked a chain of cosmic events that in time, would free the atheistic state to become a kingdom of faith.

Enraged, the enemies of religion countered with conspiracy and deception. If the Red Dragon couldn't destroy the Church from without, they would try to devour her from within. First by corrupting her message, then by confusing her truths with compromise, and finally, by toppling her authority with scandal.

Rattling in his death throes, the stranger confessed to being a sleeper cell, one of many Soviet agents who were implanted into seminaries and chanceries in the fifties, trained to infiltrate the highest corridors of power within the Church for the destruction of the Church. But as it turned out, years of living among the enemy had awakened his soul to the movements of grace, and the Communist agent who pretended to be a priest, became a true priest who no longer wanted to pretend.

The Party leaders were furious. By then, he knew too much to be allowed to live. The body of evidence in this traitor had to be eliminated. The result was written in blood on the carpet floor.

"It's true that the devil has always planted weeds in the garden of God," said Teresa. "But are you saying that the problems we had in the past; those liberals and perverts who did their utmost to scandalize the faithful, that they were mostly planted by enemies of the Church?"

"No, I'm sure we were responsible for many of those bad seeds ourselves. God alone knows how many priests and theologians soiled the waters of our baptism back then. Entrusted to shepherd the people in His place, they chose instead to pasture themselves on their sheep."

The old man shook his head in disgust. He was a man of principles, gruffly honest to the point of rudeness in his integrity. And it angered him that scores of dissidents and liberals continued to fester in the Church like an ulcer when they no longer professed any belief in the faith.

"You'd think they'd have the honesty to just leave if they no longer believe, but instead they stay to infect the Church like a plague, tearing the flock apart with calumnies and lies. And the whole time, they act like they're saving the Church. I don't doubt there are many priests and religious in hell for the horrors they've committed against the people of God."

Teresa knew that her husband was not exaggerating. Such betrayals of sacred truths were too common back then. Too many bishops in the past neglected their sacred duties and became politicians and managers, filling the ranks of the priesthood with 'progressive' prophets of the new age instead of orthodox faithful men, who were often turned away for being *too* Catholic. Now the apostolic faith had all but vanished from the earth, crushed by the power of Lumen Corp.

"Paul VI was right when he said that the smoke of Satan had entered the temple of God through some crack in the wall," said Hiroshi, quoting the besieged pope of the last great Vatican Council.

At the time, the pope had lamented that the Father of Lies had found his way into the Church. Disheartened, the old Japanese man heaved another big sigh.

"Maybe *it is* true. Maybe forces hostile to the Church really did plant those bad seeds," he groaned. "Although it's not the powers of this world that I worry about."

He knew that without God, the ancient enemy would seduce the sons of men easily enough. Indeed, the very nature of seduction required the sacrifice of reason. It was true then at the Garden of Eden, it was true now. In order to taste the forbidden fruits, the nobility of divine laws had to be broken on the altar of human pride, something many people were willing to do for a chance to play God.

"You're right, those weeds were planted by a fallen angel," answered his wife. "Satan is intent on destroying the priesthood with scandal. First he sows doubt in the Church, then he sows disgust for her priests, and finally he sows hatred for the faith, knowing that souls who're disillusioned and hurt by sinful clergy will leave the sanctuary of God and be vulnerable to the real wolves that lie in wait."

Her husband nodded. "Strike the shepherd and the sheep will scatter," he mumbled.

"Then you should know why your nephew is risking his life to do what's right, and not just him but every holy priest in the Resistance who is fighting the good fight. Our world needs heroes more than ever. The enemy will not rest until he disarms and discredits every true servant of God. He wants us to stop believing in heroes. He knows that when that happens, the heroes inside us die. Clearly we need the witness of saints…"

"Even when they run the risk of being martyrs?" interrupted Hiroshi. "How many more good priests must we lose? The people of God are already suffering a drought of ministers. If this goes on, who will continue to offer the sacraments? We'll no longer have the power of the Eucharist, how then can the Church survive?"

The Japanese woman tried to appease her husband. Tenderly, she took his hand and made him sit beside her on the mat.

"Even so my love, ours is a bold mission," Teresa replied. "Fraught with danger at every turn. Every part we play is crucial, no matter how small. With all that the Church has suffered, sometimes it feels like it's impossible for us to win this war. But we stay and fight because we know that things would be a lot worse if we didn't."

"The bulk of humanity couldn't care less if we lay down and died," said Hiroshi. "They would rather demonize the Church. They think that by condemning the light, they can convince themselves that they're not living in the dark."

"Well, the vultures are always the first to smell the carrion. But you know what Gabriel told me? He said that when things are darkest, that's when you try and remember what makes it worth fighting for."

"He said that?" asked Hiroshi.

"He said that," Teresa assured him. "He also told me that he'd always be our nephew. But first and foremost, he was a priest and a son of God. Lives were at stake. In choosing to go on that mission, it didn't mean that he loved us any less, only that he loved God all the more. It hurt him deeply that you didn't understand that."

Hiroshi was castigated. The words tore into his heart and broke down the walls of his defenses like a battering ram. Perhaps it was true that he was over-protective. He was afraid for Gabriel, afraid for his safety and life, afraid of what it would mean for the Resistance if they lost another champion. And all that fear had somehow created a vortex of anxiety in his soul, sucking away every bit of hope.

He knew he had to fight against the temptation to despair. It was making him an obstacle to divine grace. He had no right to keep this servant of Christ all to himself, no matter the natural bonds that bound them together. God was asking him even now to make a leap of faith, to lay this young man on the cross.

"You taught him well, Hiro. Perhaps it's time you learn from him as well," urged Teresa. "Let go. And let God take over."

Hiroshi looked up at the altar, resting the weight of his gaze upon the suffering figure of Christ on the cross. *For God so loved the world that he gave his only begotten son.* The scripture passage leapt out at him.

For a moment he felt his spirit falter, as if the voices of fear were conspiring to reclaim his heart. But slowly, the warmth of divine love began to flood his soul, awakening the memory of a warrior who had weathered too many storms, fought too many battles against evil in his youth to turn back now in his old age.

Without warning, the shuttered windows in the room burst opened with violence. A huge gust of cold wind blew into the room and rustled all the papers and drapes, throwing everything into disarray. Things started to fall over. Lights began to flicker nervously. In the midst of all this turmoil, Teresa calmly got up and latched the windows.

The tumult settled down.

"Be not afraid," he whispered aloud, more to himself than to his wife. "Be not afraid." Just saying those words seemed to give him fresh courage.

"You're right, we need to be led by God to carry out his will every day, even when it doesn't correspond to our plans," said Hiroshi. "We need...*I need*...to trust in his providence."

He had no way of knowing if Gabriel was all right, but the least he could do was to arm this soldier of Christ with the power of faith, trusting that God would never abandon his own.

"We stop believing in heroes and the heroes inside us die," Teresa reminded him.

Hiroshi listened quietly, his eyes fixed on the small crucifix on the altar. The suffocating vines that bound his heart with fear had already begun wilting before the fire of God's love. He began to breathe more easily.

"Let's pray for our heroes then," said the old man abruptly. "All of them."

Pulling out his rosary beads, he rose to his knees before the altar and began.

"We'll continue with the Glorious mystery; the Resurrection of Christ. I'll lead," he said, "Our Father who art in heaven, hallowed be thy name..."

"Thy kingdom come, thy will be done," continued his wife.

✝

No one had said a word in the last two hours. The car was rolling along at a steady pace, carrying its bruised and tired passengers to the safety of a location that was still many miles away.

"I need to pee," alerted Chelsea.

"Hold it," said Michael, keeping his foot on the gas.

"You try holding it!"

"Then use this!"

He tossed a plastic bag into the back seat.

"You're about as subtle as a kick in the groin, you know that?" Chelsea complained.

"There's a roadside diner not too far from here," informed Gabriel. "We can stop there for a bit."

"You want to take the risk?" asked Michael.

"Trust God to protect us. We're far enough from the city, we can afford to make a short stop."

"Don't push your luck, the Corporation has a long arm and we still have some ways to go."

"You've been driving for hours, you need a break as well."

"We all do..." interrupted Chelsea.

"Let's make a quick stop, get some coffee and takeaways," Gabriel said to Michael. "I know you think your rations are wonderful but they taste like crap. And besides, the lady needs to pee."

He turned around and slipped Chelsea a friendly wink, letting her know he was on her side.

"You're not how I imagined a priest to be," said Chelsea.

"Why? Am I too good looking?" enquired Gabriel.

She tried not to laugh but couldn't hold back a giggle.

"Don't sweat it. Priests and religious who're loyal to the Church are rarely alive these days. We're an endangered species. You're lucky

208

you've got the attention of three live ones. It's like winning the lottery, except you get no money and we chastise you about loose living."

Chelsea raised an eyebrow and smirked. "Funny, I didn't think an exorcist would have a sense of humor," she commented.

"You kidding? Exorcists have to climb into the darkest pits of despair to free a soul from possession. And believe me, some of these souls don't even want to be freed. It's imperative that we have a sense of humor. I take myself too seriously and I lose my marbles in no time."

The young woman kept quiet for a while, suddenly becoming thoughtful. She ran her manicured fingers through her luscious hair, brushing it back from a stunning face that was slightly tinged with worry.

"I know you took a while to expel that thing inside of me," she muttered, sounding a little disheartened. "Maybe deep down, I didn't want to be free…"

Despite his throbbing back, Gabriel twisted around to look at Chelsea. He had something to say, and he wanted to make sure she could see his face when he said it.

"It's true that the longer a demon possesses someone, the harder it will fight to stay on. But in your case, I doubt you were carrying the evil for more than three or four weeks. It took me awhile because I had to uncover the number of spirits and their names, something the demons themselves fight strongly to resist."

"Why is that?" asked the woman.

"Every bit of truth they reveal loosens their grip on the possessed, but knowing their names and numbers gives the exorcist greater power over them. Don't worry, of course you wanted to be free…"

She looked up and saw the calm assurance in his eyes.

"I was able to do my part because you did yours," Gabriel reminded her. "We won because you fought back, don't ever forget that."

He turned around and slumped back into the front seat, keeping his eyes on the road. Chelsea continued to gaze out the window, mulling her thoughts over the passing fields.

Far ahead, something caught her attention, sparkling like gold atop the ruins of a building. As the object drew closer, she realized it was an old brass cross left over from the public pillage of monasteries and convents that raged across the country at one time.

The sight made her feel sad.

All her life, she had joined her voice to those who had pissed on the grave of religion. God was supposed to be dead, consigned to the obituaries of the major newspapers. Never in her wildest dreams did she expect him to make a comeback in her life. Since then, everything had become complicated. She had seen too much to retreat into disbelief, but she understood too little to go forward in faith. How in heaven's name did she get herself into this mess?

"Sometimes, all it takes is one bad day to take away all the good days," she thought to herself, "And I've had way too many bad days."

She glanced briefly at the three priests in the car. One was hunkered down beside her, fast asleep. The other two were seated upfront like cowboys driving a stagecoach. They were all so different, these men, and yet somehow the same. Different outfits cut from the same cloth, professing the same creed. Confident, unwavering and almost brutal in their convictions, their loyalty to God and to each other was exceptional, maybe even supernatural.

In contrast, Chelsea always felt more like a creature of accident than a child of destiny, tossed about like driftwood on the sea of life. Swept away by the seductions of the world, she had quickly abandoned every port of faith. And now that she was trying to swim back to shore, the sharks were circling in for the kill. She could scream and thrash in the waters or she could grab the hand that was reaching out to her. To leave the shadows, she knew she had to tread into the light. But after a lifetime of doubt, how does one begin a journey of faith?

Chelsea was still staring out the window when the answer came rushing by in a broken billboard. ONE STEP AT A TIME said the slogan in big bold letters, pitching a dance school that had probably long vanished from the looks of the ragged advertising.

She smiled wryly to herself. She never pegged God as having a sense of humor. Just then, the wrinkled mass of clothes beside her shifted with a groan.

"Hey, you okay?" she asked.

When Raphael didn't respond, she nudged him on the shoulder. He leaned back and the hoodie covering his head fell slightly from his face.

"Doc, you okay?" she asked again.

When the injured man didn't answer, Michael stole a quick glance in the rear-view mirror.

"How much of that stuff did you give him?" he quizzed Gabriel.

"Just the one syrette," exclaimed the friar. "I'm sure the dosage was right."

"I think you better get back there!"

The car screeched to a stop in the middle of the road and Gabriel jumped out. He squeezed into the back seat and tried to prop up his friend. By then, Raphael was slipping in and out of consciousness.

"Come on, help me lift him up," he said to Chelsea. The woman held the doctor and tried to steady him so he wouldn't fall over.

"What's wrong with him," she asked, frightened by the sudden crisis.

The Japanese friar had no idea. But he hoped that his confrere wasn't bleeding from the inside. They couldn't risk going to a hospital or the Corporation would zero in on them like a missile. At the same time, an internal hemorrhage at that point would surely be fatal, considering that the safest help was still some distance away. Needing a closer look, he grabbed the hood and pulled it back from Raphael's face.

"Oh my God," cried Chelsea in disbelief.

The victim's face was shorn of color, as if something coursing through his veins had pinched the blood from his skin.

"What is it?" demanded Michael.

"I'm not sure," Gabriel replied nervously.

Despite his experiences with the occult, he had never seen anything like this before. It left him bewildered. The skin below the doctor's jaw line was a broken web of blood vessels, cascading into twisted lines of blue and purple. The pupils were extremely dilated, as if a cruel nightmare was stalking his mind.

He felt the carotid artery on Raphael's neck. The pulse was still strong, but it was racing like a man chased by the hounds of terror. With every pounding of the heart, the victim appeared to be getting worse. A cluster of swollen veins emerged from under his collar, splintering into five tracks of nasty bruises that climbed up his neck.

Gabriel started to fear for his friend. Slowly, he noticed something else. The bluish markings surrounding Raphael's neck began to shift like a mist.

"Do you see that?" asked Chelsea, too stupefied to describe what she saw.

Uncertain if his eyes were playing tricks on him, Gabriel took a closer look. Yet there it was, clutching his confrere by the throat - the unmistakable imprint of a ghostly hand.

Suddenly, the exorcist knew what it was.

Chapter 22

The door banged open and nearly shattered its wooden frame. Out stepped the old geezer in the greasy overalls, the wooden porch creaking under his nervous weight.

Cautiously, the station owner raised the rifle in his hands. He scanned the roads in front of his establishment and was surprised that the huge flock of ravens had disappeared from view. The street was as dry and empty as the bottle of scotch in his drawer. Nothing seemed to be amiss.

The only daunting thing he felt was the weight of the gun; a monstrous12-gauge shotgun left behind by the Palestinian. That scoundrel was always bugging him to stock up on rounds. He was glad he listened. The bandolier of slugs around his chest made him feel more secure about going out there.

He squinted and shifted, but there was nothing around the station as far as he could tell. The birds had somehow disappeared without a trace, not that he was disappointed. In fact, he was plenty relieved not to have to shoot his way out of a situation. He lowered his gun and lit a cigarette.

Out of the blue, a loud squawk behind him made him jump. He spun around and the lighted fag fell out of his opened mouth, tumbling into the dirt.

"Damn turkey!" he cursed, startled to see a large raven hopping on the floor before him. He thought they had all flown away.

Catching his breath, he eyeballed the lonely bird. It wasn't doing much except squawking like a turntable with a broken needle. The noise irritated the living daylights out of him.

"Shut up!" cried the old man. He pulled the trigger and the raven burst into a ball of flames. The destruction was so complete, there weren't any feathers left to pick up.

Suddenly, it was all very quiet again, just the way he liked it. Satisfied, he grunted and blew a bunch of snot on the ground, wiping his nose with the back of his hand. He scanned the roads one last time before deciding to step back into the office.

As soon as the door was pulled opened, a gust of wind blew him inside, sending the geezer crashing to the floor in a spill. He picked himself up and covered his ears.

The noise inside the office was deafening. Thousands of screeching ravens erupted in a crescendo of chaos, swelling into a hurricane of blackness that covered every inch of the white walls. The frightened owner quickly recovered his rifle and climbed to his feet. It looked like the entire swarm of maddening ravens had flocked into his tiny station.

Squadrons of beady eyes were scrutinizing his every move, and every sharp talon in the room was clawing with destruction. The black plague was everywhere.

Seized with fear, the man began pumping rounds at the birds, scattering the scourge of feathers in different directions. Here and there, some fell like baleful angels from the sky. Most however continued to harass the old man. There were just too many to kill.

Beaks and claws and the flapping malice of a thousand ravens tore into him. His overalls shredded, his face and hands ripped and bloody, the old man quickly scampered like a country mouse into the safety of a storeroom at the back. He slammed the door shut and bolted it down. There was no other way out. He was entirely locked in, but he was safe for the moment. A glass portal on the door allowed him to see the destruction on the outside. He was still breathing hard, his flustered breath clouding up the window when he noticed something else begin to happen.

The cloud of ravens started to thicken at its core, drawn together like iron shavings to a magnet. Something was brewing in the midst of that swarm, blending the birds in a vortex of malice until every last feather in the gas station congealed into the ominous figure of a dark man.

He was richly dressed in a black three-piece suit, with diamond rings on his pale fingers and jewelry around his neck. Shading his face was a black fedora that made him look like a mobster from hell.

"Damn it," the old man cursed and chucked his cell phone aside.

He had been trying to contact the Palestinian to no avail. The phone's batteries were totally drained, despite the fact that it was fully charged only thirty minutes ago. He peeked out the portal again. The office was no longer housing an aviary of madness. Instead of demon birds, something creepy in an expensive suit was standing between him and the exit.

He grabbed the slugs from his bandolier and reloaded. If he could dash out guns blazing, he might be able to skirt the creature and make it to the safe house next door. The hidden entrance was just a few feet away. He muttered a quick prayer under his breath. "Here goes nothing," he thought.

As he touched the handle, the entire door ripped opened like a sheet of paper and flew aside, nearly dragging the old man with it. He stumbled to his knees and looked up, expecting the worse. But there was no movement from the demon in the suit. He hadn't so much as twitched.

Quickly the owner scrambled to his feet and blasted a few rounds in the general direction of the creature. He ran along the wall, clumsily knocking over shelves and equipment. As he hobbled passed a full-length mirror, he caught sight of a reflection that made him stumble. He did a double take, thinking he had seen the impossible. But there was nothing behind him except the cold stirrings of fear.

Yet he could smell the scent of a woman, her powerful pheromones awakening his dormant appetites. He staggered with mounting desire, his eyes darting around like a teenager on heat. In the confusion, something soft and velvety lashed around his ankle and yanked him into the air, dangling the poor man like a trapped animal. Before his mind could decipher what happened, his senses were already buzzing with an intoxication he hadn't felt for quite sometime. He wasn't all that young but his heart was leaping like a wild stallion, consumed by a raging fire of lust that devoured his body. The passion was so strong that it felt like his loins would burst into flames.

He knew this wasn't natural. This couldn't be real. The stench of sulfur was all around. Cursing, he fired randomly, hoping to clip whatever it was that had turned his world upside down. The barrel chugged away, spewing lead in every direction. It was hard to see clearly while swinging like a pendulum, but he could hear the rounds shatter everything in their path…everything except the intended target.

Without any warning, the coil around his ankle tightened and his body flew across the room. His mouth kissed the concrete floor and split opened, knocking the concupiscence from his hijacked libido.

"Geezuz!" he cried out, his teeth on the deck, blood dripping down his chin.

Unfortunately, there was nothing to keep the apparition at bay.

The voluptuous vixen approached, her long shapely legs eating up the floor with a poise that sent the unchaste fire storming back into his heart.

He stared at the creature. Her luscious hair cascaded over her naked body, sweeping around her flawless bosom like a living thing. Her breasts, her hips, her sensuous curves all seemed to whisper his name, reeling him in like a drunken wretch. He tried to resist but he couldn't. His will was paralyzed with craving. She was more than perfect; she was divine. And then slowly he noticed her eyes - two empty pools of pale white that sucked in all the light in the room. The sudden recall struck him like a rock. This was no Goddess. This was a succubus. Yet try as he might, he couldn't tear himself away from the femme fatale. His spirit was willing but his flesh was weak. He knew he would be damned if he gave in to the vision. With the few teeth he had left, the old man bit down on his lip and felt the searing pain of freedom cut through his brain. For a few seconds the spell was broken, ripped apart by the outpouring of fresh blood.

He grabbed his rifle and let loose a barrage of fire. The naked entity took the full impact of the brutal blasts without even flinching, her glossy red locks shielding her like a protective cape, swatting away the bullets like flies.

Undaunted, the frantic man grabbed a vial of holy water from his pocket. The Palestinian had passed it on to him from one of the priests. He flung the contents at the female form and she retreated in rage. The water splashed harmlessly onto the floor and missed the angry specter by a foot. Swallowing his fear, the old geezer felt his mouth go dry. All he had managed to do was piss off the lurid thing even more. He knew the payback was going to hurt…

And he was right.

A surge of smoldering cracks began to peel open her heaving bosom, causing blood to trickle out of the succubus like molten lava. Her comely breasts split apart like rancid melons reeking of maggots and decay. Burning fissures erupted all over her body, melting away her sensuous curves and stripping away the skin to expose the actual creature inside.

Without question, the old man was terrified. He gasped in horror at the rotting corpse in all her putrid reality. All that he had found titillating before, now struck him with immense disgust, causing him to retch like a poisoned dog. Indeed, the demon of impurity stood revealed as she truly was.

Running her wasted fingers through her hair, the lustful nymph pulled out clumps of her scarlet mane. These fell to the ground and slithered like a bed of venomous snakes.

"Come to me, my love," breathed the unclean spirit. She opened her arms wide to embrace him.

Alarmed, the old man kicked and floundered, striking at the den of serpents that swirled around his feet. When he tried to crawl to safety, a tall black figure grabbed him brusquely by the neck and pulled him up.

Suddenly he was face to face with the opulent demon in the fedora, except there was no face that he could actually see.

Beneath the wide brim of the black hat was an empty space where a visage should've been. There were no discernible features, no contours of flesh, just a fearsome void that stared back at him from the darkest pits of hell.

Desperate to break free, he pointed his weapon at the creature's head and pulled the trigger. The barrel exploded and the rounds passed right through. From the empty blackness, human features began to form.

Stunned, the old man recoiled in panic when a gruesome face suddenly appeared. First one, then another, and another, until numerous faces lay flickering like burnt images trapped within the facial cavity of the demon head.

He knew none of the ghastly faces personally and yet somehow recognized them all. In life, these were covetous and grasping souls, ruthless and conniving. In death, their avarice endured beyond the grave, and their souls, now shackled by their ill-gotten wealth, became imprisoned forever inside this mammon of greed.

"Guilty…guilty…guilty…"

Shrieking with despair, the wretched spirits cursed the station owner, calling him by name. The sight of this frightful cabal accusing him was altogether too much to bear.

"God help me!" wheezed the petrified owner, trying to break the stranglehold on his neck. In return, the diamond encrusted fingers tightened like a metal vice and the shotgun slipped from the old man's grasp.

"God is not here," mocked the demon, his voice cackling like a legion of lost souls.

At once, the owner choked and gagged as if a stream of metal shavings were bubbling up his throat. Sure enough, a gush of minted coins began pouring out of his mouth like a jackpot machine, swelling into a torrential river of money and blood until his beating heart washed out of his gullet and splattered onto the floor.

At the same time, the man's stomach burst open and thousands of dollars cashed out from his ruptured belly, accompanied by his entrails. The poor man collapsed in agony and died, his face frozen in terror. The last thing he saw was his still beating heart quivering like a leaf, buried in a mound of hell notes.

✝

The impure light surrounding the dagger began to simmer, the angry faces on the pommel once again frozen in steel. The little girl let out a guttural sigh, like the rasping noise of a departing soul who had taken her last breath.

Her eyes opened wide and the blankness returned. She stood just outside the gas station, on the porch fronting the office.

"Well done, Magdalene," said the Lumen Commander. "The master will be pleased."

The girl looked up and said nothing, her face drained of all emotions. Whatever innocence and light still breathing inside of her were locked away by the parasitic terrors ruling her own body.

"I'll take that for now," said the Commander, reaching out his hand for the Tibetan Phurba.

The little girl tried to pass on the dagger but the blade refused to cooperate. It attached itself to her hands and refused to leave. An echo of soft voices emanated from the pommel, humming a strange tune.

The Commander attempted to pry the weapon from her fingers and immediately, a terrible pain shot through his arm like a bolt of lightning. Cursing loudly, he quickly invoked the formula given by Chambers and the terror began to subside. This thing was more than a just conduit for evil. The influence it swayed over life and death was palpable. For now, the incantations had managed to bring the powers to heel. But once unleashed, it was always difficult to persuade evil to return to its cage.

He quickly restored the dagger to its dark wooden case, almost relieved to close the lid on the fickle blade.

"Sir, we found the safe house. They were definitely here,"

reported a Praetorian officer. The gas station was then crawling with Lumen troops.

"We also found this," said the man, pulling out a digital tablet. "The data is encrypted but we should be able to break the security programming."

"Good! Strip the place, take whatever is useful and burn the rest of it to the ground. But make sure you hang the old man on a flagpole. Let it be a warning to anyone who's thinking of helping these fools. I want the Resistance to know that we'll hunt down every soul who so much as offers them a drink of water."

The officer raised an eyebrow, afraid to question his superior but keenly aware that such a move would only alert their prey to the hunt. Weren't they ordered by Chambers to keep their distance?

"They already know we're following the crumbs," assured the Commander, aware of what the man was thinking. "If he's as good as he used to be, he would've figured it out by now."

"Sir?" asked the Praetorian officer. He had no idea who his boss was referring to.

The Commander scowled and replied, "They may be able to run for now but the beast will eventually find them."

Chapter 23

As they approached the edge of town, the vehicle cruised off the main road and detoured down a street of deserted buildings. The pavements lining both sides of the lane were cracked and overcome with weeds. There were tomes of graffiti etched across every corner, cursing God and man.

It was clear that this place was a leprous outpost, inhabited only by memories of the dead. As the gravel groaned beneath their wheels, Michael looked out the window and remembered how it came to be.

Once an urban hive, decades of crime and violence had packed the local morgue to capacity, forcing many to abandon the area ages ago. The federal government had made some effort to save the town back then. But when the druggies, hookers and gangs refused to tow the line, the authorities decided to pull the plug once and for all.

At the time, he was part of the military crew that was sent in. Their orders were simple – kill the rats and clean out the human cesspool.

The next few days were a blur. But it was said by some that the streets were paved with corpses that week. No one survived the purging. The blood of those human lives, tainted though they were, still clung to the calluses of his mind.

The car went over a pothole and jolted Michael from his thoughts. He straightened the steering, pulled out his whiskey and took a big gulp. Sadly, the faces in his mind were still drowned in blood.

Behind him in the backseat, the mood was equally solemn.

"How is he?" enquired Chelsea, stunned by the rapid deterioration of the doctor.

"You can see he's getting worse," replied Gabriel.

"Is he possessed?"

"I don't think so. But he's afflicted with some kind of curse. His soul is under siege.

"You mean like a hex?"

"Something like that, but a great deal more powerful. I've dealt with genuine hexes before but I've never seen sorcery like this. Whoever is powering this spell is someone high up in the dark realm; a bona fide warlock."

"You can't be serious," said Chelsea. "You're telling me some guy with a pointy hat and a wand is doing this to him?"

"I'm telling you there are more things in heaven and on earth than you can imagine," said Gabriel. "Sorcery like this often involves human sacrifice. Have you forgotten what that man can do?"

The question stabbed her in the heart. She thought she had been cured, but the residue of skepticism still clung to her like moss.

"Chambers," whispered Chelsea, almost afraid to speak his name. "I saw him do some horrible things, but a warlock?"

"Most of the top guys who run Lumen Corp are. We don't know who's overall in charge, but we do know they're all masters of the dark arts. The board of directors is nothing but a coven of evil."

"So what do we do now?" asked the woman.

"We stop the bleeding," interrupted Michael. He was searching for a place to park the car so they wouldn't be seen.

"What bleeding?" asked Chelsea, confused.

The priest pulled the handbrake and the tires screeched to a sudden stop, throwing the vehicle into a precise spin that parked it under the arches of an abandoned complex. Both men jumped out and secured the area. Michael flipped off the safety on his rifle and scanned their surroundings like a hawk. Only when he was sure that the coast was clear did he give the signal to hurry back to the transport.

Once again, Gabriel reached into the car and grabbed hold of his confrere. He could feel the torn muscles in his back ignite.

"Help me get him inside," he said to Chelsea. "We need to bind the wound right now!"

"You said earlier that he wasn't bleeding," cried the woman. "Why is he bleeding now? I don't see any blood, what's going on?"

"It's not physical, it's spiritual. But the effects are the same."

The girl was baffled. "I don't understand," she said.

"Think of the spell as a long wicked knife. You stab a man with a blade like that and he'll bleed like a stuck pig. Father Raphael has been stabbed by a powerful spell and he's leaking 'blood' all over the place. We have to staunch the flow, stop the spiritual bleeding or the Lumen dogs will track us down to our front doors."

"You have to be kidding me."

"I wish I was," Gabriel commented. "But a spell like this leaves a supernatural trail for miles around. Every hellhound in the vicinity will be able to smell the stink."

"But how could…"

"Enough," said Michael, butting in. "Both of you stop your yapping and get inside!"

He pushed past Chelsea, slung his rifle and pulled Raphael to his feet. In the process, the woman lost her balance and nearly tripped. She recovered but said nothing, her face pallid and strained.

"Come on," said Gabriel, extending his arm to the young lady. "We're running out of time."

She grasped his hand and stumbled forward. Michael had already carried Raphael through the front doors of the derelict building. They needed to catch up. As Chelsea neared the entrance, she noticed the battered sign fronting the façade. The letters were distressed and faded but something about the moldy sign stopped her dead in her tracks.

"What is this place?" she cried out in alarm.

"Take it easy, it's just an empty old building," said Gabriel, trying to calm her nerves.

"What was it previously?" she pulled away, demanding to know.

"Some kind of medical centre. It's been abandoned for years, like the rest of this ghost town. We can stop here for awhile, it should be safe."

Chelsea remained unconvinced. Something about this place haunted her.

"Come on," urged the friar, losing his patience. "I assure you, there's nothing in there but cobwebs. Besides, we're not going to stay long."

She resisted and looked up at the sign again, as if reading an omen.

"Miss Shields, let's go!" repeated Gabriel more urgently.

This time he grabbed her by the arm and dragged her into the darkness. She faltered after him, and the two disappeared under the looming arches of a grimy plaque that read – New Life Women's Clinic.

✝

Inside a modest chapel at the Vatican, a lone figure in white knelt on a prie-dieu before the tabernacle, with his face nestled in the palms of his hands. Resting before him on a small working desk was a white zucchetto. Beneath that, stacks of letters from around the world piled up like a great wall of troubles.

The old pontiff glanced at them. Some were official reports, the rest were urgent letters requesting help or authorization, and still others brought news of fresh Lumen atrocities.

From country to country, most of these communicated pain and desperation, while a few indeed were written in blood. Upon them all, the elderly man prayed intensely. And then gently he held the papers to his forehead, wearing their painful contents like a crown of thorns.

He sighed and looked up at the tabernacle. *A disciple is not above his master*, he recalled scripture saying. He closed his eyes and prayed. Once again he offered his own sufferings in union with the sacrifice of Jesus on the cross, embracing the world to himself.

Suddenly, a thought occurred to him. In fact, it rushed upon his mind like a tsunami sweeping away all other concerns. The pope was surprised at the strength of the inner locution. It was as if an angel had not whispered, but had shouted an urgent message into his ear. There were no voices, no words, only the pressing force of a conviction that began to swell in his heart until he was no longer able to bear it.

"Giacomo!" called out the pontiff.

The papal secretary came running into the chapel.

"Your Holiness…"

"Prepare the altar for Mass right now," ordered the pope. "There's something I must urgently commend to the Lord!"

"What's wrong Holy Father?" asked the worried secretary. But the pontiff was in no mood to explain.

"Please do as I say, my son," pleaded the pope. "And hurry."

The American archbishop turned to his aides and snapped his fingers.

"Bring in the sacred vestments," he told his staff. "And prepare a set for me as well. I will concelebrate with the Holy Father."

"And monsignor," said the pope.

"Yes, Your Holiness?"

"Contact Joseph Li."

†

Gabriel unpacked his portable Mass kit and removed the sacred vessels from their case. He threw a linen cloth over some wooden crates that Michael had stacked up for use as a makeshift altar and pulled out his priestly stole.

"What're you doing?" asked Chelsea.

"Preparing for Mass," answered the exorcist.

"Why are you wasting time playing church? Shouldn't you do an exorcism, get this thing out of his system?"

"He's not possessed," replied Gabriel. "At least I don't think so."

"You don't think so? You mean you're not sure?" she postured.

"Without my Roman Ritual, I can't be sure."

"What do you mean?"

"The Rite of Exorcism is more than just a treatment, it's also a helpful diagnostic tool for demonic possession. Sometimes when I'm not sure if a person is really possessed or not, I recite the prayers anyway, but without the patient knowing. If a demon is really buried in there, the prayers will usually force the spirit to expose itself. Unfortunately, my Ritual's all ripped up and lying on the cathedral floor with a bunch of dead Lumen guys."

"So what, don't you know all this stuff by heart?" she snapped, her tone deeply offensive.

Gabriel looked up with annoyance. "I don't do this on a daily basis. Contrary to popular belief, possessions don't fall out of the skies."

"I know, I know," she scoffed. "Only wicked angels do."

"That's right," retorted Gabriel, losing his temper. "Like I said, I believe this is something else. Someone is praying to Satan for his demise and we have to try and interrupt the effects, break the spell before it gets worse."

There was a loud groan in the room. Raphael was stretched out on the dusty floor like a wounded beast.

One minute, he was writhing like a prisoner strapped to a burning grill. And the next moment, he was shivering like a man lost in a blizzard. In between, the victim would mutter incoherently, his mind besieged by a curse that was dragging him to the brink of insanity.

Chelsea placed her hand gently upon his tortured brow, wiping the cold sweat from his face.

"Well padre, whatever you need to do, you better do it quick," she said. The blue veins around Raphael's neck had begun to rise up to his face.

Just then, Michael returned to the room with a communicator in his hand.

"Did you get the Prelate?" asked Gabriel with hope.

"No luck, something's jamming the signal," said Michael. "We're on our own."

Laying aside his sword, Gabriel proceeded to prepare the 'altar', pouring wine and water into their respective cruets and unfolding the corporal; a square piece of linen cloth that the Host and Chalice would be placed upon during the actual consecration.

Michael looked at Chelsea and her face showed the disdain in her heart. He knew what she was thinking.

"If anything will stop the bleeding right now, it's this," he told her. "Don't underestimate the holy sacrifice of the Mass, it's the most powerful prayer in the Church's arsenal."

"Actually, it's the most powerful prayer on earth," corrected Gabriel. "In the Mass it is Christ Himself who is praying to God the Father. The greatest miracle takes place each time the words of consecration are pronounced by a priest acting *in persona Christi* (in the person of Christ) when ordinary bread and wine are transformed into his body, blood, soul and divinity."

"Look, if I wanted a doctrine class, I would've asked for it," said Chelsea. "Do what you have to do and let's get the hell out of here."

She gritted her teeth and cast furtive glances around the room, like she was expecting to see something unpleasant.

"What's wrong with you?" Michael growled.

Chelsea didn't answer. She tried to shake off the growing frustration but her anxieties only mounted with each passing second. It wasn't so much that she didn't believe in the power of prayer, but something about this morbid place was gnawing at her nerves. She felt a deep sense of oppression and a frightful hollow in the pit of her stomach.

The men were oblivious. *Why couldn't they feel it? Was she the only one to sense that something was awry?*

She looked up at Michael. The priest frowned and turned his face away.

"We've wasted enough time," he grumbled to Gabriel. "Let's get this show on the road."

The Japanese friar removed his jacket and threw the simple stole over his shoulders. Under the circumstances, it wasn't possible to observe all the vesting rubrics. The clock was ticking.

As Gabriel crossed himself and began the liturgy, Chelsea caught sight of something from the corner of her eye. Her vision darted all around the room, searching for the source of her disquiet.

There was nothing. The only sounds she heard came from the priests celebrating Mass and the poor broken man whimpering by her side. But she knew something was lurking in the shadows. She couldn't see it, but she could sense it. The creepy sensation of being watched encircled her like a noose.

Gabriel read the scriptures aloud and entered into that part of the Mass known as the liturgy of the word. Despite the air being as dead as the iron nail on a coffin, one of the two candles that were lit on the makeshift altar suddenly blew out. Michael noticed this and relit the wick. At the same time, he discreetly unbuckled the holster catch on his sidearm. The temperature in the darkened room had plunged a few degrees. It wasn't freezing, but it was chilly enough to send shivers down their spines.

"This is the gospel of the Lord," proclaimed Gabriel, holding up the scripture text.

"Praise to you, Lord Jesus Christ," said Michael, making the ritual response. Both men could see their breaths vaporize in the cold.

That instance, a small shrieking figure suddenly spouted from the shadows and ran up to Chelsea. The unexpected appearance of this terrible troll sent the beautiful woman tumbling back in fright. She lost her balance and slammed into the concrete floor. Before she could catch her breath, the ghastly creature was upon her.

Seized with panic, she grabbed the katana lying nearby and drew the sword, swinging it madly like a woman fearing for her life.

"Stay calm, put the sword down!" shouted Gabriel.

"You get this thing away from me!" she shouted back.

"*You get this thing away from me,*" mimicked the tiny imp, its voice snarling with rage and contempt. "*No want…no want!!!*"

Chelsea was startled to hear the thing talk. Its body was shrunken and small, with a spindly neck that supported an impossibly large head. Its skin was mummified and grey, and the creature looked over a hundred years old but sounded eerily like a child, except no human child ever sounded like that.

"Whump!" – the walls literally shook and trembled. "Whump!!!" – again the thunderous noise exploded like a cannon. To all, it seemed like something was trying to smash its way out from behind the concrete walls.

"Heads up," yelled Gabriel. "We have company!!!"

Chelsea twirled around and her jaw fell open. From out of the darkness, a congregation of horror had gathered around the altar. There must've been about fifty to sixty tiny goblin babies crawling all over the floor like rats, their oversized craniums knocking about like bowling balls with eye sockets full of suffering and grief. There was no mistaking the shape and appearance. Deformed and grotesque, they looked like abominations suckled from the breasts of some hellish whore.

"Toyols," whispered Gabriel, distracted from the celebration of the Mass.

"You've seen these things before?" asked Michael, pointing his gun at the sea of monstrous heads.

The exorcist nodded. "But never this many," he gasped.

Gabriel knew the Malayan people commonly used these things as spirit slaves to steal things or harass their enemies, but he had never encountered these ghouls outside of South East Asia. A toyol wasn't nearly as dangerous as a demon, but a dead fetus animated by black magic was still a spawn of evil. And if they made the wrong move, things could get nasty very quickly.

Suddenly a terrible shriek interrupted his thoughts. The samurai sword went clattering onto the floor as Chelsea flailed her arms in panic. The toyol had leapt onto the poor woman and had sunk its teeth into her hand. She tried desperately to shake it off but the creature refused to let go.

In a flash, Michael jumped into action and pulled the wrinkled baby from her arm, tossing it away like a smelly wet rag.

"Ugh…" exclaimed Chelsea.

The bruise wasn't that bad, but the mucus dripped and slobbered off her skin in disgusting gobs. From that point on, things got rapidly out of hand. The circle of ghouls began to close in like a constricting mob. There seemed to be so many of them.

Gabriel glanced up and saw movement on the ceiling and walls. Even Michael started to look worried. They weren't just surrounded. They were in danger of being overrun by these entities. The only thing holding back the swarm of terror was the flickering light from the tiny candles on the altar.

"Throw me my sword," Gabriel shouted to Chelsea. He was eager to fly into battle but Michael restrained the friar and gave him a look that kept him grounded.

"Finish the Mass," he ordered. "We'll hold them off."

Reluctantly, Gabriel obeyed. He needed every ounce of his will power to keep from leaping into the fray. But Michael was right, he had to complete the liturgy or Raphael might not survive the hour. But seeing as how things were, he wasn't even sure if any of them would live through the ordeal.

"You said this place was empty," Chelsea rebuked. "You said it was safe…"

Gabriel had no answer. He had taken shelter here before but nothing like this had ever happened. Pushing everything out of his mind, he refocused on the ritual of the Mass.

"*Holy, holy, holy, Lord God Almighty,*" he intoned the prayer of the angels. "*Heaven and earth are full of your glory, Hosanna in the highest. Blessed is He who comes in the name of the Lord, Hosanna in the highest.*"

In answer, the toyols charged the group like a tribe of warring pygmies.

"Stay near the altar," Michael shouted as he dragged Raphael into the light of the sacred flames. Chelsea did all she could to fight off the leeching creatures with her bare knuckles. Gabriel's katana was now lost in the mound of screeching, wriggling bodies. And the only thing keeping them safe was the glowing luminance from the makeshift altar.

Try as they might, the toyols could not breach the hazy circumference of light. They stayed in the shadows, grinding and gnashing their teeth. But Michael was taking no chances. He grabbed his automatic rifle and held it to his shoulder.

"What're you waiting for? Shoot the damn things!" cried Chelsea.

Surprisingly, Michael didn't blast away. His bullets had all been dipped in chrism oil and consecrated for battle, he knew they would cause some damage if he squeezed off. And yet something kept him from shredding the creatures.

"*Therefore, O Lord, we humbly implore you: by your Spirit graciously make holy these gifts we have brought before you for consecration,*" said Gabriel, stretching out his priestly hands over the bread and wine. "*That they may become the body and blood of your Son our Lord, Jesus Christ, at whose command we celebrate these mysteries.*"

Again the flames on the candles flickered wildly when no wind could be felt. The toyols became even more aggressive and rambunctious. They jumped and screeched like a horde of monkeys but no amount of angry protest could put the fire out. Like a pair of angels holding flaming swords, the candles remained lit and continued to burn even more brightly as the Mass proceeded. Nevertheless, this didn't stop the throng of goblins from trying to get closer.

"Back off!" shouted Chelsea, swatting a creepy hand away with a rusty pipe she picked off the floor. The toyol in question hissed angrily and threw a loose stone at the woman, narrowly missing her face.

"Do something," Chelsea pleaded with Michael.

Cursing, the priest finally unleashed a warning burst over the massive heads of the creatures. The bullets slammed into the walls and tore up the concrete, the plaster disintegrating without trouble. In that moment, all the anxiety in the room collided like a train wreck. The flashlight attached to Michael's rifle exposed a hill of abominations behind the fake wall.

Chelsea shook her head in disbelief, the blood draining from her face.

"No…" she gasped, refusing to acknowledge what she saw. Rows and rows of medical jars lined up against the broken shelves, stuffed to the brim with human fetuses floating in the slimy muck of some embalming fluid.

Even a seasoned mercenary like Michael was taken aback. He looked at Gabriel and saw that his friend was equally stumped to see the tiny corpses bloated and carved up, their little faces frozen in suffering and death. Each morbid jar was sealed by a strip of talisman wrapped around its lid, imprisoning the bodies of the innocents in a slavery of evil.

"No…*this isn't happening*," mumbled Chelsea, her tone as dead as the babies in the jars.

In response, the toyols reassured the woman that they were indeed real and present. Picking up objects in their hands, they began stoning the group. Salvos of mud and gravel bombarded the team without mercy. The mystery was deepened when no such matter could be found on the floor for them to hurl. It seemed almost as if these missiles were conjured out of thin air.

Michael and Chelsea did their best to shield the altar from the filthy bombardment, buying time for Gabriel to consummate the Mass. It was at this point that Raphael suddenly sat up and screamed in pain, the veins in his neck bulging like steel cables.

"Hold him!" cried Gabriel, instructing Michael to keep the victim from thrashing about.

Whatever dark magic was poisoning the doctor, it was getting worse. This was spiritual warfare and Gabriel knew their only saving grace at this time rested in his hands. He looked down at the small white host held between his fingers and prayed fervently for Raphael, offering the holy sacrifice of Christ for his liberty and deliverance. Then holding the host aloft, he began to recite the consecration prayer.

"On the night he was betrayed, he himself took bread, and giving you thanks, he said the blessing, broke the bread, and gave it to his disciples, saying: Take this, all of you, and eat it – for this is my body which will be given up for you."

In accordance with the rubrics, the Japanese priest raised the circular piece of wafer up high like the rising sun.

To Chelsea's consternation, a blinding flash of light exploded from the host and flooded the entire room. It lasted barely a second, but it was so bright that she covered her eyes in fright. When she finally dared to look again, she stole a peek at the priests and realized that they were unaware of what had just happened.

Gabriel genuflected and continued to pray under his breath. Michael struggled to calm Raphael who was grimacing in pain. No one seemed to have noticed the strange phenomenon except her.

"My God," she said, looking at the host. It must be the adrenaline. She had to be dreaming. But a quick glance at the menacing throng confirmed that she was not.

The toyols had seen it too, and were very much afraid. There was chaos among the ranks. The circle of darkness around the altar peeled back in panic with hundreds of wriggling bodies falling over each other in retreat. The imps were terrified, they were screaming and crying as children do when frightened and confused.

Chelsea locked her eyes on Gabriel, her heart drumming with expectation for what might happen next. Did they understand that this place was an abortion mill? Did they know that she murdered her offsprings in a place like this all those years ago? None of that seemed to matter right now. She sobbed.

The Japanese priest took a small chalice of wine into his hands and prayed fervently yet again, this time begging God to free the memories of the children trapped in this den of evil. Once more and with great reverence, he intoned the consecration prayer.

"In a similar way, when supper was ended, he took the chalice, and giving you thanks, he said the blessing and gave the chalice to his disciples, saying: Take this, all of you, and drink from it - this is the chalice of my blood, the blood of the new and eternal covenant, which will be poured out for you and for many for the forgiveness of sins. Do this in memory of me."

As before, he raised the chalice with both hands, lifting the blessed cup over good and evil, indeed over the whole world. In his heart he knew that the wine was gone, replaced only by the blood of the Son of God.

The gold chalice began to shimmer at first. Then without warning, the same blast of light exploded from the cup and washed over the room. Chelsea shielded her eyes in panic. There was a great noise like the rush of a mighty wind and before she knew it, a powerful squall swept down and caught hold of her hands, pulling them away from her face. Against her better instinct, she opened her eyes. It was bright, so bright that it seemed like the light of a thousand suns were burning through her retinas.

This time, the blinding flash lingered for quite some time. How long had she been staring into this mysterious brilliance? There was no sound, no motion, and no sight that was not consumed by this intense brightness. Pain and fear had ceased to exist. Time itself appeared to be frozen in this limbo of light.

Then slowly she began to hear voices. Giggles...laughter...the sounds of children at play. She blinked and found herself standing in an opened field. The grass was soft and beautiful, and a gentle breeze rustled the blades with little caresses. Wherever she looked, the colors were vibrant with life and beauty. To her left, a running stream cascaded over shiny pebbles, sparkling like diamonds in the spring. To her right, a great multitude of children frolicked on the green. And everywhere, there was the sound of joy and innocence.

Willing herself to stay calm, she took a deep breath and gazed around. A profound sense of peace overwhelmed her, a peace that the world could not give. If this was a dream, she was loath to wake up from it. Gently, she felt the tugging of little hands and glanced down. And two beautiful faces looked up at her - a boy and a girl.

Bursting into tears, Chelsea dropped to her knees and hugged the children. She had never seen them before until now, but deep in her heart she knew. She just knew.

"Are you okay?" she asked, her tears drenching her cheeks in a mixture of joy, guilt and relief.

The children nodded and smiled. "We're okay," they said. "Don't worry, mommy, we're okay…"

She clung to them like a castaway holding on to dear life, refusing to let go lest she drowned in the murky depths of despair yet again. In return, the children threw their arms around the young woman, kissing and hugging her.

Chelsea began to sob uncontrollably.

"We forgive you…we love you…don't cry, mommy…"

The words embraced her like a healing balm, untying the knots of depression in her soul and setting her free. She would've gladly stayed in that garden of grace, pressing those children close to her heart. But there was another voice in the background. It was so soft at first that she could barely hear it. Yet she could sense it calling to her.

In response she clung even more tightly to the two beautiful children, desperate to hang on.

"It's okay mommy, you can let go," said the girl smiling.

"You don't have to be afraid anymore," said the older boy by her side. "We're safe."

Overcome with emotion, Chelsea was speechless. She caressed the two siblings with great affection, nodding quietly through her tears, her lips trembling with a longing that shook her to her toes. Filled with contrition, she felt the years of grime and regret wash away from her soul.

As the children embraced her one last time, she could feel them slowly slip through her fingers with the sands of time. Her pulse quickened with fear and she tried to grab on to the moment, but eternity would not leave them in her hands just yet.

Little by little the man's voice returned like a faint memory getting stronger, until she could recognize the distinct cadence of the Japanese priest reciting the words of the Mass.

"*Behold, the Lamb of God, behold him who takes away the sins of the world. Blessed are those called to the supper of the Lamb.*"

Like a bolt of lightning, there was another flash and then suddenly she was back in the room. She looked up, her face soaked in wonder as she saw Gabriel lift the host and chalice together into the air.

"My Lord and my God," she cried out, her eyes swimming in tears.

She couldn't understand what had just happened, but she could feel a tremendous weight lifted off her chest. For the first time in a long time, she no longer felt bound by the shackles of guilt. Casting her gaze around the room, Chelsea noticed that the shadows didn't hold the same terrors for her as before. There was no trace of any toyol, no signs to suggest that they were very nearly engulfed by a legion of those things. The tiny terrors were simply gone. Above all, the stink of decay that accompanied the creatures had been purged by a fragrance that she found inexplicable; an odor of sanctity that flowed from the altar.

Gabriel drew near to Raphael who had been convulsing with fear. Taking the consecrated host in his hand, he brought it near to the face of the wounded priest.

"*The Body of Christ*," whispered the exorcist, holding the small white host between his thumb and forefinger.

At this, the ghostly hand around Raphael's neck reached over his mouth and clamped his jaw shut. The infernal spell coursed through his veins like poison and bubbled up like a muzzle over his face, refusing to admit the bread of life.

Michael grunted a prayer and did his best to pry open the victim's mouth. Even then, he barely managed to open a slit.

"That's all I need," said Gabriel, quickly slipping in the host. The effect was instantaneous.

The blue streaks across Raphael's face rolled back like Venetian blinds. His body broke into spasms, throwing the suffering man into a violent fit. Doubling over in pain, he gagged and choked cruelly until he coughed up a spiky glob of blood that rolled onto the floor.

Chelsea, who had been watching on the sidelines, was astonished to see the blood clot squirming around like a tiny octopus. Before she could point that out, Michael dug his booted heel into the mess and felt the thing pop beneath his weight.

In that moment, Raphael let out a groan and collapsed like a man struck down in battle.

"Father!" the woman cried out in alarm, worried that the doctor priest was no more.

"Come on buddy," encouraged Michael, smacking his friend on the face. Slowly, color returned to his cheeks and life began to take over from the reins of death.

"Is he going to be okay?" asked Chelsea.

Michael rapped his fingers over the man's face a few more times, slapping the sleep from his eyes.

"Come on you lazy mule, wake up," said Michael.

Raphael stirred and finally opened his eyes.

"Stop slapping me," he grumbled.

A loud sigh of relief escaped everyone.

"Thank God," said Gabriel, rejoicing. He crossed himself and proceeded to finish the thanksgiving prayer after communion.

Even a sourpuss like Michael managed a tiny grin. He grabbed Raphael by the collar and helped him to sit up.

"How're you feeling?" asked the soldier priest.

"Just peachy," said Raphael, trying to recover his balance.

Still dazed and confused, the doctor felt like he had just climbed out of his own grave. When he saw Chelsea, his eyes lighted up a little.

"Miss Shields," he nodded, smiling weakly.

The woman was crying too much to say anything at first, but it was clear that she was overcome with joy.

"Good to have you back, Father," she finally replied.

Without hesitation, she threw her arms around him and hugged him.

Chapter 24

Marshall Chambers stood quietly before the stone altar, his sallow face dunked in a pool of boiling rage.

Dressed in a black alb and liturgical vestments, Chambers looked every bit the parody of a Catholic priest at Mass, with the maniple deliberately worn on the opposite arm and the chasuble embroidered with a large inverted cross. Even more conspicuous than the religious garb was the sight of his hands dripping with blood.

Flanking him were two female acolytes who shifted uncomfortably in their robes, afraid to make eye contact. Norman, the Lumen aide, also felt the unnerving glare of his master and shivered with dread.

"Come," said Chambers, his voice snagging Norman like an icy hook.

The Lumen executive bowed low and approached the sacrificial dais, taking care not to step on the splashes of body fluids on the floor. Only five minutes ago, he was cavorting with a beautiful blonde on the upper deck of the mansion's private lounge. Now he found himself summoned to the basement crypt, a vault of sorcery whose corridors he had seldom been allowed to darken, and where the Christian Rite of the Eucharist was demonized and perverted.

He looked about nervously. Above the sacrificial altar hung a wooden crucifix from the low ceiling, supporting not the corpus of Christ but the grisly carcass of a dead baboon nailed to its rotting beams.

Beneath that hideous figure, the gruesome remains of a young child lay butchered like a pig. Its face was smashed in, its bowels torn apart, and its entrails scattered all over the floor. Six burning lamps flickered around the fresh corpse, dancing with glee at the human sacrifice served up on the table like a macabre dish. There were big puddles of blood everywhere, dripping from the carnage of the altar and permeating the crypt like a slaughterhouse.

As Norman climbed the steps to the altar, the acolytes descended and floated past him. Both women were completely naked under their flimsy robes. Long mysterious hoods covered their faces but the rest of their garments barely covered anything else. The anxious assistant could see the paleness of their breasts pushing out from behind the pentagrams on their cloaks. He felt the sudden pangs of lust but quickly doused the fire for fear of losing his head. This was no time to let his loins out for play.

"Mister Vice-president," said Norman, prostrating himself before the austere visage of Lumen Corp's high priest.

Chambers gazed down at his servant in contempt. He could hear the man's heart scurry like a rodent trapped in a cage. And as always, the smell of fear excited his cruelty.

"Come closer," said the Lumen VP. His hands were awash in blood, his fingers grasping the pulpy remains of a human heart.

"Do you know what annoys me the most, Norman?" asked Chambers. "That the Vice-president of International Affairs is saddled with a local pest problem because his aides are too useless to do their jobs. You'd think that the most powerful Corporation in the world would have managers who could clean up their own backyards. But no, I have to step in and clear the shit in their sewers. Do you know how that makes me feel?"

He crushed the heart in his hand and the fleshy organ squirted through his fingers like an overripe fruit.

Norman knew that his master was furious. The death spell binding one of the priests had been broken, and now Chambers was on the hunt for a scapegoat. It didn't matter that no one had forced the Lumen VP to embrace this task. He had taken a personal interest in destroying The Archangels as a challenge to his vanity.

Unfortunately, what should've been an easy foxhunt was proving to be a blemish on his record. And he - high priest of Moloch, the demon prince of the underworld - would not suffer the taunts and humiliation of the other warlocks on the Board of Directors.

Corporate politics demanded that he acquit himself before the scheming tongues of his colleagues could reach the ears of the Chairman. He had worked too long and hard to lose his throne in the new world, not when the Antichrist himself was standing at the gates of New Babylon.

"These priests are starting to annoy me. They've got more miserable lives than a cat," Chambers grumbled. "Do you know what it would take to break a spell this powerful?"

Norman knew that his boss wasn't expecting an answer. He kept silent and bowed his head, careful not to raise his eyes.

"We can still track them, sir," claimed the balding executive. "The Praetorians have intercepted their communications. We know where they are. I've ordered the Commander to keep close. Once they make contact with the Chinese, we'll move in and take them alive…"

"Finish them now," interrupted Chambers. "No more games, Norman. Tell the men to kill those cretins on sight. I want their stinking skulls on my desk by midnight."

Norman was appalled. This wasn't the plan. He knew that disobedience to the Board was punishable by worse things than death. High priest or not, Chambers' influence did not extend to immunity from Lumen justice. There were far greater evils pacing the corridors of power in the Corporation, and he wasn't about to stake his life on the wounded pride of one despot. As much as he feared the Vice-president, he feared the collective wrath of the Company Directors even more.

Norman swallowed hard and decided to risk the question…

"What about the Chinese, sir? The masters were explicit that we should not jeopardize the operation until we captured the old man. The Board won't be pleased if we pulled the plug now. He *is* after all the voice behind the Resistance. He's still our real target, isn't he?"

"The target is who I say it is," retorted Chambers. "Or have you forgotten that?"

"Of course not. But I fear the Board will not understand your lordship's eagerness to solve their problems."

"Spare me your mockery, worm."

"I wouldn't dare, my lord," said Norman, groveling. "Your will is my command, I mean no disrespect."

He grabbed Chamber's hand and kissed the blood-soaked fingers, hoping to mollify the growing tension.

"It's just that…well," he hesitated. "I only wish to remind your lordship of certain realities."

"And what realities would those be?"

"Begging your pardon, sir, but you promised the Board that you would give them the head of the Catholic resistance, and they've made it clear that they would accept nothing less. As it is, the rebels are constantly on the move, shipping men and equipment, abandoning bases and transporting weapons and more. The old man is too well hidden by those who protect him, but he cares about these priests. If we kill them now, we may never lure him out into the open. "

Chambers sighed and bent down. He took Norman's face into his bloody hands and cradled it like a child.

"My dear man, has anyone ever told you that you worry too much?"

All at once, Norman began to panic. His desire for self-preservation had unwittingly placed him in the line of fire. Having foolishly walked into a trap, he was now desperate to climb back out.

"Forgive me, my lord," he said apologetically. "It's just that the Board of Directors won't take kindly to failure, and I want so much for you to succeed. You alone deserve the confidence of the Chairman, not those posers who conspire against you. Surely you know you can trust me, sir. I'm loyal only to you."

"But I haven't failed, my trusted and loyal assistant," said Chambers. "Those meddling priests may have forced my hand early but I'm not beaten yet."

"Of course not…I…I didn't mean that," Norman stammered. "You know I wouldn't suggest such a thing."

The Lumen aide laughed nervously and tried to salvage his downfall.

"You're absolutely right," said the terrified official. "The Board doesn't know the situation on the ground. We should kill those bastards now that we have the chance. I was blind not to see that. Let's not give them any more time to regroup…"

Chambers said nothing. Instead, he stroked the man's face affectionately.

"My lord, please…I'll…I'll get right on it. Give me another chance," Norman pleaded.

"Calm down, my dear fellow. No need to stress out. We don't want you to get an aneurism now, do we?"

"But sir, we've got them where we want them. Let me contact the troops, it'll be exactly as you command. I'll have their heads on a dish for you by this evening. I promise…"

"Shush, you've done more than enough," said Chambers, smiling. "Perhaps it's time you took a break. Get some well-deserved rest…"

He leaned over and kissed Norman on the forehead, as if saying goodbye to a friend.

Almost right away, streaks of blood started pouring out from the victim's eyes. Flooded with pain, he could barely stay conscious. All he could hear was Chambers muttering a litany of mantras under his breath, his voice rising like a volcanic eruption. And the more the high priest chanted, the louder Norman screamed, shrieking like his head was about to implode.

"Master, please," cried the poor soul, clawing desperately at the hands cupping his face. "Let me live, I'll make it up to you!"

"Oh you've done quite enough," replied the Lumen VP. "I think it's time for you to retire."

He gave one final squeeze and like a rotting cantaloupe, the man's head burst wide opened. Splotches of brain and fluid splattered onto the altar like the sprinkling of unholy water.

Chambers laughed and released his grip. And the former aide dropped to the floor.

Chapter 25

"I'm really sorry about that," said Chelsea, looking genuinely contrite. Gabriel tried to appear nonchalant but it was obvious that he was devastated. With a heavy heart, he picked up the family heirloom. The scabbard was intact but the blade was broken in three places. Something had happened to the katana when the toyols overwhelmed it like a flood. In some mysterious way, the evil animating those creatures had sullied and ruined the sword.

"If I hadn't touched it, this wouldn't have happened," lamented Chelsea. "Can you fix it?"

Gabriel shook his head. "It's okay, what matters is that you're safe."

He tried to smile but the girl could see the grief in his eyes. A samurai's honor was in his sword. To wield it recklessly was an act of blasphemy.

"I'm so very sorry," she repeated.

Gabriel nodded and looked down again at the shattered blade in his hands. As much as it felt like a part of his soul had been rend asunder, he was equally baffled by the breakage. The katana had been forged in the fires of baptism. In the hands of his warring ancestors, it had battled the forces of hell for centuries. He couldn't understand how the sword could be so easily destroyed by a bunch of impish ghouls when the sacred steel had long defeated demons by the dozen.

It might have something to do with the fact that those creatures were born from the unjust slaughter of innocents, which could have compromised the blade's resistance against the tyranny of evil. Or it might have been due to powerful sorcery at work, strengthening the assault of the toyols with unholy prayers. Either way, he would never really know. The supernatural realm was still mostly uncharted territory. The more he knew, the more he realized there was to learn.

"There's terrible magic at work here," Raphael commented weakly. "Best to leave this place to phantoms and ghosts, don't you think?"

His friend was right of course. The sword couldn't be re-forged, not here, not now. And Gabriel was sure there would be more nasty surprises before the day was over.

"By the way, you okay?" the friar asked his confrere. "We almost lost you back there."

Raphael took a deep breath and became pensive.

"I'm not sure I can describe what I felt," the doctor replied. "It was more like a nightmare that I couldn't wake up from. After awhile, I had no control over my own body, like I was a stranger to myself. I wasn't sure if I was dead or alive, or whether I was awake or in a dream. All I felt was the greatest despair overwhelming me. Whatever was doing this wanted more than just my death, it wanted my soul..."

"Listen, you don't have to say any more," Gabriel intervened, seeing how his confrere was struggling with the experience. "Rest, we've got a long day ahead of us."

Raphael nodded slowly and slumped back against the wall. He might've been freed from the painful effects of the curse but his ribs were still cracked and his face a violent mess from the Lumen torture he had received hours earlier. Despite that, it wasn't his body that protested. His spirit was beginning to feel the burden of battle. The memory of evil was often a hard thing to recall without feeling like you were descending back into madness.

As an exorcist, Gabriel understood that. There were times in his battle with evil that he sensed the most appalling darkness invade his mind. It wasn't a darkness that was part of the room or in the shadows around him. It was more like a burning desolation that devoured his hope and courage to live, like a cruel hand twisting a serrated knife into his soul, severing all attachments to faith.

To this day, the memory of those vile encounters would sometimes take their toll on him. And he often needed more than a few deep breaths to collect himself.

"Is he going to be all right?" Chelsea whispered to Gabriel.

"I hope so," said the friar. In the worse cases, he had noticed that evil this dark didn't always go away completely. Sometimes a stubborn residue would cling to the victim like a virus remaining dormant in his system for years, seemingly conquered, only to break out again when his spiritual resistance was low.

"We'll have to wait and see."

No doubt the divine presence in the Eucharist was powerful enough to free anyone from any evil, but God's wisdom often challenged the frailty of human plans. Sometimes total healing and deliverance took a little longer. In the end, it would be the Lord who decided when and how they would triumph over evil.

"*Kyrie eleison*," Gabriel uttered in his heart. "Lord have mercy."

A crackling boom broke the silence and rumbled through the empty halls of the former abortion clinic, rattling the shuttered windows and throwing the concrete walls into a shudder. Chelsea blinked in fright as flashes of lightning stole into the room and sliced through the shadows. Three successive times, the thunder roared like a voice from heaven, shaking the foundations of the building.

There was a storm coming. Countless lives had already fallen beneath the brutal heel of this war, but the first casualty of evil had always been truth. The lies and deceptions, the conspiracies and campaigns of sin had long darkened the minds of men to the light of God.

As the world continued to thunder and flash around him, Gabriel clutched the small wooden cross around his neck and felt the place where he had carved those words as a young boy – "*In hoc signo vinces*".

He closed his eyes and whispered a silent prayer. Moments later, the heavens opened up.

Michael came in from the rain, drenched to the skin and cradling his soaking gear under his arm.

"Did you get a signal?" asked Gabriel, looking up. The covert satellite comms had lit up like a Christmas tree earlier, prompting Michael to rush outside for better reception.

"Barely," replied the tall muscular priest. He threw the communications device on the floor and stepped over it. It had gone dead.

"But you got through to the Prelate?"

"He got through to us, though I'm not sure how. I didn't pick up any feeders or patches but there was enough juice jamming our signals to block out our secure lines, which means the Corporation has probably got a fix on our location. We have to go."

Raphael stirred from his corner. Despite his relief from the painful effects of the spell, his injuries were still serious enough to cause some concern.

"So our lines weren't that secure then," the doctor grumbled. "I thought the gear you ripped off the military were top of the line?"

"It's always a game of cat and mouse," admitted Michael, "The

Corporation owns the military. Whatever improvements we make over their technology…"

"They make improvements over our own," said the doctor tartly, "So the game continues…"

He slumped against the wall and groaned, his body bruised and broken, his spirit now beginning to buckle with exhaustion.

"What did the Prelate say?" Gabriel asked Michael. "Did you tell him we need a supply drop?"

The friar knew they were running out of time. The longer they stayed out in the open, the more vulnerable they were. They had to get to a safe house. The Underground Church had a few cozy spots that were practically fortresses. They could hide there, nurse their injuries and collect their strength until they figured out what to do.

"He wants us to come in," replied Michael.

Gabriel was stumped. "What do you mean he wants us to come in?"

"Get ready to move out," said the priest. He grabbed his guns and told everyone to pack up.

"Wait a minute," objected Gabriel. "You said the Corporation has a fix on us. If we meet up with the Prelate, we'll only lead the wolves right to the shepherd."

"Or they could come in any minute and kill us right now," noted Chelsea. "We can't stay here either."

"She's right, we've got our orders," Michael declared.

"Screw that, I'm not putting the old man in danger," exclaimed the friar.

Michael was irate.

"Listen, no one knows the risks more than *the old man*," said the priest. "He has his reasons for calling us in. Besides, we can't survive this on our own. We can't keep dodging bullets out in the open, not in our present conditions. We need backup and you know it!"

"We're fine! We can beat this, we just need some help getting to a shelter," argued Gabriel.

"Really?" Michael snapped. "We're fine???"

"I can take them!!!"

As soon as Gabriel said that, a searing pain shot through his injured back, causing him to stagger and wince.

"Don't be a moron! You can't even take me right now," said Michael.

Gabriel didn't like the sound of that. And all too soon, the quills of his temper began to bristle with indignation. In answer, he grabbed the bigger man by the collar and threatened…

"Like I said, I won't endanger the old man to save our hides," the friar insisted.

"You know something, Father," Michael remarked. "You've got the heart of a lion but the stubbornness of an ass!"

Livid with anger, the Japanese friar raised his fist. Both men squared off like two gladiators about to clash.

"Stop it! Both of you," shouted Chelsea. She wedged herself between the two priests and tried to push them apart.

"Of all the times to be arrogant and pig-headed! It's not enough that you have to fight demons, now you want to fight each other?" she admonished.

When it seemed like neither man would desist, she exploded.

"You hypocrites, what happened to your faith in God? Are you no longer priests, do you no longer belong to Christ? After all you've been through together, is this what it boils down to, your egos?"

The startling outburst was unexpected. But it did just the right thing; it defused the tension. Gabriel felt a wave of shame slowly rise up to his cheeks. He released his grip on the older priest. Michael in turn remained silent but he lowered his eyes.

"She's right, we're all wounded and exhausted, our tempers are frayed," Raphael joined in. "But save your energies for the devil. You're both sacred ministers, you should know better than to let anger come between brothers."

Raphael grimaced and pushed himself up. His broken ribs continued to grate against his sides, causing him great distress.

"I agree with Michael. I don't think we'll be able to handle another assault," the doctor added. "I can barely stand. And both of you look like shit. The Prelate has a good team of people protecting him, we stand a better chance of surviving this if we stick together."

Chelsea turned away from the squabbling priests and helped Raphael to one of the wooden crates where he sat in pain.

"So…" asked the doctor, gripping his sides. "Are we still brothers?"

The question hung in the air with some embarrassment.

Gabriel took a good look at Michael. And for the first time, he noticed that the man's jacket wasn't just soaked in rain, fresh blood was dripping down his sleeve.

"You're hurt," he said, somewhat surprised.

"It's nothing," mumbled the old soldier. "The stitches are just torn. Your uncle was a lousy medic."

A knowing smile crept over the young Toshigawa. It was true. Despite having had so much practice, Hiroshi was terrible when it came to first aid.

Gabriel looked down at the shattered remains of his sword on the floor. He picked up the broken blade and cradled the metal pieces in his hands. Meanwhile, the blood on Michael's sleeve continued dripping like precious seconds of time.

The friar recalled what his uncle had told him as a young boy – the samurai spirit of Bushido did not rest in the cold steel of a sword, but in the burning hearts of men who sought not their own will, but the will of their divine master.

Indeed, the Prelate had ordered them to come in. As a priest in obedience, the will of his religious superior was the will of Christ. It would be dishonorable for a samurai, much less a Catholic priest, to refuse his Lord and Master.

A deep sigh of remorse escaped his lips.

"All right," he whispered, almost to himself. "Let's do it your way. So what now?"

"Now we try to catch a train," said Michael.

Chapter 26

"Ring-a-ring-a-roses," chanted the little girl, her voice dancing in a gentle cadence. "A pocket full of posies…"

The deck of tarot cards floated into the air and circled the child in a ring of mystic symbols, spinning slowly around her like a carousel of charms.

"Hush…hush…" said the girl.

The cards began to spin faster and faster, whirling into a blur. Her tone started to grow deeper and deeper until a chorus of guttural voices slipped from her throat. By then, the tiny human voice had become a whimper in the great cacophony of malignant spirits.

"Hush…HUSH!!!" said the demons, as if hiding some dark secret between the lines of a nursery rhyme.

Five tongues of blue flame emerged from the cards and hovered before the girl like ghostly wraiths. She opened her mouth and the vaporous fires rushed in.

"And they all fall down," said the possessed child. One by one, the tarot cards lost their luminance and fell to the floor; all except one.

Magdalene reached out and took hold of the remaining card. It was the mystical picture of the pope, the Hierophant. And it was still levitating in mid-air. As her tiny fingers grasped the image, the paper burst into flames and disintegrated in her hands.

"Ashes to ashes, dust to dust," said the morbid girl, grimly. She blew on the smoldering flames and they flickered like the embers of a funeral pyre.

"What do you see, Magdalene?" asked the Commander, folding his arms.

He glanced at the tarot images on the floor. The five cards from which the blue flames emerged earlier were now blank, as if the mystic symbols on the paper had taken flight.

"What does the oracle say?" the Praetorian leader wanted to know.

The child had already armed him with a forecast of what was to come, but he was eager to discover more. From previous rituals, the spirits had prophesied that the Church would be reduced to ruins. The woman, Chelsea, would be overwhelmed by despair. And most of all, *The Archangels* would be brought to their knees weeping. Nothing pleased the Commander more than the thought of standing over their torn and bleeding bodies.

But now despite his insistence, he couldn't get the child to prophesy. They were inside a large trailer hooked up to a traveling convoy. It was built as a military command center for this operation. And apart from the possessed girl, there was no one else in the insulated room at the time except for the Commander and a few of his senior staff.

Groaning, Magdalene snapped her head back in a vicious way, making some of the men in the room uneasy. At the same time, her jaw dislocated itself and broke free, only to swing back in place with a crunching jolt, giving her an expression that could only have come from hell.

"Come on kid!" urged the Commander impatiently.

He pulled out a large knife and ran the naked blade across his palm. Placing his wounded hand over her head, he insisted, "Tell me what you see!"

Straight away, the blood began to flow past her long lashes and into her eyes, turning them into deep pools of crimson red. Her speech flowed from a cauldron of demonic voices - each distinct, each cursing and riling against the other in some hellish dispute, as if a terrible clash of personalities was erupting inside the girl.

"Hush…hush…no more telling, no more secrets for unraveling…Lest the Christians flee our wrath, lest Michael rise to call our bluff…"

At the mention of Michael, the girl threw herself onto the floor and writhed like a snake.

"This is bullshit!" said the Commander. "I'll take care of that scumbag priest. You tell me what I want to know."

Magdalene snapped her face towards the Commander and growled with demonic rage.

"*Careful with your tongue, you insolent fool,*" screeched the multitude of spirits. Her face had become an icy throne of evil while her body continued to be savaged in a horrific tug of war between unseen dragons.

The Commander took a cautious step back from the thrashing girl on the floor. This had never happened before. Given the right spell, these demons had been obliging, talkative even. Something or someone was clearly hampering the divination process.

"Every time you use her to foretell the future, you're shortening her life," said a voice from the back. "Demons don't give out anything for free, there's always a price to pay. You should know that by now, Commander."

Taken by surprise, the small group of Praetorian officers whipped around and drew their weapons.

"Put your guns away, gentlemen," said the intruder.

Instead, the request was curtly answered by the intimidating noise of weapons being cocked.

"Hold your fire!" barked the Commander. He pushed his way to the front of the group and came face to face with a pair of Lumen agents.

The unwelcomed guests appeared to be Asian twins, both of the same height and built. And both dressed in their signature Lumen suits and ties, although one was mainly decked out in white and the other in black. Looking like androgynous clones in heavy makeup, there was nonetheless no mistaking the strong presence of danger lurking beneath their effeminate smiles.

"How did you get in here?" demanded the Commander. None of his men, including himself had heard so much as a door creaking. And security at the command center was anything but easy to breach.

"How we got in isn't as important as who sent us," said the agent in black. "The Vice-president has told us to give you boys a helping hand. So far, it appears your progress in this matter has been unimpressive."

The Praetorians were seething like a nest of vipers.

"Stand down," ordered the Commander. It took a few moments before his men would grudgingly comply.

The rivalry between the Praetorians and the Agents was more than just a fight for bragging rights. It was a struggle for dominance in the new world. In the hierarchy of things to come, the capricious loyalties of most mercenaries meant that neither group was ready to lose their Lumen advantage.

"Tell Mr. Chambers that all is proceeding to plan. There's no need for your interference here," said the Commander, his tone filled with loathing for the trespassers.

"That's not what it looks like," replied the agent in white. He pushed past the cabal of military officers and walked towards Magdalene.

Seeing the Lumen agent, the child sprang up like a marionette, her motions jerky and convulsive, her face lost in the dungeons of her possessed state.

"It seems that the success of your mission rests on the predictions of a little girl. I didn't know you to be superstitious, Commander," the agent said sarcastically. "Or are you simply not confident of your plan?"

"So you're the bastards who messed with the oracle," realized the Commander, fuming.

The man in the white suit laughed. He pulled out a small strip of yellow paper inscribed with Chinese markings and plastered the talisman on the girl's forehead, mumbling an incantation as he did so.

At once, Magdalene began to simmer down. The fire in her eyes went out and color returned to her cheeks. She was not free from the darkness roosting in her body, but at least she was no longer a puppet tossed between monsters that would gladly rip her apart as payment for a prophecy.

The black suit stepped up to the Praetorian Commander and added, "The Catholic Resistance is highly trained, highly organized..."

"That's right, we agree on that," interrupted the Commander. "We're not dealing with buffoons like yourselves, we need all the information we can get. It doesn't hurt to know our fortunes going into the next fight."

"Except the future is a fickle mistress," argued the agent. "The more she reveals, the more she hides. No oracle can guarantee its own predictions. Besides, you keep dipping your big hands into the tiny cookie jar and you'll break it. I'm sure Mr. Chambers won't appreciate you taking such liberties with his pet."

As the agent said this, his white twin stood behind Magdalene and smirked, gently stroking her hair like a man trying to calm an unstable beast. The girl had regained some degree of calmness, although her face still betrayed the darkness imprisoning her senses.

"I'm warning you, don't mock me," said the Commander. "We do what we must to win this war. The Vice-president knows that I'll stop at nothing to complete this mission."

The agent scoffed. "Nothing is what I hear you've been doing," he retorted.

Before the man could blink, the Commander had one hand

clutching his throat and the other ready to shove a blade into his gaping mouth.

"Take it easy, we're all on the same team here," said the other twin.

The Commander snorted. "Are we?" he asked, pushing the steel tip of his blade against the agent's cheek.

Despite the intimidation, the Lumen agents refused to tamper their rhetoric.

"Come now, don't kill the messenger just because you don't like the message," said the man in white. "Mr. Chambers has given you until the end of this week to deliver the goods. If you fail, one of your darling officers here might be looking at a major promotion."

The Commander scowled. He withdrew his blade and threw the black suit onto the floor. The stakes were too high. If he killed these men while they were acting as Lumen emissaries, there was no telling what the boss would do.

"Get off my trailer before I feed you to my dogs," he threatened.

The agent in black chuckled and calmly stood up. He smoothed out the wrinkled collar of his expensive suit and said, "Remember, until the end of the week…"

"And just to make sure you don't screw up," said his partner in white. "We'll be tagging along for the ride. Think of us as an insurance policy in case your *fortunes* take a dip. After all darling, we're here to help."

The twins broke into raucous laughter, looking like mirror reflections of each other.

"Stay out of my way," the Commander hissed. "Go back and tell Chambers we've got a good track on the priests. We should bide our time, wait until the enemy grows complacent and then strike. If we move too soon, we'll lose them."

"Ah yes, patience is bitter but its fruit is sweet. Unfortunately that's a virtue the Vice-president doesn't have, so you can tell him yourself if you like," replied the man in white.

"But tick tock tick tock, you handsome devil," said his partner, contemptuously. "It's only when the Christian world gets a true taste of Lumen justice, when their heroes lie broken and dead, will the Resistance die. If I were you, I'd stop playing with little girls and go kill me some Catholic priests."

The Commander was dead silent. His face was stone cold. It was difficult to gauge his expression under the silicone mask, but his entire body was tense with rage. The anger in the room was boiling to the point of peril. It was obvious that a line had been crossed.

Sensing this, the twins decided to retreat.

"Time for us to leave," announced the agent in black. "Wouldn't want to keep these fine gentlemen from doing their jobs."

Without delay, his twin partner tore the yellow talisman off Magdalene's forehead and stuck it onto the vest of a Praetorian sergeant like a used piece of gum.

"She'll be fine for now," said the agent as he walked past the Commander. "But careful you don't break her…"

"Or I assure you, she'll end up breaking you," taunted the black suit.

A few of the Praetorian officers shifted nervously when Magdalene turned and looked at them. But there was nothing to suggest that she would lash out. The demons within her had been duly contained, at least until the next time their destructive powers would be called upon.

"We'll be in touch, gentlemen," said the agents, purring.

As they both turned to leave, the Praetorian Commander brusquely grabbed one of them by his silk tie and grunted, "You will give me your names, agents. I will speak with your superiors!"

"Call me Yin," said one.

"Call me Yang," replied the other, his delicate voice suddenly turning gruff.

Then looking around at the Praetorians, he added scornfully, "Among men like yourselves, we have no superiors."

And muttering a spell under their breaths, they both vanished into thin air.

Chapter 27

The Lafayette Grand Central was one of the country's most iconic train stations. It was built over a century and a half ago and stood like a gothic castle overlooking the city square. Huge, majestic and even foreboding in its architecture, its size and dimensions were dwarfed only by the countless numbers of passengers who wormed their way through its many tunnels and halls each day.

Hour after hour, the massive structure swallowed hundreds of thousands of passengers who pushed and shoved their way into the bowels of the subway system, even as elsewhere in the building, thousands more were excreted from its metal entrails, flooding the streets with people too self-absorbed to realize that the soul of their city, and indeed the whole human world, was in danger of being devoured by sin.

On this day, beneath the watchful gaze of the stone gargoyles high above, three renegade priests and a beautiful woman staggered into the station looking for refuge.

"Where do we go?" asked Chelsea, trying to look inconspicuous.

The hood of her jacket was drawn over her head while a large pair of sunglasses helped shield her stunning features from passersby. She was still a famous celebrity, and it was unlikely that the world's most desirable woman would go unnoticed in a crowded station for too long. Whoever their contacts in the Resistance were, they needed to find them fast…before a rowdy fan, paparazzi, or worse, a Lumen spy should find her first.

"Over there," said Michael, pointing to a phone booth. He had been instructed earlier to wait for a call.

As the group pushed their way to the wall of public phones, the crowds pressed in against them like a surging tide. The noise of chattering commuters, plus the smell of so many sweaty bodies crammed together inside an old musky building was nauseating. Chelsea began to feel claustrophobic. She clung to Michael's arm while Gabriel lent a supporting shoulder to Raphael.

When they finally reached the phones, Michael turned around and furrowed his brow. "Damn it," he cursed, "Where'd they go?"

Chelsea felt a pang of panic. They had been separated from Gabriel and Raphael. The heavy flow of bodies engulfing them made it impossible to spot the two priests. Every second brought them farther apart, risking their situation even more.

Just as Michael was about to dive back into the crowds in search of his missing companions, the phone rang. He promptly answered the call.

"Don't worry about your friends, they'll be fine," assured the female voice on the line.

"Where are you?" asked Michael, detecting a slight Russian accent in her tone.

"No questions, just listen," ordered the woman curtly. "Ten feet to your left, there's a janitor in blue overalls and a white cap. Do you see him?"

"Affirmative."

"Go. Follow him now," instructed the voice urgently.

Before the priest could reply, the line went dead. Michael hung up the receiver and took hold of Chelsea's hand.

"Come on, let's go," he said, keeping his eyes on the subject.

At the same time, he reached under his jacket and unclipped the holster catch on his sidearm. All these years of working in black ops had taught him the value of caution, even among supposed allies.

Pushing their way through the traffic, they drew near to the janitor. As they approached the contact, the man in the overalls started to inch away, slowly cutting a path through the crowds with his cleaning trolley.

Michael and Chelsea followed close behind. Anytime the crowds got too dense, the janitor would stop and tarry for a while, giving them a chance to catch up. Not once however did the man draw attention to himself or acknowledge his pursuers. Instead he shuffled along the congested path until he turned a corner in the passage. Then parking his trolley by the side, he retrieved a jumble of keys from his belt and unlocked the grubby door before him.

Sporting an old baseball cap that looked more weathered than his grizzled face, he was the sort of individual no one would take a second glance at. His stooped posture, stubble and stained overalls made him invisible in a city too wealthy to notice another cleaner in the gutter.

Patiently, the janitor waited until the priest and the woman caught up before pushing his trolley into the darkness. Once they were all inside, he slammed the door shut and threw the switch on the wall.

"Welcome to purgatory," he said, making a grand gesture with his arms.

A long row of ceiling lights flickered to life, showering the dank corridor with a greenish hue that accentuated the mildew encrusted on the walls. Lined up along the sides were two rows of dented storage lockers, battered and tarnished with age. The whole corridor looked depressing and cold.

"Purgatory?" mumbled Chelsea, a little disconcerted.

The janitor looked at the woman and smiled. "It's just code for this here sanctuary. You ain't dead," he said. "Least not yet."

He walked up to one of the metal lockers and pulled noisily at the door, yanking the rusty cover open. The screeching noise, like nails on a chalkboard, only made Chelsea grimace even more.

"Where are my confreres?" asked Michael abruptly.

"Don't worry about the padres. They'll be fine," swore the janitor. He reached into the heavy locker and tugged at something. There was the sound of a lever dropping and almost immediately, the weighty metal closet slid aside like a screen door to reveal a small iron hatch hidden beneath.

"Platform five, carriage 401," said the janitor, stuffing a small tracking device into Michael's hand. He squatted down, unlocked the hatch on the floor and jerked it wide open.

"Don't tell me, more tunnels," complained Chelsea. "I swear, you guys are taking this *Underground Church* thing way too literally."

The janitor rose to his feet, clearly amused. "Funny girl, I like her," he said to Michael.

"It's the only reason I keep her alive," the priest grunted back. "Come on, princess, let's go."

He reached for the woman but she slapped his hand away.

"Don't touch me," Chelsea remarked. She grabbed a flashlight hanging from the trolley and lowered her legs into the opened hatch.

"You coming or what?" she asked Michael.

Before he could answer, she slipped into the hole and disappeared altogether.

"Betcha' didn't expect that," said the janitor, chuckling. He reached for an extra flashlight and gave it to the priest.

"Don't keep the young lady waiting," he teased. "No telling what she might do next."

Looking a little peeved, Michael turned his back on the cleaner and dropped his muscled frame down the hatch.

✝

"Shit!" said Chelsea, looking disgusted with the muck on her shoes.

"Guano to be exact," said Michael, trailing a short distance behind her. "Bat shit."

Hearing that, Chelsea gasped and shone her flashlight at the darkened roof. The heady beam of light danced around the disused tunnel, frantically cutting through the shadows and confirming her anxieties.

"Damn it, I hate bats!" she said, shuddering.

As it turned out, the bats were more afraid of her. Spooked by the voices and the flashing beam, the noisy colony fled their perches and fell like a squadron of dive-bombers, squeaking furiously as hundreds of leathery wings brushed against her.

"Ugh," cried Chelsea, utterly revolted. "Go away, shoo!" she shouted, swatting furiously at the cloud swirling above her head.

"Stop fooling around," said Michael, appearing like a phantom from the dark. He picked her up like a doll, pulled her through the flapping mass and dropped her into the clear.

"Thanks," said Chelsea, looking quite disheveled. "Those things always give me the creeps," she confessed. "I'm going to ignore that you dropped me on my butt though..."

"That makes two of us," replied the priest.

Indignant, Chelsea flashed her torch at Michael's face. He glared back, his visage lost somewhere between a smile and a scowl.

"I'm glad you're enjoying this," she griped.

The guilty smirk on his face only widened with pleasure. "What can I say, I hate bats too," Michael quipped. "Good thing you went first."

"You're such a douchebag," exclaimed Chelsea, pretending to sound livid.

Secretly however, she was delighted that the priest was warming up to her, even if she didn't know how long it would last. Despite her misgivings, she was curious about the cleric.

"So tell me, why'd you become a priest? You don't exactly strike me as the priestly type."

Michael looked at her. "Long story," he said.

"Long walk," answered Chelsea, noting that the abandoned rails under the station seemed to stretch on forever.

When Michael didn't say anything more, she continued, "Raphael told me you were in the military. Were you a soldier?"

"Among other things," admitted the priest.

"So what happened?" she pressed on. "What gave you religion?"

True to form, Michael started to clamp up. "You talk too much, you know that?" he grumbled. "I prefer the bats."

"Well you talk too little," she pouted. "But you're right, the bats would make better company than you."

Before she could say more, the tunnel walls began to shake and rumble. Bits of plaster broke off the ceiling and plunged to the ground. The earth itself seemed to shiver with fear. Chelsea felt her heart race. Had they been discovered? Was this the prelude to another demon attack?

"Don't panic, it's just the trains running," said Michael. "Noise and tremors get amplified down here in the tunnels."

As he said that, the shrill whistle of a metro train echoed all around them. Hearing that, Chelsea looked over her shoulders with some anxiety, expecting to see several tons of steel carriages barreling down towards her. Instead, all she got were more bats fluttering through the empty cavern.

"Relax, this section of the rail has been shut down for years," explained Michael, checking the map on his tracking device.

"How can you be sure?" confronted Chelsea. "How do you know there isn't a train coming up behind us?"

"I can't, so I suggest you talk less and walk faster," said the priest, striding ahead.

Chelsea trotted after Michael. "Look, I know that polite conversation isn't your strong point but..."

"But what?" the priest responded gruffly, clearly in no mood to oblige.

"You know, we're not that different, you and I," remarked Chelsea. She was determined to press on.

"How'd you figure that?" asked Michael.

"You said yourself, the Corporation owned the military, just like they own the fashion and media industries. Whether we admit it or not, we've both had our fair share of serving the Lumen cause, don't you think?"

"So what?" demanded the priest.

"So what made you give up your old life?" she asked defiantly. "I'm no expert on the military, but I'd heard that the Corporation used Army units to hunt down and destroy religious groups in the past. If the rumors were true, what turned you from a soldier of fortune to a soldier of God?"

The question seemed so intrusive that Michael didn't answer at first. He merely looked at her with some perplexity.

"That's pretty obvious, don't you think?" he said, hoping to quell the dialogue.

"No..." replied the woman.

"Which part of not wanting to serve the powers of darkness don't you understand? These people are Satanists and monsters. They work with demons to usher in the reign of the Antichrist to enslave the world. I refused to be part of that. What more do you want to know?"

Chelsea could see that Michael was getting upset. And yet, she clung doggedly to the questioning, refusing to give up.

"At the time, did you *know* they were monsters? Because like everyone else, I sure as hell didn't get the memo," she retorted. "Thanks to the Corporation, I didn't even believe in the devil until a few days ago."

"And how has that worked out for you?" asked Michael bluntly, deflecting the topic from himself. "Considering that the path to eternal life is a moral life."

Chelsea was stunned by the rejoinder. She looked as if she had been slapped across the face.

"You're right, it's true," she said softly, sounding chastised. "I deserved the misery and suffering that came with rejecting the truth about my soul..."

She said nothing else for a while, her eyes growing moist in the darkness. Then taking a deep breath, she regained her composure. And when she spoke again, there was a great depth of contrition that quietly disarmed Michael.

"I've gone through my whole life never thinking about my Creator or questioning the meaning of my existence. As soon as I was old enough to think for myself, I was an atheist. I couldn't get out of religion fast enough. I just did what I wanted, whenever I wanted. I was free to live my own life without rules or judgment. Only, I wasn't free. The more I got what I wanted, the more imprisoned I felt. And pretty soon, you get to a place where you think you'd never be able to climb out of the shit hole you buried yourself in. Then things happen to open your eyes, to make you change your mind. The last thing I want now is to go back into that hole…"

"Then don't," replied Michael. "It's not how you begin, it's how you end."

"That's my point, I don't just want to make a change. I want to make a change that will last. Everything I know today convinces me of the truth about God. I know that from everything that's happened in the last few days. But somehow, I'm still holding back. All my life I followed my heart and my heart betrayed me. How do you walk away from fear when it's the only thing you've ever known?"

"What matters right now is the choice you make today. Nothing in this life counts for anything if the next life is lost. Leave the past to the past," advised Michael, hoping to end the discussion.

"And what about you, have you left the past to the past?" asked Chelsea.

"You're not going leave this alone, are you?" Michael responded with annoyance.

"Why? What'd you have to hide? Every saint has a past. Every sinner has a future. That's what they say, isn't it?"

The priest furrowed his eyebrows in distress. In spite of the dimness, Chelsea could see the cruel lines of suffering etched across his face like an epitaph. Instantly, she regretted her brazen comeback. She realized her constant digging for answers had unearthed a casket of open wounds for the man. Without meaning to, she had stubbornly pushed and prodded until she broke down the walls of his private grief, all for the sake of satisfying her thoughtless curiosity. The pangs of remorse began to slice into her heart. Duly ashamed, she hung her head and apologized.

"Look, I'm sorry. I just thought maybe there was something you could tell me, something from your own experience that could help me right now," said Chelsea.

She tried to salvage her dignity, brushing back a lock of stray hair from her face. But the color on her cheeks only deepened with shame, causing her eyes to well up with tears.

Angry and surprised at her own emotions, Chelsea kept silent for a few seconds.

Eventually she mumbled aloud, "I'm sorry, Father, I was way out of line. Please forgive me."

With that, she shone her flashlight into the darkness and soldiered ahead, her cheeks burning with disgust for herself. But Michael caught her gently by the elbow.

The woman stopped and looked at the priest. Instead of scorn and judgment, she saw something else. There was an unexpected softness in his face, a tenderness that wasn't there before. And for the first time, Chelsea saw the man behind the cloth.

"You asked me what made me give up my old life," noted Michael grimly. He turned his face away from the woman and stared into the darkness, as if drawing his thoughts from the shadows.

"You're right, I worked for the government. And the government worked for Lumen Corp. When I was a soldier, I pulled the trigger as much as I had to in order to get the job done. There was no right or wrong, no good or evil. There was only the mission, and the mission was to break the Christian Resistance and take out their leadership…"

He dropped his tired frame onto a concrete ledge and sat there like a gloomy sculpture, his broad shoulders drooping with angst.

"You wanted to know. So I'll tell you…"

The tone in his voice was such that Chelsea regretted stoking the embers of this fire. But it was too late. She had already pried open the furnace of his pain and his grief began to leak out.

Michael told her what happened the night of the operation; how they had cornered some Underground Christians in a derelict church. His orders were to assassinate the 'renegade bishop' and round up the rest for deportation.

"I was trained to kill for the regime. For me, death was just part of the job," said Michael in remorse. "But I learned something the night I pulled that trigger. For a priest, death was the only way he could truly retire."

Michael described how the blood of that holy man poured out like an oblation on the altar. But no one else was supposed to die that night. Most, if not all, would be sentenced to prison or re-education camps.

Unfortunately, there was a young Praetorian officer, a lieutenant whose monstrous appetite for malice would be sated only by the butchery of innocents. Cruel and avaricious, the junior officer had heckled him to take no prisoners. But Michael was a captain, and he refused to allow the massacre.

Then there was the little girl, a child barely old enough to understand danger, who had become separated from her mother in the mayhem. In the chaos, the future priest had hoped to shield the youngster from the attention of the Praetorian officer, who bristling with disgust and defiance, had begun to pummel the prisoners with savage blows, only to be stopped by the cold steel of Michael's gun pressed up against his skull.

"I ordered him to stop. He wouldn't listen," grumbled the former captain.

As soon as Michael turned his back, the lieutenant turned his rage on the little girl. And the deafening blast of a shotgun tore life and limb from the hapless child, shredding her body into a pile of bloody rags.

Stunned and furious, Michael tore into the lieutenant like a spirit of vengeance, riddling the culprit with hundreds of bullets until the gurgling blood drowned out the screams of the guilty man. Almost as quickly, every weapon in the room jumped up in aggression. To avoid a massacre between his own troops and the Praetorian detachment, Michael surrendered himself to Lumen justice. Taken into custody and court-martialed, he was charged with treason, stripped of his rank and thrown into the dungeon.

"There in solitary confinement, I thought I was done with violence and death," said the priest. "But death wasn't done with me."

As Michael spoke, his breathing became labored, each word dragging up a shoal of memories too brutal to voice. Still he carried on, trawling the passages of time for something to help Chelsea understand.

He knew the Praetorians would never stomach the slaughter of their own by an outsider, and he was right. In the dead of night, they came and took him from his cell. They beat him and dragged him off into the shadows for execution. But he broke out of his shackles and escaped into the boondocks, trailing a pack of Lumen killers on his tail.

For days, he was hunted like a wild animal. He ran until his injuries took a desperate toll on his strength. Weak from the loss of blood, he stumbled into an alley and fainted behind a dumpster. There, lying on a mound of waste and sewage, he should have died. But providence had other plans. A strong pair of hands reached down and pulled him out of the filth. For a long time afterwards, he languished between life and death, delirious and paranoid, until the fever broke and he emerged from the darkness gasping for light.

Later on, Michael learnt that the old couple who sheltered and nursed him back to health were in fact Underground Christians, part of the Resistance that he had persecuted without mercy. Filled with confusion and shame, the former soldier felt his defenses break down. And it was then that the scales began to fall from his eyes.

In the weeks that followed, he grew stronger, nourished by the Christian faith and generosity of his benefactors. The old couple ran a diner where they hid the wounded soldier in a secret room in the basement. They were Japanese. They spoke little and asked even less, but they cared for him with great charity - healing and changing his bandages without rest. Above all, they prayed fervently for him.

Gradually, the gift of faith began to peel away the myth of Lumen lies. As his body slowly recovered, his soul started to come alive as well, until the time came when he could do no less than ask for the waters of baptism.

"After that, when the Truth became a living part of me, when I realized God was real, joining the priesthood was the only thing that mattered," he declared. "As a soldier, I spent my life trying to destroy Holy Mother Church. As a priest, I would gladly sacrifice my life to protect her."

Yet despite Michael's convictions, Chelsea could see that the priest struggled to absolve himself of his violent past. She knew with a woman's intuition that he still carried the burden of guilt resulting from the death of that innocent girl.

"I know it's ironic that I became a Christian and a priest," said Michael softly. "Maybe I'll never be able to atone for the lives I've taken. But I'll be damned if I let the Corporation destroy my soul anymore than I already have…"

With that, he reached into his pocket and pulled out a small crucifix. Raising it to his lips, he kissed the cross with all the zeal of his priestly vows. Then saying nothing more, he put away the sacramental, locked away the pain and got up. And quietly continued down the tracks, as if the silence between them had never been broken.

This time, it was Chelsea who reached out and caught him gently by the arm, holding him back from disappearing into the darkness.

"It's not your fault that young girl died, you tried to protect her," she remarked.

"And who protected the rest I had a hand in killing?" demanded Michael, his self-loathing clearly evident. "Before these hands were consecrated to Christ, they were dedicated to the murder of Christians. Do you know what it's like to mourn the deaths of your victims?"

"I know you were a soldier and soldiers obey orders," responded Chelsea, hoping to reason with him. "What choice did you have?"

Michael looked down and rubbed the palms of his hands, as if they were stained with blood.

"We always have choices, even when we don't realize we do," he said, critically. "We can lose our way, become so fascinated by evil that we don't recognize what's good anymore, even when we're staring right at it…"

"So for the rest of your life you're going to tie a noose around your neck and lynch yourself in guilt, is that it?" asked Chelsea. "Is that how you plan to go on?"

"What do you care?" scoffed the priest, making no attempt to hide his anger.

"I care because we're both victims of Lumen Corp, we both carry the seeds of doubt over our pasts. I thought maybe if we shared that darkness, we could help each other crawl into the light. But all you want to do is flagellate yourself with blame. If that's faith, if that's hope, then count me out!"

Stung by the rebuke, Michael knew her resentment was justified. He had tried to convince her to leave the past behind, only to have her turn the tables on him. By then, he had had enough of her questions and taunts.

He rose to his full height and growled. "Don't pretend you know me, you've no idea what I'm capable of," said the priest, raising his voice.

But Chelsea was not intimidated. She folded her arms and shot back in frustration.

"Why do you insist on punishing yourself," she retorted. "What makes you so special from everyone else who's ever done wrong?"

"Because I know the evil that still burns within me. A man who forgets his own history is doomed to repeat it. I have no intentions of forgetting who I was or what I did!"

"But…"

"Enough!" cried Michael, cutting off the woman. He would allow the subject to be broached no more. Cursing under his breath, he stomped off into the shadows.

For a while, both walked on in silence, saying nothing to each other. Michael brooding in torment, Chelsea thinking that the toughest thing she ever had to do was just allowing herself to be loved. But ever since the mystical vision of her children in paradise, she had begun to see that even though she still doubted herself, she had no reason to doubt the mercy of God.

Then something happened. Prompted by the whisperings of grace, the woman stopped the man, reached out and gently held on to his face. In turn, Michael didn't resist the touch of her hand. His features were still contracted with angst, but he chose not to pull away from her gentleness.

"Maybe we're *not supposed* to forget," Chelsea said to the priest, recalling her experience at the consecration of the bread and wine during Mass.

"Maybe we're supposed to forgive ourselves for who we were!"

Chapter 28

It was a foolish mistake, something no experienced operative would've tolerated, much less commit. But the station owner was not the only fool to be drunk on the wine of his own arrogance and complacency. Kaz realized his own hubris had laid the stumbling block for the fall. He had imagined all his contacts to be as firmly entrenched in the fight against evil as he was, when in reality some were more interested in profiteering from the conflict than winning the war.

As it was, a sloppy conscience on the part of the station owner gave way to sloppy procedures. It didn't take long for the enemy to break the encryption codes left behind by the old geezer. The data stored in the digital tablet revealed names, transactions and distribution channels, everything the Corporation needed to close down Kaz's operation.

The Palestinian rebel shook his head. Looking at his monitors, he could hardly believe his bad luck. One careless contact toppled another like a line of falling dominos, and before Kaz could properly assess the damage, three safe houses and more than a dozen collaborators had fallen under the scourge of Lumen justice.

But there was something else in the reports, something more menacing than the crunch of Praetorian boots. Those that survived the dragnet spoke of fearsome creatures on the prowl.

Kaz studied the recordings from the cameras on site. He had made it a point to hook up a secure link to their surveillance equipment from his own systems. Looking at the blurry images, there was no denying what they were.

The weapons dealer was deeply disturbed.

He was no theologian but he knew enough about spirits to know that they couldn't be plainly captured on any electronic device. Someone clearly wanted him to see this. The Corporation was diabolical to be sure, but they had always been careful about concealing their infernal roots. This new contempt for discretion could only mean one thing. The battle for souls was quickly reaching a new zenith. More people were going to die. Sheltered inside the secret walls of his bunker, Kaz felt safe enough from any sudden invasions. A host of security measures further ensured that nothing would get into the complex without triggering its defense systems. Unfortunately, the same could not be said for his collaborators who fell victims to the Praetorian attacks. Watching the images unfold on his monitors, the hardened warrior felt shaken to his bones.

Again and again, the same terrifying scene was played out. A menagerie of dark spirits descended upon the rebels like a storm, devouring their victims in a whirlpool of violence and fear. Armed with weapons and prayer, some of the victims tried to put up a fight. But there was no contest. Even though the vicious carnage captured on screen forced Kaz to look away a few times, he saw enough to perceive the presence of demons in the fray, each corporal and distinct, each frightful to behold. And when the dice of destruction had rolled to a stop, five malignant players stood out in this game of death.

Kaz had never seen an evil cluster like this - a naked succubus with a head full of snakes, a dark spirit wearing an empty face, a small impish boy with a swollen skull full of maggots and a grey sluggish creature with leathery skin. There was even a pair of grotesque spirits conjoined like Siamese twins, who raged and spat at each other as they cut through their victims like a double-edged sword.

He felt his blood grow cold. Hell had dealt his partners a cruel hand. Now it was up to him to gamble his own odds of survival. While he pondered this danger, Kaz noticed something else. There was another face hidden in the background, frozen in the glass reflections like a phantom witness to a crime scene.

He zoomed in on the digital image and saw a young girl in orthopedic braces, the same one he had seen lingering in the sewers when they escaped from the cathedral the night before. The computer tallied the various screen caps and confirmed his suspicions. She was there in every attack, swaying and quivering in the shadows, almost buzzing like a lightning rod channeling the evil.

Kaz had no idea who the mysterious girl was, but he knew without hesitation *what* she was. Demons normally needed a talisman of some kind to act as a portal into the world. Often it was a small statue, charm or medallion. But he suspected that the portal in this case wasn't a mystical object at all. He had heard stories of how innocent children were sometimes stolen or sold into the service of the devil, most when they were just infants, some when they were still cradled in the wombs of their mothers. In return, those who pledged to sacrifice these innocents were rewarded with wealth, mystical powers and other dark favors. Over the years, the possessed child becomes a slave to Satan, consecrated to the Father of Lies as a powerful conduit for his minions.

Studying the expression of the young girl, Kaz realized that she was trapped between life and death, too scared to live but too scared to die. Unlike a statue or medallion inscribed with magical runes, this was a symbiotic feast between spirit and flesh. The older the girl got, the stronger the influence of the demons. In truth, the child was as much a hostage to evil as she was an aggressor. Cursing, the devout Muslim frowned at the complication. How do you sever the portal without taking an innocent life?

He had to warn Michael. His fingers raced across the digital console, but before a connection could be made, the computers suddenly went offline. One by one, the systems began to shut down. The central processing unit groaned like a wounded animal while the lights in the bunker flickered and died, snuffed out by a power surge that erupted from nowhere.

Before the man could draw another breath, the room was entirely pitch black. In the silence, the Palestinian slowly reached for his gun. As he grabbed his weapon, he could hear the back-up generators kick in. Seconds later, the hum of energy spread throughout the room and the systems came back to life.

Kaz got up slowly and paced the floor, his rifle at the ready. Everything looked the same as before. He glanced at the monitor and noticed that the bunker's defenses were back online and operational. None of the security measures appeared to be breached. He leaned over the console and engaged a scan. The answer came back negative. Creepy as it was, there was no reason to suspect that this was anything more than a freak power surge. Even so, he was cautious. He raised his weapon and scanned his surroundings.

Minutes ticked by and nothing happened. The more he waited, the more his pulse began to calm down until finally, he smiled and breathed a sigh of relief. It was then that he noticed something odd. His breath was vaporizing like steam. A numbing chill began to creep back into his heart, sending shivers down his spine. He looked at the thermostat and the readings were completely normal. Yet somehow, the bunker had turned icy cold in less time than it took to reboot the systems.

Kaz wasn't sure what was going on, but he was certain of one thing. He was not alone.

✝

"The world is going to hell!" said the woman with the Russian accent.

"It certainly is," observed the man sitting next to her. He looked down at the small prayer book in his hands and ran his fingers lightly over its wrinkled pages.

The Russian smirked. She was a tall leggy blonde with a short crisp temper and even less patience.

"And despite all your prayers too. It hardly seems fair," she scoffed, flicking the ash from her cigarette while her other hand rested gingerly on a submachine gun in her lap.

"Fair's got nothing to do with it," replied the middle-aged man. Dressed in a staid black sweater with glasses hugging the bony ridge of his nose, he could've passed for a boring college professor instead of the hardened revolutionary that he was.

"Then what does?" asked the woman. "We've been fighting the night for so long, I've forgotten what the day looks like." She took an angry drag on her cigarette and blew out her frustration.

Patiently, the man closed his prayer book and tried to fan the pungent smoke from his face. The woman chose not to notice. She drew another puff of tobacco and exhaled in his direction.

"I never thought I'd say this, but how much blood does it take before the Almighty acts to save his people," she grumbled. "This crazy war has made too many martyrs already, young men and women dying before they've had a chance to live. The virtuous suffer while the wicked continue to prosper and mock everything that's holy. No wonder so few people believe in God."

Restless and annoyed, she flipped on the safety catch for her weapon, pulled out the magazine to check that it was fully loaded and then vigorously slammed the rounds back into their chamber. Her growing angst was not lost on her companion as he tried to calm her down.

"Defending the truth is never an easy thing," he asserted. "Only those who seek it and love it can know the value of sacrificing life

267

itself to defend it. Besides, atheism is a condition that is easily cured by death. As for the wicked, *the sinner's road is smoothly paved but it ends at the pit of Sheol...*"

"Enough with the preaching," she groaned. "Don't you ever tire of parroting those lines? The weight of the whole world is pressing down on us and meanwhile, the enemy grows stronger and more dangerous. It's enough to test the patience of saints, and I assure you, I am no saint!"

"You believe in God, don't you?" asked the man. "The enemies of God wish ardently that the Church would be forced back into the catacombs of the first century, dismissed totally from public life. And in many ways they have succeeded because many Christians are either too lazy, fearful or indifferent to defend their public right to faith and expression."

The woman scoffed.

"Don't tell me about public faith, my parents were Orthodox Christians. *They* believed in God, so much so that the Corporation had to silence their very public faith. I'm not religious, never have been. But I believed in them, and in everything that they stood for. It's not revenge I seek, comrade. It's the defense of their memory that I fight for. Yet does God believe in us who fight to defend his name?"

The man kept quiet. He could understand her pain. "Your parents," he paused. "You were close?"

"I owe them everything," she replied without hesitation. "There's nothing I wouldn't do for them."

He nodded his head. She never shared the details, but he knew her parents had been arrested for stubbornly defending their Orthodox faith. Sighing, he removed his glasses and wiped them against the frayed edges of his old sweater. When he finally returned the spectacles to his face, there was a faraway look in his eyes, like he was recalling something from another time.

"We all face temptations at one point or another," he shared. "The temptation to lose faith, to lose trust in the nearness of God. Yet no matter how dark the night gets, the sun still rises in the morning. It's precisely when you remain steadfast in faith, when giving in would've been so much easier that you finally know who you are."

"You think so?"

"I know so, or I wouldn't be sitting here talking to you,"

answered the man. "Especially when you're trying kill me with all that smoke."

The lady laughed and nodded, but she made no attempt to extinguish her cigarette. She knew the man had been thrown into prison and tortured more times than he could remember on account of his Christian faith. And yet, almost miraculously, he survived every Lumen attempt to silence him thus far.

"You know as well as I do that evil cannot be ignored or shoved aside," the man continued. "It must be confronted and overcome, both with faith and with reason."

Just then, the metal doors separating the train carriages slid opened. The blonde looked up and saw a burly sentry at the doorway beckoning to her.

"They're here," confirmed the woman.

She flicked the cigarette onto the floor and killed the flame under her boots. Then picking up her weapon, she followed the guard into the adjoining carriage. Her companion in the black sweater got up and quietly tagged along. They entered a passenger car that had been hastily modified into a mini command post. Various surveillance apparatus were crammed into the small working space. Most of the plastic seats had already been removed to make room for computers and equipment. Hunched over the sensitive data was a small team of men and women keeping their eyes and ears open for the first sign of trouble.

The tall Russian lady motioned to the sentry keeping guard. He reached down and yanked the rusty side door open. In stepped Gabriel and Raphael, sandwiched between two hulking metro cops in full uniforms.

"Welcome, gentlemen. I trust the police escort made it easier for you to avoid the crowds," said the towering blonde.

She had learnt of Raphael's weakened condition from her sources and had sent the cops in to help.

"Indeed, where did you get the official threads?" enquired Gabriel, noting the impressive details on the police uniforms.

Each officer was issued a holographic badge that couldn't be replicated without breaking the Lumen codes. And that wasn't always easy to reproduce.

"Oh, I assure you, Officers Blackwell and Cope are real cops. Not everyone who works for City Hall is a Lumen thug. Besides, the enemy has been walking among us for years, disguised as our brethren. It's time we had our own spies in the dragon's den, don't you agree?"

She pulled out a fresh cigarette and lit up. "Thank you gentlemen," she muttered, without looking at the men in blue. The two massive cops saluted and returned to their stations.

Gabriel and Raphael glanced at each other. Without a doubt, this woman carried herself with authority. Her chic blonde hair and Slavic features made her look voguish, but the calluses on her knuckles and the way she cradled her weapon suggested nothing less than secret service or military, maybe even the Russian mafia.

Gabriel leaned over to his confrere. "Whoever she is, I'm glad she's on our side," he whispered.

Raphael remained silent but he too observed the same thing. In a fight, she would be as deadly as she was beautiful, he thought.

As he pondered this, the woman slung her rifle and pointed to some chairs. "Have a seat, Fathers. Don't stand on my account," she said, plunking herself down on a small armchair.

Carefully, Gabriel lowered his wounded friend down on a cushion, but he continued to eye the people in the room with mistrust. He had met the Prelate's team before, but he didn't recognize anyone in this new group. Plus the old man himself was nowhere to be seen.

Again, the blonde woman seemed to have read his mind. "Relax, you're among friends," she said.

"Anna is quite right, you're among friends," repeated the stranger lurking behind her.

Since the time they came in, the man in the black sweater had been staying in the background, letting the woman take charge while he observed everything with quiet detachment. But now, he stepped forward like a general taking command.

"I'm Father Robert Pike, Society of Jesus. And this is Anna Koslov, our new head of security."

"What happened to the old head of security?" asked Gabriel. He had met the previous incumbent once. The man was renowned for his courage and loyalty to the cause.

"Death comes for us all, padre. Even for legends, he comes," said Anna, flicking the burning embers from her cigarette.

She glanced up at the friar, hoping to catch a reaction. But Gabriel was impassive, his deadpan expression giving nothing away. Raphael on the other hand struggled to his feet and confronted the stranger in the black sweater.

"As far as I know, the Jesuit known as Robert Pike was also executed in a re-education camp some time ago. If you are who you say you are, how did you escape?" enquired the skeptical doctor.

The man chuckled.

"I'm sorry that my freedom from that gulag disappoints you, but the rumors of my demise have been greatly exaggerated. It seems providence has made quite a habit of breaking me out of Lumen prisons. And this time, with the help of an archangel, I might add..."

"He's telling the truth," came a familiar voice from the opened doorway. Assisted by the sentry, Michael climbed into the carriage with Chelsea in tow.

"I was there when they broke him out," admitted the priest, relieved to see that his two confreres were alive and well.

Beaming with joy, Gabriel and Raphael were thankful to see Michael. For a minute, all three were lost in a huddle of eager handshakes, as if they couldn't believe their good fortune in having survived the litany of evils thrown at them so far.

"Truth be told, your friend here led the entire rescue operation," declared Father Pike. "No doubt I would be lying in a ditch somewhere with a bullet in my skull if he hadn't."

"You got that right," said Michael, extending his hand to the man he helped rescue.

Father Pike ignored the handshake and grasped his fellow Jesuit by the shoulders with great affection. "It's good to see you too, brother," he exclaimed.

In the happy chaos, the men forgot all about the young damsel idling nearby. Anna Koslov was the only one to notice that the girl was growing impatient.

"I don't mean to break up the reunion," grumbled Chelsea. "But can someone please tell me why we're here?"

Lost in the din of their conversations, none of the priests gave her the attention she desired.

"Listen, why are we standing around wasting time?" Chelsea griped. "Can we get on with meeting this Prelate, whoever he is?"

But when no answer was forthcoming, Chelsea began to feel the emotional strain of the last few days creep up on her. Overcome with fatigue, her temper started to slip down the blistering slopes of a meltdown.

"YOU dragged me halfway across the country, into sewers and

tunnels, chased by demons and warlocks, so you can meet and chat about old times?" she accused the men. "Have you forgotten that we're still being hunted like dogs?"

"Pipe down," warned Michael, surprised at her outburst. But Chelsea refused to be hushed. A wave of frustration bubbled up and she started cursing.

"Don't get your panties in a twist," Anna interrupted. "When you do what they do, growing old is a damn near privilege these days. Good priests are dying out faster than we can ordain them. Anytime one survives a bad situation, it's cause for us to celebrate. Cut them some slack."

Chelsea glared at the woman and fired back. "I'm guessing you're no priest, so tell me again, who the hell are you people?"

Unperturbed, the blonde Russian shoved a stool towards Chelsea with her booted heel.

"Take the load off, princess. Sit down before you fall down," she urged, making no attempt to hide the disdain in her voice.

But Chelsea refused to buckle. She stood tall like an Amazon staring down her opponent.

"Forgive us, Miss Shields," Father Pike apologized, trying to defuse the tension between the two women. "This war has taken a toll on our good manners. Please, do have a seat."

He motioned politely to a chair. After what seemed like an eternity of sulking, Chelsea finally relented and sat down.

"The Prelate has arranged for all of you to leave the country," announced Father Pike, dropping the news on them like a ton of bricks.

The group didn't know what to make of this. They were caught, by surprise.

"What're you talking about? I'm not going anywhere," protested Gabriel.

"In case you haven't noticed, there's a war going on," Michael reminded Pike. "And we need every hand on deck. You don't abandon your station when the shit hits the fan. I need to stay here. We all do."

"*You need to stay alive* is what you need, all of you," argued Anna Koslov. "After your dance with the devil the last few days, you've got the entire Lumen army on your backs. How much longer do you think you can run before the wolves catch up to you?"

Michael recognized her Russian accent from the payphone

conversation they had earlier. She was the one who had split them up.

"Take the girl, by all means," he grumbled, indicating Chelsea. "Get her somewhere safe. But our place is right here, on the battlefield…"

"Hello??? Am I invisible?" asked Chelsea, annoyed. "Does anyone even want to know what I think?

"No!" echoed Michael and the Russian, much to the chagrin of Chelsea.

"Listen to me, the streets are getting too hot for you," Father Pike responded. "You've been on the run so you may not know this, but the headlines have been raging with anger and outrage. The media has been blasting the high profile kidnapping of Chelsea Shields by Christian fundamentalists. They've got the entire city screaming for your blood…"

"And if they can't find you, they'll take the blood of any Christian *they can find*," said Anna, chiming in.

"So that's why you reeled us in, because you don't want to lose any more people on account of us. How noble," Chelsea remarked with sarcasm.

Anna replied frostily, "One, I didn't *reel* you in. And two, that's not what I meant."

"Please, everyone, calm down," appealed Raphael. "We've got enough problems without any of us adding to it."

Somewhat exasperated, he turned to Father Pike. "What do you mean calling for *our* blood?" he asked with concern.

"For one thing, your pictures are all over the news," informed the Jesuit. "They've got you on surveillance cameras dragging Miss Shields through the sewers. The Corporation leaked those images so you won't be able to stay on the surface much longer without being recognized."

"So we'll go underground. Haven't we always done that?" asked Raphael, struggling to talk. Despite his recovery from the curse, his strength seemed to be failing him, and his breaths were coming in short gasps.

"For how long?" Father Pike asked the doctor. "Lumen spies have been compromising some of our sanctuaries in recent months. Sooner or later, someone will spot Miss Shields, and then those Christians hiding you will suffer even greater violence and treachery. Do you really want to make more martyrs for the Church because you're too stubborn to leave for your own good?"

At this point, Gabriel felt his ire rising. He didn't like the tone the man was using with Raphael.

"So you'd rather we cut and run, ditch our mission because the wolves are circling and leave the flock to fend for themselves?" he retorted angrily.

"I know how you feel, but we can protect the flock better if you leave the country. This is no place for you to be right now," pleaded Father Pike.

"This is exactly where we need to be," insisted Gabriel. "On the front lines, in the thick of it, fighting the good fight. I have no desire to risk our people any more than you do, but this is a war. And in every war, the price for victory is going to be high. Running away won't stop the killings."

Father Pike didn't answer. There was a moment of quiet frustration amongst all. Then Anna got up and pulled a digital device from her jacket. She opened a press article on the screen and handed the piece to Gabriel.

"Read this," she said.

The Japanese friar looked at the tablet and said nothing, but the lines around his mouth tightened like a vice.

"Go on, read it to your friends," insisted Anna. "Let them know what we're facing."

Gabriel hesitated.

"What is it?" asked Chelsea, fearing the worse.

The friar glanced furtively at Michael and Raphael, and saw that the two priests gaped back with all the impatience of a bull in a china shop. They too wanted to know.

"Read it!" Michael grunted.

Grudgingly, Gabriel cleared his throat.

"A murderous conspiracy by Christian fanatics to punish our best and brightest is underway," he read aloud. "Pictures of the brutal slaying of Rock legend, Max Sparrow, has also been released, with rumors that the police has uncovered a plot by religious extremists to sow panic among the city's bourgeoisie…"

At the mention of Max Sparrow, Chelsea snatched the tablet from Gabriel and enlarged the picture on the screen. Every livid pixel in the photo leapt out like a thousand needles stabbing her eyes. She couldn't believe what she saw. Frame after frame, her brother's naked body lay crucified to the wall of his bedroom, held aloft by metal spikes driven into his hands and feet. A gaping wound in the form of a cross lay carved on his torso, festering like a cesspool of hate. She wanted to scream and yell, but her tongue remained strangled in pain, for scrawled in blood over the rotting corpse hung a cruel epithet in gruesome red letters. It read – SINNER!

"Thanks to the media, the public thinks you're responsible," said Father Pike. "Max Sparrow was an international star. The entire country cries out for vengeance, and soon enough, the whole world will be screaming bloody murder as well. Right now, every law-enforcement agency in the land is gunning for you, not to mention the Praetorians sniffing at your heels…"

"We've been on the run before, we can lie low. I have friends in this town, we'll manage," answered Michael.

But Raphael wasn't so convinced. "No, they're right. There's nothing the Corporation wouldn't do to flush us out. We have to leave, at least for now. Staying put will only focus the eye of evil on those brave enough to shelter us, and we can't risk more innocent lives than we already have."

He turned and looked at Chelsea, expecting her to agree. Instead, all he got was an angry flood of tears.

"You too?" cried Chelsea, burning with scorn.

She gave Raphael a look of disappointment. And despite his personal convictions, the doctor felt chastised. Although she was still trembling in shock at the grisly desecration of her brother's remains, the woman was determined not to flee.

"Listen, what they did to Max was only the beginning," Raphael tried to persuade her. "If we stay, they'll go after everyone we care about until they get to us."

"Then let them come," said Chelsea, refusing to concede the argument. "I know we're endangering ourselves and others if we stay. I know sooner or later, they'll find us and kill us. But haven't you been telling me that even though we may be knocked down, we still need to stand up to evil? To show the enemy that nothing comes easy?"

By then, every face in the carriage was turned towards Chelsea, including the operatives who had looked up from their machines in curious silence. Wiping the tears from her eyes, she returned every gaze in the tiny command post with a fierce and awesome dignity.

"They may take our lives and burn our bodies, they may kill our families and loved ones. But for God's sakes, show Satan that when he messes with the cross, he'll get the sharp end of the stick. You're supposed to be children of light. Fight back, dammit. Fight back!"

When Father Pike tried to reason with her, Michael pulled out his battle cross and popped the huge blade from its shaft. Flipping the weapon over, he slammed the dagger into a side table and left it standing like a crucifix on the altar.

"I concur," he snarled, prompting Father Pike to back down.

"He who lives by the sword, dies by the sword," said an ancient voice from the back.

The steel door behind Michael had slid opened to reveal a passageway connecting the other carriages. The old man shuffled in painfully, escorted by a small team of Anna's elite guards.

Once inside, two of the guards took up positions by the windows while the rest left to secure the perimeter. Anna herself got up and offered her chair to the Prelate.

"We cannot fight the evil one with his own weapons," cautioned the old man. "Our weapons must be prayer and faith. With these, you do more to crush the powers of hell than if you resort to violence."

Helped by the Russian, the elderly Prelate dropped his body onto the cushioned seat. At once, Chelsea noticed the brown mittens on his hands. The wool was cut away to expose the fingers while the palms remained shielded from prying eyes.

"Yet we surround ourselves with armed guards. Forgive me, monsignor, but I don't need you to tell me this is a just war. I know it is," countered Michael.

"Just or not, we must be careful not to lose ourselves in rage, no matter how warranted our actions may seem," said the old man. "As much as you strive to do, pray even more that the devil may not exploit a chink in your armor. It's not against human enemies that we have to struggle, but against the Sovereignties and the Powers who originate the darkness in this world."

"So what, bring them on!" Chelsea barked with emotion. "God is on our side, isn't He?"

"I'm more concerned that we should be on God's side," the old man answered kindly. He looked at the three priests known as *The Archangels*.

"Nevertheless, it's good that you're all here. I thank the Lord for keeping you safe from harm. And I pray that he continues to keep you so. More than ever, the world is in need of your courage and witness," he told the men.

"As for you, Miss Shields, God has saved you from darkness and brought you into the light. And we shall do all we can to protect you from those who would drag you back into the dark."

The Prelate removed an episcopal ring from his pocket and slipped it onto his finger. One by one, the priests came forward to kiss the ring with respect, acknowledging his office as bishop and pastor.

Suddenly it occurred to Chelsea who the elderly stranger was. "Wait a minute, you're the guy Marshall Chambers has been hunting for; the one they call the Chinese..."

"I am Joseph Li, the shepherd and governing prelate for the Underground Church," replied the old man, his grey eyes smiling with an inner light. "On behalf of the Prelature of St. Lazarus, I welcome you to the League of Angels."

Chelsea knew the gospel story of Jesus raising Lazarus from the dead. It was a fitting name for a Church struggling to rise from the tomb. She was more cautious about the League however. It wasn't the first time she had heard of the group. Like everyone else on the planet, she had been informed by news reports that they were fanatics and terrorists, crusading to purge the world of everyone who didn't believe in God.

"Is this true?" she asked, her face looking deeply sullen. "You're all part of the League?"

Sensing her disquiet, Father Pike volunteered to clear the air. He shared that in the beginning, the local resistance was little more than a badly organized militia, a hodgepodge of splinter groups lacking proper training to be effective. Most were earnest but ill prepared to deal with the Corporation, and their efforts only invited more Lumen tortures and executions.

Then rumors started emerging that someone was striking back at the enemy in ways that seemed impossible, often taking the fight into the dragon's lair to rescue souls in need. No one knew who they were, or even if they were working together. But when tongues started wagging that they were Catholic priests, the excitement among Christians erupted through the ranks, as if someone had dumped a barrel of gasoline on the dying embers of their faith. The roar of enthusiasm was explosive.

The Prelate knew at once they had to harness this great fire while it burned brightly. Although none of the three priests fell under his jurisdiction at the time, contact was made and alliances were formed. By then, the exploits of the men had become legendary. Stories of their courage and triumphs grew taller with each Lumen skirmish, giving strength and comfort to those who were praying for God to send down his avenging angels. And like true angels, these heroes of the faith sought out the lost sheep, defended the sacraments, and battled demons for the souls of men.

In time, Michael, Gabriel and Raphael became living icons of the fight against evil, uniting the fractured resistance in a merger that went beyond faith and creed. For the first time since the battles began, the different religious groups who strove to take down the Corporation were now eager to join the coalition known as the League of Angels, driven by the common goal of forcing back the tide of evil.

The name seemed appropriate. Scripture had described angels as a large gathering of ministering spirits created to serve God's divine plan, to protect man from evil and help him safely to heaven. To all who persevered against the tyranny of the Corporation, the brave and powerful example of The Archangels had finally given the Resistance their fighting edge. They were at last a movement and a force to be reckoned with.

But now that the enemy was closing in on the priests, the League was in danger of losing their champions.

"You're reading way too much into this," cautioned Michael. "The League is bigger than any of us, and it'll live on without us."

Father Pike started to respond but the Prelate raised his hand and interjected.

"The truth is, the League will limp on without you," said Joseph. "You three mean more to the Resistance than you know, both as priests and as symbols of defiance against darkness. You give more hope than you realize. Don't go throwing your lives away when you don't have to."

Chapter 29

"Have you found it?" asked Chambers.

The Lumen VP was seated behind a large working desk in his office. Before him, the windows opened up to a magnificent view of the city from his perch high above the rest of humanity. There was nothing opulent about the furnishings, although a stately majesty permeated the room with a distinct sense of power. The walls were adorned with plaques and artwork that were reminiscent of a head of state rather than a corporate big wig. And Chambers himself was dressed in a modest dark suit - nothing flashy, just the right amount of poise and style to convey a princely dignity.

"Not yet sir, but I'm certain this is the place. Our experts tell us we're not far off," said the voice on the speakerphone. "There're indications we're digging in the right spot. We should have something for you in a couple of weeks."

"You're taking much too long, professor," replied Chambers.

"But we're going as fast as we can, sir. The areas around the excavations are very treacherous and the men are exhausted. Give us time, they're working as hard as they can," pleaded the voice.

"You're a man of culture and learning so inspire them, professor," said Chambers. "The hills around the excavations are beautiful. If they're too tired to go on, it's the perfect place to go to sleep. After all, the holes are already dug. They can rest for eternity if they so desire…"

"Sir, please. If we could just have a little more time."

"Ah yes - time - so much to do, so little of it," sighed Chambers. "It's a pity you won't meet your deadline."

"But you promised us six months," squawked the man in alarm.

"Perhaps I should come down there myself, give the men a little encouragement. What do you think?" asked Chambers.

There was a sudden lull in the conversation. The only sounds escaping from the speakerphone were the frightened murmurs of desperate voices in the background.

A moment later, the professor cleared his throat and anxiously replied, "It will be done as you say, sir. We'll double our efforts!"

"Triple them, professor. Triple them!" said Chambers. "Or I'll fill those excavations with your bones."

✝

"You all right?" asked Michael.

Chelsea didn't respond. She just sat in her corner and cried, trying to forget the gruesome desecration of her brother's remains. Her lips were still white with anger and shock. Every few minutes, she would rub her temples and curse, mourning the absurd tragedy of her situation. She kept on this way for quite a while. Until finally, tired of her own self-pity, she looked up and noticed the markings for the first time.

Michael's forearms were heavily tattooed. She didn't recognize the symbols but thought they looked military, the kind Special Forces units might have used to identify their own. His torso was stripped bare. And his skin was stitched together like a world map of every conflict he had fought in. It was hard to imagine how anyone could've survived such a history of violence. But nestled against the cruel branches of terrible scars and markings, Chelsea noticed one unique emblem among the rest. She had seen it before as a child, but had since forgotten its meaning.

The tattoo over Michael's breast was the burning symbol of a heart on fire, encircled by a crown of thorns and topped by a flaming cross. Beneath the pious ink were the Latin words, *Gesu, confido in te* - which meant: Jesus, I trust in you.

"What's that?" she asked, pointing to his chest.

"Mercy," replied Michael, not bothering to elaborate.

He examined the new bandage over his upper arm. The wound still hurt like hell but at least the deep gash had stopped bleeding. His shoulders and back were also treated for major cuts and abrasions.

"I don't see any serious damage to the muscles," said the medic. "But like I said, take it easy and look after yourself. If the stitches pop again, it's going to get real messy."

"No problem, I'll be sure to floss after every meal as well," Michael replied sardonically.

The medic shook her head and blurted out, "Listen or don't listen, it's up to you, Father." She packed her medical bag, got up and left the room.

"Are you a natural talent at being an ass or do you actually train for it?" Chelsea asked Michael. "Seriously, all she did was ask you to take it easy."

"You think Satan takes holidays? We're at war," the priest muttered. "And we'll be at war until the end of time. I'll take it easy when I'm six-feet under."

As he pulled a clean shirt over his bare torso, Anna Koslov came in with an inventory of weapons. She handed the list over to Michael.

"It's all packed into your new vehicle. I suggest you dump the old ride," she instructed.

Michael scanned the weapons list.

"Armor-piercing rounds, concussive burst energy shells," he said, raising his eyebrows. "How'd you get hold of these?"

"How else? Providence," replied Anna, smirking.

"What about the other stuff?" Michael enquired.

"Blessed salt, incense grenades, consecrated rounds, all your special toys are in there as well," Anna assured him. "And just in case, you might want to hang on to this."

She tossed him a silver knuckleduster. Michael caught the weapon in his hand and turned it over. Inscribed on the contact points were Greek exorcism prayers.

"Might come in handy," she said.

Michael grinned, enjoying the thought of dishing out some heavy punishment to any creature dumb enough to cross his path.

"Where're the rest?" asked Chelsea, indicating Gabriel and Raphael.

The two priests had left with the Prelate over an hour ago. She was starting to worry. The place was a graveyard for disused carriages, and it was easy to get lost in the labyrinth of twisted steel and rotting metal.

"Don't worry about them, they'll be fine," replied Anna. "Your friends have got some serious battle scars. It'll take more than a medic with a first-aid kit to help them. Leave it to the old man."

✝

Elsewhere in a different compartment, Gabriel sat facing Monsignor Joseph Li, the Prelate of the Underground Church.

"You say a demon threw you on the ground," whispered the old man.

The friar nodded. The torn ligaments and muscles in his back were still throbbing with pain.

"Show me," instructed the Prelate.

Putting aside his jacket, Gabriel lifted up his shirt with difficulty. And sure enough, there was a haunting bruise in the shape of a hand on his back.

"Does it hurt?" asked the old man.

"Only when I laugh," the friar answered.

Joseph smiled.

"I'm glad it hasn't injured your sense of humor," he said to Gabriel. "Come, let us pray. The sooner we call on the Lord's name, the faster we can purge you of this corruption."

Discreetly, the Prelate took off his woolen gloves and revealed the bloodstained marks of the crucifixion on his palms. There were rumors that the old man had borne the yoke of the stigmata for some years. He wasn't the first person in the history of the Church to be mystically imprinted with the wounds of Christ in his own flesh. There were others in the past. Most were simply tricksters and frauds. Many were found to be delusional. Still others were diabolical. And the rest - the ones that really mattered - they were saints.

Gabriel himself had never seen the phenomenon up close until now. He tried not to stare, although he couldn't help but be fascinated by the wounds. He had noticed that the scabs were dry. There was no bleeding even though the holes in both hands were clearly noticeable. As an anthropologist, he was trained to understand before he could believe. But as a man of faith, he knew he had to believe before he could understand.

"Sorry," mumbled the friar, realizing that he was gawking at the holes in the Prelate's hands. The old man gave no indication that he noticed the friar's embarrassment. He laid his hands gently on Gabriel's back and began to pray.

The train compartment was dimly lit, but the soft glow of the portable lamp seemed to burn brighter as Gabriel felt something like a current flow into his tortured back. Slowly and steadily, the Prelate continued to invoke God's blessing under his breath, his voice barely audible now as he fell into an intimate conversation with the Lord.

"Restore your servant to full health, Heavenly Father. Remove all fear and doubt from your priest by the power of your Holy Spirit, and may you, Lord, be glorified through his life. In the name of Jesus, drive out all infirmity and sickness from his body."

Gabriel tried to join in the prayer. Yet the more he raised his heart to God, the more his thoughts converged on Raphael. He knew that the death spell was broken, and whatever dregs of darkness still clinging to his friend was there only by the express permission of God. In spite of many difficulties, his faith encouraged him to trust the wisdom of divine providence. Nevertheless, he shivered to imagine what horrors still plagued his brother priest. At the moment, the doctor was being treated for his physical injuries next door. But there was no telling how quickly his condition might deteriorate if the spiritual malady continued to linger.

"No one climbs to a higher level of life without death to the lower," Joseph responded cryptically. "Your friend will get worse before he gets better."

Gabriel wasn't at all surprised that the Prelate knew what he was thinking. But he was distressed to hear that Raphael's condition would not only persist, it would get worse.

"So the curse is still active then," the friar remarked unhappily. "What did you sense when you prayed over him earlier?"

"Evil always brings fear and discouragement. There is much of both in him," admitted Joseph. "The spell cast on our friend was intended to cripple a soul with despair, driving the victim to take his own life eventually. No doubt, the strength of the curse has been broken, but it hasn't entirely been dispelled. Little by little, he will feel the terror rise up again..."

"Then tell me how to stop it," said Gabriel, turning around. "Show me how to cast out this spirit of fear!"

Joseph looked at the young priest and his heart swelled with compassion. He knew that Gabriel was an exorcist, and he understood that few things wounded the friar more painfully than seeing his friend still enslaved by the chains of evil despite his best efforts to free him.

"Help him, monsignor," pleaded the friar.

Joseph closed his eyes and paused for a second, trying to find the right words. When he spoke again, it was with some hesitation.

"Listen to me, the path to his liberation does not lie with you or me. It lies in the hands of Father Raphael himself. The Lord has decreed that it must come from him. All we can do is pray for our brother, support him in our love."

"But we can't just leave him defenseless either, waiting for this evil to awaken," Gabriel argued. "Isn't there some ritual we can consult, some antidote to this poison?'"

"What does the bible say about overcoming fear?" Joseph asked patiently. *"There is no fear in love; but perfect love casts out fear.* Do not worry, my son. This sickness will not end in death. It's for the glory of God that our friend remains in this dark night as yet."

Gabriel took a deep breath and sighed, his arms akimbo, his frustration growing. Gently, Joseph placed his stigmatized hands on the shoulders of the young priest, coaxing him to calm down.

"Be patient, padre. Even if the Gates of Hell appear to prevail, those who believe in God know that evil and death do not have the last word. Stay close to the Lord. Stay close to your brother, Raphael, so that when the time comes, you'll know what to do."

Saying that, the old man got up and restored the gloves to his hands, veiling once again the mystery of Christ's passion in his flesh.

"Before I forget, they told me you lost something priceless in battle," said Joseph. "That samurai sword was in your family for many generations, was it not?"

Gabriel nodded sadly. "It was a sacred relic for the Toshigawas, passed down from father to son, from warrior to warrior, down through the centuries. I would've preferred to have lost my life than to have lost it."

"I understand your sorrow," said Joseph, empathizing. "The katana was more than just a sword, it was the soul of your ancestors."

With difficulty, Joseph got up and approached a steel box resting on a side table. He carefully lifted the heavy lid and removed a large object from within. It had a rectangular base and was covered in red velvet. Turning around, he motioned for Gabriel to approach.

"Help me with this, my son," said the old man.

"What is it?" asked Gabriel as he drew near.

"A gift from the Holy Father."

When Gabriel heard that it was from the pope, his pulse began to quicken. Taking the case from the Prelate, he felt the weight of something powerful flow through his hands.

"Go on," urged the old man. "Open it."

Encouraged by Joseph, the friar removed the velvet covering from the wooden case. He cradled the box in his arms like a newborn and read the ornate inscription on the polished oak. The carving was in ancient Latin.

"It can't be," he mumbled to himself.

"Oh, but it is. I myself was surprised when I first saw it," said

Joseph. "Believe me, your eyes do not deceive you."

Wasting no time, Gabriel opened the wooden case. In his exorcisms, he had often invoked the intercession of this powerful saint. And each time, the demons have cowered at the name of this legend. To behold this precious relic, this symbol of the warrior spirit, was something the Dominican friar had never imagined, much less thought to handle with his own hands. He tried to speak but he couldn't find the words. All he could do was let his jaw fall slack with astonishment.

"The blade of St. George," Joseph confirmed in a sonorous voice. "I thought you should have it."

"But why?" Gabriel managed to utter. "This is too precious to leave with me."

"Isn't it obvious?" asked the old man.

As Gabriel lifted the ancient sword from the reliquary, the blade began to shimmer in his hands, as if recognizing a kindred spirit.

"Listen to what it's telling you," said Joseph. "This relic survived an age not too different from our own."

Gabriel continued to marvel at the sword. Entranced, he ran his fingers lightly along the steel. To his amazement, the metal edge was still sharp.

"Then as now, Christians were not persecuted for religion, they were charged with hatred of the human race," explained Joseph.

The Japanese friar knew this to be true. Even as ancient Rome touted its place as the enlightened capital of the world, it continued plunging its citizens into moral decline. Sexual debauchery, murderous policies, serial abortions and the practice of exposing unworthy newborns to death plagued the empire from dawn to dusk. Despite threats and torture, the early Christians stood firm against the decay of the day, choosing instead to witness against the depravity of Nero, his sordid lovers, and his cohorts.

"And for that, they were accused of creating a climate of hate and declared enemies of the State," said Gabriel, lifting his gaze from the sword. "I understand the uncanny parallels between the past and the present, but I still don't understand why you're entrusting me with the sword of St. George."

"In every age, the culture of death returns to make war on God's children. Should it not be fitting that the sword of the dragon slayer be passed on to a new knight who will champion the culture of life today?" asked the old man.

Gabriel shook his head and protested. "I'm not worthy of wielding this. I'm just a simple priest," he stammered.

"You're a fine Christian and a good priest," Joseph reminded him. "An exorcist and the son of samurais. You and your ancestors have fought the infernal dragon countless times through the centuries, often giving your own lives to defend the Lord's name and honor. You're more than worthy, my son. That's not the question. The question is whether you're willing."

Gabriel dropped his eyes and caught his own reflection in the blade. Against all logic, the ancient metal now seemed to shine even more brightly than before. Something about the sword gave him courage. When the friar looked up again, his face was all burnished like bronze.

"Understand this, the world is being reshaped by evil," the old man warned. "The Church is being persecuted like never before. If I should be arrested and charged with treason for holding fast to divine truths, I pray they'll have enough evidence to convict me. Even though these last days have unfolded with great confusion and darkness, trust that the Lord is in the thick of the battle with us. Like David facing Goliath, if you remain brave, if you keep the faith, you'll see astounding victories in the midst of what may look like total defeat."

"I know the Lord chooses the weak and small to confound the great and mighty," Gabriel replied. "But sometimes, I wish we could just kick the enemy's butt all the way to kingdom come already."

The Prelate was sympathetic.

"As do I, Father. But in this war, victory is won through our weakness and total dependence on him. Regardless of the odds against us, hell will never prevail. Now enough, no more pessimism! Come, you have a trip to make and we don't have time to waste."

Gabriel returned the sword to its reliquary and carefully laid it down.

"But the Corporation has a grip on every corner of the world," said the friar. "Even if we leave the country, where can we safely go?"

"You go to Rome. The Holy Father awaits you," Joseph replied. "If there's one place you can still find shelter at this time, it'll be at the Vatican."

Gabriel was stunned, and it took him awhile before he could ask why.

"Why what?" prompted the old man.

"Why risk so much to protect us; first yourself, and now the Holy Father? Don't you realize that the Church needs you more than she needs us?"

The old man shook his head in disagreement.

"Father Gabriel, we're all shepherds, not hirelings. Each and every one of us is precious to the Lord, and none of us will abandon the sheep entrusted to us for fear of the wolves. It's our calling to love each other in the Lord, to give our lives for one another. By this, they shall know we are Christians. After all, why do you and your brother priests take such risks to protect the young lady, if not to leave the ninety-nine in safe pastures and save the one that is lost? The Church needs you too, my son."

"You sure I can't stay?" asked Gabriel, pushing his luck.

Joseph frowned and gave him a look of annoyance.

"Okay, okay, I got it," exclaimed the friar. "Obedience pleases God more than sacrifice."

"Indeed it does," said Joseph, with a twinkle in his eyes. "Try not to shorten the life I have left."

Gabriel grinned like a mischievous schoolboy. But a second later, he caught a flash of something red. "Monsignor, you're bleeding," he gasped.

Joseph looked down at his hands and saw that his gloves were soaked in fresh blood. He peeled off the wet mittens and exposed the scarlet pool dripping from his palms.

"Why is this happening?" asked Gabriel, visibly upset.

"With St. Paul, *I fill up in my flesh what is lacking in the afflictions of Christ, for the sake of his body, which is the Church,*" Joseph answered from scripture.

The pain was always excruciating, but the Prelate had hoped not to draw undue attention to his daily martyrdom. Unfortunately for him, there was no hiding it this time. The wounds were bleeding more than usual.

"I'm not sure I understand," confessed Gabriel, baffled by the blood trickling from the stigmata. "Is there anything I can do?"

"It's nothing, my son. The Lord is simply telling me that my prayers have been granted."

Gabriel ripped the ends of his shirt and tried to use them as new bandages. "Does it hurt?" asked the anxious friar, not knowing what else to say.

Joseph winced and gave him a quizzical look. "What? You think the Lord gave these to me for good looks?" he groaned indignantly.

The remark caught Gabriel by surprise, and he stopped fussing with the bandages. Thinking he might have offended the Prelate, the friar hung his head and apologized. But the old man chuckled with affection.

"Come here," said Joseph, beckoning with opened arms. The friar got up and felt the hearty embrace of his spiritual father.

"You're much too young to be so serious, my boy," the Prelate chided him.

Feeling a little embarrassed, Gabriel laughed quietly to himself. It was only after a few moments that he realized something was different.

For the first time since the injury, his back was no longer in pain.

Chapter 30

The station's majestic tower stood at attention, keeping watch over the public square. The damaged clock face had recently been restored and was running again, although the city council had silenced the antique bells from adding to the noise pollution in the area.

Down below, the roads were congested as always, with traffic snaking through the central district and coiling round the Lafayette in constricting lines. Thousands of commuters poured in and out of the station regularly, lumbering like drunks too intoxicated with their own poison to look up from their cell phones and digital devices. Most, if not all, were numb to the human souls next to them and blissfully unaware of the tidings of war rumbling beneath their own feet.

Outside the station, the sun was burning bright and the humidity was climbing. The crowds milling about at noon seemed lethargic and confused, as if the heat from the tarmac was baking them to a drunken stupor. Even the air in the open piazza was heavy with a stillness that strangled every leaf in the park, choking the city with the stench of its own decay.

High above the city square, the iron hands of time struck twelve on the clock. On the horizon, dark clouds gathered with speed.

Guardedly, a sniper team from the Resistance peered out from behind the glass façade of the clock face, making sure their gun barrels scarcely peeked out from the safety of their cover.

"See any wind?" asked the sniper, staring down the length of his rifle.

Click by click, the spotter carefully adjusted the settings on his scope. "Nope," he answered with casual detachment.

Both men seemed calm and unflappable, but their furrowed brows betrayed hidden lines of unease. Outside, there were no rustlings of leaves or paper, no coat tails flapping in the wind. Every loose piece of trash in the piazza was frozen to the ground. Even the banners usually flying atop the station were strung up like corpses hanging lifelessly from their poles. All around the city, the heat was oppressive, with hardly a breeze blowing. And yet…

"Those clouds are moving pretty fast," said the spotter, studying the gloom in the distance.

"Yup," the sniper agreed reluctantly. Just to make sure, he double-checked his ammo to confirm he was fully stocked before dropping his attention back to the crowds below.

"Looks like a storm approaching," he cautioned his partner. "We better bolt down the hatches."

✝

"A time of great darkness is coming," the booming voice cried out. But it was unlike any sound she had ever heard before. The noise of it bypassed her ears and slammed viciously into her mind like a beastly locution on a rampage.

"Darker than what already is?" asked another. Again, the voices crashed inside her skull and tore up her psyche, splintering her sanity into a crazy maze of twisted sounds. The throbbing was unbearable and it sent her crumbling to her knees. She cupped her ears and screamed, only to be answered by terrible echoes of scorn and derision.

"No!" she yelled back, refusing to listen. Struggling to keep her thoughts from exploding, she shoved off and ran, her heart beating wildly with every fumbling step. Behind her, the darkness closed in like a pack of wolves, their brutal chops snapping at her naked heels, their tongues slobbering with frightful desire for her flesh. She stumbled and fell, and the howling became louder and more aggressive as the canines grew drunk with the pungent scent of her fear.

Panic-stricken, Chelsea clambered to her feet and pushed on, barely escaping the unseen presence lunging at her legs. She turned her head briefly and saw nothing but blackness trailing in her wake. And yet something was pursuing her, its unholy breath snorting like a steam engine, its flaming nostrils chugging down the tracks like a beast on wheels.

Turning a corner, the woman slipped and slammed into a wall that appeared from nowhere. Bleeding and confused, she tried to back away from the dead end. But when she spun around, the open path was no longer there. Instead, a massive ring of ghoulish mirrors had blocked off her escape. She was trapped, hemmed in by a legion of her own reflections that the mirrors simply ate and regurgitated with shocking distortions, tearing at her humanity.

"Come home, my love," said a voice dripping with lust. "Come home to papa."

Alarmed and disgusted, Chelsea picked up a loose rock and threw it at the shimmering wall. The jagged stone hit the silky surface and passed seamlessly into the murky depths, scattering the ghostly images like tadpoles in a pond. Surprised, she staggered back and tripped against a rusty chain coiled up in a corner. In desperation, the woman snatched it and flung the iron links like a whip, intending to smash her way out of the glass prison. She threw the full weight of the chain into the mirrored wall and it snagged. Instead of shattering into a hail of broken shards, the glass swallowed the ends of the chain and held taut.

Before Chelsea could react, she was jerked off her feet and hauled entirely into the unknown. Shrieking, she crashed with surprise into a waiting bed and found herself in the familiar trappings of her childhood home. The wall of mirrors was still there, though she now looked in from the other side, and what she saw in the reflections made her blood run cold. Without knowing how, she had abruptly become a child again; a trembling eight-year-old in her pajamas cowering under her sheets, terrified of the monsters in the hallway. She could hear their encroaching footsteps above the frenzied beating of her own heart. Overcome with dread, she called out to God to save her, to stop the monsters from coming into her bedroom. But there was no answer from heaven.

Instead, one by one they came - her father leading the pack, the smell of alcohol on his breath, his stubby fingers groping beneath the sheets for the quivering prize between her legs. He whispered her name, calling her his princess, cooing all the while that this would be their little secret. Then came the form teacher at school who called her his pet. He made her sit on his lap and kissed her, thrusting his tongue into her mouth, telling her how beautiful and special she was, and she believed him. Just as she believed the elderly priest who said God loved her. And he showed her just how much by slipping his wrinkled old hand under her dress, calling it a gentle caress from the Lord. The faces kept changing over the years but the attacks didn't. She pleaded with them to stop but the laughter only grew louder.

As she struggled to push back, Chelsea caught a glimpse of herself in the mirrors and noticed that the trembling child was gone, as were those who robbed and savaged her innocence. In their place was a naked young woman drowning in a sea of disembodied hands.

Startled, Chelsea twisted and fought and tried to break free. But the hands that groped, squeezed and tossed her about like a plaything ravaged every nude inch of her body until finally, her spirit vanquished and her will broken, she fell back and surrendered herself to a bed of iniquity.

"A time of great darkness is coming. No one can save you. No priest can protect you. We will find you. And we will devour you."

The noise of screeching metal crashed inside her skull like a train wreck and jolted her awake. At first, Chelsea wasn't sure if she was dead or alive. Her eyelids fluttered awkwardly like the broken wings of a wounded bird. Slightly dazed and confused, she tried to sit up. All at once, the room spun like a top and she slithered back into her seat, slain with vertigo.

"Darker than what already is?"

The Prelate nodded. "Indeed, men will not see the darkness for what it is. They'll look at the blackest night and think it the brightest day. They'll celebrate the destruction of the good and holy and think they're championing a new dawn of justice. In many places, black will be white and white will be black. And relativism will rule nations like a lukewarm mother, indifferent and careless of what evil might besiege her children. They'll not see the noose of sin that hangs about their necks and wear their damnation proudly like shiny medals before the world…"

"And the world, led by the Antichrist will applaud them for it," said Father Pike softly.

His comment shook the final drips of slumber from Chelsea's mind and she sat up like a drowning woman breaking the surface for air. As yet, no one in the carriage had noticed her rousing from her seat – not Pike, not Gabriel or Michael who were huddled around the Prelate like novices around their master. Everyone assumed she was still caught in the shackles of sleep, burdened by the day's trauma of having seen pictures of her brother desecrated in death.

"Monsignor is right," said Gabriel. "There're people who hate for the sake of hating. The tragedy is they don't even realize it. They often think they're righting some injustice or making the world a better place. Innocence can be so corrupted that some people will stop at nothing to get what they want."

"Stop them. Please don't let them get what they want," Chelsea suddenly mumbled aloud, her face shrouded in the cold light of the portable lamp.

The Prelate and his priests looked at her in surprise. They thought she was still asleep and didn't expect her to be listening. When it became clear that the young lady was trembling with cold sweat, Gabriel got up slowly and walked over to her. He knelt beside the woman and gently laid his hand on her shoulder.

"Chelsea, what's wrong? Are you all right," he asked in concern.

She scoured the faces of the men in the room and her skin began to crawl. There was no reason for her to distrust them, not after what they had gone through for her. But still, the nightmare had awakened memories of a terrible childhood that left her feeling more than vulnerable. She shook her head vigorously, trying to dislodge the vivid hallucinations from her past.

These priests were different, she told herself. Not like those others. Not like that cruel imposter who stole her innocence in the shadows of the sanctuary lamp. These ones were genuine. She could trust them to understand, to pull her from the icy darkness she felt embracing her. But the more she tried to believe that the League would defend her, the more her doubts grew, bolstered by a nagging thought whispering in her ear.

"Who are you people? Why do you risk everything to protect me?" she found herself asking.

Her guardians looked at her strangely like she was spouting gibberish. This time, it was the Prelate who tottered forward and took her by the hand.

"Tell us what's bothering you, my child," the old man encouraged. "Perhaps I can help."

Slowly, Chelsea felt the chills of her anxiety thaw in the warmth of his voice, and she began to weep openly. She told of her ghastly nightmare, of the betrayals she endured as a child, and how as she grew into success and fame, she had tried to drown those terrible memories in a mind-numbing cocktail of drugs, crude sex and dangerous men. But the hurt only got deeper...

"Each time I found myself in a place with no light, each time things only got worse. Those animals put me in a living hell and I chose to stay there. I tried to escape all those feelings of hate and disgust, but all I did was fence myself in. They drew first blood and I continued to let them bleed me from the grave. I'm my own worst enemy," she sobbed brokenly.

"Shush my dear," said the old man, patting her arm softly.

"Life without love is death. What is hell but the suffering of being unable to love?" said the Prelate. "But you're safe now, you're among people who love you. I love you."

The old man took off his mittens and stroked her hair. She said nothing but wondered why he wore those things. There was nothing wrong with his hands. They were smooth as silk, like the hands of a newborn babe. Why did he try to hide them?

"What're you doing?" she asked as the Prelate began sliding his fingers down towards her cleavage.

"I just want to show you how much I love you," said the old man. Without warning he cupped his hand over her breast and squeezed hard.

Chelsea was completely taken aback. For a shocking moment, she found herself frozen between fear and confusion, unable to decide what to do. But when the old man tried to force his drooling mouth over her lips, her instincts kicked in and she broke free of his embrace.

"Stop it!" she cried out in anger and turmoil. "Why are you doing this?"

"Because I love you," purred the grinning Prelate.

He flung her to the ground and crudely pounced on her. His strength was incredible for his age, and his flabby body pressed against her like a sack of cement, trapping the poor girl under a mountain of throbbing flesh.

When Chelsea tried to resist, the old man tore open her blouse and ripped off her brassiere, dangling her naked breasts before the mocking laughter and catcalls of the other priests. The young woman bawled at Michael and Gabriel, aghast that they stood idly by while she continued to be mauled by the Prelate. But her desperate cries only drove her former guardians into frenzy. Snapping and howling like a cackle of hyenas, they leapt into the fray and fought each other for the prize, tugging and clawing at the screaming girl for a naked piece of flesh.

"Wake up!" shouted Michael, his rugged features distorted with unbridled lust. Chelsea shut her eyes in revulsion and turned her face away, prompting the priest to shake her even harder. "Wake up, woman," he roared.

Large powerful hands grabbed hold of her and pulled her to her feet. The sudden jolt of motion surprised her. She gasped and opened her eyes.

"Get up," growled Michael. "We're under attack!"

The carriage was full of people scurrying around. The surveillance equipment had indicated a breach in security. Their perimeter had been compromised. At the moment, the command post appeared to be boiling with urgency, but Chelsea wasn't sure if she was still dreaming. She saw people moving about but they looked like trees. She heard Michael barking her name a few more times, but it was only after he slapped her on the cheek that her vision came back into focus.

"Snap out of it!" said the priest. Just then, Anna Koslov barged in.

"You'll want to see this," she said, handing him a small device. "It's all we got before we lost contact."

Chapter 31

"What the hell is that?" asked the first man.

"I don't know. But that's no cloud!" answered his partner.

The team in the clock tower quickly ditched their sniper rifles for their backup weapons. There was no way they were going to do any damage by firing single shots into something that big, moving that fast. Their best hope was to spray the oncoming swarm with short bursts from their carbines and keep their heads down.

The dark clouds they saw on the horizon closed the distance and made a beeline for the clock tower, storming the men with such speed that neither one had time to radio in a warning. Squeezing their triggers, the men blasted the swarm with everything they had. It was all they could do to keep their faces and limbs from being ripped to shreds by countless beaks and talons raiding the loft.

Down below, the afternoon crowds milling about the piazza were surprised to see the sky darkened by the presence of so many large ravens in one place, their enormous black wings almost blocking out the sun. Gaping with awe, most people were unsure of what to make of the sudden flock of huge birds teeming above their heads. A minute later, it became clear to the gawking crowds that the thing to do was to run.

Inside the venerable train station, it was business as usual. The busy commuters remained oblivious to the frightful scourge of feathers and claws falling from the skies. The trains continued to run like clockwork. The passengers poured in and out of the steel carriages with no inkling that the world outside was covered in darkness. Earlier on, the League had positioned several guards at various points in the station. Blending into the crowds, they were supposed to stay low and call in at the first sign of trouble. So far, no one had made that call. Like Officers Blackwell and Cope, they were all silent, their throats slit, their blood draining away behind the closed doors of some forgotten broom closet.

A pack of hellhounds was also stalking the station. It was just as well that the bulk of humanity remained blind to the ghostly wraiths trotting among them. Indeed, only those with the eyes of faith or the eyes of iniquity could see these fearsome creatures cloaked by the veil of dark magic. Quietly, the hounds mingled with the crowds, sniffing through the forest of human souls for the scent of their enemies.

In the hidden corridors of the Lafayette Grand Central, a Praetorian legion was already tearing through the storage lockers looking for the concealed switch. The cleaner who had led Michael and Chelsea was locked in a chokehold, watching helplessly as a burly guard repeatedly slammed him against the wall with relish.

"You won't get anything from me!" croaked the janitor.

The guard tightened his grip and snarled. "We won't have to."

A charge of explosives decimated the lockers, exposing the tiny lever guarding the trapdoor to the tunnels below. The janitor was instantly crestfallen. He had just enough time to make a silent act of contrition before the long blade of a Praetorian dagger pierced through his lower jaw and sliced into his brain.

✝

Michael's bearing was severe, his muscles taut with unease. He hooked the small digital device up to the monitor and played back the recording on the big screen. The image was gritty but recognizable.

As soon as it came on, the grimness of the message was apparent. Between warnings of a Lumen trap, Kaz was raging on about demons, his frantic cries punctuated by ghoulish noises baying all around him.

"It's an ambush. They've been tracking us," Kaz whispered into the camera. "You have to get out of there now!"

The sound of something scuttling behind him made the Palestinian turn around. That very second, the ceiling lights began to flicker like crazy, as if the whole bunker was about to blow up.

Kaz slowly reached for his weapon. It was obvious that fear had penetrated his heart. He looked at his hands and they were shaking. He was no coward, yet something in the room had infected his courage.

"Allah, preserve me," he prayed. Calling on his faith for strength, he turned his attention back to the monitor and tried to finish the task.

"I'm patching this through," he said. "They're using the kid as some kind of portal. To stop the demons, you'll have to take her out!"

The surveillance video popped up and hijacked half the screen, replaying the slaughter from the night before. Michael squinted and made a quick tally. There were five demons, not counting the two terrors that nearly killed them in the sewers. The priest was worried. If they had barely survived those two previous battles, what chance did they have of surviving five more? And then he saw the tiny girl in black, and once again his heart skipped a beat. She was lurking like a ghost in every scene, a lightning rod conducting the armies of hell to the frontlines of this war.

Michael clenched his teeth...

Kaz was right. It made more sense to blow up the bridge than to fight the demons once they crossed over. But what if the girl was an unwilling victim, a hostage to evil? What then? He couldn't risk the life of another innocent child, no matter what.

Just then, Joseph Li entered the command post with Gabriel tagging beside him. The old man squinted at the demons and instantly recognized the gruesome evil on screen. Christian tradition warned of seven deadly sins, each incarnated by a demon that used to be an angel of virtue before the fall.

"It appears the child is a vessel for the Capital Vices," the Prelate mumbled under his breath.

The whole cabin heard the old man say so but no one thought to ask him how he knew. Instead, they were all caught up in the horror of watching the drama unfold. By now, the bunker with Kaz was drowned in shadows. The backup lights had failed and the Palestinian was eager to flee the scene. Something snickering in the darkness however stopped him cold. He tracked the eerie laughter with the spectral scope on his rifle and saw nothing. Whatever it was, it was toying with him.

"They killed the rest, now they're coming for me," he told himself. He knew he had to move fast. Quickly, he launched a volley of stun grenades to clear a path. The assault rocked the room with a loud bang and ejected a suffocating cloud of incense. Almost right away, the darkness seemed to writhe and groan, as if choking from the effects of the sacred smoke.

Seeing this, the Palestinian unleashed a blinding flash of gunfire and took a manic dive for the exit. Unfortunately, he never made it. Something diabolical snatched the poor man into the air and dragged him cursing into the shadows. A second later, the screen went dead.

"Where's the rest of the video?" demanded Michael.

"That's all we got," replied Anna. "We lost all contact after that."

"Damn it!" Michael shouted, banging his fist on the table.

A hush descended on the room. No one dared to utter a word. Even Chelsea who had suffered so much from Lumen hatred simply rested her hand on Michael's shoulder. She wanted desperately to console him, to rage against the cruelty of it all. But she knew all too well that nothing would assuage the pain and loss of that moment.

"You must go now. There's a plane waiting for you at the coordinates. Leave quickly," said the Prelate. He gestured for Michael and his team to hustle. Before he could say more, the surveillance equipment buzzed with alarms and whistles.

"They're in the tunnels!" reported one of the rebels monitoring the computers.

"What? How'd they get past the guards?" Anna asked in disbelief.

She never heard the answer for just then, the fiery sounds of combat reverberated down the long passage. The enemy had made contact with the perimeter defense. Judging from the echo of explosions and gunfire, she estimated that the battle was just a few hundred yards away. Time to evacuate.

Grabbing her rifle, she turned to Michael and Chelsea. "Why are you still here?" she scowled.

The soldier priest strapped on his private arsenal and clipped his crucifix dagger to his gun belt. "We'll hold them off. You get the Prelate to safety," he answered gruffly.

But the old man wouldn't approve. "No my son, you must leave now. Don't test my resolve. And above all, don't try the Lord's patience!" Joseph scolded him.

The stern rebuke caused Michael to pause and breathe hard. He turned to Gabriel looking for support but the Japanese friar was nowhere in sight, having run off earlier to retrieve his brother priest from the sickbay next door. He returned a moment later hauling Raphael over his shoulder. The wounded doctor was trembling and barely awake, a sign that the frightful malady had begun to reclaim his soul.

That same instant, Father Pike rushed in with a squad of armed guards from the League. They were fully stocked and ready to engage. Turning to Anna, he said, "We'll buy you some time…"

"Copy that, we'll get the Prelate to the extraction point," she replied. "Make sure you get there yourself!"

She quickly barked instructions to her team to set the plan in motion. Within seconds, the entire command post was stripped down and dismantled, the armed rebels taking only what was necessary and rigging the rest with explosives.

"Come on, let's go!" cried Chelsea, tugging at Michael's sleeve. "They've got this covered, they'll be okay."

When Michael hesitated, Joseph stepped forward and traced a big sign of the cross over the priest. Reluctantly, the former soldier dropped to his knee and bowed his head. He knew what was coming.

"I remind you of your promise of holy obedience," said the Prelate solemnly. "Go now with my blessings, Father. And may God be with you."

✝

Down in the tunnel, the devastation was immense. The rebels holding the perimeter defense were all torn up. The battleground was sticky with blood and strewn with body parts. Human entrails lay scattered like grisly confetti before a parade of hellhounds trotting over the bones of the dead, hungry for the souls of the living.

Praetorian Guards drew up behind them checking for survivors. In one corner, a young resistance fighter crouched in the shadows and tried painfully to staunch the bleeding wound in her side. She looked around at her fallen comrades, many dismembered and dead. Like them, she had fought hard for the freedom to believe in God. And like them, she would soon give her life for the faith.

As she pondered her final moments, a terrifying howl dispersed her thoughts. She watched helplessly as a demon dog appeared, baring its razor-sharp fangs. The air in the tunnel was pungent with the stench of rotting flesh. Shuddering, the wounded rebel quickly reached down and pulled out her sidearm. She knew regular bullets did nothing to stop these creatures, but her lead casings were anointed with chrism. At the least, pulling the trigger would give this rancid canine a ferocious headache.

She fired off a few shots. Between the terror in her heart and her loss of blood, she could scarcely keep a steady aim. The wretched hound ducked and sped towards her, knocking the weapon from her grasp. Leaning down with its massive jaws, it growled and exposed a cavern of serrated teeth inches from her face.

"Where're your friends?" asked a creepy voice from the back. From the corner of her eye, she saw a skinny man in a white suit ambling forth. He approached the giant mastiff and stooped over the petrified woman. His delicate features were heavily made-up.

"I've been meaning to get this puppy a brand new chew toy," purred the Lumen agent. He stretched out his hand and patted the monstrous dog, tousling the matted fur on its mane.

"Fortunately, he seems to like you," said the agent, smirking. "Tell me where your friends are hiding the old man."

"He's long gone by now," the woman stammered. "I don't know where he is."

"Liar," said the man in white. He struck the rebel with his fist. And quite by chance, the hellhound next to him blew up.

The impact threw the agent several feet into the air and splattered the woman with a violent dose of shock. She turned around and saw a dozen metals balls sail over her head. These ignited before they hit the ground, scattering a huge cloud of sodium nitrate all over the tunnel.

The ghostly pack of demon dogs imploded like rotting flesh in a furnace, their moldy skins flaming away in agony as one by one, the howling mastiffs dropped to their knees and succumbed to the exorcised salt in the air.

Father Robert Pike quickly grabbed the wounded rebel and dragged her to safety while the League advanced with their guns blazing. The Praetorians flipped on their visors and fired back, rocking the tunnel with tracers and death.

"Hold them off!" shouted the priest.

He passed the woman to a comrade and ran back to join the squad. By then, the hellhounds were starting to regenerate. The sodium nitrate had dissipated, blown away by an eerie gust of wind that appeared from nowhere. The priest pulled out a crucifix and invoked the blood of Christ. With one knee on the ground, he held up the cross and chanted the binding prayer in Latin. Armor-piercing rounds whizzed by and tore through some of his men, leaving him miraculously unscathed.

The Jesuit squeezed his eyes shut and focused, his voice rising in cadence. In response, the hellhounds roared and burst into flames, sparking a wild inferno that scorched their putrid remains into clouds of magical runes, sending the demon mutts limping back to perdition with their tails between their legs.

"Pull back!" shouted Father Pike.

His men were holding fast but the Praetorian assault was too strong. As bullets ricocheted off the walls, the priest ordered a retreat, only to find that his troops would rather die fighting than to back down from evil.

All of a sudden, the enemy fire ceased. A flash of white somersaulted over the heads of the Praetorians and landed in the thick of battle.

The man known as Agent Yin stood among them completely transformed. His face was ghostly white. His elongated tongue wriggled like an eel swinging from his mouth. There was nothing human behind those demonic eyes. He looked like a pagan god thirsty for blood. Summoning the powers of darkness, the agent swung his arms in a wide arc and several of Pike's companions toppled with opened wounds slashed across their chests. Again the man in white exploded in a flurry of strikes, and two more Leaguers lost their heads and slumped to the ground.

Laughing, the Lumen Agent pretended to lick an unseen blade in his hand. And for a staggering moment, Father Pike glimpsed the deadly edge of a phantom sword dripping with the blood of his men.

"God help us," the priest exclaimed with horror. He picked up a rifle and tried to blast the agent. But Yin dodged the clumsy attack and lunged for the Jesuit. In seconds, the creepy man had his fingers throttling the victim's throat.

Father Pike could hardly breathe, suffocated by the prospect of a ghostly sword rushing towards his skull. He felt the tip of the unseen blade almost reach his face when something snagged the aggressor by the wrist and yanked him back.

Yin flipped into the air but quickly landed on his feet. Hissing like a cat, the agent was furious to see his wrist lassoed by a metal chain studded with spikes. On the other end, a tall muscular rebel kept the noose tight and fought to reel the enemy away from Father Pike.

Like a great white shark tugging against a fishing line, Yin struggled to pull the intruder into the kill zone of his blade. But something caught his attention. The retractable chain cutting into his wrist was anchored to a large crucifix in the hands of his opponent.

"What'd you know, another stinking priest!" heckled the agent. He twisted and rolled, looking for an angle to shove the ghostly sword into the spiked chain. But Michael deftly blocked the move and swung the white figure into a group of Praetorians, sending them all crashing like bowling pins.

"What part of stay out of sight don't you understand?" Father Pike yelled at Michael. "I told you we've got this!"

"The only thing you've got is a losing fight," Michael bellowed. "Get your ass off the ground!"

He shouted for the remaining squad to grab Father Pike and retreat. In the commotion, the Lumen agent twisted his arm and broke free of the rosary chain.

"Leaving already?" said Agent Yin, his eyes seething with deep pools of odious black. "Stick around, the party's just getting started!"

He screeched and flung his hands at Michael. A dozen strips of yellow paper shot out of his sleeves and landed on the carcasses of the fallen troops. As soon as the talismans came into contact with the deceased, Yin chanted an arcane spell and swung his mystical blade like a conductor raising a chorus to death.

"What sorcery is this?" Father Pike cried out in alarm.

Slowly, the slain bodies of warriors from both sides of the conflict began to stir. One by one they clambered to their feet like empty husks, their human shells taken over by unclean spirits.

Michael shouted for Father Pike to get behind him. He couldn't launch a grenade into the throng; the battlefield was too small to endure a ballistic blast. They were packed like sardines in the tunnel and the shrapnel risk was too great. What he needed was a distraction. He looked to his left and right. The small rebel squad refused to yield and fought on valiantly.

Michael shouted above the tumult of gunfire. "At my signal, fall back!"

The priest then pulled a weapon resembling a flare gun from his harness. Aiming above the heads of the undead, he fired off. A blinding flash of luminance erupted and scores of tiny round pellets rained down on the Lumen horde. The ejected contents fell upon the enemy troops and clung on, covering both the living and dead with thousands of miniature discs that stuck to their clothing and skin.

Quickly, Michael flipped on the switch on his flare gun and the phosphorus pellets ignited simultaneously, splattering the Lumen force with thousands of little explosions that flamed out and scorched deeply into their skins. Cursing, the Praetorians stripped off their armor and tried to put out the chemical burns engulfing their bodies. Only Agent Yin and his army of living dead remained impervious to the attack. Still in a trance, the man in white laughed boisterously and sent the burning corpses galloping in for the kill.

Michael shouted for the League to retreat. At once, the squad grabbed their wounded and raced back down the tunnel. Father Pike stumbled after them, leaving his fellow priest to bring up the rear.

"Move!" Michael roared at the rebels.

The chilling howls of the dead echoed behind them. Michael glanced over his shoulder and saw the tide of evil gaining speed. But instead of running faster, the priest whipped around to face the oncoming terror.

"That's it. Come a little closer," Michael whispered. He reached for a gadget in his gun belt and gripped it tight.

The priest knew that the reanimation of corpses was different from the possession of the living. Only the bodily remains were despoiled by dark magic, the souls of the faithful departed were safe in the mercy of God, making it easier for him to end this sacrilege.

Tracing a benediction in the air, he muttered, "You are dust and to dust you shall return."

As the desecrated bodies stormed into range, he detonated the charges he had placed in the tunnel earlier. The walls exploded in a huge fireball, spitting flames into the walking cadavers. The powerful blast threw Michael back and brought the roof down on the corpses, turning the narrow passageway into a funeral pyre of metal and stone. Trapped beneath the burning rubble, the blistering bodies of the dead fought furiously against the raging inferno. But the only freedom to be found was in the searing fires of cremation.

Michael struggled to his feet and brushed the dirt from his jacket. He wiped the blood from his cheek where a large rock had made a deep cut. Although a mountain of debris now separated the squad from their Lumen enemies, the revolting smell of burnt flesh continued to waft through the cracks.

"Eternal rest grant unto them, O Lord," he prayed aloud. "Let thy perpetual light shine upon them. May they rest in peace."

For now, the rebels appeared to be safe. Father Pike lurched over to Michael, his face contorted with pain.

"I can't believe you rigged the walls to blow. You could've brought the whole place down on us," he complained.

At that moment, the ceiling began to rattle with tremors, causing the Jesuit to look about nervously.

"Maybe we should get the hell out of here!" he said in distress.

"Can you rendezvous with the Prelate on your own?" asked

Michael. "I have to get back to my team."

"Just go already, we'll be all right!" Father Pike insisted. "Your brothers will need you in this fight."

As Michael turned to leave, the Jesuit grabbed hold of his arm and muttered, "By the way, thanks for bailing us out. That's twice I owe you my life."

Michael nodded gravely. "Try and *hang on to it*, there aren't many of us left," he grunted.

Chapter 32

Beneath the beating pulse of the metropolis was another city, a network of catacombs and hidden passages long forgotten by everyone, except those who lived in the shadows in order to preserve the light.

Gabriel sped through the entrails of the train station, dragging Raphael as fast as he could. Chelsea hurried along behind the priests, watching their backs. They reached a metal door at the end of the tunnel and stopped to catch their breaths.

"Hang on, we're almost there," said Gabriel, giving the others time to rest.

Raphael lifted his head weakly. "Where's Michael?" he groaned.

"Don't worry, he'll catch up. Let's go."

But the doctor wouldn't move. He grabbed his confrere and insisted, "We're not leaving without him."

"Let's hope we won't have to," replied the Japanese friar. He kicked the steel door opened and all three of them stumbled into a concrete clearing.

They were in a basement parking space that hadn't been used for quite some time. The place was dimly lit. The smell of mildew and water seepage lingered in the air. A few parked vehicles languished in the shadow of rust and decay, save for one that sparkled like a beacon of hope.

"That better be our ride," said Chelsea, gesturing towards a black muscle truck in the middle of the complex.

"Come on!" urged Gabriel, making a push for the vehicle.

Before they could reach the truck, Raphael started to choke and gag. Blood sputtered from his lips and trickled down his chin. He made a great effort to stand but his knees buckled beneath him. The strangling blue lines of the wicked spell had begun to reappear on his neck.

"Please God, not now," said Chelsea, terrified that the doctor might die before they had a chance to ferry him to safety.

"Why bother? He won't make it, you know," a voice echoed in

the cavernous hall. "In fact, none of you will."

A girlish laugh darted around the concrete pillars, making it tricky to pinpoint the exact location of the source.

Chelsea couldn't tell where the voice was coming from. She looked over at Gabriel and saw him calmly unbuckle the small sack he was carrying behind his back. Slowly, the Japanese friar pulled out a pair of oriental daggers, each balancing a single pointed blade amidst two sharpened prongs

"Get Father Raphael into the truck and stay with him," Gabriel instructed sternly.

She didn't like the idea of leaving him alone to face whatever was out there. "But..."

"Don't argue," Gabriel raised his voice. "Do it now!"

Chelsea grabbed hold of Raphael and dragged him towards the truck. The doctor cringed in pain as he leaned heavily on her shoulders. Together, they hobbled to the safety of the vehicle.

"Aw...c'mon, don't be like that. Come out and play," said the effeminate voice.

"Stay in the vehicle!" Gabriel shouted back to his crew.

Peals of laughter erupted in mockery. "Yes, stay in the vehicle," the darkness taunted them. "Beyond this point, there be dragons!"

Gabriel stepped into the light and twirled his weapons like a pair of batons. He had gotten two brand new sai from the Resistance and the daggers swung easily in his hands.

"You're not afraid of me, are you?" teased Gabriel. "Show yourself!"

The basement exploded with laughter. "Oh goody, a challenge. I like that," replied the disembodied voice.

From behind a pillar emerged a tall figure cloaked all in black. The thin man sashayed into sight and stood facing Gabriel, a wide maniacal grin on his face. The blackness of his clothes made his pale complexion seem almost translucent, like the ghostly membrane of a decaying corpse.

"All right hero, let's see whatcha got," said the creepy man.

Gabriel crossed his daggers and assumed a defensive stance.

Agent Yang giggled hysterically. "That's so cute," he gushed. "It's a pity I have to kill you."

He snapped his fingers and instantly, the bulbs in the ceiling burst in rapid succession, quickly drowning the basement in a sea of shadows. In a matter of seconds, the parking complex had become an arena of darkness, with barely a flicker of light pulsing through the yawning space.

Gabriel got the chills and retreated slightly, squinting into the gloom. He could barely see his own hands, much less his opponent. And yet, the darkness seemed to be crawling with moving figures, like an army of evil had suddenly surrounded him.

"Ready or not, here I come," laughed the Lumen agent.

Almost immediately, Gabriel felt the brutal force of a blunt object smash into his sides, knocking him to his knees. He tried to get back up but the shadows wouldn't let him. A flurry of pain erupted all over his arms and legs, as if a pack of wild beasts were digging their claws into his flesh.

With each merciless blow, a blistering tide of sacrilege assaulted his ears. His body crumpled like a rag doll but his soul refused to be intimidated. Blind and confused, the friar lashed out against his opponent. But the points of his deadly sai caught nothing but thin air.

"He'll be killed if this goes on," Chelsea shrieked inside the truck.

Her heart pounded madly as she watched the blackness rip into the friar. Beside her, Raphael crossed himself and looked out the glass window. He could hear the painful cries of his confrere ring out in the dark, striking his own heart in agony. The doctor closed his eyes and placed a trembling hand against the armored door, begging for light in the midst of so much darkness.

"Lord, save your people," he pleaded. "Help me to help him."

As always when he prayed like this, his breathing became shallow and his pulse often slowed to a crawl. In contrast, the visions came hard and fast. They flashed before his mind like snapshots from a camera pushing back the darkness one frame at a time. He gasped. He could see the terror stalking his confrere.

Outside the truck, Gabriel was feeling the sting of defeat. His body throbbed with cuts and bruises. Despite his combat skills, he could barely raise a fist against the onslaught of shadows. At times, he felt like he was battling a pack of wild beasts than a single man in a black suit.

Yang continued to cackle and curse, mocking the soldier of Christ. The young friar tried to retaliate. He blocked and parried, twisted and slashed, but he was fighting blind. The shadows always seemed to slip beyond his reach. Again and again, the blows rained down on him, pummeling him to the floor with ruthless violence.

Once flat on the ground, the stench of sulfur was overpowering. Gabriel fought to keep from blacking out.

"This is so much fun, I can do this forever," said the Lumen agent. "But alas, I'm a busy man. Places to go, people to kill. Tick tock, tick tock. Are you ready to die?"

A torrent of blasphemies accompanied his laughter. Clearly Yang was not alone. But neither was the Japanese priest.

In that moment, Gabriel heard someone talking in his ears. Raphael's voice echoed so softly that the friar thought he was hallucinating. The ancient battle mantra known as the breastplate of St. Patrick resounded over and over in his mind. It was a mere whisper at first, but it was loud enough to drown out the sacrilege pouring into the basement.

Christ with me, Christ before me, Christ behind me,
Christ in me, Christ beneath me, Christ above me,
Christ on my right, Christ on my left...

Gabriel shook the pain from his head. Was he dreaming? Surely the beatings had taken a toll on his instincts. Even so, he could feel a mysterious presence embrace him. And then suddenly it happened. A powerful surge of energy blazed through his limbs and scattered the shadows. The jolt was so strong that it drove his opponent back a few feet.

Startled by the outpouring of grace, Yang fell to the ground cursing. The Lumen agent was stumped by this unforeseen change of events. He jumped to his feet and dramatically called on the powers of hell, rallying the wounded shadows to his defense.

Nevertheless, Gabriel was now able to see through the darkness. In flashes and in spurts, the visions came to him as they came to Raphael, tethered by a common thread of prayer. In some mystical way, both men were bound together in sight and sound. Chelsea however still saw the basement shrouded in darkness. But she too noticed that the friar seemed more equipped to battle the abomination rushing at him.

There was an explosion of punches and kicks as both combatants tackled each other. Gabriel had suffered much from the earlier thrashings, but he was determined to bring some payback to the fight. The two warriors battled like pugilists in a death match, with the friar pressing his advantage with the consecrated weapons in his hands. At one point, Yang screamed when Gabriel punctured flesh and bone, forcing the man in black to retreat.

"You stinking cockroach! I'll crush you for this," cried the agent. He recited some mantras and dived into the shadows, snatching metal from the darkness. Incredibly, an ancient Chinese weapon materialized in his hands.

Gabriel was flabbergasted. He recognized the long pole with the heavy blade attached to one end. The Kwan Dao was capable of cleaving a man in half, but this was no ordinary weapon. It flickered and flamed in the grip of evil like something conjured from the armory of hell.

The friar took a prudent step back.

"What's the matter?" scoffed Agent Yang. "Afraid to lose your head?"

Boiling with rage, he swung the mighty polearm and rushed at the priest. Both men clashed in a furious tangle of muscle and steel. There was a massive barrage of swift and deadly moves. Between the two warriors, it was hard to tell who was the more skilled.

However, the long reach of the Kwan Dao kept Gabriel from getting close enough to do any serious damage. Instead, Yang launched wave after wave of unrestrained violence. At one point, the terrifying polearm skimmed over the scalp of his enemy and tore into a nearby pillar, smashing chunks of concrete from its core.

Pelted by debris, Gabriel lost his balance and stumbled backwards. He recovered just in time to see his opponent swoop down like a monstrous bird, driving the flaming pole towards his skull. Instinctively, he raised his daggers to ward off the blow. Sparks flew as the impact of the Lumen blade snapped off the steel prongs of the sai, battering the friar with the prospect of certain death.

Yang didn't let up. He pressed down hard, determined to end the fight. But Gabriel held up the weight of the polearm with the twisted frames of his daggers. With death inching ever closer, he struggled to push the deadly load away from his face. At the last second, the Japanese friar noticed that the broken prong on one of his weapons rose up like a jagged spike. Without hesitation, he dropped to his knee and plunged the shattered rod into the foot of his enemy.

Agent Yang squealed like a stuck pig. Before he could threaten to punish the priest, powerful beams of light suddenly blasted into his eyes. Blinded and stunned like an animal caught in the headlights, the Lumen assassin stood impaled by the steel prong trapping him to the ground. By the time he realized what was happening, the truck was already bolting towards him at high speed. The vehicle slammed into his body and tore him off the floor, leaving much of his foot still skewered to the ground.

Gabriel had jumped out of the way. He rolled to the side and watched the Lumen agent cling helplessly to the muscle truck until it crushed him against a pillar. Yang screamed in agony and dropped the Kwan Dao. The polearm clanged to the floor and burst into flames, vanishing like a phantom blade. The engine growled. The truck reversed like a rhino backing off from an injured prey. Groaning noisily, the agent slid off the front grill and slumped to the floor.

Again, Gabriel watched in disbelief as the truck rushed forward with vengeance, squashing the man in black beneath its massive wheels. The basement echoed with the sounds of painful torment. Amid the screeching of tires, the side door suddenly flew opened and Michael shouted from the driver's seat.

"Get in!"

Gabriel wasted no time hurrying to the truck. When he got near, Chelsea reached out and pulled him in. The door slammed shut and Michael jammed his foot on the accelerator, gunning the wheels over the splattered remains of the Lumen agent while he sped towards the exit.

Having ensured that Raphael and Chelsea were strapped in, Gabriel glanced out the rear windshield and saw Agent Yang recede into the shadows. The black figure wasn't getting up. Relieved, he turned back to Michael and punched him in the arm.

"Nice of you to show up," he groused at the priest.

"Nice of you to stay alive," said Michael, gassing the pedal.

The speeding truck shot up a ramp and crashed through a large gate. With a thunderous roar, the vehicle burst into the open sunlight and drove into oncoming traffic. It was still daylight and the roads were swarming with cars. Swerving madly, Michael dodged a few near misses before slipping into the right lane.

"Everyone okay?" he asked.

"Everyone not okay!" Chelsea shouted back.

Michael glanced at the rear-view mirror and saw Raphael wilting away. The blue veins grasping his neck had blossomed into a cluster of distressing vines. The clairvoyant priest was gasping for air, as if his intervention in the battle earlier had somehow worsened his condition. Every time the vehicle jolted, the priest cried out in agony.

"He'll die if we don't stop somewhere and fix this," Gabriel

311

insisted.

"Stop now and we all die," Michael replied. "We need to get away from here first!"

As soon as he said that, the truck screeched to a halt. All along the road before him was a quagmire of motorized steel and bumpers, aggravated by commuters pouring out of the train station. They were stuck in traffic like sitting ducks. Michael blasted his car horn and a fleet of angry horns blasted back. They were going nowhere.

Frustrated, Chelsea leaned out the window and yelled. "Get out of the frickin' way you morons!"

Quickly, Gabriel turned around and yanked her back in. "Stay in the truck! You want the whole city to recognize you?" he scolded her.

Then something no one could've expected happened. A heavy object fell on the car next to them, brutally crushing the bonnet like tin foil. The noise of the impact was startling.

"What the hell?" Gabriel blurted out in shock.

When Chelsea saw the human form all shredded and torn up, she screamed in fright. The crowds on the sidewalks also broke out in pandemonium. Seconds later, another lifeless body plummeted down and smashed into the roof of the taxi in front of them, splattering blood and brain all over their windshield. The sniper rifle bouncing off the hood told Michael everything he needed to know. He jammed his foot down and drove the armored truck like a runaway tank, bulldozing vehicles out of the way.

"Look out!" Chelsea cried as they mounted a sidewalk and rumbled towards the terrified crowds.

Young and old scrambled to jump free. Michael swerved hard and brought the metal beast back on the road.

"Hang on!" said the priest.

He forced his way through the congestion, ramming into bumpers like he was charging through a demolition derby. There was panic on the streets. People were desperate to dodge the seeming lunatic behind the wheel. In some places, the cars were packed like sardines. Yet Michael smashed his way through the bedlam of steel and blaring horns, leaving a trail of wounded vehicles bleeding fuel in his wake. Eventually, the truck burst through the chaos and tumbled onto the open road.

Meanwhile, the clock tower high above the station had been cleared of rebel snipers. The broken glass face on the north wall recalled the recent demise of the two men thrown out like trash.

Even so, the room was hardly empty. A detachment of armed guards gazed down upon the streets below, watching Michael and his crew race away to freedom.

"Bravo. Looks like old soldiers never die," said the man in the silicone mask. His tone suggested a hint of admiration, but his creepy face expressed nothing but scorn. He stretched out his hand and a Praetorian officer passed him a comlink. He took it and held the device up to his ear.

"Is it done?" he asked.

On the other end, a senior guard answered firmly into the transmitter, "Yes Commander, the package has been secured."

All around him, members of the Resistance had piled up in carnage. The small band of militia protecting the Prelate was decimated, leaving their shepherd in the hands of Praetorians. Several guards bound and dragged the old man through the bloody remains of his fellow Christians, intending to humiliate him.

Joseph Li refused to lose his composure. He kept his serenity, praying softly for the souls of the dead as the enemy led him towards a waiting van. But just before they shoved him in, the old shepherd turned back and glanced into the shadows, his eyes brimming with compassion. It was as if he was looking at someone hiding in the dark. One of the guards lost his patience and slapped the elderly man. The rest pushed him into the van and pulled the sliding door shut. With that, the Prelate was gone.

"Let me speak to her," the Commander snarled into his comlink.

The guard beckoned to a tall woman lurking in the dark. Cautiously, Anna Koslov emerged and took the device from his hands. She pressed it to her ear.

"You did well," said the Commander, preening with satisfaction.

"I did what I had to," Anna shot back. "You left me no choice."

The Commander laughed. "If it makes you feel better, you can say the serpent made you do it."

His mockery only deepened her shame and enraged her. But she held her tongue.

"Still, you did an excellent job of infiltrating the Resistance," he continued. "Your intelligence background with Moscow served you well in this mission. Unfortunately, I don't imagine your friends will forgive you for this. So tell me, how does it feel to be a traitor?"

Despite her instincts for survival, Anna was in no mood to play games. "Listen to me, you freak," she retorted. "The deal was I give

313

you the old man, you give me my parents. Where are they?"

"Ah yes, dear old papa and mama," whispered the Commander. Anna couldn't see his expression but she could sense a smirk rising from his tone.

"As agreed, I've given orders for them to be released from prison. They're a little worse for wear but I assure you, they no longer suffer the tortures of our dungeons…"

"*Where are they?*" she demanded loudly, refusing to be coddled. But the Commander would not be rushed.

"First, there's the little matter of The Archangels," he said.

"The truck has been fitted with a tracking device," she confirmed. "You'll find them easily enough."

"What about the Jesuit named Pike?" the Commander asked.

"I don't know, I didn't see him. Pike wasn't part of the deal," she snapped impatiently. "If he was, I would've taken care of it."

The Commander chuckled. "It never fails to amaze me," he remarked. "Given the right motivation, a woman's treachery knows no bounds."

"Just keep your end of the bargain," Anna hissed. "You promised to return my parents. I want them now!"

The Commander kept silent for a while, prolonging the tension, knowing that every extended moment was anguish for the woman.

"Very well," he finally said. "I always keep my promises. In fact, your parents have been waiting impatiently for you."

Anna heard the sounds of shuffling feet and turned around. But her parents were nowhere to be seen. Several troopers stood facing her, their muzzles aimed at her chest.

"You son of a bitch!" she shouted, realizing too late that she had drawn the blade of betrayal only to fall on it herself.

The woman quickly reached for her gun, forgetting that she had already surrendered her weapons. When the holster came up empty, her usual calm and logic abandoned her. An ocean of misery crashed against her heart and trapped her in a whirlpool of anger and despair. Shaking with emotion, she dropped the comlink and it clattered noisily to the floor.

The Commander's voice crackled through the tiny speaker. "Enjoy the family reunion," he sneered. "Tell your folks I said hello."

But Anna didn't hear any of that. The last thing she heard was the sound of retribution riddling her body. And then all was quiet as she collapsed in a pool of her own blood.

Chapter 33

Father Pike tried to lay low, keeping his body as flat to the ground as possible. They had narrowly escaped a Praetorian ambush on their way back, but the enemy was still within earshot. Quietly, the priest turned his head and placed a finger over his lips. The rebel beside him crawled back and gently wrapped his hand over the mouth of a wounded confrere. The muffled groans were immediately stifled.

It was a miracle that the small group of stragglers had managed to dodge the attention of the Lumen forces. Had they arrived a minute earlier, the entire team would be massacred. For now, they were still breathing. Father Pike whispered a prayer of thanksgiving to his guardian angel, but there was no way for them to make the rendezvous in time. The path ahead was blocked by a contingent of Praetorian Guards. There were at least a dozen troopers in that group; hardened killers who would just as quickly slit a man's throat than look at him.

As the Jesuit pondered his next move, he noticed movement on the enemy front. Something was happening. The sergeants were baying like wolves and rallying their pack to move out. Father Pike inched closer for a better look. In his heart, he was worried. He knew that such urgency could only mean one thing. Either their enemies had cornered the Prelate and were calling for reinforcements, or they had already captured the old man with success. Whichever the case, God seemed to have abandoned them.

Straightaway, he felt the claws of depression grip his mind. Making a brief act of faith, he tried to push back the growing despair. Knowing that sadness was an ally of the devil, he would not allow doubt to creep into the secret sanctum of his heart. He would trust still in the Divine Will. As he peered through the night vision goggles, he saw the Praetorians close ranks and get ready to leave. Within a few moments, the Lumen forces had efficiently regrouped and vanished into the dark, disappearing as quickly as they had arrived on the scene. Keenly aware that this could be nothing more than a trap, the Jesuit led two of his best scouts forward to ensure that the coast was really clear.

For the next half hour the men crept along, their hearts thumping within their chest. The rest of the surviving team followed at a safe distance, shadowing them as closely as possible. The progress was painful and slow, with many of their comrades still bleeding from battle wounds. At the slightest hint of danger, the group would pause and hug the ground, mixing their labored breathing with prayer. Eventually, after what seemed like a really long time, the whole squad managed to make it to the assembly point safely.

As soon as he arrived, Father Pike could see signs of carnage everywhere. The ground was soaked in fresh blood, the tunnel walls were pocked with bullet holes, and although the Praetorians had hidden away the dead bodies, the most damning evidence of tragedy lay sparkling on the ground. Solemnly, the priest knelt down and picked up the shiny object. It was partially encased in dirt but he recognized it immediately as belonging to the Prelate.

Years before in a private audience, the pope had granted the old man the gift of his own pectoral cross, a symbol of episcopal authority. In his humility, Joseph had never worn it openly, preferring instead to keep this treasure safely tucked away in his breast pocket. Even so, Father Pike had often seen him clasping the cross to his heart in moments of fervent prayer. As such, it seemed strange that this carefully guarded treasure should be found littering the ground like a discarded trinket.

Unless of course…

The Jesuit turned the object over in his hands. Despite the filth and grime, it was gleaming like a beacon of hope. Joseph might've deliberately dropped this to signal that he was still alive when they dragged him away.

"The Prelate is alive," Father Pike repeated to himself. He was tempted to breathe a sigh of relief when he caught sight of the blood-soaked gravel beneath his feet.

Reality returned like a raging bull and gored the poor man with grief. He was reminded that the day was drenched in battle. Indeed the smell of death still clung to the air like a bad dream. The Jesuit gazed at the pectoral cross and his jaw tightened with emotion.

He knew the Resistance had suffered a terrible blow. With the loss of so many brethren, the Underground Church was mortally wounded. Although the world was already in dire straits, things would be so much worse without the League doing what they could, striking back with guerilla tactics, spoiling the plans of the Corporation whenever possible. But now with the Prelate in Lumen chains, the powers of darkness would get bolder and more reckless in the days ahead.

Looking at the signs of butchery all around, Father Pike hoped desperately that Michael and his team had survived this nightmare. He knew that things would only get worse from hereon.

"Do not be silent, O Lord," he cried, pressing the pectoral cross to his lips. "Do not forsake us in our time of need."

✝

"Make haste to help us, O Lord. In your mercy, grant us your strength and salvation," said Gabriel, reciting the words from memory.

The Japanese friar had clambered into the backseat and was doing all he could to stall the evil contagion. In response, Raphael struggled like a child battling a nightmare, whimpering in fear and trepidation. Gabriel held down the doctor and imposed his hands on the victim's forehead, praying the rest of the formula in silence. After a few minutes, the older man calmed down.

Chelsea looked on with worry. Anxious to help, she rested her hand on the shoulder of the wounded priest and prayed along. Although she didn't know what to say and felt clumsy in her efforts, she tried her best to invoke God's help. The bumpy ride however did nothing to calm her nerves.

As the truck passed the city limits, Michael entered the coordinates into the onboard computer. The special console on the dashboard lit up and a digital map unfurled across the windshield. A tiny blip revealed the location of a secret airfield.

"Hang on," said Michael. "We're about two hours away."

Two hours, Chelsea thought to herself. With all they had gone through, two hours seemed like forever. Armageddon could unfold in that time. She closed her eyes and tried to stay calm, her heart and soul reaching out tepidly to the Christ whom she had denied for most of her life.

She looked at Raphael. The priest was drifting in and out of consciousness. His eyes rolled back and his breathing was labored and harsh. The woman felt a pinch of depression. She wanted earnestly to pray, but could only offer up grasping moments of desperate pleas. With tears in her eyes, she begged God not to look upon her sins but the faith of the Church, and to spare the man who had suffered so much to save her.

Gabriel noticed this. "You all right?" he asked.

She wiped the tears from her eyes and remarked, "Do I look all right?"

Gabriel tried to comfort her. "Don't lose hope, something good will come from this," he said.

Chelsea looked at the friar as though he had gone mad. "Something good will come from this? Like what?" she demanded to know.

The friar didn't answer immediately. He closed his eyes and continued to pray for Raphael. Only when he was done did he reply the woman.

"I'm saying we shouldn't be discouraged by our difficulties. We don't always know why God allows us to suffer humiliation and pain. But we know that the Lord is faithful even when we're not. If he allows us to endure evil, it's because he can bring greater good out of this sadness. We have to trust him."

Chelsea made no attempt to hide her skepticism. If it was true that Raphael was afflicted by a spell of terror, then the encroaching dread was starting to infect her courage as well. She glanced at the doctor and saw him boiling with fear, his features twitching horribly with the tortured look of paranoia. At one point, his visage became so painful to watch that she had to turn away.

"How do you do it?" she asked Gabriel, her voice trembling. "How do you keep your faith alive when people around you keep dying?"

The friar remained unruffled. He tugged at the sleeve of his jacket and dabbed the cold sweat from Raphael's face.

"I know things are looking bad. It's true that Raphael could die. But our greatest injuries are not physical but spiritual - the loss of our souls to the powers of hell. We need to increase our faith and keep praying. Don't lose hope. We'll get through this."

Chelsea looked at the suffering man lying between them. She was struck by how fragile he seemed.

"I wish I could believe that," she said miserably. "All I can feel is dread."

The sadness in her voice moved Gabriel to pity. As mired in sin as her previous life was, it was familiar and safe, conformed to her passions and beliefs. But now, faced with the reality of God and the volatility of the last few days, she was struggling to find her footing between hope and despair.

Reaching around his neck, the friar untied the small wooden cross he wore over his heart, the same one that he had carved as a souvenir for his aunt. For a few moments, he stared wistfully at the memento. Then gradually, he lifted up the item in his hand.

"In hoc signo vinces," he said, pointing to the inscription on the wood. "In this sign you shall conquer."

He leaned forward and placed the sacred object around Chelsea's neck. As he tied the cross in place, he spoke to her warmly as a father would.

"When you're at the crossroads of life, you have a choice. Either you continue down the same path or change. Try to make an act of faith," he encouraged her. "It's not always necessary to understand in order to believe. Sometimes you have to believe in order to understand."

"You learned that from your books?" she asked, trying to resist a smirk.

"I learned that from my uncle and aunt," he said simply.

Chelsea kept silent. Quietly, she reached for the wooden cross around her neck. The crude carving felt harsh and raw against her skin. She clasped the small object and ran her fingers lightly across the grain, feeling for the rough inscriptions. She stared blankly into the distance, her mind jostling with a litany of self-doubts.

"Don't be afraid," said Gabriel. "Many favors and blessings are hanging from heaven to relieve our worries, if only we'd cut them down with the sword of our trust in God."

Chelsea took a deep breath. She looked up, her eyes brimming with emotion. It took all her energy not to give in to despair.

"In hoc signo vinces," Gabriel reminded her. "In this sign you shall conquer."

She held on to the cross tightly and repeated the words after him, "In hoc signo vinces."

Without warning, Raphael exploded in a bout of painful spasms, thrashing wildly between them.

"What's happening?" Michael shouted from the driver's seat. From the rear-view mirror, he could see Gabriel and Chelsea struggling to hold down his confrere.

Raphael was tossing and flailing like a man under attack. Every muscle in his body strained in the opposite direction, threatening to tear him asunder. His face had become a ghastly grimace of intense battle. Something inside of him was clawing for his soul, and the doctor priest was fighting back.

Gabriel knew his confrere was under siege. Quickly, he rummaged through his pouch for the oil of anointing. He took the bottle of blessed chrism and began to mark Raphael on the eyelids and earlobes, nostrils, lips and palms, begging God to have mercy on the poor man. Already, parts of his body were becoming rigid and cold. His lips had turned blue and the tortured veins around his neck appeared to be tightening like a noose.

For a while, the ritual of anointing revived the victim somewhat. The violent thrashings ceased and color returned to his cheeks. Even his arduous breathing became more subdued. Unfortunately, this only proved to be the calm before the storm. Shortly after, terrible spasms once again rocked the sick man. A dark shadow flew over his face, punishing him with excruciating pains. Crippled with agony, Raphael coughed and sputtered until blood dribbled down his chin.

"Come on buddy, hang in there!" cried Gabriel.

The friar was desperate to staunch the effects of the wicked spell, but nothing in his short career as an exorcist had prepared him for this. He was stumped for answers. The Prelate had assured him that Raphael would not die, that when the time came, he would know what to do. And yet as the minutes slipped away and death drew ever closer, the quest for liberation seemed anything but doomed.

Nevertheless, Gabriel refused to give up. He placed his hands on the victim's chest and prayed harder, invoking all of heaven for their intercession. As he recited the Litany of the Saints from memory, Michael loudly took up the ritual responses from the driver's seat.

Chelsea watched with curiosity. The holy titles and names of the saints were lost on her. And yet with each invocation, she found herself wondering if all the citizens of heaven would actually descend into the tiny cabin at that moment. What if the saints and angels were indeed embracing them right now, echoing their desperate pleas with a single voice directed towards the throne of God?

She brushed the thought aside. Surely this was absurd. The saints were dead people. How could they possibly help? Yet these Christians believed that those who died in Christ would rise with him. And if this was true, the saints were hardly dead at all. They were alive in every sense of the word, stripped of their imperfections, deeply united in prayer as a family of God. Perhaps, they were really not alone. There was a spiritual unity between those who had won the crown of victory and those who were still fighting the good fight. And right now, she was part of that family. She was still pondering this when something else caught her attention...

Having fallen into a daze, Raphael mumbled incoherently. Over and over, a single murmur escaped his lips like a broken chant.

Chelsea had to interrupt the men. "What's he saying?" she asked abruptly.

Gabriel and Michael were too busy praying the Litany to pay any attention.

"Both of you, stop and listen!" she shouted. "He's saying something."

Finally, Gabriel paused and lowered his face to the sick man. By all reckoning, he knew that a miracle was needed to save his friend. The man's mortality was hanging by a thread, and everything the exorcist had done up till then had borne little fruit. But as he hunched over the dying priest, his eyes brightened at the sound of something familiar.

The friar inched closer, listening carefully. The rasping noises, punctuated by terrible groans, continued to rattle like a death knell. But beneath the anguish and fear, a single word pulsated over and over like a beacon of hope. It was hardly audible at first, but with every painful breath, it grew in strength and fervor until it dawned on Gabriel that the poor man was not really repeating a word at all. He was calling out a name.

"Dear God, why didn't I realize this sooner?" he thought aloud. *"There is no fear in love. But perfect love casts out fear..."*

No doubt they were dealing with an unusually malevolent spell, but the Prelate had already given him the remedy for fear. Only now did he recognize the concrete cure. The friar jumped into the front seat and quickly accessed a new location on the digital map.

"What're you doing?" Michael protested. "We don't have time for this."

"You have to get us there," said Gabriel, thumping his finger at a new blip on the windshield.

"Too far. We can't afford the risk," Michael observed.

At this stage, he knew that a detour would cost them severely. Every holdup in the journey would bring the Corporation dangerously close. And this side-trip might just be the thing to bury them all.

"We don't have a choice," Gabriel shot back. "Do you want to save him or not?"

"And how do you suggest we do that? By digging him a new grave?"

"I don't have time to explain," Gabriel replied. "You'll just have to trust me."

Michael glanced in the rear-view mirror. Indeed, Raphael was rapidly fading like a ghost. If there was some way to keep him alive, they would have to act now. As the old soldier grappled with his decision, he caught sight of Chelsea staring at him in the reflection. The woman was cradling his friend like a wounded child. Her cheeks were flushed and her lips were parted, as if she wanted to say something.

In the end, it was her eyes that did all the pleading...

Despite his misgivings, Michael found himself conquered by her gaze. He understood that she would not risk the death of the ailing priest, nor was she ready to give in to despair. Without uttering a single word, she had convinced him that they would either all make it together, or not at all.

Somewhat admonished by her loyalty, he turned back to Gabriel, whose burning resolve had only grown more urgent.

"All right, we'll do it your way," he told the friar.

Throwing caution to the wind, Michael pushed the truck into high gear and gassed the pedal hard, swinging the vehicle around for the state cemetery.

"I just hope you know what you're doing," he growled.

"So do I," said the Japanese friar.

Chapter 34

It had been a long night. The doctor was just finishing up his rounds, exhausted by the endless queries and demands. Everyone seemed to be clamoring for his attention. Every suffering soul insisted on his utmost care. All through the wards, the sounds of hope and anguish melted into a common cry for help. But this was no public hospital shackled by budget cuts. This was a bastion of exclusive healthcare for the rich and famous. Behind the walls of privilege and privacy, the nursing staff did their best to calm a powerful clientele of patients used to getting what they wanted. And what they wanted now was the attention of the miracle man in the white coat.

The leading matron shook her head. There were other skilled doctors standing nearby, specialists gifted in their craft. Yet the entire team stood huddled in a corner like extraneous pieces of medical equipment, rendered obsolete by the growing status of their new colleague from uptown.

For some time, the young man's fame as a healer had preceded him. He was rumored to be an exceptional physician, but the last two years really cemented his glowing reputation. Cases that baffled the city's brightest medical minds crumbled before the clarity of his diagnosis. When no one else could find the cure for an illness, he was always ready with a remedy. It was as though he could touch the very marrow of human suffering and expose the decay creeping behind each disease. More than once, the renowned doctor had untangled the deadly knots of incurable maladies and freed patients from the noose of death.

For the man whom science, medicine and magic seemed to converge like a lightning bolt, it didn't take long for success to fill the coffers of his ego. He could treat almost every illness and save just about anyone. But when it came down to it, *just about* wasn't good enough.

Laying in an intensive care unit was a woman hooked up to tubes and machines. And despite his best efforts to help her, she was dying. The young doctor sighed. He had garnered more wealth and respect than he ever imagined possible. And yet, all that seemed to weigh like a giant millstone around his neck. The bristles on his chin were peppered with streaks of premature gray. Rubbing his eyes, he scratched the day old stubble on his face and tried to disguise his grief as fatigue.

"Carmichael - room 24," said a large woman, interrupting his thoughts. She handed him a medical file.

He refused the dossier. "I'm done for the day. Give it to one of the others," he grumbled to the Director of Medical Services.

"He asked for you," she replied, with some jealousy. "They always do."

She pressed the file into his hands and told him to get moving. The other doctors turned towards their colleague with some envy, watching to see what he would do next. No one knew about his secret, how he had always managed to read what was hidden from everyone else. Beyond the clinical tests and procedures, the young man had a gift for knowledge and wisdom. He could somehow tap into a reservoir of information that would not show up on charts and reports, often just by touching his patients.

"If I was superstitious, I'd say you were in league with the devil," said the woman, half joking. "Still, I suppose what matters is that you get results, even if your methods are less than kosher."

The young doctor smirked. "You know I don't believe in God or the devil," he said brusquely. "But I do believe my shift is over."

He stuffed the medical file back in her hands and walked away.

"Now hang on, you've got a responsibility to your patients," she reminded him. "Don't think you're special just because…"

The man turned on a dime and glared at her.

"Just because what?" he retorted gruffly. "The only patient I need to see right now is holed up in the intensive care unit, and you've got me treating your cash cows the entire day. Like I said, my shift is over. I'm done here."

The Director was tempted to reply but she held her tongue, knowing that she couldn't afford to antagonize the young doctor, not when a dozen hospitals in the country would kill to have him on their staff.

The doctor strode away without turning back, his shoulders stooped with frustration. By the time he had taken the elevator to the intensive care unit, his thoughts had once again returned to anguish. He stared morosely at his hands, resentful of the fact that they had healed so many but were incapable of helping the one person that really mattered. In a fit of rage, he slammed his fist into the metal doors and cut his knuckles on the cold steel. The stinging pain took some of the angst away, relieving the pressure building up in his heart.

The elevator bypassed the general ward and kept climbing. When the doors finally opened, a single private room took the entire floor. The doctor composed himself and stepped out. At the end of the hall, a woman lay in a bed of pain, surrounded by nurses and a host of beeping machines. When she saw him approach, she lifted her head and tried to give him a smile. But her cheeks were so sunken that the effort made her look grim and macabre instead.

The doctor came close and sat beside her. Taking her hand into his own, he brought her gaunt fingers to his lips and kissed them. The warmth lingered on her fingertips as she gazed at him with love.

"How're you feeling?" his eyes seemed to say.

She nodded slightly and squeezed his hand. The tracheal tube in her throat made it hard for her to speak. But still she tried, though she could only manage a guttural sound scraping through her airway.

"Shhh," he admonished her. "Don't talk."

He reached down and gently brushed her cheek. The gold ring on his finger shimmered as he did so, reflecting his love for the woman whose finger bore the same beautiful wedding band. She looked at him lovingly, as she had always done. On his part he tried to appear brave, but the tears welled up in his eyes. They had only been married for five years. And for half that time, the young doctor labored furiously against the bizarre illness that ravaged his wife.

Through it all, he knew of the gossip brewing behind closed doors and whispered along busy corridors. Here was the great miracle worker, the atheist doctor whose genuine skills at healing bordered on the supernatural. Some say he was a clairvoyant, others that he was a trickster and a fraud. Personally, he thought of his gifts as a psychic impression. The charisms started manifesting when he was a teenager and grew stronger with age, even as he traded the faith of his ancestors for the altars of ambition. In truth, the man himself did not know how or why he came to possess these unusual talents, only that he could sense the hidden and see the invisible, and often heal the sick when science itself had long given up the fight.

Now in the evening of his bright career, doubt and confusion had begun to assail his mind. He had saved others but he couldn't save his own. *Physician, heal thy wife. What we hear you do for the rich and famous, do for your own.* The jealous voices giggled behind his back, mocking his fame and success. But he cared nothing for the insults. All his heart was now locked up in the shriveled form of his beloved, the same woman who now grasped his hand, pleading with her gaze for him to believe.

Months ago when she was still healthy, when the brilliance of his future had dazzled him blind, they had argued and debated about God. She believed and he did not. She cared deeply about the Church and he could hardly care less.

"Have we loved the truth?" she had asked him one time. "Or have we betrayed the truth by surrounding ourselves with people who only want to help us make peace with sin and error?"

He was annoyed with her that day. "I've told you before," he said. "These people are our friends, they're not our enemies. Without their support, we wouldn't be enjoying any of this right now."

"Does it not matter that your friends also support killing off God and religion?" she asked, knowing that his golfing buddies were funding nationwide campaigns to destroy organized religion.

"That's not fair," he grumbled at her.

She said nothing in return. But he could sense her disapproval.

"All I want is to give you the good life," he told her. "After all these years, it's finally starting to pay off. This is everything my heart desires for us. Please don't ruin this by bringing your God into it."

Her eyes glistened with emotion. "All I want…all I need is you by my side. I don't need these other things, my love."

"Maybe not, but why should we reject it?" he asked, taking her into his arms. "Look at our lives now. How can this be wrong when it feels so right?"

It was true. Life was good. They had more wealth than they knew what to do with. Their stock among the social elites was rising everyday. But she was worried for her husband, worried that the adulation lavished at his feet was turning his heart to idolatry.

"Our hearts can be deceived, my love," she cautioned him. "We can't simply follow our longings. We have to lead our hearts by the light of virtue, so that what we desire in life is true and good, and not something that will lead us to perdition."

He didn't want to hear it at the time. It was bad enough that the woman he loved persisted in believing in superstitions, but to risk everything he had worked for to assuage her scruples was asking too much.

In the weeks that followed, they would dialogue back and forth. Mostly he tried to defend his choices. And mostly, his justifications melted in the fire of her faith and charity.

Despite their differences, he loved her madly. Her innate goodness balanced his natural cynicism. She was that rare creature in an age of disbelief - a pious Catholic and a devoted Christian. And even though she respected his freedom, she made no secret of praying for his conversion. He objected at times, reminding her of the hypocrisy and scandals in the Church, to which she would calmly reply, "Just because there are traitors in our ranks is no reason to condemn the whole Church."

Nevertheless, the doctor was no believer in the mysteries of faith. And he thought little of the Catholic Church. As far as he was concerned, the entire thing would be better off razed to the ground.

"If you want to see the face of Christ, look for the Church that is most persecuted," argued his wife. "And there you'll find the truth. Anything less is no threat to the powers of darkness."

The young man tried not to scoff. There were millions of souls in the world who cared nothing for the Church's mission against darkness. He had seen enough vice and betrayal among priests and pastors to quench the light of faith for entire generations. How could anyone trust the message when the messengers themselves were soiled in sin?

"It's just that I find it hard to believe in a Church that claims to speak for God when some of her shepherds are anything but godly," he replied. "How can anyone feed from a tree whose fruits are rotten to the core? There's enough filth in the Roman Church to stink all the way to high heaven."

The woman smiled and answered simply, "Would you destroy a whole garden if disease and worms have spoilt a few flowers? You know as well as I do that we'll always have Judases among us. Yet you don't judge the Church by those who betray her teachings, you judge the Church by those who're faithful."

He shrugged and pulled her close.

"Well if they were all as faithful as you, the whole world would be on fire for Christ," he said, chuckling. "Still, I suspect if it wasn't for the storm on the outside, no one could stand the stink on the inside."

"The sins and miseries of some, regardless of who they are, are no reasons for me to lessen my faith in the Church that Christ founded," said his wife. "Men do not govern her, the Holy Spirit governs her. And the Lord himself has promised that he'll remain at her side until the end of time."

The doctor grinned and nuzzled her neck.

"Well, I'm happy as long as *you* remain by my side. Anyhow, I've got no time to become a saint. That's your job, to pray for your ungodly old man," he teased.

She laughed and threw her arms around him with great affection.

"It doesn't take much time to make us saints, darling," she replied gently. "It takes only much love."

With that, she leaned into his lips and kissed him. Despite their differences about religion, they were very much in love. And they were happy.

But it wasn't long after, that a strange malady began to take hold of his wife. The young doctor had come home one day to find her in bed with a cold. He had thought nothing of it, trusting that a course of antibiotics would put her back on her feet. The sniffles became worse and she began coughing. Within days, her condition had deteriorated greatly. The first traces of pneumonia clung to her lungs like the herald of bad things to come.

Immediately the doctor warded his wife, taking every precaution to ensure her recovery. But the stress of his job made it clear that she would not be his only patient. Torn from her side by the demands of clients who would not tolerate his prolonged absence, he had placed her in the care of colleagues he trusted, confident that her illness would be treated easily enough.

For a while, she had seemed stable. Each day after looking in on the rich and famous, he would rush to check on her condition. Tests were done but the results were always ambiguous, compounded by the fact that she had lost a disturbing amount of weight.

Despite that, her smile and serenity never left her. She would joke and laugh, appearing in good spirits. As always, she had known how to calm his fears when the ground beneath him trembled with doubt. Nevertheless, he had been unable to diagnose the cause of her illness and it troubled him immensely. He had laid his hands on her like he did with the rest, searching for the source of her ailments, and each time he had come up empty. That had never happened before. And it frightened him.

In time, her condition worsened with new complications. There were more scans and procedures, more tried and tested methods. Yet nothing dismissed the grim reaper from hovering over her wasted frame. By then, the doctor had forsaken all others to save his wife. But try as he might, he could not expose the darkness threatening to extinguish her flame. Again and again he fought to lift the veil of her suffering in order to see clearly.

Again and again, he failed.

The young man was utterly dismayed. All his efforts to heal her crumbled like sandcastles in the storm, washed away by the riptides of a cruel fate. For weeks, the illness ravaged her body but left her soul shining with peace.

"My love, when I am dead, you will return to the Catholic faith and become a Franciscan priest," she had scrawled on a piece of paper. He had dismissed it as the wishful ramblings of a woman drunk on medication.

"Darling, you know my sentiments. I despise God and religion. And I always will," he had told her. In return, she smiled and patiently ran her fingers through her rosary beads.

At times, she seemed crucified to her bed. Like incense burning before the throne of God, her life was slipping away in the fragrance of prayer. All her waking moments seemed to be pierced through with pain. On some occasions, she resembled a martyr dying in place of some poor soul. And yet through it all, her peace had never left her.

Pale with anguish, the doctor tried to be brave. But little by little, his courage grew dim. Eventually he fell to his knees in a painful vigil by her side, dreading the unavoidable.

"Despite all my skills, I can't even save the woman I love," he broke down and cried.

With pen and paper, she had written her response: "Perhaps you're not supposed to save me. Perhaps I'm supposed to save you."

Her breathing became labored. Her complexion grew more pallid. In her last moments, he had clasped her to his chest, pleading with her to hang on. Her eyes were large and luminous. They seemed to glow like orbs of fire even as her body succumbed to the disease. For days, she had not been able to speak, silenced by the tracheotomy meant to help her breathe. But when the moment came, she looked up at him with all the affection in her heart, and mouthed the only words that really mattered.

"I love you," she whispered. And then slowly, she closed her eyes. The poor man didn't move from her side. Nor would he allow anyone to touch her. For hours, he clung to her cold body and drenched the night with tears. Only with great difficulty did the nurses finally succeed in helping him to let go.

In the days after the funeral, the doctor was lost in a stupor. The shock lasted several weeks, the grief lasted a lifetime. When he finally got around to sorting out her things, he found her private diary in a package addressed to him. On opening the book, he flipped the pages to her last entry and read the lines that would change his life forever.

"My love, a year ago, I asked God to send me sufficient sufferings to purchase your soul. On the day that I die, the price will have been paid. Greater love than this no woman has, than to lay down her life for her husband."

That night, feeling the acute sense of loss in the empty space beside him, he broke down and cried like a child, burying his face in his pillow. A swarm of emotions dragged him through the tortured corridors of his mind, pulling him back to the image of the tiny chapel where his grief was laid opened like a raw wound in the days during her wake. Again, he found himself kneeling in the front pew before the casket of his wife, uncertain if he was dreaming or wide-awake.

The chapel was empty of people, leaving the doctor all alone with his memories. A single wooden cross hung over the mortal remains of his beloved. Raising his eyes, he noticed that the walls were lined with two rows of oil lamps. A soft gentle light suffused the aisles and sanctuary, pushing back the shadows. Around the casket, a sacred silence settled like a balm, broken only by the tender sobs escaping from his heart.

Without warning, a loud crash shattered the night as the chapel doors flew open. Startled by the noise, the doctor turned and glanced behind him. The doors had been ripped off its hinges. And a palpable darkness stood over the threshold like an enemy at the gate.

Frightened and confused, the doctor tried to rise from his knees. Immediately, he was struck down with vertigo and nearly fell to the ground. An icy gust of wind surged into the sanctuary and stole the breath from his lungs. Gasping, he held on to the pew, struggling to steady himself.

From the corner of his eyes, he saw the blackness crawl in with a fiendish hunger. The darkness began to take shape, looking like a huge lion prowling for fresh meat. As the evil approached, the burning lamps hugging the walls began to go out one by one.

Stricken with horror, the doctor panicked and felt the impulse to pray. Yet he stubbornly resisted, thinking he had gone mad with grief. When all the lamps were extinguished, the evil assumed the form of a person and drew near. He could sense the unspeakable hatred brewing within this specter.

Without warning, he suddenly felt the dreadful touch of death grasping his neck. The phantom threw him to the floor and throttled him like a bag of straw. He couldn't breathe. A nest of blue veins engulfed his throat, sucking the life from him. In desperation, the doctor finally relented and called out to God for help. To his amazement, the choking slowed to a crawl. He saw a vision of his wife leave the casket and slowly relight the chapel lamps with a small candle. The apparition calmly continued down the aisles, pausing before every lamp until the entire chapel was lit. At that point, the strangling darkness cried out in fury and vanished without a trace.

The doctor sat up in cold sweat. Everything in the chapel had returned to what it was before the intrusion. He twisted around and saw that the doors were still shut and undisturbed. Despite the trembling in his legs, he pulled himself to his feet and gazed around, uncertain of when reality last left him.

Perhaps it was all just a nightmare, he thought. And yet there she was, standing upon the altar steps, looking a thousand times more radiant than he remembered her. Unwilling to trust his eyes, he gawked at his wife like a man doubting his own sanity.

"My love," he mumbled in disbelief. "You live…"

"I live," the vision agreed. She smiled at him, and he felt his heart burst with joy. "And so shall you," she prophesied.

There was a gentle breeze like the soft caress of a woman's love, and then his wife was gone. The doctor found himself back in his home and in his own bed, his body quaking with emotion.

"Don't leave me," he cried into the pillow with his eyes shut tight, hoping to preserve the memory of his beloved. In his heart, he feared that he might never see her again.

"I love you," he repeated over and over, tears flowing down his cheeks.

"I know, I'll always love you too," he heard his wife say. Her voice sang lovingly in his ears and settled like a warm kiss upon his lips. Slowly, his heart found courage and his spirit reawakened.

A deep sense of warmth surged through his very being. When he opened his eyes again, the sky was weeping with sympathy. All of heaven seemed to be sharing his grief. The rains came down like a torrent of tears, drenching him to the bone. Yet his blood was burning with hope. The pain was still there. But amidst the suffering, there was also a baffling sweetness. For a while he remained kneeling in the mud, disoriented, unsure of where he was. Then slowly, he heard someone call his name...

"Father," the woman's voice sounded through the rain. "Father Raphael!"

The doctor looked up and saw familiar faces staring back at him. Michael and Chelsea stood to the side while Gabriel knelt in a puddle next to him. The rain was pelting down on all of them. There was no one else in the cemetery, not on a day when lightning split the skies and the earth seemed to be drowned in a deluge of sorrow.

"Are you all right?" Chelsea asked with great concern.

Raphael felt a lump in his throat. He said nothing for a while. He merely stretched out his hand and touched the tombstone before him, tracing his fingers against the name etched across the grey marble slab.

"*Greater love than this no woman has, than to lay down her life for her husband,*" he whispered from memory.

With tenderness, he leaned over and kissed the name on the tomb. When he got back up, he noticed that the rain was drizzling to a stop.

Chapter 35

"I think the danger is over," Gabriel declared with some relief.

He had carefully examined Raphael and found no trace of the curse. The bulging blue veins around his confrere's throat had also vanished like the morning mist.

"You gave us quite a scare, doc. We thought you were a goner," said Chelsea.

Raphael looked pensive as he approached the waiting vehicle with the rest.

"I guess the Lord isn't done with me yet," he said wistfully.

When the doctor had first emerged from his ordeal, he requested that they leave him alone for a while. The rain was still coming down in sheets, drenching the party. But he remained kneeling before the tombstone, allowing the cleansing waters from heaven to mingle with his tears. A part of him wished he could've stayed with the memory of his wife forever. Though he was now a priest, he had never stopped being a husband and a man. And in his sorrow, he missed her dearly.

"I'm glad you're back," Gabriel told him. "But we're not out of the woods yet. We need you to hang tough."

Michael was busy scanning the surroundings in the meantime. But nothing stirred beyond the rustling of leaves. The deathly silence of the cemetery gave him enough cause to lower his weapon. When everyone had gotten into the vehicle, the priest jumped behind the wheel and pushed the truck into high gear. He was impatient to get away. They had plenty of ground to make up and not much time to do it.

As the transport lurched into motion, Raphael suddenly staggered like a man clubbed with a wooden bat. He grabbed his head and groaned, feeling as if someone had torn a living page from his consciousness. The rupture in his mind continued to bleed images and thoughts that filtered through the cracks of his psyche. He knew what it was. Even though a mystical fracture like that was rare, it was usually a portent of something dark and ominous.

Gabriel noticed this and wondered if the doctor was succumbing to another demonic attack. "What's wrong?" he asked urgently.

"I don't know," Raphael answered. "I see a sanctuary lamp, the flame is flickering. Something is trying to snuff it out."

Then quite suddenly, the doctor opened his eyes and gasped. "Where's the Prelate?"

At that moment, a green light on the onboard computer started blinking, signaling that a message was patching through.

"I thought you covered our tracks," Gabriel murmured.

"I did," said Michael.

Ever since they left the train station, he had thrown up a shield around their communications, bouncing frequencies off a few satellites and scrambling all traces except for a highly secured window for monitoring police bandwidths. The fact that this call was coming through an open channel made him frown. Someone was mocking them, trying to tell them their security was useless. And he knew right away who it was.

"Let it through," Raphael said in a firm voice.

Michael tapped a button on the dashboard. Right away, the computer opened a small screen on the windshield and a video image popped up.

"Wow, I'm surprised at how quickly you picked up the call," said the man on the screen. "I was expecting at least a couple more minutes of groveling in fear."

"What do you want?" Michael grunted back.

"Straight to the point, I like that," said the Lumen V.P. "What I want is for you to give up this senseless charade. It's time we stop the pretense. You know there's nowhere for you to run. Give up now and I'll spare your precious Prelate."

"Don't listen to him, he's bluffing," Chelsea spoke up. "The old man escaped with the rest, I saw them leave."

"Did you, sweetheart?" responded Chambers. He looked at the woman with a delicious smile. "And by chance, were these the ones he escaped with?"

The screen suddenly became flooded with raw footages of the rebel massacre hours earlier. The grounds were saturated with blood. Dozens of bodies lay crumpled in the dirt, faces mutilated, body parts mixed with empty cartridges in a carnival of carnage. Through it all, the tyranny of Praetorian Guards gloated over the butchered remains of the dead like vultures.

"What's the old saying?" Chambers postured fiendishly. "A knife that cuts that deep usually comes from the back?"

Before any of them could figure out what he meant, the image of Anna Koslov appeared onscreen, only to be cut down by a barrage of gunfire.

"So you see, your Prelate is safe with me," Chambers sang with contempt. "I promise to show him a good time."

Michael flew into a rage when he heard that. "You son of a bitch, where's the old man?" he exploded. "What have you done to him?"

The V.P. shook his head in mocked disgust.

"Tsk, tsk, such language from a priest. Calm yourself, Father," said Chambers. "What I do with him depends on what you do for me. Quid pro quo…"

"Save your breath! We don't make deals with the devil," Gabriel brusquely cut in.

Chambers pretended to be miffed. "But you haven't seen the offer," he said with disappointment. "There's something for everyone, even the little princess in the back gets a Lumen discount."

Frightened but determined not to show it, Chelsea scoffed. "You expect us to believe you'll release the old man once we turn ourselves in? You're so full of shit, it's not even funny."

Chambers laughed hysterically. "That's because you haven't heard the punch line. It's all a matter of perspective. From where I stand, it's hilarious."

Through it all, Raphael had restrained himself from speaking. Now he spoke with a voice brimming with authority.

"Son of perdition, you may have won the battle today. Yet the Lord himself will win this war. Regardless of how much we suffer, the League will never give up its mission to save souls. Whatever the costs, we'll fight you to the very last man. We'll do everything in our power to awaken mankind to the truth. Believe me, you cannot win."

Chambers hovered over the screen like a brooding animal, his eyes betraying the beast within. Clearly, he was enraged by Raphael's quiet audacity, which seemed to flow from a wellspring of power that not only surprised him, but also deepened his rancor.

"Believe me, your childish faith has made you a fool," he sneered. "Don't you realize that we've already won? Did you really think we could operate on this scale without the support of the people? The souls you've been fighting to save all these years are the same ones who beg me to peel the flesh off your bones and to drink the blood from your skulls. And you thought you could awaken them with your heroics?"

Chambers leaned forward like a lion licking its chops, snarling with the anticipation of the kill.

"The truth is, you've had your chance to kneel before me, to know what it's like to surrender and live," he growled. "But like the old man, you chose to defy the inevitable. You put up this futile resistance when you're nothing more than insects. And you know what happens to insects..."

Gabriel felt the hair on the back of his neck stand up. Without question, a sudden dread began to stalk his heart.

"What have you done to the Prelate?" the friar dragged out his words.

"Why don't you ask him yourself?" suggested Chambers.

In a move that shocked even a former mercenary like Michael, the Lumen V.P. reached over and propped up the severed head of Joseph Li.

"Say hello, old man!" he laughed, grabbing the slack jaw and yanking it like a puppet.

"*Hello*," the Vice-president replied in a falsetto, mimicking the Prelate.

Gabriel was struck to the bone, horrified by what he was seeing. The sight was so traumatic that Chelsea felt like her blood had turned to ice. With every ounce of his fury, Michael wanted to reach into the video and kill the man responsible for this murderous sacrilege. Only Raphael remained focused, unyielding, refusing to submit to the blunt brutality of this nightmare.

"There is no escape. Even now, my shadows surround you," Chambers threatened.

"Then let them come," Raphael answered boldly. "We'll never give up."

The Lumen V.P. laughed hysterically.

"Oh but you misunderstand. I don't want you to give up. I want you to die. Go ahead, shrink away into the dark corners of your fears. Surrender to the terror that's coming for you. Let me see you panic. Let me hear you scream. Come on, give it to me!"

Michael slammed his fist into the console and killed the transmission, plunging the screen into an abrupt silence. He stomped on the brakes and the vehicle screeched to a stop. Without exceptions, everyone unbuckled their seatbelts and jumped out of the truck, stumbling onto the road like people who've had their guts ripped out of them.

For a long time, no one said anything. Each felt like their psyche had been poisoned, stabbed, and shot by the same psychotic villain. The memory of the Prelate's demise clung to their minds like an open wound, bleeding them of any clear sense of direction.

Eventually, Gabriel broke the silence. "Looks like everything has gone to hell."

Michael caught his gaze and frowned. He knew there was no longer any point in making the rendezvous. In all likelihood, the pilot was already dead. The trigger was pulled the moment Anna Koslov turned her back on the light. At this point, they could either keep running until they were caught, or they could stand their ground and fight. Either way, things were not looking good. He was still mulling over the options when Chelsea suddenly spoke up.

"We have to stop running," she said. "I've got enough blood on my conscience."

Gabriel looked at Chelsea. "You can't stay here. The Prelate ordered us to bring you to safety…"

"Screw the order, the old man is dead," she cried out. "Just like everyone else!"

"Calm down!" Michael grunted, somewhat annoyed with her outburst. But the lady refused to be hushed.

"Stop telling me to calm down!' she snapped. "Don't you get it? If we keep running, they'll keep coming. They won't stop until we're all dead. If I die, I die…"

"You're not going to die," Michael brusquely interrupted.

"*If I die, I die,*" she repeated in defiance. "But I won't risk the lives of any more people."

"Well you're not dead yet, so stop being dramatic and get a grip on yourself," Michael exploded. He was perched on a stone fence like a gargoyle, his face frozen in a scowl.

"No, she's right," Gabriel cut in. "We can't keep running, even if there're still people we can trust to hide us. The enemy is counting on us to lead them to every safe house and contact we know. The League won't survive another attack."

"So what do you suggest we do?" Michael growled.

This time, it was Raphael who answered.

"We stand our ground and fight. Be steadfast, put on the armor of God and face the darkness that comes. It's our vocation to overcome evil. To do that, we must confront it. The rest we entrust to God's mercy."

Michael jumped down from the fence and grimaced. There was a wet stain on his wounded shoulder where the stitches barely held together.

"We're outgunned and outnumbered," he reminded them. "If we stay and fight, we might not survive this."

"And if we don't, we'll probably live to regret it," said Raphael. "We took the bait and walked into this trap. Now the devil is hoping to catch as many of our people as he can. We've got to break the line before they reel us all in."

Michael stared at Chelsea. He could tell that she was scared. "You sure you want to do this?" he asked her.

The young woman took a deep breath before answering…

"I've lived my whole life caring for nothing - not God, not anyone," she told him. "If I have to die, let me die caring for something!"

Gabriel agreed with her.

"If we have to choose between two paths, either of which leads to death and defeat, we have to choose the one where we die fighting for justice and honor," he said.

Michael kept silent and glanced at the surrounding hills. He seemed distracted, like a man seeing the vestiges of a bad dream.

"What'd you say, Father," Chelsea persisted. "Will you help us fight back?"

The tall rugged priest furrowed his brows.

"If we do this, we do it my way," he declared. "We don't hold back, we don't take prisoners. We finish this once and for all. Got it?"

The rest nodded their heads. Everyone agreed that it was time to get some serious payback. But time itself seemed to be running out. Shadows were drifting down into the valley. As a bird squawked in the distance, Gabriel turned his attention to a gathering of clouds on the horizon. The gloomy sight made him nervous. When he spoke again, his voice took on a fresh impetus.

"So where do we take the fight?" he asked. "We can't do it out here in the open. We need cover and we need a battle plan."

"Don't forget, we'll be going up against demons," Raphael added. "We'll need time to fortify the place to our advantage."

Michael checked the ammo on his weapon. "What we need is a

castle," he said gruffly. "Something that'll give us a tactical high ground."

The others paused and looked at each other.

"You're kidding, right? Where're we going to find a 'castle' around here?" Chelsea asked, incredulous.

"She's got a point," said Gabriel, checking his digital map. "There's nothing out here but cornfields and dirt roads."

Michael turned his eyes to the hills and frowned. "I know a place," he revealed. "It's not on the map, but it'll do."

Chapter 36

They drove along the ridge in silence until they reached the brow of the hill. Michael turned a corner and pulled up next to a big oak tree. There, across an old courtyard and looming above them were the remains of a large decrepit church. The walls were boarded up with planks that were rotten to the core. Its windows peered out like empty sockets bereft of any soul. The marble and art that once adorned this beautiful temple of God had long been stripped off and carted away to raise monuments to the city of man. All that remained was the cold husk of religion standing in the encroaching gloom, its hallowed halls no longer resounding with praises to heaven.

Chelsea got out of the vehicle and stared at the wounded structure. In some places, the walls were badly smashed up. There were huge gaping holes in the roof. And the front door itself was barely clinging to its hinges. The whole place looked like a desecrated tomb.

"This is where we make our final stand?" she gasped in disbelief.

"Come on," said Michael. "We don't have all night."

They grabbed their gear and approached the massive door. It was a bulwark of decomposed wood held together by rusty grills.

"It's locked," said Raphael, pointing to the chains and padlock.

There was a vicious bang as Michael stoutly kicked the door. The damaged grills flew off like matchsticks in a storm, pulling the doors down in a cloud of dust.

"It's opened," said Michael. He stepped over the threshold and entered the church, followed closely by Chelsea.

Raphael was surprised at how easily the huge doors came off. He turned and looked at Gabriel.

"Well come on, old timer," said the friar, slapping his friend on the arm.

"Old timer?" Raphael muttered, shaking his head. He grabbed the younger man and shoved him along. "Don't make me kick your butt."

Gabriel chuckled. He was grateful for the tiny bit of humor in this dark time. But as soon as they passed from the courtyard into the building, the gravity of their situation became obvious. If the external structure looked desperate, the interior was a veritable nightmare. The church rustled with all kinds of vermin scuttling across the floor. Pillars were shattered and overcome by creepers, and cobwebs clung to every nook and crevice. The smell of death lingered in the musky air like the ghostly trappings of a violent past.

Chelsea couldn't remember the last time she walked into a Catholic church. Many of the State approved 'churches' were little more than sanctuaries of immorality, endorsed by Lumen Corp and supported by renegade clergy railing against the orthodoxy of the Underground Christians. Their worship halls echoed with hateful rhetoric for traditional doctrine, their pulpits preached disgust for moral laws while their barren altars celebrated that unholy alliance between the sacred and profane.

But this was something else. The community who once worshipped here had truly believed in God. And like so many others across the land, they had paid dearly with their lives. As Chelsea stumbled around the nave, she slipped and nearly fell into a large hole. Michael snatched her from the yawning pit just in time.

"Be careful," he said, pulling her back.

The woman looked down and gasped. The jagged hole at her feet exposed the existence of a basement dug into the rocky foundation. In the semi-darkness, there appeared to be a small chapel down beneath. Apart from a few broken pews, almost everything else had been reduced to ashes and the floor was stained with soot. At some point in its history, a fire seemed to have gutted the small room, even though the flames appeared to have stopped short of the sanctuary with the makeshift altar.

"What is this place?" she whispered.

Michael said nothing. He started descending into the basement through a craggy decline of rubble and twisted metal. Chelsea followed him quietly. When they reached the bottom, the priest walked on ahead until he came to the edge of the communion rail.

"Hold on," cried the woman, trotting up to Michael. When she caught up to the priest, he was already on his knees before the sanctuary. The altar itself was still draped with the linens of the past. Curious stains permeated the dusty old cloths, leaving dark blotches of what appeared to be dried blood.

Although Chelsea had never been in the chapel before, there was something familiar about the setting. She glanced around. There were bullet holes in the walls and debris everywhere. Scattered here and there were dirty slivers of clothing, evoking the memories of the dead. And then she saw it - tucked away among the rubble like a casualty of war - the ragged remains of a child's soft toy.

Suddenly, all the different pieces began to click. The story Michael had told her in the tunnels came alive. Chelsea turned to look at the priest and saw the tension in his face. Whether his head was hung in prayer or in sorrow, she couldn't tell. Her heart swelled with compassion. Without making a sound, she knelt down and placed her arms around his shoulders.

Back in the main church, Raphael and Gabriel stood in astonishment, their eyes transfixed upon the monolith standing before them. Clad in a suit of armor with his spear held high, the massive angel towered over the sanctuary like a guardian long forgotten.

"Have you seen one this big?" Raphael whispered in quiet awe.

Gabriel shook his head. Without taking his eyes off the colossal statue, he began reciting the ancient prayer to the Archangel…

"Saint Michael the Archangel, defend us in battle. Be our protection against the wickedness and snares of the devil. May God rebuke him, we humbly pray, and do thou, O Prince of the heavenly host, by the power of God, thrust into hell Satan and all the evil spirits who prowl about the world seeking the ruin of souls."

"Amen," replied Raphael. Both men finished up by signing themselves with the cross.

Just then, Michael reappeared on the upper level with Chelsea in tow. The rugged priest looked weathered and pale. He pulled out his whiskey flask and took a swig. Wiping his mouth on his sleeve, he nodded gravely to the other two.

"Let's go, we have work to do," said Michael.

With barely an hour before sunset, and no way to know when the guillotine would fall, the group rushed to fortify the church compound with traps and defenses. Michael teamed up with Raphael to secure the perimeter with remote weapons and explosives, erecting a gauntlet of high-tech sensors and gadgetry.

At least, Anna Koslov had given them a chance to fight back. Most of the weapon caches in the truck were gleaned from the military black market. And Michael knew just what to do with them.

"If we're going down, we're taking as many of them with us as possible," insisted the priest.

Raphael agreed and activated the next sentry gun in their arsenal. The weapon was remotely controlled, and capable of chewing out the landscape with pinpoint accuracy. As he put in one booby trap after another, the doctor followed Michael's instructions to the letter. The cruel irony wasn't lost on him. He had spent his entire medical career working to save lives. And now he was fervently laying a path for death. There were laser guided projectiles and anti-personnel mines, devices that maimed and destroyed without mercy. Alongside the remote turrets were cluster bombs that flew into the air, only to rain annihilation on anyone hapless enough to loiter below. Like it or not, this was war. And the survival of the League was at stake. If they couldn't win the battle, they were going to try and cripple their opponents one way or another.

Elsewhere in the ruins, Chelsea and Gabriel were busy setting up defenses of their own. Slinging a pouch full of spiritual weapons, he went from doorway to doorway, niche to niche, inserting tiny Benedictine medals into crevices, and sprinkling exorcised salt along hallways and entrances. In many places where there was a threshold, Gabriel instructed Chelsea to stash a relic or to mark the grounds and doorposts with chrism oil.

On his own, the exorcist went about blessing the place with Holy Water. He paused before the statue of St. Michael and traced the sign of the cross over it. Like most churches, the sanctuary with all its sacred images had been desecrated when it fell victim to Lumen sacrilege. Now it was time to reawaken the spiritual power within those walls.

"You think all this is enough to handle what's coming?" asked Chelsea.

"I guess we'll find out," said Gabriel.

He knelt down and removed a long wooden case from his backpack. Laying it across the floor, he opened the box and drew out an ancient Roman sword. Despite its venerable age, the weapon looked imposing and battle worthy.

Gabriel lifted the sword and swung it a few times to get a feel for its weight and balance.

"Where did you get that?" Chelsea asked in amazement. She noticed the blade sparkle as it caught the evening light. If anything, it seemed to come alive in the hands of the young man.

"This sword belonged to St. George," replied Gabriel. "He was a warrior and a Christian, a saint and a martyr. Legend has it that he slew a dragon with this very blade. I'm counting on him to help us slay a few more tonight."

Chelsea looked at the sacred relic. Having witnessed the snapping jaws of hellhounds and the horrifying guises of demons, the story of a saintly warrior killing a dragon didn't seem all that farfetched.

"Does anyone else know you have this?" she enquired.

The friar gave her a roguish grin. "What matters is that the Corporation doesn't know we have it," he said. "That's the kind of advantage I like."

Gabriel stood up and sheathed the blade. "We better go find the others," he told the woman.

"No need. We found you," a deep voice grunted from the shadows.

Chelsea was startled by the sudden appearance of a man. He was garbed in a long dark cassock with a stiff white collar. He wore a gun belt around his waist while the lower half of his black robe remained unfastened. As he walked in, the opened folds of his garments flapped behind him like a small cape.

"Listen, don't creep up on us like that!" she shrieked. "Next time, make some noise or something. You nearly gave me a heart attack."

Michael bared his teeth and growled at her, prompting laughter from Gabriel. The friar turned to Chelsea and chuckled. "You okay?"

"I'm glad you're enjoying this," she said, fairly embarrassed by her own reaction.

Gabriel shrugged and turned his attention to Michael. "Where's the doc?" he asked.

"Over here," said Raphael, striding in through a portico. He tossed a small bag to the Japanese friar and remarked, "Better suit up, we haven't got much time."

Gabriel dug into the bag and pulled out his Dominican habit. The garment looked medieval, consisting of a long white tunic and scapular with a black capuche and cape.

Raphael himself was clothed in the brown habit of a mendicant friar, with a simple knotted cord around his waist. He wore a shoulder holster where the gun was partially concealed by his capuche and hood.

Watching the men, Chelsea was more than a little puzzled. She had rarely seen a priest in a cassock or religious habit. For far too long, clerical clothing had been outlawed in the land. To wear one was to risk imprisonment or worse.

"It's not Halloween, guys," she remarked. "What's with the fancy dress?"

Gabriel pulled the white tunic over his head.

"They're not costumes, Chelsea. They're visible signs of our vocations," he said, donning the rest of his habit. "They signify the Religious Orders we belong to."

Chelsea made a face.

Sensing her bewilderment, Raphael did the introductions.

"I'm a Franciscan, Father Gabriel is a Dominican, and the dark knight over there," he said, nodding towards the roguish priest. "He's a Jesuit."

Cloaked in his long black cassock, Michael looked like a huge bird of prey crouching in the shadows.

"But you're all priests, aren't you?" Chelsea tried to clarify.

"And we'll all die as priests. No sense in staying anonymous," Michael answered.

Chelsea gazed at the elaborate outfits. "So you figured you might as well dress up for the party," she quipped.

"Something like that," Gabriel replied. He smiled wryly and put the finishing touches to his black cape, securing the sheath holding the sword of St. George to his back.

Somehow, the calm and resolute ideals of the three men only flustered the woman even more. She was perturbed. Of all the times to be impractical, this was surely the one night where it would be silly to face the enemy dressed like that.

"Listen, I get that you want to make some kind of pious statement," she groused. "You want to show the world you're bold and courageous priests. That's great. But wearing these things only make you stand out. If you want to be easy targets, why don't you just paint a big red cross on your chests?"

Michael took his battle crucifix and thrust it into a scabbard harnessed to his torso. It hung over his heart like a sacred badge.

"In life and in death, we must not be afraid to witness to our faith," explained the former mercenary. "The world needs people who'll fight for justice and truth. But more than that, it needs the courage of people who trust and believe in God."

"Father Michael's right," said Raphael. He approached the young lady and placed his hands gently on her shoulders.

"Chelsea, you believe in God, don't you?" he asked softly.

The woman said nothing. Instinctively, she reached for Gabriel's wooden cross that she wore around her neck. Raphael noticed this and tried to encourage her.

"In the dark nights of our lives, we should always cling to the symbols of our faith," the doctor maintained. "Not because of fear or superstition, but because the dawn can come quickly for those who believe."

✝

When the sun finally tipped over the horizon, the night came on with a rush of vengeance. The hills were quickly drowned in a sea of gloom that washed over the entire valley.

Chelsea had never seen the earth covered in such darkness. The moon was shrouded in a heavy mist, plunging the land into a black abyss from which no living creature seemed able to escape. Even the rustlings of leaves and the songs of nightjars floated in the winds like a sad and terrible dirge. The only sounds that comforted the young woman were the voices of the priests.

Although split up into teams, she could hear the others through the comlinks they wore. She was crouched low with Michael in one of the twin bell towers rising over the remains of the church, while Gabriel and Raphael had disappeared into the maze of rubble beneath them. Slowly and softly, the men recited their prayers in common.

> *"Soul of Christ, sanctify me*
> *Body of Christ, save me*
> *Blood of Christ, inebriate me*
> *Water from the side of Christ, wash me*
> *Passion of Christ, strengthen me*
> *O good Jesus, hear me*
> *Within Thy wounds hide me*
> *Suffer me not to be separated from Thee*
> *From the malignant enemy defend me*
> *In the hour of my death call me*
> *And bid me come unto Thee*
> *That with Thy saints I may praise Thee*
> *Forever and ever*
> *Amen."*

346

And then the voices on the comlinks fell silent. Strict radio discipline was the order of the night. From where they were, Chelsea could see the valley spread out before them. Or at least she would, if the night wasn't so saturated with darkness.

She turned and looked at Michael. The priest was prone beside her, his face partially obscured by the infrared binoculars he held to his eyes.

The winds had begun to pick up. Chelsea shivered and pulled her jacket tighter around herself. Being so high above the ground made the young woman feel vulnerable. She looked up and noticed that the skies were laden with storm clouds. She wanted to mention it but the first drizzles of rain had already started pelting down on the church.

Chelsea shifted her weight and retreated farther into the shelter, hoping to stay dry. She looked at the man beside her. His rugged features were handsome but weathered with pain. There was almost a sense of self-imposed exile on his face.

"Do you ever get lonely?" she asked out of the blue.

Michael turned around in the darkness. "Do you ever shut up?" he asked with an edge of irritation in his voice.

"I'm just saying. Don't you miss having a woman in your life?"

"Not at this moment," Michael groaned.

"Look, I know you guys take vows of celibacy. You don't get any sex. You give up having a family of your own so you can devote yourselves completely to the family of God. It's a total act of dedication. I get it. But don't you ever wish you had a wife, or just a woman you could cuddle up to? Doesn't it get lonely trying to do it all by yourself?"

Michael put away his binoculars and sat up.

"First of all, we're not vowed to celibacy, we're vowed to chastity for the sake of the Gospel. There's a difference. The reason we don't marry is to be more available for the mission and to be a radical witness to the gospel. We don't have sex not because we're celibate, but because we try to be chaste like every other good Christian who's single. "

"All right chill, you don't have to give me a long lecture," Chelsea grumbled. "I was just wondering. That's all."

She frowned and kept quiet for a while. A few seconds later...

"I'm curious, do you find me attractive?"

Michael started to get really annoyed. "What's the matter with you?"

347

"Nothing," said Chelsea.

She was hungry, tired and cold. And desperately in need of some warmth to lift her drooping spirits. She wanted to confide her thoughts and feelings to him. But all she could think of saying was…

"You probably think I'm a real nuisance, don't you?"

The priest looked at her. His face was chiseled like stone, but there was a vivid softness behind his eyes.

"Everyone gets lonely now and then," he said quietly. "Even for us who are consecrated to God. But in my experience, divine grace has always been more than sufficient. For me, the mission comes first. I try not to dwell on myself."

Chelsea said nothing. She simply returned his gaze. They looked at each other for a few moments. And from where she was sitting, she could feel his genuine concern, even though his face was partially hidden in the shadows. However, she could tell that the priest was growing somewhat embarrassed by his emotions. He broke eye contact and swiveled back to face the open night, acting as if something else had caught his attention.

There was an awkward silence. And then he cleared his throat.

"For what it's worth, I do find you attractive," he mumbled with his back turned towards her.

Chelsea started to smile. "I'm sorry, what was that?" she asked. "Did you just say I'm attractive?"

Michael quickly regretted his remark.

"Knock it off," he grunted. "I'm celibate, I'm not blind."

The woman chuckled with amusement. "Why do you have to be such an ass all the time?" she asked.

Before the priest could respond, she clambered over and sat beside him. Neither said a word to each other. The winds were picking up and the night was growing colder. Chelsea inched closer and leaned her tired head against his shoulder. She half expected Michael to stiffen up with disapproval, but the old soldier simply lowered his muscled frame to make it easier for her to rest.

"I'm just going to close my eyes for a few seconds," she said.

"Go ahead," Michael whispered. "I'll watch over you."

But Chelsea didn't hear him. She had already drifted off to sleep, overcome by the strain and anxiety of the day.

He glanced at her and took a deep breath. The smell of her hair lingered in his mind like a page from the past. In his days as a mercenary, he had known love as a man. But he had also known war to be a jealous mistress who would accept no rivals for his attention. It wasn't true that those who lived by the sword always died by the sword. Sometimes they survive only to see it plunged into the hearts of those most precious to them. The victims of violence are always the ones closest to home.

Michael cradled his rifle and sighed. He kept his eyes fixed on the horizon, trying to forget the ghosts of those memories. Outside, the darkness was frigid and harsh. But inside, his heart was welling up with mixed emotions. He kept still and let her sleep for a while, almost afraid to disturb her rest.

Sometime past midnight, Chelsea awoke to the sound of thunder. She sat up in a fright and nervously looked around. Only when she realized that Michael was still beside her did she begin to calm down. Groggy with sleep, she peered outside the tower at the moonless night.

"How much longer before they come?" she asked.

The priest looked at her.

"Does a burglar warn you in advance before he breaks into your house? No, he comes like a thief in the night. But I wouldn't be surprised if they stuck to the hour of Satan."

"The hour of Satan?" she asked. The phrase alone gave Chelsea goose bumps.

"Jesus died on the cross at three in the afternoon," explained Michael. "Therefore, those enslaved by Satan often choose to do their worst at three in the morning. It's their way of mocking the saving mission of Christ and the divine mystery of the Holy Trinity."

3 A.M. - Chelsea had often heard it referred to as the darkest hour of the night. "So you think that's when they'll come?"

"It wouldn't be the first time," said the priest.

The drizzle had given way to a downpour. The cold air whipping at their faces caused Chelsea to shudder. Seeing this, Michael pulled out his whiskey and took a big swill of the brew. When he finished gurgling, he wiped the mouth of the flask with his grimy hand and offered the lady a drink.

The woman looked appalled and shook her head. In that instant, a crackling roar shook the spire as lightning lit up the countryside. Chelsea felt her heart jump out of her chest.

"Give me that," she cried, snatching the flask from the priest. It took more than a few gulps to calm her nerves.

When finally she composed herself, she found the courage to ask

Michael.

"You're worried about that girl, aren't you?" she exclaimed. "The ghoulish one in the black dress..."

Michael didn't flinch, but she saw the vein in his temple throb ever so slightly.

"I know you think she's a hostage to the devil," said Chelsea. "But as long as she's alive, she'll be the death of us."

"And what would you have me do, kill her? You should know better than to suggest that," said the priest.

Chelsea turned her face away. She understood what it was like to be tossed between the devil and the deep blue sea, where the only path left was the one nobody wanted to take.

"Chambers tried to have her aborted as a baby but she survived," the woman tried to explain. "Now he's using her as some kind of weapon. I know that makes things a lot more complicated, but if we don't finish her..."

"We do nothing of the sort," Michael cut in. "The choices we make tonight will mark us for eternity. We can't afford to spill innocent blood."

"And those demons inside of her, are they innocent too?" Chelsea asked in defiance.

Michael shook his head and looked at the woman. She was expecting a flash of anger on his face. Instead, all she saw was the deep compassion of a man who had seen too much violence and suffering to ever forget.

The Jesuit priest took a deep breath and replied, "When I was in the Special Forces, it was common for insurgents to use children as living bombs. They were taken from villages and then brainwashed to do nothing but deliver death to our camps. They starved the kids at first. Then they told them we've got food and candy. Eventually, they'd send them running over with big smiles on their faces and explosives strapped to their backs. And when a child got close enough to a squad of soldiers, the bastards would detonate. Often there would be nothing left. Just a crater of blood and guts."

He paused, carefully weighing his next words.

"We may have a young girl running towards us with a ton of demons strapped to her body tonight," he continued. "Do we save our own skins by blowing her head off, or do we do everything in our power to save her as well?"

There was an awkward silence between the two. Chelsea felt the remorse of her own lost children rise up again like an accusing ghost. She gritted her teeth and brushed the thoughts aside.

"You can't save everyone," she mumbled.

"I suppose I can't," Michael admitted. "But it doesn't mean I won't try to save this one."

Chelsea remained thoughtful, letting her mind simmer on what the priest had just told her.

"Sometimes, the only way you can save yourself is to lay your life on the line," Michael shared as an afterthought.

The woman didn't argue. She gazed at the wall in quiet thought, pondering deeply until something peculiar caught her attention. Curious, she tried to focus on the tiny specks of black crawling on the bricks. It was uncommon to see flies buzzing about at night, especially in the middle of a thunderstorm. But the more she stared at the creepy crawlies, the more she began to cringe. There was something weird about these bugs – the misshapen bodies and monstrous heads – they resembled the ones in her brother's bedroom the night Raphael tried to save him.

Alarmed, Chelsea tried to warn Michael but the priest had also seen the signs. Right away, he too knew what would grimly follow.

"Crap, they're early," he muttered.

Chapter 37

A shattering roar of gunfire erupted near the perimeter walls. Down in the hidden ramparts of the church, the gun turrets went to work and tore up the intruders with thousands of bullets ripping through the darkness. The incendiary blasts lit up the stormy night. Despite their stealth, the Lumen forces could not evade all the sensors already set in place. Many fell victim to the onslaught of armor-piercing rounds.

Up in the bell tower, Michael triggered a few more surprises for his guests. The entire compound was remotely wired to the console that he wore on his wrist. He ran his fingers over the screen and a fleet of cluster bombs shot into the air, scattering a cloud of lethal debris that exploded on contact with the troopers caught beneath. The smell of burning flesh wafted into the sky as several Praetorians burst into flames and crashed in the dirt. Others were blown apart by a maze of anti-personnel mines.

The fierceness of the battle illuminated the courtyard below. Chelsea could not tell if the blinding flashes came from the lightning storm or the explosions chewing up the night. She inched closer to the small window, trying to catch a glimpse of the skirmish.

The Lumen forces were not completely vulnerable. They got close enough to set off an electromagnetic pulse that neutralized some of the gun turrets, paving the way for the guards to storm the courtyard. But where were they? She could barely spot the Praetorians advancing in the dark. The winds whipping at her hair made it hard for her to see clearly, so she leaned out for a better look.

"Get the hell down!" Michael cried out in alarm.

He grabbed the woman and pulled her back. In that instant, a rocket-propelled grenade slammed into the tower and threw them both against the wall. The ancient brick and mortar crumbled around the pair, plunging Chelsea and Michael into the blackness. Dropping down a shaft of rubble, the priest tried frantically to break his fall. By chance, he grabbed hold of a wooden scaffold that broke his momentum and tossed him roughly onto a landing on the second floor. He hit the deck hard like a bag of cement and felt a crunch in his ribs.

Grimacing with pain, Michael struggled to his feet and shouted for the woman. Amidst the chaos, he heard a faint cry a short distance away. He looked across the chasm and saw Chelsea clinging to a ledge on the other side.

"Hang on!" he bellowed.

There was some distance between them and no room to take a running jump. But there was enough scaffolding wedged between the debris to bridge the gap. Michael grabbed hold of a wooden beam and swung himself across, latching on to a few supports until he landed squarely on the platform next to Chelsea. He reached down and pulled the screaming woman from the forty-foot drop.

"Easy, I've got you," said the priest.

Chelsea clambered over the edge and clung to Michael. She was still breathing hard when she saw the damaged console on his wrist.

"Damn it!" she cried out, looking at the busted device.

The Jesuit stripped off the broken console and tossed it aside. "Come on, let's move!"

✝

Outside, the forces of darkness were rallying their strength. The Commander stood on a rise overlooking the assault. More guards poured into the courtyard, stepping over the smoking corpses of their fallen dead. The church's remote systems had all but shut down, severed by the powerful electro-magnetic blasts that the Praetorians unleashed against Michael's defenses.

To do that, the Lumen troops had to get close enough for the radiation field to be effective. But here and there, an old-fashioned mine planted beneath the muddy foliage would send an ill-fated guard hurling into the night, his limbs and guts flying in all directions.

"That's your big plan, littering the lawn with the carcasses of your men? Stop being a pansy. Let me send in the dogs already!" the Lumen agent taunted.

The Commander grabbed Agent Yin by the throat and hissed. "Watch your tongue or I'll gladly cut it out," he threatened.

The paleface broke free of the other man's grasp and cackled like a crone.

"Sticks and stones may break my bones, Commander," he

scorned. "But your threats and your pussyfooting won't get the job done. It'll only get Mr. Chambers real mad!"

Agent Yin was brewing with unbridled hate, with every sinew in his body straining for malice. He thirsted for revenge, eager to drink from the blood of those who fatally mangled his twin. Enraged that the assault was going too slowly, he decided to intervene.

"Tell your men to get out of the way," he snapped angrily. "Any fool can swing a hammer. What you need is the elegant blade of a surgical knife."

The company of guards surrounding their Commander began to shift with menace towards the garish man in white.

"No," said the Commander, waving them down. "Let him send in his puppies. I want to see this."

Agent Yin snapped his head back and rolled his eyes. Grasping an amulet around his neck, he started summoning the hounds of Hades. The cryptic incantations grew louder until the glow of mystic runes began to appear in the air. In no time, a fearsome pack of canine creatures had emerged from the phantom mist.

Dripping with decay, the monsters growled with murderous intent. Their ghastly fangs protruded like tusks through a quagmire of blistering skin and bones. The noise of their claws brushed against the grounds like whetstones grinding on tampered steel. All about their flaming bodies, the rains sizzled and steamed.

It was obvious that these were not the usual hounds. Each of these appalling creatures shouldered two grisly heads, much like a Chimera stripped of its skin. Every savage howl came from a terrible jaw belching fire, their spiked tails and colossal fangs smoldering like hot coals on a massive body of burning larva.

"Hmmm, upgrades," observed the Commander.

Noting that they were much larger and more ferocious than the average hellhound, he shot Agent Yin a cynical smirk and nodded to his men to step back.

"Let's see how they do."

Giving the creatures a wide berth, the guards pulled back their forces and watched the hideous pack leap into action. The canines bolted for the church like blazing meteors leaving a trail of fire and destruction in their wake.

When they reached the entrance of the church, they paused and growled. A couple of hounds circled the compound looking for a way in. The building wasn't intact to begin with. There were gaping holes in the walls as well as windows whose shutters had long been consumed by age. Nevertheless, the creatures were seized with hesitation. None made the effort to leap through the opened breaches or even trample down the barricades blocking the entrance. Something powerful and unseen was keeping them at bay.

"What's the matter, Agent Yin? Your wolves are trembling like rabbits," said the Commander.

The Agent in white did not reply. Instead, Yin pulled a strip of talisman from his pocket and wrapped it around the amulet. Shaking with rage, he increased the power of the incantations and tried to bend the monstrous dogs to his will.

"You will obey me," he shouted with venom. "I command you to enter and attack!"

Compelled by the dark magic, the canines howled like a pack of whipped curs. Flames spouted from their nostrils as they dug in their claws and attacked, driven forth by the angry lashes of a sorcerer impatient for revenge.

The first beast to leap into an opened window slammed into a wall of bright light. The lightning flash threw the creature back onto the ground, leaving the monster writhing in a cesspool of hurt. Muscle and bone collapsed. Strips of rotting flesh peeled off in thick globs that dribbled down to the earth. One by one, the hounds that attempted to break into the church ended up hurling themselves into a fortress of pain. Many were shredded by the firestorm of booby-traps. Others shattered like glass when they clawed against the sacramental shield encircling the building. The wall of spiritual defenses burned the unclean spirits and seared the corrupted flesh off the revolting beasts, reducing some to a bubbling mess of putrid slime.

Yet as soon as the monsters hit the ground, they began to reassemble as quickly as they had been torn apart. Already one or two had struggled to their feet, empowered by the sorcery running through their veins. But something else was unfolding...

Before the creatures could gather their strength, the courtyard became submerged in a sea of electrical bolts, unleashed by a volley of capsules launched from inside the church. The crackling brightness of hundreds of thousands of volts filled the night, as did the shrieks of the tortured hounds lost within its embrace. In the midst of this chaos, a barrage of gunfire rained down on the dogs, sending a hail of consecrated rounds ripping into the demon pack.

Agent Yin watched in fury as his spell began to unravel. He shouted more incantations at the canine hordes to keep them from breaking down. But it was too late. Between the onslaught of firepower and the crippling effects of the sacramental weapons, the howling beasts fell apart like a shredded deck of cards.

From where he stood, the Commander could see that the hounds were turning back into magical runes and returning to the source of their enchantment.

"Looks like your babies are coming home," the Praetorian leader taunted. "And I'm guessing they're not happy with the trouble you've caused them."

Yin panicked and clutched his amulet. He tied another strip of talisman around the trinket, chanting madly to deflect the vengeance that would come.

"Stop, I command you!" the agent shouted in desperation. "Yield to me!"

In response, a terrible sound like the baying of wolves was heard in the middle of the storm. The ghostly runes separated in the sky and plunged down like lightning, piercing the agent in white. Yin staggered and gripped his chest. The amulet tore free of the talismans and fell to the sodden ground, sinking into the sludge.

Gasping, the sorcerer struggled to breathe. His tongue flopped out of his mouth like a dead eel while the blood drained from his face, leaking from his pores until his flawless white suit was drenched in red.

Crying like a ghoul, Agent Yin buckled to his knees, his eyes rolling back with unspeakable pain.

"Help me," he pleaded, his voice muffled by the obstruction of a bloated tongue.

"But of course," answered the Commander.

The huge Praetorian leader casually stepped behind the suffering soul. In one fluid motion, he pulled out the Phurba and deftly sliced the man's jugular. All remaining life from the victim gushed out like a broken sprinkler, soaking the mystical dagger with the taste of blood.

Smirking, the Commander withdrew the blade and shoved the agent aside. The slain man collapsed in the mud like a butchered pig. In a matter of seconds, his bloody remains began to sink into the earth; following the path of the lost amulet until there was no longer any sign of the agent or the floating runes that once summoned the hellhounds.

"Have we taken care of the perimeter defenses?" asked the Commander.

"Yes sir, the EMP guns took out the last of the remote turrets," replied one of his men.

"Then it's time we deliver the package," said the Praetorian leader. "Hand me that bazooka."

✝

Gabriel stalked the shadows and kept close to the wall. His black cape covered most of the white on his habit. Raphael was on the other side of the room. Both men glanced at each other, somewhat surprised that they had survived the assault thus far. Neither was sure at first that the spiritual defenses would hold out, but the sacramentals did more than just weaken the hellhounds, they broke the spell binding the spirits to the host and made it easier to deliver the coup de grâce.

Nevertheless, the storm was just breaking. And already, the cracks in the fortress were beginning to show. Bits of plaster rained down from the domed ceiling as the battle raged on. The priests exchanged gunfire with the Lumen hordes outside, taking accurate aim at anyone who got too close.

"We can't hold them off forever," Chelsea contended. She had stayed behind in the choir loft as Michael slipped off to do some damage.

"Just stay out of sight," Gabriel insisted over the radio.

"And pray!" said Raphael.

Through the cracks in the wall, Chelsea could see the Praetorians advancing. More than once, a couple of guards lost their kneecaps to sniper fire before they lost their lives. She knew that the priests were doing their best to avoid making direct kills. Unfortunately, there was nothing to stop the enemy from trying to do the opposite. Bullets and shrapnel whizzed by as the prospect of death edged closer

"You've already lost, you know," shouted the Commander from outside. "I could persuade you to surrender; tell you that you won't suffer, that the end will come quickly…"

He shouldered the bazooka and laughed. "But then, where's the fun in that?"

Michael recognized the threat. "Get down!" he screamed into the comlink.

Downstairs, Gabriel and Raphael leapt out of the way as the blockade covering the entrance blew up. The impact tossed the two men aside and buried them in debris.

From where she was, Chelsea could see the extent of the damage. Where the entrance used to be, there was now a massive crater smoking like a doorway to Hades.

"God, if you're listening, please help us," she cried out.

In her anxiety, she tried to scuttle down to the priests to pull them out of the rubble. But Michael suddenly appeared from behind and restrained her.

"Stay put!" he ordered, stuffing a machine pistol into her hand. "If they get too close, just pull the trigger."

Chelsea knew that the slugs were blessed and coated in chrism, but she knew nothing about guns. She tried to protest but the priest had already vanished. In the meantime, a dozen guards had rushed in through the smoky entrance and were taking up positions. The young lady was frightened for Gabriel and Raphael. But as far as she could tell, the two men had freed themselves of the debris and were nowhere in sight.

The remaining Praetorians spread out when they entered the church. Dogged and armed to the teeth, they scattered like vermin ushering the plague. Flashlights from their rifles cut through the cavernous space looking for prey. Still, it wasn't totally dark in the building. Flames from the burning debris danced all about, casting shadows on the roof.

Chelsea tried to keep her head low. But when a beam of light suddenly struck her in the face, she panicked and pulled back. In her haste to retreat, she lost her footing and crashed through a rotten beam. The poor woman tumbled in the dark until the concrete floor rushed up to greet her.

The impact knocked her out for a few seconds. When she came to, she found herself on the ground staring at a pair of tiny shoes with dainty black ribbons. The sight confused her at first until she looked up and saw the porcelain frown of a little girl staring back at her.

The spooky child pointed a pallid finger at the woman. "Murderer," she murmured.

Startled, Chelsea recoiled in dread. The vision of Magdalene perched like a giant raven caused her to blanch. She snapped around and saw herself surrounded by men whose faces were obscured by frightful masks. Eventually, a man looking more demonic than human reached down and dragged the woman to her feet.

"Well, well, well. The brighter they shine, the harder they fall," said the Commander. "Then again, I've always known you were a nosey skank."

He leaned over and squeezed her bottom. "Where're your friends, sweet cheeks?" he asked in a hoarse whisper. "Tell them to come out and play."

Chelsea could smell the stink of his hot breath. It reeked of sulfur and brimstone. But rather than cower, she spat in his face.

"I'm not afraid of you!" she pretended, though in truth she was terrified of the creep.

The Commander wiped away the spittle. "That's because you don't know me like I do," he said, grinning. "Let's get acquainted."

Again he pulled out the Phurba. Grabbing Chelsea by the hair, he poised the dagger over her face.

"Call them," he ordered. "And don't forget to scream!"

When she refused, the Commander wasted no time driving the blade down. In that moment, a rifle shot rang out. The bullet ripped through his hand before he could draw blood, hurling the demon steel to the floor. In the process, the muzzle flash gave away Michael's position on the rafters.

"Get him!" the Commander roared.

Quickly, the Lumen troops hunkered down and unleashed their fury. Hundreds of tracer rounds hammered into the darkness.

Michael threw himself against the scaffolding, barely able to dodge the assault. Down below, a dozen metal spheres suddenly shot out from the shadows and sped towards the Praetorians.

As soon as the metallic balls got close enough, they flew off the ground and leached themselves to the body armor of the troops. Once attached, the devices triggered a wave of tiny explosions that stunned the victims and threw up a cloak of white smoke.

Chelsea coughed and collapsed in the thick haze. She could see nothing but intermittent flashes from above. Michael was taking the opportunity to pick off the guards with sniper fire. One by one, bodies began to fall around her. But there was something else striking at the heels of the Praetorians as well, moving with the swift motion of a cobra. She could hear the sounds of metal clashing against steel, and the gruesome cries of men facing the cutting edge of a naked blade.

At one point, she was relieved to hear Gabriel's voice grunting above the din of combat. He was fighting his way towards her. She caught a glimpse of his black cape but saw nothing else. Her mind began to race. Even with all their equipment, the Lumen troops were stumbling blind. How then could the priests see through all this smoke? That very instant, a hand grabbed her by the collar and pulled her back. She looked up and saw Raphael dragging her to safety. The doctor was chanting, his face aglow, his eyes channeling a vision that only he could see.

At once, Chelsea recalled how the power of prayer had bonded the clairvoyant to his confreres, allowing him to share the gift of supernatural sight. What he saw in his visions, Michael and Gabriel were able to see in flashes. Surely this was enough to tip the odds in their favor.

The woman allowed herself a small sigh of relief, but soon discovered how wrong she was to be optimistic. In no time, the white cloud shielding her from the enemy started to dissipate, as if blown away by some breath of malevolence. Before long, the haze was entirely lifted, leaving her and the two priests exposed to the cold glare of evil.

Chapter 38

Gabriel stood facing Magdalene with the sword of St. George in his hand. The pristine white of his tunic was speckled with blood. All around him, the bodies of Praetorians lay crumbled in agony or death. The Commander himself was nowhere to be seen, having abandoned his men for the safety of the shadows.

But there she was, the little girl in black, her eyes shining like orbs and her skin stretched taut like leather. Giggling insanely, she stepped forward and picked up the Phurba. Immediately, the Tibetan dagger came alive in her hands.

"Stay back!" Gabriel warned Chelsea and Raphael as the gruesome faces on the pommel started to snarl.

Above them, Michael fixed his crosshairs on the possessed girl. His instincts told him to pull the trigger but his conscience kept his finger at bay. Most of the Lumen force had been decimated. The few Praetorians left standing appeared nervous, with some glancing back at the spooky girl and others looking like they would run. Everyone knew the demons would manifest but no one knew what to expect.

All of a sudden, the shadows embracing Magdalene started to warp and flex, as if a portal had ripped opened the fabric of hell. One by one the wraiths emerged from the darkness and promptly took shape...

Lust was the first to flaunt her passions. Greed was the bottomless pit without a face. Envy was a pair of bickering banshees joined at the hip. Sloth was a hairless ghoul with the power to paralyze. And Pride was a tiny golem with a bloated head of rotting sores. Only Wrath and Gluttony were missing, banished by the priests in the sewers under the old cathedral.

Faced with this menagerie of dragons, Gabriel felt his heart leap with anxiety. He gripped his sword and prepared for the worst.

Raphael told Chelsea to hang back while he took his place next to the Japanese friar. The doctor was grim and geared up for action. In one hand, he clutched an automatic pistol. And in the other, he held his Benedictine cross.

By then, pandemonium had struck the Praetorians. The guards panicked when they realized that fallen angels had no sympathy for loyalties. It quickly became obvious that no one would be spared. Terrified, the troops opened fire as the five demons tore into their company, shredding them limb from limb and ripping their hearts out from beneath their armor.

Chelsea was horrified. She gawked at the bloodbath and trembled. "We're dead, we won't survive this," she cried out.

"Trust in God, we'll be okay," said Raphael, trying to bolster her faith.

"Demons are still creatures," Gabriel added quietly. "There are limits to what they can do. On hallowed ground, their power is greatly weakened. They can't harm us any more than what God permits. As long as we don't falter in our faith, we can fight them."

Michael rappelled down from his perch at that point and landed next to his confreres. The noise distracted the ghouls from their feasting and they turned their attention to the priests.

"Great, you've interrupted their supper," said the friar. "We're next on the menu."

Michael said nothing in reply. He simply pulled a shotgun from his harness and fired at the darkness. The shells exploded with rock salt and sent the demons screeching. Chelsea covered her ears. The cries from the unclean spirits sounded like the shrieks of a thousand tormented souls.

"I think you just made them mad," Gabriel remarked. He sheathed his sword and switched to a small cannon in his arsenal.

"Shut up and shoot something!" Michael ordered.

At that, everyone pulled out their weapons and blasted the creatures. Even Chelsea retrieved her fallen pistol and unloaded her cache of blessed ammo. None of that seemed to make a difference. The demons dropped the gruesome remains of the Praetorians and turned on the rebels.

With unnatural speed, Lust threw herself at Gabriel and tore the gun from his hand. Massive coils of hair snaked around his arms and neck, wringing the life from him while her naked breasts swelled up to excite his senses. The friar felt his passions explode. He could barely think, much less fight back.

"There is no joy in holding back. Give in to your desires," whispered the demon. "Take what you want. Take it now!"

Gabriel squeezed his eyes shut. It took every ounce of his

willpower to deflect his passions long enough to draw out the sword of St. George. Immediately, the succubus recoiled at the sight of the holy relic. Yet the creature refused to let go. It strangled the poor friar like an octopus throttling its meal.

A few feet away, Michael grappled with a demon intent on stealing his strength. The priest had lassoed the bald creature with his powerful rosary chain, intending to lynch the monster with the triggering spikes. But the scuffle drained and sapped him of his will to fight. He dropped to his knees, crushed by the weight of indifference poisoning his whole spirit. There and then, he would've lain down and given up the struggle had Raphael not rushed in at the last minute.

The doctor pointed his gun and fired on the chain, shattering Michael's bondage to apathy.

"Get up!" Raphael shouted as he tried to hold off the attacks of Sloth.

Michael struggled to shake off the lethargy. He looked up just in time to avoid the razor-sharp claws of a pair of Siamese twins barreling towards him. The two-headed demon missed their human prey and tore off a pillar instead.

Twisting around, the priest grabbed his shotgun and squeezed off until he was empty. The rock salt in the shells splattered the creatures with pain, but did nothing more than to annoy the entity.

"Something's wrong, the sacramentals aren't working!" Michael blurted out.

Blessed salt always crippled an unclean spirit, or at the very least, it would burn a demon like raw meat in an acid bath. Instead, the hideous twins only cursed and argued as to who most deserved to feast on his priestly entrails.

"To hell with it," said Michael. "We'll do this the old fashioned way."

He dropped the shotgun and yanked out his side arms. Praying for a miracle, he was about to charge with gusto when Raphael flew past and slammed into a pillar.

"Doc!!!" Michael cried out in alarm when he saw the impact of the crash.

Torn and bleeding, the Franciscan spat the blood from his mouth and struggled to get back up. He pulled out his crucifix and faced the demon that tossed him. Greed was an empty face lurking behind the dark rims of a black fedora, its body laden with burial riches that gleamed like a tribute to death.

Meanwhile, Gabriel had freed himself from the crushing embrace of Lust. A grisly clump of braids lay wriggling like serpents at his feet. The demon had been driven back by the ferocity of the ancient sword. But already the succubus was reviving and the pungent scent of pheromones once again filled the air. Even the blessed shurikens buried in her naked torso did nothing to slow her down.

"Mary Immaculate, help us!" Gabriel whispered.

He was horrified to see that Michael was right. Their usual stock of supernatural weapons was barely making a dent, though the succubus seemed genuinely afraid of the sword of St. George. This could only mean one thing - the demons were feeding off the evil enclosed in a cursed object nearby. The friar looked around and spotted Magdalene standing in the middle of the storm. The child was completely lost in a trance. Her eyes were glowing white and her hair was flying in all directions. Most of all, the Phurba was flashing like a lightning rod in her hands.

"Get the dagger away from her," Gabriel called out. "We need to shut down the portal!"

Without delay, Michael made a dash for Magdalene. But the fighting was too intense. The chaos of combat kept him from getting to the girl. Were it not for the aid of his religious clothing, he would've been torn apart by the demons. Instead, the Jesuit was surprised to see that his black robe protected him.

It wasn't sufficient to repel the evil, but like a chain mail it took away some of the bite. The priest knew that his cassock had been blessed when he first entered religious life as a novice. He knew that this was true for Gabriel and Raphael as well. Perhaps, this traditional ritual performed years ago now gave them a spiritual shield. As he was thinking this, a bone-chilling cry of hatred rent the air.

Again, the fury of the Envies bore down on him, punishing the soldier priest with blistering wounds. Not once did the ghastly twins halt their attacks, nor did they stop bickering over which one of them was the greater. Like a pair of hyenas jostling for food, the mauling was savage and competitive.

Over and over, Michael defended himself as best as he could. At one point, he ran out of ammunition and pulled out his massive cross. The retractable blade popped out of the crucifix and gleamed in his hand.

"What're you waiting for?" said the Jesuit, goading the she-devils.

"Come on!"

The vile creatures gave the battered priest a look of scorn and laughed.

At the far end of the room, Raphael gazed into the empty face of Greed and saw an army of souls trapped within. He recognized the features of many who were deceased. All of them were gnashing their teeth. To his right, the gristly form of a sluggish creature crept towards him, unfolding its wings like a leathery tent.

Without betraying his fear, the doctor held out the Benedictine cross and prayed aloud. As he did so, the medal embedded in the wood began to stir. The symbols of exorcism inscribed on its surface lit up like a torch. Immediately the two demons snarled and backed off, as if the warm gentle light reached out and burned them.

Raphael himself was suddenly taken with ecstasy, his visions coming hard and fast. The power that he normally felt coursing through his veins grew beyond anything he had ever known. Inspired by a vision of St. Michael, he knelt down and placed his palm on the floor. As he did so, his mind was opened to understand what was happening.

It was true that the remains of the old church had been deconsecrated. But no amount of time or purpose could completely erase the sacred character of a place that witnessed countless celebrations of Holy Mass. All that was needed was a jolt of grace to awaken its spirit.

"St. Michael the Archangel, defend us in the day of battle," Raphael pleaded. "Be our protection against the wickedness and snares of the devil. May God rebuke him, we humbly pray…"

And he felt a ripple of power spread out from his palm. Like a powerful blast of radiation, a mystical white light flooded the building and swept over flesh and stone, sending the demons reeling with agony and dread.

When Raphael looked up, he saw that the course of battle was changing. The spirit of Greed still glowered like a mobster with a vendetta, but its power and confidence seemed to wane. The demon started to shed its human disguise. It flickered and morphed until it no longer resembled a man. Instead, a gruesome creature remained in place, its naked body and sinews made up entirely of tiny faces stitched together in a fabric of pain.

The doctor was aghast to see so many damned souls trapped in the clutches of this vice. But the ominous sight only deepened his faith in the light. Raising his crucifix, he traced a large cross over the specter, uttering the Latin words of benediction as he did so. The effect was instantaneous...

A blazing scourge of fire struck the demon and ripped opened its bowels, causing stacks of burial notes and funeral coins to gush out like entrails. The accursed creature screamed and fell to the ground. Clutching its ruptured belly, it tried to pull itself together. But the clairvoyant priest pressed on and repeated the blessing. And this time, the monster shattered like hot coals before a sledgehammer.

Raphael shielded his face from the burning embers. When he lowered his hand, a dark shadow suddenly rose up before his eyes, wrapping him in a stranglehold. He lost his footing and fell to the ground, swathed in the leathery wings of Sloth. He couldn't breathe. He couldn't move. A blanket of loose skin covered him from head to toe. He was suffocated, paralyzed, and inches from having his windpipe crushed. Through it all, the demon laughed and poured on the inertia. As the doctor crumbled under the weight of his own mass, his ribs began to groan. His lungs threaten to collapse.

And then suddenly, Raphael heard the sound of gunfire. The abomination screeched and released its grip. But Chelsea continued to pull the trigger.

"Get off him, you sack of shit!" the woman screamed. She fired rapidly at the creature's head until its cranium exploded with violence.

The noise made Gabriel look. Chelsea had given the demon a vicious lobotomy and was now dragging Raphael from the carnage. She had wisely gone into hiding the moment the fight began. But as the conflict escalated, her sense of loyalty had drawn her raging into the fray.

"Sometimes, the only way we can save ourselves is to lay our lives on the line," the Japanese friar had told her previously. She caught his eye across the hall and nodded, as if reading his mind.

Gabriel had no time to return the gesture. A scarlet trail was gushing down his face onto his white habit. His battle with the succubus had been a clash of frustration. Her preternatural gifts far surpassed his natural agility and speed. The creature was deftly avoiding all his attacks with the sword. She scuttled up the walls and clung to the rafters with her hair, swooping down every few seconds to claw a handful of flesh and blood. The friar knew he had to act quickly or the demon would tear him to shreds.

Keeping a firm grip on the sword, Gabriel kept his focus on the banshee scurrying above. The menace was keeping her distance, clearly aware that her victim was not totally defenseless, now that the sacred imprint of the church had become alive again. But no demon could resist the temptation to sow death and destruction. And once again, she plunged like an angel of hell to rip the flesh off the young priest.

As she dived from the ceiling, the friar pulled off his black cape and flung it over the unclean spirit. The religious garment snagged the succubus and held on, forcing her to tumble blindly to the floor. Squawking like an animal caught in a trap, the demon cursed with fury and unleashed a torrent of blasphemies. But Gabriel was already crouched behind the struggling beast. Catching hold of the cloth, he drove the sword of St. George into the shrouded figure and twisted the sacred blade. A sickening wail of agony exploded and shattered all the windows in the building.

Gabriel repeatedly yanked the sword out and drove the blade in again until the succubus collapsed in agony. When he finally lifted the cape, he was shocked to see the demon revealed in all her decadence. The creature languished in a body of putrefaction, having shed her human form to unveil the true horror of lust.

"Kiss me," said the demon, hissing like a snake...

She exuded all her powers of concupiscence, attempting to drown the friar with unbridled passion. But Gabriel had had enough. He was nauseated by the stench of sin. With one stroke, he swung the blade and sliced off her head.

There was a terrible cry of fury from the shadows. Every time a demon was dismantled, it seemed to weaken the rest, as if the corporeal bonds of evil were breaking up. Even then, the battle was far from over.

Trapped in a corner, Michael had his hands full. It was hard to tackle one embodiment of Envy without getting slashed by the other. Their chilling talons kept the priest at bay. Despite that, the former soldier managed to do some damage with his cross blade, prompting the evil twins to retaliate with venom.

They swooped in on the Jesuit, forcing him to pull back. In the skirmish, the stitches on his shoulder ripped opened and his whole arm felt like it was on fire. His cassock soaked up most of the blood but the pain was crippling. He could barely raise his hand.

Ignoring the injury, Michael pulled out a small grappling gun and fired. The line shot up to the roof and caught a beam. As the demons charged, the priest reeled out of the way. He barely skimmed the heads of the Envies when he flipped around and dropped onto their backs. The creatures cursed and screamed, and wrestled for the priest. But the Jesuit hung on.

"I've had enough of you two," Michael declared. "It's time you split up!"

He wedged the large blade between their torsos and gripped the crucifix tightly, letting his weight drag the knife all the way down. By the time he hit the floor, the monster was cleaved in half. Instead of falling down, the two halves of the demon scuttled off with fire flashing in their teeth. It didn't matter that each only had one leg to stand on. They were leaping madly like lions on the kill.

"Crap!" Michael swore as he dodged a crushing blow to his skull. He turned his face and saw Gabriel jump in with a terrifying battle cry. The friar brought his sword down on one demon and struck off its head, throwing the other into complete hysteria.

The remaining twin balked at the sight of the sacred weapon. It fled from Gabriel and turned its wrath on Michael. At this, the friar quickly threw the sword of St. George to his confrere. The priest caught it in the nick of time and brought the blade down like a guillotine. There was a loud shriek and then the creature's head rolled off its shoulders.

"Thank the Lord, I think we got them all. We actually won," said Gabriel, relieved to see the carcass fall over. Like all the rest, the atrocious remains began to break down into a putrid mess.

"I wouldn't say that," Michael exclaimed.

He tossed the sword back to the friar and reloaded his guns. All around, the slain bodies of the unclean spirits had begun to take flesh and reanimate, strengthened by the conduit of evil left opened. The two men glanced at each other and suddenly remembered.

"The dagger!!!" both echoed with alarm.

They looked for Magdalene and saw Raphael and Chelsea already on the scene. The woman was trying to pry the Phurba from the girl but the child was gripping it like a vice.

"I can't get it off her," Chelsea cried.

The iron faces on the pommel growled and tried to sink their teeth into her fingers, forcing Chelsea to let go. Raphael took over immediately and wrapped his consecrated hands around the Tibetan dagger.

Ever since the doctor broke free from the spell of death, he had felt the fervor of his charismatic gifts increase tenfold. Invoking his authority as a priest, he prayed aloud…

"In the name of the Lord Jesus Christ, by the power of his cross, his blood and his resurrection, I bind all curses, hexes, spells, satanic rituals, incantations and evil wishes, and I break their influence by the power of the risen Christ, and I command these curses to go back to where they came from…"

At the sound of the verbal command, the Phurba started to quiver and jump. It shook violently and shot out of Magdalene's grip like a missile. The dagger flew up to the ceiling. When it finally fell, it plunged into the large hole on the floor and vanished into the chapel below.

Raphael caught Magdalene as she collapsed. The girl was pale and rigid as a corpse.

The doctor quickly checked her vital signs and realized that she was still breathing. But before he could do more to help her, the hairs on the back of his neck started to bristle. Something was wrong. He felt a presence lurking just beneath the edge of madness. It was toxic and overwhelming, saturated almost with insane pride.

"Father, behind you!" Chelsea tried to warn him.

Raphael spun around and took a terrible blow to his chest. The impact threw him against a pillar for the second time that night. He crumbled to his knees. When he looked up, he saw a small ugly golem with a massive head of boiling sores. In the chaos of the fight, they had all forgotten about Pride. It was the most insidious of all the vices, the root of every sin. And yet the creature before him looked just like a tiny child, though its expression beamed with a wickedness that frightened even the priest.

The doctor struggled to his feet and reached for the crucifix tucked in his belt. As he grabbed the Benedictine cross, it felt slimy and alive. Looking down, he was startled to see a large toad squirming in his grasp. Raphael dropped the creature and quickly found himself surrounded by vermin of every kind. Out of nowhere, clusters of lizards and insects appeared and invaded his brown Franciscan robe, clinging to the coarse garment with pestilence and grime. Some had begun to crawl onto his face, sending the priest into a mild panic. He collapsed on the floor, feeling the misery of a million teeth sink into his flesh.

Chelsea rushed to his aid but the priest barked at her to keep away. He was grimacing in pain, claiming that the parasites on his body were carnivorous. Yet as far as she knew, she could see nothing tangible attacking the man.

"Get up! It's not real," she shouted, tugging at his habit.

But the doctor was drowning in the illusion, unaware that the plague seizing his body was merely a phantasm.

Meanwhile, the demon lumbered towards them like a gargoyle brought to life. Desperate, the woman bent down and picked up the cross Raphael had dropped. She held it up before the small golem...

"I'm warning you. In the name of God, back off!" she cried out.

The demon looked at Chelsea with an arrogant sneer.

"You need faith for that. And we know the only thing you believe in is yourself, don't we?" the creature mocked her.

"That's not true!" Chelsea retorted angrily.

"That's my girl," said the demon, laughing. "Too proud to even admit you're mine."

The golem then proceeded to rip apart its own rotting skull, peeling away at its cranium until another face emerged from beneath. Chelsea was horrified to see her own features staring back at her. Frightened, she backed away and tripped over herself, dropping the cross. For a moment, the floor trembled and looked like it would burst open to swallow her whole. But the strong arms of Michael caught her and pulled her back from the illusion.

Her heart was still beating wildly when she turned and saw the rugged priest standing behind her. She glanced to her side and noticed Gabriel lifting the doctor to his feet. The prayers of the exorcist had purged the infection from his fellow friar. And now, Raphael too was free of his imagined torments. He bent down and picked up his crucifix.

"Fall back," Michael said to the woman. "We'll take it from here."

To Chelsea, the three men looked like angels robed with divine justice. Raphael was brimming with holy vengeance, his hands anointed with a mystical light. Gabriel wielded the sword of St. George like a bolt of lightning. And Michael towered over the rest, his guns ready to blaze with punishment.

But the creature shook off its human face and puffed up like a giant toad, certain that it could devour the battered priests easily enough. After all, perfection such as itself could tolerate no defeat. It had waited until it was the only demon left to deal with these insolent fools. Why indeed should the spoils of victory be shared with any other? Was Pride not the greatest among the Deadly Sins? What the lower vices failed to achieve, it would rise up and accomplish on its own.

In response to the demon's arrogance, Gabriel muttered audibly, "You made a mistake thinking you can handle us by yourself."

The creature cackled. "Such conceit in a priest," it replied in a guttural voice. "Oh yes, you three will make an excellent meal."

Chapter 39

Michael was unleashing his own brand of divine justice, emptying his guns at the demon. His confreres were brutally swept up in battle. All three had thrown themselves completely into the task of taking down the evil. The last thing Chelsea heard was Gabriel yelling for her to stay back. Without really knowing why, she found herself greatly offended by his brusqueness. Her emotions began to play havoc with her logic and in no time, her face had become flushed with anger.

"Don't talk to me that way!" she shouted back. Did the men really think that she was useless, that she was nothing but a damsel in distress?

The very thought made her furious. How dare they forget that it was she who rescued Raphael from the embrace of Sloth? If it weren't for her, the doctor would've been crushed to death. Yet instead of praise, she had received only scorn. Perhaps it was time to show these pompous priests what she was capable of.

Consumed by a reckless need to prove her worth, she rushed towards the gaping hole on the floor. She had seen the Phurba plunge into the basement chapel and knew that the dagger was still there, concealing itself like a wounded dragon waiting for an opportunity to take flight.

Driven by this dread, Chelsea was determined to find the dagger and destroy it. She had to break the talisman and banish the last of the demons. And then finally when she stood tall and triumphant over evil, she would force the priests to admit that she was worthy of their admiration. Grinning like a woman unhinged, she pulled out the gun that Michael had given her and slowly descended into the darkness. As she climbed down into the basement chapel, she caught a glimmer of something tangled up in the rusty chains of a sanctuary lamp.

A smile washed over her face. She couldn't believe her luck. The Phurba was just dangling there, waiting to be plucked from its forbidden perch. As she crept towards the broken altar, the violent sounds of battle echoed from above, distracting her. She took her eyes off the dagger and glanced up at the ceiling, curious to know how the priests were doing against that terrible golem. When she looked down again, the weapon was gone.

Chelsea was appalled. She stopped in her tracks, livid at the thought of being robbed of her victory. But unknown to her, her proximity to the sacred sanctuary began to break down the illusions of self-importance she had contracted from the demon. The closer she got to the bloodstained altar, the more Pride abandoned her captive mind until eventually the woman broke free from the spell. Like a patient waking up from a coma, she looked around the room and wondered why she was standing alone in the darkness of the basement chapel.

"Looking for this?" she heard someone ask.

The voice sounded familiar. Chelsea shook the daze from her eyes and tried to focus. Her brain was still muddled, but as soon as she saw the Commander step out from the shadows holding the Phurba in his hand, she quickly raised her pistol and pulled the trigger. In her panic, she missed completely. And before she could squeeze off another round, the beastly man was upon her. He snatched the gun from her hand and struck her in the face. The blow sent her flailing into a row of broken pews.

Thankfully the benches had long fallen prey to termites and the hollowed wood crumbled beneath her weight and absorbed her fall. Chelsea looked up like a trapped animal. She tried to crawl away but the Commander reached down and grabbed her by the hair. Without mercy, he yanked her to her feet.

"Look at you. You were offered a role in this conquest, a throne in the New World," the Commander blustered with contempt. "You could've reigned supreme. Yet you spit in the face of destiny."

Disgusted, he hurled the woman to the floor. She tumbled and smacked her head on the broken tiles, opening a gash on her forehead. Blood began to trickle down her face, which pleased the Commander very much.

"You useless tart! With the final descent of man, the world will fall into chaos and destruction. Then we who kneel before the beast shall rise to rule the land. Now tell me, sweet cheeks, where will you be then?"

As if to answer his own boast, he brutally kicked her in the stomach. Crushed with pain, Chelsea curled up into a bundle of quivering flesh, her tortured guts nearly spilling out in agony. She gagged and coughed, barely able to see through the blood and tears. And still she found the courage to retort...

"I've got news for you," she stubbornly cried out. "I don't care about who I was, or who I was meant to be. And I don't give a shit about the role you think I should play. To hell with you and your Corporation, I choose my own destiny!"

At this, the Commander dragged the woman to her feet and laughed. He stole a kiss by forcing his odious mouth on her lips before shoving her roughly against a wall, making sure to keep a firm grip on her neck.

"Chambers wanted to give you another chance. He saw great potential in you," said the man in the silicone mask. "Me? I see nothing but a whiny bitch. And like all stray dogs, you deserve to die."

Chelsea gasped as the lascivious man pulled out the Phurba and slid the cold steel between her thighs. Still squeezing her neck tightly, he traced the sharpened tip of the dagger up her body until it rested over her plump cleavage. The faces on the pommel were aroused at once and lusted for blood. The woman was scared. Choking under his grasp, she tried to call out for help.

"Oh it's too late for that," the Commander declared. "Pray, plead, beg, whatever suits your fancy, you worthless slut. It won't save you."

Once again, Chelsea watched the dagger rise over her breast. She stopped breathing and expected the worse. Without warning, the Praetorian leader abruptly flew off his feet, tackled by a force of vengeance slamming into his body. The attacker was a tall muscular figure in a black robe, and the impact lifted both men into the air and threw them viciously to the ground.

Michael was the first to recover. He glanced over at the woman to see if she was okay before setting his sights back on the enemy. Groaning, the Commander clambered back up like a zombie rising from the grave.

"How rude. Didn't your mother teach you not to interrupt someone when they're about to make a kill?" asked the man with the Phurba.

Michael scowled and pulled out his guns. Unfortunately, the chambers of his pistols were empty and he was flat out of ammo. The battle against Pride had taken a toll on his bullets. As it was, Gabriel and Raphael were still wrestling with the demon upstairs. That spiritual combat continued to play out. But down here in the ruined chapel, it was up to the Jesuit to tie up loose ends.

The priest threw down his guns and drew out his crucifix, launching the blade as he did so. In response, his opponent smirked and twirled the Phurba in his hand.

"Just like old times," said the Commander, grinning. "The way you rushed in here, I'm starting to think you miss me."

For a moment, Michael wondered if he had walked into a trap. As soon as he realized that Chelsea had vanished, he had gone looking for the woman. The thought of some new peril lying in wait for the young lady was too much for him to bear. Without realizing it, the priest had grown emotionally attached to her. But now as he stood before the evil in the silicone mask, something told him he had just taken the bait.

"Bless me, Father, for I have sinned," said the Commander, crossing himself with mockery. "And now it's time to make you pay for yours!"

Both men charged at each other like gladiators nursing a grudge. Steel clashed against steel - the demon dagger in the grip of the Commander fighting the cross blade in the hands of the priest. In no time, the sounds of battle coming from above were drowned out by the violence unfolding below.

Chelsea tried to stand with Michael, but every inch of her body was racked with pain. She held on to the altar and pulled herself up, refusing to stay down. There wasn't a great deal she could do at the moment. All the same, she wasn't content to be excluded from the fight. The stubborn roots of her character would allow no such admission. Marshalling all her faith, she began to pray - clumsily at first - then gaining strength until her voice sounded like a bugle call to heaven.

†

Outside, the storm was growing ever stronger. Peals of thunder rocked the foundation as lightning flashed across the walls.

Inside, Gabriel and Raphael had lost sight of the demon taunting them. The upper levels of the church were suddenly overgrown with vines and briars that sprouted rapidly like some kind of phantom weed. The walls were dripping wet with moss and the floors were covered with slosh that reeked of a decaying wetland. Insects and creatures of every imagination scuttled and slithered across this landscape.

Realizing that the illusions had grown in strength, the friar looked at the doctor and they both agreed to stay close. Pride was in their midst, and there was no telling how much of what they were seeing was born from their own poisoned minds. Every step they took was mired in filth. Every effort to move was hampered by the vines of resistance.

"Can you see anything?" asked Gabriel, hoping that the charismatic gifts of his confrere would clear a path through the deception.

"My visions are clouded. I can sense evil close by, but I can't focus with all this distraction," said Raphael.

In fact, his mind was boiling with desperate notions of pride, as if some insane fire was lit beneath the cauldron of his human ego. The doctor struggled to pray, fighting to regain control over his will and emotions. He glanced over at Gabriel to see if the friar was feeling the same, and saw that the man stood rigid like a block of marble. The only expression on his face was a look of manic glee that suggested something had gone wrong.

"Gabriel," the doctor whispered in concern. "In God's name, are you all right?"

Without answering, the younger man raised his sword and rushed at his confrere. Raphael ducked and jumped out of the way, falling into a patch of thistles that clung to him like the grasping claws of a wild animal. Tugging hard, he tore free of the thorns and looked up to see the friar leap in for the kill.

"Wait!" Raphael gasped as the blade stopped inches before his face, blocked by the gleaming steel of another sword.

Someone wielding a weapon had intercepted the strike. Blow after blow, the unknown warrior drove back the senseless attack of the Japanese friar, giving the doctor a chance to escape.

Raphael tried to see who it was that saved him but the shadows were dripping with darkness. There was nothing to be seen. It was only seconds later when a brilliant flash of lightning lit up the murky halls that things were thrown into focus. Incredibly, the doctor saw two Dominican Friars hurling themselves at each other, both identical right down to their ancient swords and the bloodstains on their white tunics.

Pound for pound, sin was impersonating grace. Good and evil were so entwined in this epic struggle that it was impossible to tell the demon from the priest. To all appearances, Gabriel seemed locked in battle with the splitting image of himself.

"And the Devil did grin, for his darling sin is pride that apes humility."

That line from Samuel Taylor Coleridge echoed like a siren in Raphael's mind, reminding him of the craftiness of the evil one. Again he tried to discern the imposter from the real Gabriel, but all he could perceive was chaos and hate. And the frightening sense that just a few feet below, a great darkness was also engulfing the rest of his friends.

✝

Michael was struggling to get the upper hand in the basement chapel. He had stabbed his opponent half a dozen times with his dagger, but the Commander was still standing. The deep gashes left by the crucifix blade were still opened, but there was little or no blood. At that point, the priest wondered if the Praetorian leader was even human.

"For someone trained to kill, you're not doing a very good job," said the Commander with a treacherous smile on his face. "Would you like me to show you how it's done?"

Michael ignored the taunting. Without question, he knew that the battle could end badly. The wound on his shoulder was still throbbing. He was weakened from all the blood loss. And in spite of his best efforts, the threat before him refused to die. The priest was still figuring out his next move when his opponent vanished into the shadows and reappeared right next to Chelsea, catching the woman by surprise. Astonished, the Jesuit rushed to ward off the attack but the Commander already had her in his grasp.

"You're slowing down, old man," said the enemy, shaking his head. "Perhaps a little incentive will help you pick up the pace."

Michael watched as the Commander tightened his grip on Chelsea's throat. She began to choke and sputter, looking desperately to him for help. And for the first time that night, the soldier priest felt his heart tremble.

"Let her go," he roared. "This is between you and me."

The Commander sniggered.

"Oh Captain my Captain! After all this time, you're still trying to save the little girl. That was fifteen years ago. You didn't save her then, you're not going to save her now. Still, that was a naughty thing you did back then – betraying your own men for a cute little bunny. Then again, we know what happened to that bunny, don't we?"

Michael tried to remain impassive but chills ran down his spine. He wasn't surprised that the enemy knew of his grief. After all, Lumen Corp had a deep memory and a wide network of spies. But even so, there was something crudely familiar about this psycho tormenting them.

"Hold still now, we don't want you to get hurt," the Commander said to Chelsea as she struggled to break free. "Or maybe we do," he added, laughing.

Michael motioned for Chelsea to calm down. He didn't want to risk the Commander snapping her neck like a twig.

"If anything happens to her, you die," said the priest.

The Commander grinned like a maniacal clown.

"Oh death doesn't frighten me, old man. In fact, I welcome it. You see, I was murdered years ago, my body riddled with bullets, my soul lost in despair. I thought I was finished, but the bosses at Lumen Corp had other ideas. They saw a great man of talent after their own hearts. So they bargained with hell for my soul. They used their sorcery to ransom me from Hades. My stinking corpse was taken back and stuffed in a vat of demon blood, left to rot in a pool of dark magic until I could climb back out and reclaim my throne in the new world. What a comeback, huh? Cursed never to see the light, reborn never to die again."

Michael looked grim but undaunted. He pulled himself up to his full height and kept a firm grip on the cross blade in his hand. By then, he had no doubts as to who this man was.

"I've killed you before, I can do it again," the soldier priest threatened.

Once more, an appalling cackle drifted through the chapel like a cry of desecration.

"Don't flatter yourself. You and your kind are doomed to fail," said the Commander with scorn. "In case you haven't noticed, the world lives in darkness and darkness lives within the world. The masses are feeding on their neighbors like rats on a sinking ship, starved of everything but the rotting flesh of their own passions. They've feasted on lies for so long, they've lost all taste for the truth. And the more they devour each other, the stronger we get."

The Commander brandished the Phurba like a butcher's knife and ran the steel playfully across Chelsea's throat.

"You think you can stop us? You can't even stop me from sticking this whore like a pig," he snorted.

In truth, Michael was hesitant to act. He knew the Commander would rip through the woman if he made any sudden moves. At the same time, the burning tension on Chelsea's face pleaded with him to do something. The priest was caught in a bind. He needed an opening, but it was one that only she could give.

"You know what I've always hated about you?" said Michael, buying some time. "Beneath all that arrogance, you're still just a windbag, an empty uniform who doesn't know when to shut up."

A spark of insanity flashed over the Commander's face as he drew his lips back in a snarl. For a moment, Michael regretted his remark. But the startling noise of an explosion suddenly shook the chapel like an earthquake. The blast had come from above, dislodging debris from the ceiling. The distraction was brief. But it was enough for Chelsea to try and scratch out her captor's eyes.

The woman's impulse surprised the Commander and he turned away on reflex. When he looked to the front again, Michael's dagger was flying directly for his face. The cross blade impaled itself into his cheek and snapped his head back with such force, it drove the Praetorian back a few steps.

In the process, Chelsea managed to break free, giving Michael all the room he needed to take down the enemy. But before the Jesuit could make his move, the Commander regained composure and yanked the blade from his face. As the steel came out, it pulled off a big chunk of the silicone mask, exposing the repugnant face hidden beneath.

Michael recognized the frozen visage from all those years ago. The hateful countenance of his old lieutenant was still the same, except that the pallor of death had eaten away every semblance of life in his skull. The shrunken face stretched horribly into a sneer, mocking the living with its poisoned wells of hate.

"Face to face, man to man. I'm tingling all over," said the Commander. He glanced at the crucifix handle in contempt. Spitting at the image of Christ, he threw Michael's dagger into the shadows.

"You're still as ugly as I remembered you," said the priest. "This time, I'm going to permanently wipe that stupid grin off your face!"

"Go ahead, old man," replied the Commander, smirking. "Nothing pleases me more than to see you fail."

Chelsea watched as the fight erupted with vengeance. Michael had lost his cross blade while the Commander still had the Phurba in his hand. The two militants clashed like titans staking a claim on the world of man – one for the City of God, the other for the Thrones of Hell. Back and forth they tussled and fought, with the priest straining to dodge the demon blade. In the hands of the Lumen killer, the darting steel was swift and unrelenting, and eager to taste the blood of a Jesuit.

"Be careful!" Chelsea shouted. She was anxious for Michael, who was unarmed.

But her fears were somewhat assuaged when the priest slipped his hands into a pair of knuckle-dusters that he pulled from his cassock. They were the only weapons left in his arsenal, thanks to Anna Koslov. Michael clenched his fists and the metal bracers gleamed for action.

The Commander laughed. "So you're down to punching your way out of here, are you? You're going to have to do better than that, padre!"

The enemy rushed in with the Phurba and tried to cut the priest to pieces. But Michael blocked the cursed blade with his brass knuckles and fell back. Here and there, he faltered and suffered slash wounds to his upper body. Stumbling and hurting, the priest was barely holding his own when he managed to land a lucky punch.

Everything changed when Michael connected with the Commander's jaw. The ferocious impact lifted the brute into the air and hurled him against the wall. Even the priest was taken aback by the power of the punch. He glanced down at the carvings on the brass knuckles and saw the inscribed prayers of exorcism glowing like hot coals.

Across the chapel, the Commander struggled to his feet and fell back down. He was stunned and confused, feeling as though a truck had slammed into him at high speed. Grimacing with pain and disbelief, he looked up to see Michael charging at him. The priest rained down his punches, landing several combos that pulverized his opponent like a sledgehammer. With every blow of the brass knuckles, the words of exorcism sent shockwaves rippling through the undead soldier, shattering the very essence of his darkness.

"Come on you son of a bitch!" cried Michael. "Let's see what you're made of."

The Commander tried to repel the attack, but his broken body was too fractured to ward off the violence. Still he slashed and jabbed, and tried to stab the priest, only to have the Phurba knocked out of his hand. Michael wasn't about to take any chances. Again and again, he pounded the enemy, savaging the man until the beast within cried out for mercy.

The Jesuit priest threw an upper cut that sent the Commander flying into the pews. Before the battered villain could even stir, Michael was already upon him.

"Stop!" shouted the Commander, his eyes bulging with panic. Whatever was left of the silicone mask was hammered into oblivion. All that remained was a twisted visage of pain and hatred.

"If you destroy me, you're no priest," cried the Lumen scoundrel, panting like a wild animal scourged to submission. "You're just a sham, a murderer like the rest of us!"

The words cut Michael like a knife. He roared and slammed his fist on the floor, narrowly missing the man's head.

"I'm nothing like you!" the priest shouted back, his eyes burning with fury.

The Commander saw an opening and grinned.

"Don't kid yourself. We're not so different, you and I," he said. "You're just a coward hiding behind that collar, afraid to face up to the truth of who you really are. You're a killer. You've always been a killer. And nothing you do will ever wash away your guilt."

Michael was incensed. He knew better than to let the enemy get inside his head, but his heart was boiling with too much rage to see the Commander snatch a rock from the scattered debris on the floor. By the time he noticed the danger, he felt the severe blow of concrete smash against his skull. The force struck him to the ground.

Stunned and bleeding, the priest opened his eyes a few seconds later to see his attacker poised with an even bigger rock raised over his head. Without mercy, the Commander brought the rubble down with all his might, hoping to squash his prey like a bug. He cursed when the target rolled away and dodged the impact.

Infuriated, the attacker lifted the massive rock a second time. Michael tried to climb to his feet but the Commander stepped on his bleeding shoulder to secure him.

"Stay still captain, it's not like I have all night to kill you," grumbled the Praetorian. "Besides, this thing weighs a ton."

"I'll tear you apart if it's the last thing I do!" Michael bellowed.

He attempted to throw off his opponent, but the Commander dug in his heel, causing the Jesuit to scream in pain.

"Sorry, but there's no time for empty promises or last rites. How about I whistle you a happy tune while you die?" said the assailant, laughing.

He raised the jagged rock up high. But before he could destroy the priest, a searing pain shot through his back. The Commander cried out in shock and dropped the heavy load. It fell and smashed into pieces right next to Michael.

Without waiting, Chelsea rushed in and stabbed the Praetorian leader a second time. The frightful man howled like a beast whose spine had been ripped out.

Racked with agony, the Commander fought to stay on his feet. His face was shriveled from years of dark magic coursing through his veins. But the grisly decay couldn't hide the haunted look of a man who suddenly realized that the light at the end of the tunnel was an oncoming train. He looked up at the woman, astonished to see her standing before him like an angel of death, the demon blade grasped firmly in her hand.

Chelsea had picked up the Phurba when no one was looking. Twice, the blade had pierced the Commander and each time, he felt an inferno rage through his body, draining his life form. The Tibetan dagger wasn't merely a conduit for evil; it was a weapon that could destroy a cursed spirit even as it butchered the body. The woman stood firm before her enemy, watching the eyes of the wounded man narrow into slits while his arteries burst with excruciating pain.

The Praetorian leader couldn't believe his bad luck. Of all the people who would stop him, it had to be the one he least expected.

"You kill me in cold blood and your soul will be damned," he groaned like deadwood crackling under fire. Already, his skin was peeling back and returning to dust. And the harsh light in his eyes was waning.

Chelsea watched the hideous man start to crumble. And all the anguish and misery she endured came flooding into her mind, kindling her anger with the memory of her brother tortured and desecrated...

"You're already dead," she said in a voice throbbing with anger. "You just don't know it."

And with both hands, she plunged the demon dagger into his skull. The Phurba pierced the rotting cranium and drove the Commander to his knees, rousing the wicked faces on the pommel with pleasure. The cries of agony were inhuman, prompting Chelsea to step back as the vile creature clung desperately to his mortal form. His body convulsed with frightening spasms, as if brutally savaged from the inside.

Even Michael was appalled at the gruesome sight. The Commander was drowning in his own skin, his face dripping in a river of pus and disease. All that was human about him was decomposing quickly, spurred on by the eerie voices emanating from the carved images on the dagger. The wretched soul cast a furtive glance at the priest...

"I'll see you burn in hell!" cursed the enemy, his jaw barely holding together.

Gritting his teeth, Michael climbed painfully to his feet.

"Hell would be heaven if I can spend eternity making you pay," said the Jesuit.

In one swift motion, he kicked the Commander in the chin and the man of perdition burst into flames. The vicious fire consumed the living corpse and incinerated all his flesh. Even his bones were not spared. Like molten wax, the skull collapsed upon itself. The body was reclaimed by the ghostly inferno, until the burning figure was reduced to a boiling pool of malodorous sludge.

Michael saw the Phurba fall loose from the cranium and topple into the putrid mess. Before he could grab it, the cursed dagger had sunk into the muck and slime, dragging the entire slush that used to be the Commander into the cracked and splintered floors of the chapel. Within moments, man and steel had vanished into the earth, drawn into the consecrated soil of holy ground. There was no sign of the mystical blade or the mortal remains of the enemy. Both were imprisoned in the foundation of the church.

A chilling silence followed, as if darkness itself was woefully surprised that they had survived a homicidal maniac from the grave. Chelsea was still shaking from all the adrenaline coursing through her veins. But she was relieved to know that the priest was safely in one piece.

Michael caught her looking at him. "You saved my ass back there," said the Jesuit, nodding his appreciation.

He tried to remain aloof. But amidst the thrashing his body endured, his heart had also been struck free from its frozen exile. They had both come treacherously close to losing their lives. And in that moment, Michael wanted nothing more than to put his arms around the young woman. If only to protect her, he told himself.

Chelsea picked up on that and smiled. Brimming with emotion, she limped over to the priest and cupped his rugged face in her hands.

"Do me a favor. Stop being a hero and stay alive," she chided him gently. "I don't want to lose you either."

Chapter 40

The explosion was unexpected. In the throes of battle, Gabriel and his doppelganger had most likely tripped one of the sacramental booby traps still remaining inside the church. With the phantom foliage creeping over every inch of the cavernous hall, it was hard to recall exactly where the devices were placed.

Regardless, the fallout from the blast was crippling. Raphael's ears were still ringing when he opened his eyes. The doctor gazed around and was stunned to see both versions of his bleeding friend lying wounded on the floor - one knocked out by the physical concussion while the other brought low by the spiritual effects of the trap.

But which was the real one? As each began to stir, Raphael grabbed his automatic pistol and braced himself for whatever came next. With one hand, he felt for the crucifix tucked in his belt. With the other, he took aim at the nearest Dominican fallen at his feet. In spite of his efforts, he was unable to strip away the illusion and expose the imposter. His head was still too clouded with anxiety to discern the truth. So the doctor cocked his weapon and hoped to God that he had the right target.

Groaning in pain, one of the two Gabriels attempted to get up. But the feeling of a gun pressed against his head stopped the man in his tracks.

"What're you doing? It's me!" said the Dominican. He pushed the barrel aside and motioned to his nemesis. "That's the imposter."

Across the floor, the other Gabriel was reaching for his sword.

"Drop it!" Raphael cried out as he swung his gun between the two.

If he pulled the trigger now, a powerful burst of explosive shells anointed with chrism would tear apart his target. Man or demon, the gun was not designed to discriminate, only to destroy.

"He's playing you, don't listen to him!" said one.

"Finish him off! Do it now before it's too late," said the other.

It went on like a tug of war, each friar zealously insisting that the other was the imposter, but neither giving Raphael any real confidence that he was telling the truth. Left to his own judgment, it was hard for the doctor to recognize his friend from his foe. Again he tried to discern the truth with prayer, but the fulsome voices in his head were too disruptive for him to focus. He could barely contain his own temptations to pride, much less drive out the deception before him.

In the end, it was the Benedictine cross in Raphael's hand that loosened the threads of trickery spun by the evil spirit. The priest noticed that when he brought the crucifix too close to one friar, the man would flinch, as if seared by the heat of a burning coal. It was barely perceptible, but it was enough to give the doctor an idea...

Keeping his gun barrel locked on the friar, Raphael thrust the small cross before the startled man and insisted, "Kiss it! Venerate the wood of the cross."

"Don't be an idiot, we don't have time for this!" Gabriel growled in return.

"Kiss it!" Raphael demanded at gunpoint.

When the friar refused, he brought the cross down on the Dominican. There was a shrill cry of terror, and then all hell broke loose.

The slightest touch of the crucifix proved too much for the pretender. Forced to humbly kiss the image of Christ, the spirit of pride reverted to its hideous form and spat at the cross instead.

"You shouldn't have done that," Raphael cried out. He wasted no time pulling the trigger.

A deadly burst of gunfire exploded from the barrel. But even then, the demon managed to dodge the attack with shocking speed. It jumped out of the way as Raphael chased the golem with a trail of bullets tearing up the church. At one point, the doctor ran out of ammunition before the creature could be brought down.

The spirit of Pride turned a revolting face to him. "Not so tough without your little toy," said the golem, smugly.

Raphael tried to reload. In his hurry, he dropped the ammo clip and the magazine clattered to the floor. The doctor was horrified. He looked up and saw the demon lunge, and instantly his blood ran cold. The golem had transformed itself into a large fearsome beast intent on slaughtering the priest. But death never came.

Instead, Raphael watched the enemy slam into the marble deck, its twisted body embedded with shurikens. Bursting with rage, the creature attempted to rise. But the blessed medals at the core of the blades kept the demon down. The fires ignited by the Latin inscriptions on the medallions combusted with terrifying violence, engulfing the unclean spirit with a vengeful flame.

In the meantime, Gabriel's voice rang out like a siren. "Ab insídiis diáboli, líbera nos, Dómine!"

He leapt out of the darkness and buried his sword in the creature's back, jamming the blade in with all his might. There was a crack of lightning and a thunderous roar. A burning column of light erupted from the entry wound and the demon howled with terror. Trembling with unspeakable pain, the dark spirit whimpered and cursed, reacting as if St. George himself had reached down from heaven and bludgeoned it. Before the creature could resist, Gabriel yanked the sword upwards and sliced the golem in half.

The corporal form of Pride crumbled like burning ash, breaking the bonds of iniquity that kept it on earth. Without a tangible form, the demon found itself recalled to the underworld. But Raphael wasn't taking any chances. He stumbled forward and prayed over the smoking remains, asking God to bind the nefarious spirit and remove any prospect for its return.

Holding his crucifix high, the doctor blessed the scene before him. Right away, the smoldering carcass burst into flames and scattered like dust. At the same time, the jungle of darkness clutching the upper level began to shrivel, withering as quickly as a field of shadows burnt up in the light of the divine sun. The swampy foliage melted away until no hint of illusion was left defiling the walls of the church.

Gabriel stood aside, watching order and sanity return to the hallowed halls. To all appearances, Raphael seemed to have recovered much of his mystical gifts to peel away the deception.

"It looks like you've got your mojo back," he said to his confrere.

Raphael glanced at his hands and felt the strength of his charism return, even as the fog in his mind dissipated with every second.

"Looks like it," replied the doctor.

"About time, Obi-wan," Gabriel exclaimed. "We could've used the force back there when we were getting our butts kicked."

Embarrassed, Raphael apologized. But the friar grinned and slapped him on the back.

"Relax doc, I was just kidding," said Gabriel, flashing a grin. "You did great back there. I mean it, you saved my ass."

The two friends clasped each other, grateful to be alive. Just then, they saw Michael and Chelsea climb out of the underground chapel and the rush of relief was even more palpable. Against all odds, the entire team had survived the night. But it took some time before they could even walk to each other. Once the adrenaline had worn off, the injuries and exhaustion combined slowed everyone to a crawl.

"You look terrible," Gabriel remarked as Michael staggered past, gripping his arm in agony. "I mean seriously, you look like shit."

"Thanks," Michael grunted. "I'd feel a lot better if you just shut up."

Gabriel laughed. "C'mon big guy, it's just a scratch. You've handled far worse than this," he said, smacking his friend on the arm.

Michael howled with pain and grabbed the friar by the collar. He looked like he was about to shoot his confrere when Chelsea interrupted.

"Where's the girl?" she asked, sounding worried. "You guys didn't kill her did you?"

Gabriel and Raphael looked at each other. They had forgotten all about Magdalene. And suddenly, the sense of panic began to rise again like an echo from the depths.

†

They eventually found the young girl crouched in a corner, distraught and crying. Her hair was matted with sweat and her skin was burning like a brazier of hot coals. Although the child was physically ill, it was her spirit that was really under siege. Pale as a ghost and wilting like a flower, her body was reacting painfully to the violence left on her soul.

Michael shook with anger. He recognized the signature of cruelty that tainted all Lumen operations. Having been a mercenary on their payroll, he knew their modus operandi well. Not satisfied with leveling the cities of their enemies, the Corporation often poisoned the earth, so that no one could bring new life to what had been taken by death. It didn't surprise him that they would lay waste to a child's body once her usefulness was over. When he tried to move her into the light, she quivered like a life about to be extinguished.

"It's okay. Let her be," said Gabriel. He signaled for the doctor to come closer.

"Can you sense what's oppressing her?" he asked Raphael. "Is

388

there something left behind?"

"What do you mean left behind?" Chelsea interrupted. "I thought we took care of all the demons."

Gabriel wasn't so sure.

"I've seen cases like this, many of them stolen from their mother's wombs and consecrated to evil before they were even born. We're talking years of spiritual abuse here. Evil imposed on such a young one for so long usually involves a malefice that needs to be expelled before she can be set free."

Chelsea was confused. "A what?"

"A malefice; something like a hex. Witches and sorcerers use it all the time to achieve their ends. It comes from the Latin words *male factus*, which means to do evil. It's usually a small tangible object that's been offered to Satan to be imprinted with his powers to harm. These cursed materials are then stashed or hidden in a victim's home or among his personal belongings. Sometimes, they're added to food and drink so the victim may unknowingly swallow it."

"So it's a corruption of a sacrament?" Michael spoke up. He had been listening intently while keeping a close eye on the child.

"You could say that," Gabriel answered. "After all, Satan will try and ape God. He will take what is good and distort it for evil. Sacraments use tangible matter as instruments of blessings and grace, like water for baptism. But a malefice uses matter as an instrument of evil and harm. It's an anti-sacrament if you will."

"And you think they left one of these things in her?" asked Chelsea.

"There's only one way to find out," Gabriel replied.

Chelsea knew what that meant. The friar was going to try and exorcise the child. She looked at Magdalene with genuine concern. The poor girl was flickering like a tiny flame buffeted by the cold winds of despair.

"She's too weak to endure this," Chelsea observed. "What if she doesn't make it?"

Indeed, there was no guarantee that the child would survive such an ordeal. She was fading faster than a candle burning at both ends.

"We don't have a choice," Gabriel answered. "If we don't expel the malefice now, she's going to die for sure."

"And how will you perform the Rite? You no longer have the Roman Ritual," Michael reminded him.

"No, but I have him," said Gabriel. He motioned for Raphael to draw closer.

"I recall enough of the Rite to begin the first blessings. After that, I'm going to need you to help me find this thing. I have no idea what it looks like or where it's hidden. You're going to have to track it down, tell me in what form and shape it's in, and where it's hidden."

"I'll try, but I can't always control what I see," said the doctor. "What is revealed is revealed, I have no power over the visions."

"It'll have to do," Gabriel answered. "We don't have much time." He turned and told Michael to hold down the child. "Put some muscle into it. This could get ugly," the friar warned.

Michael began to secure the girl. Without being asked, Chelsea knelt alongside the priest and cradled the child in her lap. The Jesuit looked at the woman and said nothing. But he could see the conflict in her eyes. The fact that Magdalene was still a hostage to evil filled the woman with distress.

Earlier on when she was driven by fear, Chelsea had thought nothing of destroying the child to save herself. In fact, she had tried to persuade Michael of the necessity for it, though in truth, the voice of her conscience was crucified with doubt. But doubt – that nagging sliver of uncertainty – didn't exist in the hearts of these men. They were committed to saving the life of this girl no matter what.

Even now, the woman knew that Magdalene was a source of danger to them all. Like a time bomb waiting to blow, there was no telling what darkness awaited them if they failed. The smart thing to do would be to leave the girl behind and run. None of the priests were in any shape to tackle anything else. They were wounded, bleeding, and crippled with pain. And still they lingered, fighting to pull this child back from the abyss.

The sight of their courage filled Chelsea with remorse. It was always that way with her. When push came to shove, she always lacked the moral muscle to do the right thing. Wasn't that how she had lost her own children? Because she was too scared to lose everything else, she thought nothing of killing her babies to save her own skin. She gazed down at Magdalene. The girl was innocent. Just like her children were innocent. The thought sank into her heart and her eyes began to brim with emotion. At one point, a large tear fell upon the girl's face.

Magdalene felt the drop of sorrow on her cheek and a tiny sigh escaped her tortured lips, as if the woman's contrition gave her some comfort and relief. Chelsea noticed this and gently brushed the tangled hair from the child's forehead. She recalled what Michael had said to her. Either we cared about doing the right thing, or we stop caring at all. There was no in-between, no tepid, lukewarm response to grace. For those who truly wanted to live in the light, it was all or nothing.

These last days, she had crossed the bridge from cynicism to belief. And though there was still much that she couldn't understand, she understood one thing. There was no room for fear in a life of faith. The night was long and the shadows were suffocating in their darkness. The storm outside seemed to have worsened in violence and intensity. Yet the priests were determined to save the child…

There was plenty that could go wrong, plenty to be afraid of. But despite the dangers, these good men refused to let fear have the last word. And in the end, Chelsea decided that neither would she.

Chapter 41

"You ready?" asked Gabriel.

"Not really," Raphael answered. "But let's do this."

The doctor was worn out and hurting. Even so, he placed his hands over Magdalene and started to pray, asking the Holy Spirit for the gift of light. Before long, his head started to throb with visions, and cautiously, Raphael freed his mind to enter the abyss.

In the meantime, Gabriel pronounced the first ritual blessings. Like surgeons focused on a vital operation, the two priests huddled over the patient in a whisper - one reciting the imprecatory prayers against evil while the other searched the depths of her psyche for the cause of her curse. At a certain moment, the exorcist prayed aloud...

"In the name of the Most Holy Virgin Mary, through the intercession of St. Michael the Archangel, the Holy Apostles Peter and Paul and all the saints, I break every occult tie of black magic, sorcery, curse, and malefice between you, foul spirit and this child. I bind every power of this spirit and I command him to leave Magdalene and go to the foot of Jesus' cross."

Gabriel had barely pronounced the formula when the prayers provoked a strong reaction from the girl. Despite being held down, Magdalene flung off her restraints and doubled over like a sick dog. Over and over, she gagged and vomited, retching with such violence that Chelsea was afraid the poor girl would disembowel herself.

"Give her some room," Gabriel instructed.

Meanwhile, the psychic link between Raphael and the child had broken off. The doctor staggered back into the light and fell over in distress.

"Easy, I gotcha," said Michael, clutching his confrere.

Covered in sweat, Raphael shuddered like a man trying to forget a bad dream. Indeed, there was something truly heinous tormenting the child, but the clairvoyant had only glimpsed the fringe of this evil before the baleful presence chased him out.

"What did you see?" Chelsea enquired nervously.

Looking pale, the doctor struggled to form the words. "Despair," he finally managed to whisper. "I saw despair."

Gabriel said nothing. He had seen this before. The prayers of exorcism can force the victim to regurgitate the malefice she had swallowed. In fact he was hoping for that to happen, but he didn't expect the intensity of her reaction. It surprised him to see the amount of filth gushing out of such a tiny body. Eventually, Magdalene stopped puking and fell over in an exhausted heap. Chelsea quietly reached out and held the girl in her arms.

"Keep an eye on her," said the friar. He squatted down and turned his attention to the vomit on the floor.

Most of it was liquid. But a few bizarre objects could be seen floating around in the muck. Gabriel poked through the contents like a soothsayer studying the entrails of some dead animal.

"Do you see it?" asked Michael.

"I'm not sure, she coughed up a lot of stuff," Gabriel replied.

Raphael approached and tried to assist the friar in sorting out the bits and pieces. He was still shaken from having glimpsed the evil inside the child, but the doctor was determined to help end this quickly. They found a few rusty nails, broken shards of glass, and what looked like a small clump of human hair. Nothing however prepared them for the strangest find of all.

"What the hell is that?" Michael asked.

It was congealed in a ball of lard spiked with what appeared to be tiny horns.

"I think we found our culprit," said Gabriel.

He noticed there were seven horns in this little globule, each of them no bigger than a tiny thorn.

"You're telling me that she swallowed all of that?" Chelsea commented. "How is that even possible?"

"We don't know exactly how this stuff works," Gabriel exclaimed. "Some malefices are ingested like food. Others are used as proxies for the curse and can often materialize from thin air when the victim is being treated. The important thing is that it's no longer dwelling inside of her."

"So what do we do now?" asked Chelsea.

"We finish this thing. We complete the healing," Raphael insisted. "It's not over yet."

Although the malefice had been expelled, the doctor was certain that the end was not near. He had grazed the depths of suffering within the girl, and felt something darker than anything he had ever encountered. Even now, his senses were rumbling with warning that the child was still very much in danger. And Magdalene herself seemed to confirm this.

The child turned blue in the face, acting like something was still strangling her. She pushed away from Chelsea and collapsed on all fours. Again the retching continued. But this time, something was different.

Instead of vomit, a thick stream of dark smoke began to spew out of her nostrils and mouth, taking shape and form, and uncoiling like a ghostly serpent slithering into the church.

"Get back, all of you!" Gabriel shouted to the rest. He drew his sword and stepped away from the encroaching form, unsure of what he was facing.

Michael grabbed Chelsea and withdrew. Raphael was nearest to Magdalene. But before he could retreat, the cloud changed direction and swirled around the clairvoyant priest, recognizing him as the one who came fishing for the malefice.

Raphael pulled out his crucifix and stood his ground. For a while the mist held back, wary of the power emanating from his hands. Then quite suddenly it rushed forward and lifted him off the floor. The doctor was swept up into the air, dangling like a mouse from the jaws of a giant snake. He fought to free himself. But the more he struggled, the more the darkness grasped him like some primeval force intent on swallowing his soul.

Chelsea gawked with panic. Once again, her world was plunged into terror and all she could hear was the sound of her own heartbeat drumming with violence. She watched as Gabriel rushed in and slashed at the column of smoke with his sword. The blade passed right through without hurting the apparition. Michael shouted for her to stay back as he too dashed into action. She saw his lips move before he jumped into the fray, but she heard nothing but the cold mockery of fear. Everything seemed to unfold in slow motion, like a dance of danger that rose and fell with the choking tension of a nightmare. Strangely enough, there was a dreamlike quality about the entire scene.

A cruel scream shattered her reverie. Gasping, she saw the serpentine form suddenly release its grip. Raphael fell back down to earth. He landed squarely on his shoulder and groaned. She glimpsed his face and her heart skipped a beat. The doctor appeared more dead than alive. A wispy trail of vapor drifted from his mouth, while his eyes drank in the darkness like two shining opals of piercing black. Sunk in a whirlpool of misery, the clairvoyant stayed frozen to the floor.

"Father!" Chelsea called out in alarm. But her voice was mangled with terror and all she could manage was a croak. She watched helplessly as the invading darkness washed over Raphael like a tide, driving the other priests back towards the sanctuary.

Michael skirted the apparition, looking for a weakness. The undulating shadow was black and hazy, and yet in certain places it seemed touchable. Gabriel muttered a prayer and flung something into the gloom. The explosion of light and incense scattered the silhouettes for a while. And then the cloud reformed itself and advanced, eating up the space between them like a swarm of locusts.

Distraught and panic-ridden, a depressing thought began to overwhelm Chelsea…

"Every time you try to fight back, every time you think you're winning, the ground breaks open and swallows you up. The darkness changes and the evil returns, surprising you in new and terrible ways. Doesn't it all feel hopeless, like one big dead end? Why keep trying, why not just give up and die?"

The temptation to despair was overpowering. Even then, Chelsea refused to give in without a fight. She clawed at her hair. She dug her nails into her hands, trying to dispel the crazy notions filling her mind. But the voices kept mocking her, squawking like a wake of vultures tearing at her dying hope.

"Behold your angels. See how quickly they fall. Such is the fate of men who place their trust in the cross."

She watched the vapors twirl around Gabriel and engulf him. The friar tried to escape the cloud but the shadows poured into his nostrils and mouth, strangling the light from his face. He dropped the sword of St. George and crashed to his knees, the whites in his eyes rolling in a sea of poisoned black. Pierced by desolation, he struggled against the anguish that was quickly devouring his spirit.

"It's hopeless. There's nothing you can do, no one who can save you," said the silky voice.

Gabriel cupped his ears and tried to block out the laughter. Nothing he did however could stop the madness from drilling into his skull. In the end, impaled by the violence of despair, the friar sank helplessly to the floor.

"Get down!" Michael shouted at Chelsea.

Wounded as he was, the Jesuit threw everything he had at the apparition. With a weapon in each hand and a bandoleer of concussion grenades, Michael leapt into the mouth of the enemy with his guns blazing...

Hailing Christ the King, he unleashed his fury on the monstrous form, shouting, "Viva Christo Rey!"

Incredibly, the sonic blasts and ferocity of the attack caught the evil by surprise. A flash of brilliance lit up the church as the storm outside thundered for the priest to fight on. And for a moment, the unclean spirit retreated before the insane courage of this man.

The terror gripping Chelsea started to yield with hope, but the smell of victory was short-lived. She watched the blanket of darkness arch over the priest and swathe him in layers of black mist, binding him like a corpse. Again, her heart began to sink. There was no way for Michael to break free. When the cloud finally lifted, the man in the cassock was no more. In his place stood a phantom, his eyes opaque with desolation like the rest. The Jesuit dropped to his knees and fell over, his breath reeking with the odor of despair.

And then, Chelsea thought she heard the shadows cackle...

She gasped with horror, realizing that she was the only one left. The menacing form took the appearance of a dragon and crawled down the nave towards her. With every step, the creature tore apart the marble flooring, becoming a tangible sign of evil in the house of God. She tried to run but her legs wouldn't move. Instead, her knees buckled and she knelt before the revolting beast like a sacrificial lamb in waiting.

Sure enough, the jaws of misery sank into her soul, grinding its teeth into her courage and bleeding her dry of hope. Her vision became clouded. Everything turned black, as if the whole world had been swallowed up in despair. There was nothing left but the clarity of knowing she was about to die. But the woman was stubborn. She tried to rise to her feet, ignoring the crushing weight of depression tearing at her soul.

"But why? Why do you still resist?" asked the voices in her head. *"This is the end. There is no hope. There is no God. There is only pain and regret for a selfish little whore like you."*

A piercing scream tore through the church like the twisted echoes of some banshee. It was soon followed by a cacophony of voices shouting at the top of their lungs. The sounds of animals and humans meshed in one unholy tumult of curses and blasphemies, giving the impression that a ghostly army had abruptly invaded the building.

Chelsea tried to block out the noise. Her heart was pounding so hard that she feared it would leap out of her throat.

"I will not die this way," she told herself. "I will not be robbed of my faith!"

"*But you have no faith,*" the dragon replied. "*All you have is a lie that cannot save you.*"

And like a dam too weak to hold back the flood, an ocean of doubt crashed upon the woman. She fell and tumbled in the currents, dragged down by the terror of feeling totally forsaken.

The air around her was drenched with decay, causing Chelsea to gag and froth with disgust. Or was that merely the dribble of madness slipping from the corners of her mouth? Maybe it was just the bitter bile of death from the crushed and twisted seeds of her shame. She couldn't tell. All she could do was gnash her teeth and cry until desperation convinced her that she could do nothing better than to kill herself.

Drunk with depression, she picked up a shard of broken glass and reached for her jugular, eager to hasten her own demise. But as she did so, something familiar brushed against her hand. Her fingers grazed the old wooden cross hanging around her neck. And for a split second, a sliver of light broke through the terrible darkness. She remembered what Gabriel told her about the words inscribed on the wood…

In hoc signo vinces – In this sign you shall conquer.

The words made her pause. With all the strength left to her, she dropped the jagged glass and clung to the cross. Her lips tried to move but her voice was lost to fear. In spite of the darkness scourging her soul, she kept repeating silently…

"In hoc signo vinces…"

The dragon was furious when he saw this. He unleashed a tidal wave of darkness upon the woman, determined to flush away all remnants of her fickle faith. But Chelsea held on, refusing to give in. She locked her gaze on the wood of the cross, whose light appeared to grow brighter with every passing moment.

The enemy responded with a brutal roar. And the weight of terror and misery pummeled her to the ground. Her lungs constricted with fear. She could barely breathe…

"*Why pretend to pray? You're no believer,*" accused the darkness.

"It's true, I have little faith," she admitted to herself, grasping the cross like a drowning victim clinging to a life buoy in an angry storm. "So help me, God, I beg of you. I need you. I know you exist," she mumbled in the agony of her tortured mind. "I'm not worthy of you but say the word. Say the word…" she pleaded, gritting her teeth with resolve.

"…And my soul shall be healed…"

Despite her prayer, her valiant cry seemed to vanish hopelessly into the void, only to rebound and slap her in the face with mockery. The voices of evil laughed and screeched horribly in her ear, urging her to stop this nonsense and to end her wretched life.

"No!" Chelsea shook her head stubbornly. She drenched the cross with her tears and screamed from the pit of her stomach, "I believe…help my unbelief…"

There was no audible sound coming from her lips and no help from heaven, just the snorting, hysterical grunts of phantoms encircling her soul. She could smell it - the huge and twisted ugliness trying to get in, tearing at her resistance like a juggernaut of despair.

Gaunt with suffering and writhing in the coils of death, a strange rigor mortis began to stiffen her limbs, tightening her body like a stringed instrument that only the Grim Reaper could play.

Chelsea could see the leering faces laughing at her pain, retching with chuckles that pitched higher and higher until she could no longer bear the ghastly shrieks. In all her desperation, she cried out…

"Lord I believe," her voice crackled like a burning log. "HELP MY UNBELIEF!

✝

The woman's voice broke through the shackles of defeat that bound Michael in his prison of fear. His spirit was still reeling from the splinters of hate, but he no longer felt the insane impulse to disembowel himself with his blade. Groggy with pain, he thought he heard Chelsea scream out to God. He tried to stand but his legs would not budge. His spirit was awakened but his body was too broken to rise. The very next moment, everything erupted in a vast crackling explosion of thunder and light.

A tremendous flash of lightning had pierced the wounded darkness and lit up the aisle, striking the base of the giant statue of St. Michael like a spear hurled down from heaven. The impact ripped through the marble and shattered the foundation, leaving terrible cracks smoldering at the feet of the archangel.

"Chelsea!" the priest cried out in alarm. But there was no answer. He heard nothing but the voices of evil screeching with panic. Like weeds in the path of an atomic blast, the shadows disintegrated with terror and confusion, leaving the dragon all alone. Cursing with rage, the monster turned upon the woman and roared, smashing the columns with violence. Even so, Chelsea would not bow before the beast. Gripping the cross in her hand, she took refuge with the statue of St. Michael.

Though unsure of what happened exactly, she knew that something inside her had changed. The massive bolt of lightning had struck more than just marble and stone; it had burnt the despair from her soul and restored her courage. Instead of quaking with fear, she had won back her voice, leaving her to cry out again and again, "My Lord, I believe. Help my unbelief!"

"Be quiet, you sniveling fool!" the dragon hissed. *"I shall devour your filthy womb and feast on the souls of your dead children."*

But Chelsea refused to give in. She latched on to the cross and repeated her cry with an urgency that sounded like a call to arms. Meanwhile, the storm outside was abating and the night was giving way to dawn. Time was running out for darkness to quench the light.

"Look around you," said the voice of evil. *"This is what your life has amounted to. Death and suffering everywhere you turn. All because of you."*

Chelsea couldn't help but notice the pain and destruction scattered all around the building. The sanctuary was in greater ruins, the Praetorians were dead, and her priestly guardians torn up and broken in their spirit. Even now, the ghastly faces of those who had died trying to protect her haunted her with guilt.

"You tried so hard to have faith, to believe in your God. But what good did it do, what difference does it make? You are destined to be lost. I will see to it that you burn for all eternity."

Chelsea tried to focus on the cross. But her hands were shaking so much, she could barely hold on to the sacramental. Her lips trembled and her prayer began to falter.

"It's okay. It's okay to despair. It's the perfect emotion. That's how you should feel. These are frightening times. Your faith is defeated. Your life is done. It's all going to be over very soon."

The woman shook her head. She wasn't ready to give up. She bit her lip and her mouth flooded with blood. The searing pain distracted her, and for a few seconds broke the spell of anguish in her mind. With all her heart, she called out to God. But the lies just kept coming....

"You have one last chance for life, away from war and grief, away from despair. Don't be afraid. Throw down the cross and I will let you live."

This is it, thought Chelsea. This is the end. With every horrible thought, with every burst of guilt and misery, she was feeding this monster, giving it the power to bring her to the edge of hell. Once more, her skin started to crawl with fear. There was nowhere to run, no place to go. The darkness would devour her heart and demolish her soul, and the pains of her desolation would never end. Not as long as she was still alive.

Alas, she knew what she had to do...

"I'd rather die!" Chelsea retorted firmly.

"And so you shall!"

The dragon flew into a rage and lunged at her...

That very moment, a terrifying clap of thunder tore through the clouds. The boom rattled the entire church and ripped new fractures into the statue of St. Michael.

And then it happened. The floor rumbled and the sculpture swayed. There was a loud crackling noise like the ripping of marble and steel. Chelsea turned around and the Archangel descended from the altar with the lance in his hands. The dragon balked and reared back. But the colossal statue threw itself upon the beast from hell. Stone upon stone shattered and crashed, engulfing the ancient serpent in a massive landslide of debris and chaos. The demon shrieked as the spear of St. Michael pierced its wounded pride, trapping the unclean spirit in the dungeon of its corporeal form.

Across the nave, Gabriel and Raphael were jolted from their slumber of despair. Michael too was suddenly freed from his paralysis, though none of them were able to do much more than crawl with pain.

"Hang on!" the soldier priest shouted to the woman, his heart bleeding with anxiety.

But Chelsea couldn't hear him. The dreadful blasphemies of the infernal spirit had blocked out everything else. When the dust and bedlam settled, she opened her eyes. And there before the ruins of the high altar, the dragon lay impaled by a broken lance, squirming like a wretched worm pinned to the ground.

The woman was flabbergasted. The bolt of lightning must've

weakened the statue when it struck the base, causing it to break off at the crucial point. But even so, it was incredible that a mere twisted rod should hold down a demon from hell. Nothing had prepared her for this. Not only had she survived the avalanche of rubble and steel, she had emerged triumphant in faith. How could this be anything but the hand of God?

As she gaped at the dragon, the physical form of the beast began to break down. The sorcery binding the evil spirit to the ghastly body unraveled like a loose thread, spinning quickly out of control. The rains had stopped and the clouds had parted. The early light of dawn began to fill the church. At one point, the shattered lance of St. Michael caught the new sun and gleamed like a blazing torch, terrifying the creature of darkness beneath its grip.

"Our Father who art in heaven, hallowed be thy name," Chelsea prayed aloud. The words rolled over her tongue like an old nursery rhyme from childhood. Although she had neglected her youthful prayers for far too long, what she could remember now, she uttered with faith and conviction.

"...Lead us not into temptation, but deliver us from evil!"

The dragon howled with dreadful affliction. Its blackened heart, pierced by the broken lance, burst into flames. Unable to bear the humiliation of being vanquished by a daughter of Eve, the infernal beast gave up its hardened form and retreated in a haze of black smoke.

Chelsea watched the demon escape into the broken belfry in a billowing cloud. Screeching with rage, the wounded creature refused to accept defeat. It struck at the loose stones in the tower and wreaked havoc on the rafters, tearing down the roof in a spiteful act of vengeance. The more it rampaged, the angrier it became.

But already, the enemy was losing its vigor. Broken and robbed of its power to retain its draconic form, the unclean spirit found itself summoned back to the bowels of hell. Eventually it gave a woeful cry of despair and vanished like the morning mist.

Meanwhile, huge fragments of debris rained down on the church, prompting the priests to drag themselves off the floor and dive for cover. Chelsea alone stood frozen with her eyes fixed on a tiny figure a few feet away. To her astonishment, Magdalene had survived the brutal eruption of evil from earlier on. Though pale and weakened, she was still very much alive. But the falling mountain of rubble now threatened to bury the screaming child. The poor thing would be crushed to death if someone didn't help her.

Chelsea looked at the priests and saw that the men were still crippled by pain. They were barely able to move fast enough to save themselves. She gasped and turned back to Magdalene.

"Hold on, I'm coming!" she shouted.

By then, the entire roof had begun to cave in. Ignoring the danger, the woman dashed into the maelstrom, her heart beating wildly like a mother frantic for her child. A great roar of destruction rumbled through the church, as if the whole world was collapsing at that point. Yet all she could hear was the tiny voice calling out to her for help. Whatever happened, she knew she had to reach the girl in time.

"Lord, please," she cried out, her blood racing with resolve. "Help me save this child."

In the pandemonium, Michael looked up in time to see the woman rush for the girl. Just at that moment, the great dome in the ceiling collapsed.

"Chelsea, look out!" the priest tried to warn her.

But it was too late. All he could see was dust and confusion.

Chapter 42

Four months later.

Rome. Vatican City.

The piazza was still wet from rain the night before. As the first slivers of light broke over the horizon, the cobblestones started glistening like hidden gems in the morning sun. A single white dove fluttered across the obelisk, launching a bold flight over the seagulls below. It was just after dawn.

For the most part, the eternal city was still asleep. St. Peter's Square was empty except for a detachment of Swiss Guards on patrol. But already, the lights in the apostolic palace had come on. A few of the guards looked up at the papal chambers, relieved to know that His Holiness was still fighting the good fight.

If truth be told, the Supreme Pontiff had been racked with suffering in recent years. His body was broken with age and his mind burdened with worry. It was even rumored that his strength was failing and he was going blind. Yet like an old lion, he continued to roar with courage against the wolves encircling his flock. Because he was fearless against evil and resolute in truth, the Bishop of Rome had become a symbol of strength and unity for those who struggled for light. Everyday that the Holy Father was alive was a good day for the Resistance.

Behind the quiet walls of the Vatican, two visitors waited patiently for the pope in his private study. A pair of sentries with automatic rifles flanked them on each side, keeping a close watch on their scruffy guests. They couldn't be too careful with the safety of His Holiness, not when these guys looked the way they did.

In fact, the papal guards were surprised that these gentlemen had cleared security. The younger one had a terrible scar over his eye and scratches all over his face. His clothes were wrinkled and soiled, and he smelled like he hadn't showered in a while. His companion was no better. Wearing an unkempt beard and weariness in his eyes, the older man seemed nervous, like a drifter uncomfortable with the splendor of his surroundings. Both men however wore the dust of their journey like a second skin.

As the guards were thinking this, the doors opened and a tall cleric in a black cassock sauntered in. The sentries snapped to attention and saluted, but the papal secretary seemed not to have noticed. He looked straight at the visitors and stretched out his arms to embrace them.

"Brothers, it's good to see you," said Bishop Spalding.

"It's good to see you too, monsignor," said Gabriel. "This is Father Raphael, my confrere in the League."

"Welcome Father," said the bishop.

Raphael bowed with respect.

"Our apologies, Excellency. We would've been here sooner but our journey has been fraught with challenges," said the doctor.

Spalding nodded with sympathy. "I know. The fact that you're here is nothing short of a miracle."

The bishop was keenly aware that every terminal, bus station, and checkpoint in the world was infested with Lumen spies and assassins. It was therefore surprising that these men had managed to slip through the gauntlet of evil to arrive at the Vatican.

"Everyday we're getting reports that the various puppet states are trying to form one Lumen Nation. The entire world is being primed as a giant mousetrap for the faithful. It'll be even harder for us to protect our resources and people then. As it is, the devil takes no vacations, but his agents have certainly been busy plotting our ruin."

"Sounds like the wheels are set in place for Armageddon," Gabriel remarked.

"I'm afraid they're already in motion," the bishop replied. "Nevertheless, our struggle is only just beginning. Come with me, the Holy Father has been expecting you."

Spalding motioned to the sentries to fall back while he led the two men away. They walked through a series of passages until they arrived at the pope's private chapel.

The doorway was tightly guarded but the monsignor gestured for the guards to stand down. The Holy Father was kneeling on his prie-dieu before the Blessed Sacrament, totally absorbed in prayer. He had his back turned to them and his head buried in his hands.

Spalding and the men hung back for a few seconds. Then quietly, the bishop approached the pope and gently announced their arrival to him.

The old man nodded and slowly crossed himself. With the help of his secretary, he struggled to his feet and then insisted on genuflecting towards the altar. When he turned around, Gabriel was astonished to see how much the pontiff had aged. Moved by the sight of the suffering pope, the friar dropped to his knee, as did Raphael beside him.

"Come now, my sons. You didn't risk your lives coming here in order to kneel before a tired old man," chided the pope. "Let us dispense with the formalities."

The Successor of St. Peter pulled the two priests to their feet and blessed them. "I'm so happy to see you safe. I've been praying for you."

"It's good to see you too, Holiness," Gabriel responded and kissed the papal ring. He turned and introduced Raphael, who until then had never met the pope.

"Ah, Father Raphael. You're the doctor, are you not?" enquired the pope.

Raphael kissed the Fisherman's ring. "I am," he answered.

"Your Prelate told me wonderful things about you," the pope recalled. "He said you were a good and faithful servant of the Lord. That you all were…"

"As was he, Your Holiness. To the very end," Raphael replied. "We're just sorry that we weren't able to save him."

A cloud of sorrow passed over the pope's face. Through Vatican channels, he had already been told of the tragedy that traumatized the Underground Church.

"Losing Monsignor Li is a blow to all of us. He was a tower of faith and wisdom for the Church and a good friend to us all. May the Lord grant him eternal rest and reward him," the pope said calmly.

In truth, the pontiff was struck to the heart. He had admired the old Chinese bishop and loved him as a brother. But the pressing duties of holy office demanded that he conquer his own grief in order to strengthen his spiritual sons.

"Though we mourn his loss, we must do all we can to continue his good work," declared the pope. "The Prelature of St. Lazarus must not be left without a father and a shepherd. Already, the land is darkened by sin. The children of light must continue to fight the good fight. If God disappears, humanity could destroy itself. Chaos will rule the world until judgment day."

"We still have good shepherds, Holy Father. Not many I admit, but there are still apostles among us," Gabriel commented.

"Most of all, we have the Successor of St. Peter, the rock on which Christ built his Church," Raphael chimed in. "The Lord Himself has given us the assurance that the powers of evil will not prevail."

The Pontiff was moved by the encouragement and loyalty of these priests.

"Indeed my strength may be diminished and the Papacy may not be what it once was, but whatever power I still have, I intend to use it for every man, woman, and child of faith. Be assured that I won't abandon them, even if I have to give every last drop of my blood to defend the Church," said the pope.

"Let's hope it doesn't come to that," Spalding exclaimed seriously.

The Holy Father chuckled. "Don't worry, there's still some fight left in this old man," he said, patting his secretary on the arm.

"Nevertheless, the Church must pass through a final trial before Our Lord returns in triumph. And when he does, will he find faith on earth?" asked the pope.

As if burdened by this consideration, His Holiness asked to be helped to his desk. A small working area had been built into the chapel, for when the pope needed to bring the painful affairs of Church and State before the Lord. More and more, the Supreme Pontiff had found himself needing to find strength in the true presence of God. Leaning on his secretary, the old shepherd hobbled to his chair and rested his withered frame.

For a while, the pope said nothing. He merely looked at the crucifix on the altar.

"Your Holiness?" Spalding asked with concern.

Fixing his eyes on the crucified Christ, the pope gently shared his thoughts.

"Everyday, the enemy offers the world solutions at the price of apostasy. Everywhere we turn, relativism is the new religion. Man is urged to worship himself in place of God. Truth is exchanged for the indulgence of lies. And even now, entire nations fall beneath the banner of the Antichrist."

Then solemnly, the pope took his gaze from the cross and looked at his men. There was a solemn sense of duty in his eyes, like a general addressing his officers before a battle.

"Still, it remains for us to keep the faith and defend the standard of Our Lord. No doubt there'll be many casualties in this war, but we must do all we can to help as many as we can. So that failing to save all, we may at least save some."

Raphael, who had kept to the background, was actually the first to speak up.

"We stand with you, Holy Father. Not just the Christian Churches but also the other leaders in the League of Angels. They've asked us to assure you of their loyalty and support," he said.

The pope looked at him and nodded his appreciation.

"I'm deeply grateful for our friends in the League. It's true that we cannot do this alone. If people of faith do not come together to preserve the light, there'll be nothing left to defend when the night falls... But come, we mustn't forget the real reason why you're here."

His Holiness gestured warmly for the men to sit.

"Monsignor Li sent you to Rome to find refuge for the young lady you were protecting. It's true that we've received the reports, but I'd much rather hear from you. Tell me, my sons, what happened?"

Gabriel and Raphael looked at each other. Taking the lead, the Japanese friar began to unravel the tale of their journey to Rome and to cast light on the events that had befallen the Underground Church recently.

The pope listened to everything that was said, beginning with the rescue of Chelsea by Raphael to the attack on the League by Lumen Corp, to the loss of the Prelate and the battle with evil in the old Church of St. Michael. He paid great attention to Gabriel's account, interrupting only to ask about certain details...

"And the woman and child, did they survive?" asked the pope.

With a heavy heart, Gabriel related how Chelsea had bolted into action as soon as she saw Magdalene in danger. More than once, the woman had almost been crushed to death when she tried to reach the girl. But in the end, she managed to get to the child in time. It was then that the friar saw a vast section of the roof come down on the church. The terrible squall of falling debris destroyed half the apse and buried the sanctuary, kicking up a cloud of dust so thick that nothing more could be seen.

Only after the chaos had settled did Gabriel see his brother priest crouched over the rubble. Michael was frantically digging away with his bare hands to reach the woman buried beneath. Rock after rock, stone after stone was heaved away until the mangled body of Chelsea Shields lay exposed to the grim stare of the Jesuit priest.

"She took most of the damage," Gabriel recounted with sorrow. "It was bad."

As the friar continued to brief the pope, Raphael found himself reliving his own memories of that night...

From where he was, the doctor had witnessed almost everything. He could see that Michael was devastated. His face was drained of blood. His shoulders drooped with sorrow. Both his hands were torn from having dug through the stones. And yet the pain was most eloquent in the eyes of the priest as he cradled the dying woman in his arms.

Chelsea tried to talk but the blood gurgling in her throat made it impossible. Instead, she pointed to Magdalene. She had shielded the girl with her own body and was anxious to know if the child was safe.

Michael assured her that the girl was unconscious but still alive. The news seemed to give the woman some relief. Though she was hemorrhaging internally, she strained against her injuries to look into the eyes of the man holding her.

"Stay still, don't move," he warned her.

She refused to listen. Despite the excruciating pain, she raised her hand and touched his face. The priest felt her fingers tremble against his weathered cheek. She looked like she wanted to say something. But when she opened her mouth, the only sound that came out was the gurgling of fresh blood streaking past her lips. In the end, the effort was too much and she collapsed in agony.

"Chelsea!" Michael shouted. She didn't respond.

"Stay with me!" he bellowed. And this time, she rallied and gazed at him.

The Jesuit was alarmed. He hollered for Raphael to help. Though still groggy, the doctor pushed himself off the floor and staggered over. When he got there, he could only confirm what the priest had already suspected - she was bleeding profusely, her major organs were failing and she was going into shock. Chelsea was too gravely injured to last much longer. There was nothing more they could do.

"She doesn't have much time," Raphael told the priest. "We have to prepare her."

Michael was grim. He reacted as if someone had struck him in the face. A clash of emotions began to simmer in his heart. He was boiling with frustration and anger with God, and furious that they had sacrificed so much to protect her, only to have her taken away at the end. His cassock was soaked in her blood. The light in her eyes was failing. But the priest was still hoping for a miracle. He looked to his confreres for some support or encouragement...

But Raphael had already begun to administer the last rites. Gabriel had also dragged himself close enough to assist. Everyone knew that death was approaching. It was only Michael who couldn't bring himself to admit it. Instead he cursed and pleaded with God to spare the poor woman nestled in his arms.

The only reply was the soft chirping of birds in the distance hailing the new dawn.

For the next few minutes, Raphael and Gabriel quietly echoed the prayers accompanying the dying. When the time came for the friars to absolve Chelsea of her sins, Michael interrupted the ritual. As much as he struggled with the notion of seeing her die, he wanted to take it upon himself to recite the formula that restored her to the mercy of God.

Raising his hand, he traced the sign of the cross on her forehead and pronounced the words of absolution.

"God, the Father of mercies, through the death and resurrection of His Son, has reconciled the world to Himself and sent the Holy Spirit among us for the forgiveness of sins; through the ministry of the Church may God give you pardon and peace, and I absolve you from your sins in the name of the Father, and of the Son, and of the Holy Spirit."

In that solemn moment, she opened her eyes and gazed upon him one last time. Eternity was calling and she was barely able to hold on. With all the tenderness and strength left to her, she quietly mouthed the words...

"Amen..."

And like the first drop of rain before a flood, her parting gesture broke the dam in his heart.

✝

The pope listened intently and lowered his eyes, as if offering a prayer for the soul of the poor woman.

"And the child, how is she?" the Holy Father asked.

"As far as I can tell, she's totally liberated," Gabriel replied. "There's no trace of the evil that once possessed her. At the moment, she's still in our care. She doesn't remember much of what happened. But everyday, she grows stronger and more confident. With the help of God, I pray she'll recover completely in time."

"I hope you're not planning on taking care of her yourselves," said the pope, raising an eyebrow. "Apart from the serious matter of prudence, a life battling demons is no life for a little girl."

"Don't worry, Holy Father. The present arrangement is only temporary. The League is in touch with parents who've lost children in this war. Many have suffered greatly for the faith, but these families are also generous in love. Some are only too happy to welcome a child back into their lives. We'll find her a good home."

The pope seemed to approve. He nodded solemnly.

"Indeed, ensure that the child gets a loving home. See to it that the sacrifice of this brave woman has not been in vain," said the pontiff.

He leaned back in his chair and turned his thoughts to Chelsea.

"Everyone wants to leave a sign that we were here, that for a little while we did more good than bad, that our lives were worth it. Perhaps for Miss Shields, saving this young girl was her legacy of love. From what you've told me, she often wrestled with doubts about whether she was capable of real love. Even though words may enlighten the mind, it is love that stirs the heart to believe. And in the end, she made the greatest act of love, to give up her life for another. May she be counted among the blessed in heaven. I will pray for her."

Then turning to Raphael, the pope added, "Just as I pray for your late wife, my son. May she too rejoice in the Lord for her great act of love."

The doctor was stunned. He hadn't expected the pope to know about his past, but it was obvious the pontiff was well informed.

The Holy Father got up from behind his desk and gradually walked over to Raphael.

"It has been said that heaven is a city on a hill," the pope remarked. "That no one can coast into it without having to climb. People who're totally indifferent to God in this life do not suddenly develop a capacity for him at the moment of death. Indeed to be capable of God, the soul must grow and expand. St. Bernard believed that the greatness of each soul is measured by love. He who has great love is great. He who has little love is little. And he who has no love is nothing..."

The pope placed a fatherly arm around Raphael.

"Many times, the good Lord reminds us it's the women in our lives who've the greatest capacity to love. And in the eyes of God, that is everything. They've given us great examples of faith and service; that we should die to ourselves so that others may live. We must try and honor their legacies by doing the same, so that Christ may be glorified not just in our lives, but also in our deaths."

Raphael was moved. He recalled how in scripture, Jesus had made the pledge to Peter and his successors, that *whatever you bind on earth shall be bound in heaven. Whatever you loose on earth shall be loosed in heaven.*

"Thank you for praying for my wife, Holy Father. It means a lot to me," said the doctor, smiling.

"Ahem," said Spalding, attempting to keep the pope on schedule. "Forgive me, Your Holiness, but there's the other matter of succession for the Prelature of St. Lazarus."

"Indeed monsignor, thank you for reminding me," the Holy Father replied. "Yes, the Underground Church needs a new Prelate if it's to survive. Someone who can take over the role of chief shepherd and lead the flock in unity…"

Gabriel stepped forward.

"The Prelature has suffered much, but we have no lack of good priests and leaders, many of whom are faithful and wise. If it helps, we'll be happy to give you our recommendations," the friar suggested.

The pope looked at the young man thoughtfully. Then turning to Raphael he said, "My son, would you be kind enough to give me a few moments with Father Gabriel?"

Raphael was a little surprised at being asked to leave, but Spalding was already on his feet, ready to usher the doctor back into the waiting hall.

"Of course, Your Holiness," said Raphael. He approached the pope and genuflected, kissing the papal ring. "Once again, thank you for your support and prayers."

The pope reached down and pulled him to his feet.

"And thank you, Father Raphael," said the pontiff, embracing him. "For everything you've done for the Church. Please pray for me as well."

Raphael nodded. As he turned to follow Spalding out of the small chapel, he glanced back and caught a glimpse of Gabriel. The friar looked somewhat nervous.

Spalding closed the door behind them and escorted Raphael to a waiting room down the hall.

Back in the chapel, the Vicar of Christ wanted the friar to accompany him to the altar.

"Take my arm, Holy Father," said Gabriel as he offered to

support the pope.

Leaning on the young priest, the pontiff motioned for Gabriel to approach the pew closest to the tabernacle.

"Come, pray with me for a moment," said the pope, who proceeded to kneel down.

Gabriel knelt next to the old man. For a while, the two said nothing - the Dominican Friar beside the Supreme Pontiff. They both kept the stillness of prayer. Eventually, the pope pulled out an envelope from his white cassock.

"I received this about six months ago," he said, turning it over to Gabriel.

The friar took the envelope with some hesitation.

"Go ahead. Read it," advised the pope.

Gabriel gently peeled open the envelope and instantly recognized the handwriting of the Prelate on the letter. There wasn't a great deal inscribed on the paper. Nevertheless, the little that was written made him gasp.

In a firm and gentle voice, the pope added his thoughts.

"Monsignor Li always lived his life to the full. He had no illusions about his own safety. He knew that if old age didn't finish him, the Corporation would. He knew there was always going to be a chance there might not be another tomorrow. Every priest understands that. We've all gotten used to the perils of our vocation. Anyone who comes to Christ seeking comfort and pleasures has indeed come to the wrong address. Yet we know that the Lord does not abandon the Church. With every generation, hope springs afresh and courage is renewed. The struggle for truth is handed on."

"There must be some mistake," the friar stammered.

"Do you not accept the nomination?" asked the Holy Father. "I can see no reason to ignore his wise counsel."

Gabriel was dismayed. He couldn't understand how the Prelate could've suggested him as successor.

"Your Holiness, you don't understand," he groaned. "There's not a day that goes by that I don't doubt myself or my ability to stay faithful in a crisis. I don't even know what I'm doing sometimes. I'm the wrong man for this task. You have to choose someone else, someone more capable."

The pope rose from his knees and sat his tired frame on the bare wooden pew.

"We all have doubts about ourselves, Father. I should be

concerned if you did not feel humbled or even frightened by this prospect. Pride kills docility and makes a person incapable of ever being helped by God. But the monsignor was a good judge of character and he spoke highly of you. There was no one he thought more capable of taking his place."

"Nevertheless, he was wrong," Gabriel insisted.

Begging the pope's pardon, the young friar offered a litany of his failures and insufficiencies, sounding like a hapless soldier trying to escape a battlefield promotion. He was, he declared, quite unsuitable and utterly unworthy of such confidence. But the Holy Father remained unconvinced.

"I appreciate your concerns. But God does not call us to be successful. He calls us to be faithful. Every priest is imprinted with supernatural grace. Yet it's a treasure we house in a body of soft clay. To keep our vocations alive, we must continually stretch out on a cross of fire and be purified. Does this appointment frighten you so much that you'd rather climb down from the cross?"

Gabriel began to blush. The pope was gentle in his remarks, but his words had struck a raw nerve.

"Forgive me, Holy Father. I've never been afraid to confront evil nor do I fear losing my life for the gospel. But it's one thing to be a preacher, to battle demons and help those possessed by evil, and quite another for a simple-minded friar like me to be entrusted with the leadership of the Prelature. If I fail in my ministry, how many souls will be lost on account of me?"

His Holiness motioned for Gabriel to sit next to him. The friar had remained on his knees the whole time, frozen with anguish at his predicament. On the one hand, he was loathed to refuse the Roman Pontiff. On the other, he dreaded the prospect of being left in charge of so many souls.

The pope tried to reassure him.

"You know the verse from Ecclesiastes - *To everything there's a season and a time to every purpose, a time to be born and a time to die* - Now is the time to step from the shadows and lead. We must boldly confront suffering and bloodshed to bring God's light to those who need us. If we hold back from our flock, if we fear to go where we're needed, our love for Christ will surely atrophy and die."

But Gabriel refused to budge, though he wasn't sure if it was his conscience or cowardice that besought him. There were days when he did everything he could, and still it wasn't enough. For every one person he saved, how many more had to die? The things he had seen, the monsters he had fought. He had been scared before but this was entirely different. It was one thing to play the champion but another to risk the lives of others.

"I can't obey what I know to be a mistake. I know myself only too well. I can't ignore my weaknesses," bemoaned the friar.

He was sure the Holy Father would be displeased, if not upset, but the pope merely looked at him with compassion.

"Indeed, you might know yourself all too well, Father Gabriel. But the Lord knows you better. True humility lies not in denying our potential for greatness, but in obedience to the will of God. If he calls you to this, he'll give you the necessary graces to do well. You worry that you might fail the souls entrusted to you; that you might let the Church down. Yet scripture reminds us that God chose what is weak in the world to shame the strong. And that is why among men of little faith, those in religion are the worst. For though we're called to be closer to Christ, many still choose not to trust him."

At this, the friar said nothing. He merely sat through the tortured silence with his eyes clinging to the cross.

"Nevertheless, I do not wish to impose on you," the pope added ruefully. He placed his hand with the Fisherman's ring upon the sagging shoulder of the Dominican Friar.

"Our Lord respects your free will and I can do no less. The decision is yours and yours alone," said His Holiness. "But please know this; for the good of souls, we must find a new Prelate. And soon."

Chapter 43

Raphael had been waiting for the better part of an hour. He leaned against an opened window along the corridor and looked out onto the small piazza below. Where once the square was bustling with the limousines of foreign dignitaries visiting the pope, it was now empty except for a few guards on patrol. Over the ancient ramparts of the Vatican, the doctor could see the forest of modern buildings soaring into the heavens, their lofty peaks towering with the symbols of Lumen Corp.

"It's human to judge a civilization by what we see," said Spalding, standing beside him. "Those with crumbling walls are legacies of the past. Those with ivory towers are symbols of the future. And yet, the true greatness of a civilization lies with its people and their capacity for truth and justice. Because no matter how bad things get, no matter how much fear might overwhelm their hearts, those who refuse to lose hope today are the ones who can save tomorrow."

Raphael turned to look at him. "You really think we can?"

"What?"

"Save tomorrow," said the doctor.

Spalding reached into his cassock and pulled out a pack of smokes. He offered Raphael a cigarette but the doctor declined, so the monsignor lit one for himself. He took a long draw on the lighted stick and then exhaled with a sigh.

"If we don't give up, if we don't surrender, we'll get over that hill," replied Spalding. "I know sometimes we get used to the idea that we might not be here tomorrow. In many places, the Underground Church is beset from all sides. Not only are barbarians at our gates, the shadow of betrayal lurks behind our own doors. But in spite of the dangers, the Church has always done more than just survive. She doesn't simply endure evil. She proclaims hope and redemption to a broken world. As long as we remain people of the resurrection, there'll always be a tomorrow."

Raphael looked askance at the bishop. He agreed with the papal secretary to be sure, but something about their conversation made him curious. He decided to throw caution to the wind.

"Forgive me, monsignor," said the clairvoyant. "But is the Holy Father appointing Gabriel as the new Prelate?"

Spalding was surprised at the abruptness of the question. He calmly removed the dangling cigarette from his lips and tried to sound diplomatic.

"I'm not at liberty to say. You'll have to ask Father Gabriel when he comes out."

But Raphael already knew the answer. His heart was weighed down with sorrow for his confrere.

"He's a good priest, better than he believes himself to be. He has never been afraid to confront evil or to risk his life for the faith. But it's one thing to help save the day, and another to safeguard the faithful of the Prelature. Gabriel is a man who's happier giving obedience than receiving it. If I know him, he'll decline the appointment."

Spalding listened patiently. He extinguished his cigarette and put the stub away in a small metal casing he carried in his pocket. For security reasons, there were no trashcans in the corridors of the apostolic palace.

"They've been trying to get me to stop smoking," the bishop grinned. "I know I should, especially with my health. But doing the right thing is often hard, isn't it? The good that I want to do, I do not. The wrong that I don't want to do, I do anyway."

He shook his head and scoffed. The idea of a humble priest disobeying the Supreme Pontiff in order to remain a simple obedient friar seemed a little spurious to Spalding.

"But I want to share something with you," said the papal secretary. "And I trust you'll keep this between us."

"Of course," Raphael answered, wondering what it might be.

"Like most of us, His Holiness feels himself insufficient for the demands of his office. He's old and tired, he's almost blind in one eye, his health is failing and his strengths are no longer adequate for the burdens of the papacy. But for the salvation of souls, he continues to bear witness and embrace the cross."

Spalding then leaned forward and added, "We have to do the same. If we fear to go out of ourselves and tread the path of sacrifice, our love for Christ will surely diminish. When that happens, our fall will be greater than anyone else's because of the height from which we plummet. Already as it is, too many priests and religious betray the Son of God with a kiss."

Raphael took offence to the insinuation.

"With all due respects, monsignor, if there's anyone who would boldly confront suffering and bloodshed to bring freedom to those imprisoned by evil, it would be Father Gabriel. He would rather give his life than turn his back on God."

"Then let him do just that," the bishop replied firmly.

At that point, the two men heard footsteps and saw Gabriel rounding the corner, his face lost in deep thought. The friar appeared not to have noticed them until Raphael called out to him.

"Gabriel, you okay?"

The friar looked up and managed a weak smile. Raphael wasn't surprised to see a profound gravity in the countenance of his young friend. But he was stunned to notice the pectoral cross hanging from his neck, the very same one that the pope was wearing moments earlier.

Spalding smiled and greeted Gabriel with quiet satisfaction. He too had noticed the pectoral cross.

"Now if you'll excuse me gentlemen, I have to attend to His Holiness," said the papal secretary. "These men will escort you safely through the Scavi. Good luck and God be with you."

He shook both their hands and took his leave. From out of nowhere, a pair of pontifical guards appeared and invited the two priests to follow them.

The Scavi was an underground city of the dead, a necropolis long discovered beneath the floors of the Basilica. There, within a tangle of first century tombs slept the bones of the Apostle Peter, preserved within the foundations of the Church itself. A series of Christian and pagan mausoleums lined the ancient Roman streets, its corridors narrow and dim, its skies now vaulted by an earthen ceiling that shielded the city of the dead from the world of the living.

It was through this labyrinth that Gabriel and Raphael had gained entrance into the Vatican, led by men whose loyalty to the pope was uncompromised. Now, they were being ushered back into the Scavi by guards of the pontifical household. They left the Apostolic Palace and made their way through a series of passages that took them down into the main Basilica, before finally arriving at the secured entrance to the necropolis.

Along the way, Raphael had noticed a few priests and religious scattered among the Swiss Guards. Some were dressed in cassocks and habits. Many were simply praying as they went along their way, their postures worn down by suffering and fatigue, their faces fiercely determined to carry on.

"Perhaps, they too had barely survived the tragedies of the week," thought Raphael.

He wanted to mention that to Gabriel but the friar was brooding and distracted, burdened by the agony of his own thoughts. At one point, the young priest glanced down and realized that his pectoral cross was still hanging prominently over his chest. He picked up the object between his fingers and turned it over, as if looking at it for the first time.

Carved into the back was some kind of writing. The letters were small and difficult to read. But as Gabriel pored over the inscription, his eyes began to widen with disbelief. He was stunned and mortified. And it took him a while to remember that with God, there was no such thing as coincidence.

"What's on your mind?" asked Raphael, who had been watching him.

Gabriel removed the pectoral cross, kissed it, and carefully slipped it into his breast pocket.

"I was just thinking about something I told Chelsea," he whispered.

Raphael was curious. "And what did you tell her?"

The friar chuckled at the irony and smiled to himself.

"In hoc signo vinces," he replied, the uncertainty on his face transfigured by hope.

And with that, they passed through the corridors of death and made their way back to the land of the living.

†

Outside the Vatican precincts, Michael was seated on the stump of an old column jutting out from the earth like the severed finger of a colossal hand. All around him sprouted the archeological remains of the eternal city. Broken arches and shattered memories of marble and stone surrounded the priest, while across the street from him stood the glorious façade of a medieval church that now echoed with the cries of blasphemy. The sounds of skateboards and laughter, the cackle of curses and derision all rose up like a song of contempt for human decency.

Drowned in the stench of urine, this once sacred temple had long become a haven for drunks and delinquents. Like many of the ancient monuments of Christian Rome, this one had been looted and desecrated by Lumen hordes, its glorious frescos and altars stripped to feed the bonfire of sacrilege that raged through the hearts of the populace.

The only reason why many of these basilicas were still standing was so they could testify to the failure of the Christian faith, in much the same way that pagan Rome once crucified their enemies and left their bodies to rot along the Appian Way as a warning to others.

The Jesuit winced when he tried to remove the whiskey flask from his jacket. His arm was strapped in a sling and his shoulder throbbed with misery. With his other hand, he popped the lid off the carafe and took a big gulp to numb the pain. Deep inside, he knew he drank not to sedate his injuries but to anesthetize his grief. Yet the more he swallowed, the emptier he felt.

His bleary eyes tried to focus on the child a few feet away. She sat by a small patch of wildflowers that blossomed among the ruins despite the garbage strewn all around. From time to time, she would turn around and glance back at the priest. In response, he would smirk every time she showed him a flower she picked.

She looked different. In fact, everything about her seemed different. Her hair was tied back in a blue ribbon and her sundress fluttered in the breeze. She no longer required the metal braces hugging her legs. She could walk, and she could run. Her pallid skin was replaced by a rosy hue that reminded him of the first blush of spring. Little by little with prayer and patience, the priests had been able to draw her back from the shadows.

In the weeks that followed, the child grew in strength. Her physical and spiritual revival was nothing short of a miracle. Considering the horrors she endured, it was astounding that she was still alive. And yet thanks be to God, there she was, breaking into song and humming quietly to herself.

For the first time in many weeks, Magdalene was giggling like a normal healthy girl. And it made Michael feel somewhat vulnerable. Her youthful laughter broke through the ugly noises of decay coming from the neighboring basilica and reassured him that the sun was still shining. Part of him was deeply moved every time she laughed, and part of him was determined not to risk caring too much again. He knew what compromise brought. You break your own rules of engagement and the next thing you know, you're shoved down the rabbit hole where you wake up the next morning with your heart nailed to a cross. He groaned and took another swig of whiskey and ignored the fact that his gut felt like bursting into flames.

Just then, he heard the sound of broken twigs. He dropped the flask and drew his gun.

"Easy padre," Gabriel remarked.

Michael scowled. He tucked away his weapon and recovered his carafe.

"Don't you know better than to sneak up behind me? I could've blown your heads off," he complained.

"It's a good thing you didn't," replied the Japanese friar. "I've grown quite attached to mine."

Raphael started to laugh. He was happy to see Gabriel back in good form. It had been a while since the friar was able to kid around like he used to. The sufferings and losses of the previous months had taken a terrible toll on everyone. The doctor reckoned it was better to say nothing about the appointment of the new Prelate just yet, not until the man himself was ready to confirm it.

He glanced ahead and noticed the child playing by the columns.

"Mary," he called out to her.

She recognized his voice and came running like a lamb. Raphael knelt down and gave her a big hug.

"Someone's looking very pretty today," he told her.

The girl was shy but she managed to grin with delight. She didn't talk very much, mostly because she was still trying to find her real voice. After losing much of her consciousness to demons, it was going to take some time before she could discover her own personality again.

Nevertheless, Raphael was overjoyed to see how far she had come. Only a month before, he had suggested giving her a new name. He had wanted to put some distance between the dark night she had lived through and the new dawn that now seemed so promising for her. When he asked her what she would like to be called, she thought for a while and then chose the name, Mary...

"Let me guess, because you love Our Lady?" the doctor enquired. And the child readily agreed.

Since then, the Rosary had become her favorite prayer. The calming rhythm of the *Aves* and the recollection of the sacred mysteries gave the young girl peace and comfort. And ultimately, it gave her strength to overcome any residue of evil.

As he watched over the child, he began to sense that the motley crew at the ruined basilica was also watching them from across the street. Having been on their own for so long, it hadn't occurred to Raphael and his confreres that a gaggle of scruffy men in the company of a little girl might just be too conspicuous.

Even so, the tiny bunch of ruffians hardly resembled a mob. They were mostly just young punks with too much bravado and not enough common sense in their heads. The doctor glanced at his confreres and saw Michael getting irritated with the noise and taunting from across the street. Clutching his whiskey, the priest kept looking at the hooligans with an expression that bordered on hate. For a second, Raphael was worried that the Jesuit might do something drastic. Even Gabriel noticed this and feared some sort of confrontation.

"A man has to know his limitations. You ought to ease up on that," said Gabriel, referring to the drink in his hand.

"Relax, I can handle it. It's just a little gas in the tank," said the priest, sounding annoyed.

"Come on, buddy. You've had enough," Raphael chimed in and tried to take the carafe away from him.

"I told you to relax," Michael snapped, his eyes burning like hot coals.

Raphael was taken aback. "All right, calm down," said the doctor.

"Don't tell me to calm down. In fact, don't tell me to do anything!" Michael threatened.

Gabriel quickly stepped in and tried to ease the tension.

"I know you're upset. We lost good friends and comrades. It's only right that we should grieve," said the friar.

"I'm not grieving, I'm tired of this war!" Michael grunted. "We keep preaching the truth but no one listens. We keep pushing back the darkness, but it floods the earth anyway. In every mission, we lose more people than we save. Tell me this..."

He glared at Gabriel, his face twisted with pain.

"If God is our help and our salvation, where was he when we needed him? Why do we continue to fight when the Almighty himself doesn't want to get his hands dirty to help us?"

Raphael was surprised at Michael's outburst. But Gabriel thought back to his own struggles with those same feelings. It was easy to become discouraged by the overwhelming sense of futility that dogged their crusade against evil. Some days it felt like they were swimming against the tide, that the waves of iniquity would drown them even as they called out to God.

"If it wasn't for the grace of God, none of us would be alive right now," Raphael exclaimed.

But the remark only infuriated Michael even more. He scoffed at the pious 'excuse'...

"Enough of this crap! We're alive because Chelsea sacrificed herself. She was supposed to live and we were supposed to protect her. Not the other way around. When everyone else despaired, she had faith, she believed. Why wasn't that enough? Why did God allow her to survive all those days with us, only to let her die in the end?"

Raphael was tempted to answer his friend but Gabriel stopped him. In some ways, the young friar understood what Michael was going through. Their mission was to protect Chelsea and bring her to Rome. Not only had they failed to do that, the Underground Church itself had suffered a terrible wound that greatly weakened the League as a whole. The heart of the Resistance had been cut and torn out. Nations were falling under the spell of Satan. It was the worst time to be a priest....

And maybe because of that, it was also the best time to be a priest. The blood of martyrs is the seed of the Church. Where evil abounds, the grace of God abounds even more. Despite all their troubles, the friar knew that the harshness of winter wouldn't last, even when it seemed like the earth itself would be frozen in a permanent sheet of death. Eventually the sun would rise, the darkness would recede, and spring would herald a new life of faith for all creation.

"Maybe we're not supposed to ask *why*," said Gabriel. "Maybe we're supposed to ask *what*. What can we do to honor her legacy? What can we do to preserve the light? We're alive because Chelsea was brave enough to hold on to faith. To despair now would only disgrace her memory. Don't give in to hate. Trust in the wisdom of God, even if every fiber of your being cries out in pain."

"Trust him?" Michael murmured, as if the words were an insult to his ears. "There are times I'd like to get my hands on him."

He took another shot of whiskey and grimaced like someone who crawled out of bed one morning to find the whole world in ashes.

"Let it go, Michael. Don't feed the pain," Gabriel tried to persuade him. "Don't let it corrupt your heart and make you bitter.

The Lord is asking us to be strong, so that we can help Mary and others like her break free from the darkness that still enslaves."

The child looked up at the friar when she heard her name mentioned, but quickly lost interest and went back to playing with her flowers.

"Are you listening?" Gabriel asked Michael.

The Jesuit shrugged. A great deal of anger was still throbbing in his veins, but he was too weary and wounded to keep up the rage. All he wanted to do was drown his misery with the leftover brew in his hand. But before he could lift the flask to his lips, he felt a gentle tug on his sleeve. He looked down and saw the child reaching up for him.

Michael tried to ignore her but the girl kept pulling on his jacket. Realizing that she wasn't going to stop until he gave her some attention, he relented and knelt down like a man lost in a dream, his mind foggy with disinterest.

"Take," she said, trying to hand him a small bouquet of wildflowers.

He didn't respond. With his arm locked in a sling and his only good hand clutching a drink, he had no freedom to receive her gift.

"Take!" she repeated.

And when he didn't, Mary boldly snatched the whiskey flask from him and threw it aside. Before the priest could protest, the child had already thrust the flowers into his hand. Caught off-guard, he began to growl with impatience when the girl suddenly flung her arms around his neck and hugged him.

Michael was stumped. The warmth of her cheek pressed against his grizzled face unnerved him. His reflex was to pull away before her affections weaken the resolve of his heart and tear down the walls he had raised to keep it safe. But as she clung to him in her innocence, he found himself unable to do anything but remain in the embrace of this child.

"Father, don't let the darkness take me," she whispered in his ear.

Michael felt a lump in his throat. For the last few months, he had watched over her like a guardian angel. He knew the child was afraid to go back into the shadows. Often she would feel the pangs of panic when she turned around and found herself alone. As far as possible, he had made it a point to stay by her side.

Gabriel and Raphael looked at Michael with concern. It was hard to tell what he was thinking, but they could see that the priest was wrestling with his doubts. The child continued to cling to him. And slowly, the icy mask of resentment thawed in the strength of her love. His anger began to fail as the heart of a father welled up in the eyes of the warrior. The Jesuit said nothing for a long time. He simply held the girl close and tried to reassure her.

"I won't let the darkness harm you. I promise," he whispered to the child.

When he finally stood up, he carried Mary in his arm and softly kissed her on the cheek. She was emotional and tired, but content to rest her sleepy head on his shoulder. Without disturbing her, Michael carefully tucked the tiny bouquet of flowers into his jacket. He glanced up and saw the looks of distress in Gabriel and Raphael.

"You okay?" Gabriel asked.

Michael was quiet at first. He gazed down at the whiskey flask tossed in the dirt and felt remorse. It was the anger made worse by the alcohol. He was fighting with his brothers when he felt nothing but love and respect for them.

"Yeah," he replied, cradling the child…"I'm okay."

The priest lumbered past his confreres and walked on ahead. The friar and the doctor looked at each other, uncertain of whether to follow. But Michael stopped a few steps away and then turned around…

"What're you waiting for?" he asked them. "Let's go, we've got a war to win!"

Hearing that all-too-familiar grunt, the two priests smirked with relief. As they trooped after the Jesuit, Gabriel began to feel encouraged.

"What's on your mind?" Raphael asked him quietly.

The friar pondered for a while…

"I was just thinking of the words of Saint Paul; how our strength is made perfect in weakness. Whether in life or in death, we belong to God. *For the sake of Christ, then, I am content with weaknesses, insults, hardships, persecutions and calamities; for when I am weak then I am strong.* That's exactly who we are, and what we do. With our faith and our sufferings, we give witness to Christ who is our hope."

Raphael listened carefully to what the friar had said.

"Reminds me of the old poem by Henri Lacordaire," he remarked.

"Who?" asked Gabriel, unfamiliar with the name.

Raphael glanced at the friar and laughed. "He was a Dominican like you, back in the 19th century," the doctor explained.

Gabriel appeared embarrassed. "Never heard of him," he said sheepishly. "Much of our history and records were blotted out when the enemy attacked the Order. Some of it was saved and handed down by the older friars, but I've never really had a chance to go through it all."

"Well maybe you've heard of this," said Raphael. And he proceeded to recite the poem.

To live in the midst of the world without wishing its pleasures;
To be a member of each family, yet belonging to none;
To share all suffering; to penetrate all secrets; to heal all wounds;
To go from men to God and offer Him their prayers;
To return from God to men to bring pardon and hope;
To have a heart of fire for Charity, and a heart of bronze for Chastity
To teach and to pardon, console and bless always.
My God, what a life;
And it is yours, O priest of Jesus Christ.

"I like it," said Gabriel, smiling.

The doctor grinned with satisfaction. "I knew you would."

"For the sake of Christ then," said the friar, stretching out his hand.

Raphael clutched it and nodded with gusto.

"For the sake of Christ!"

Epilogue

"Show him in," Chambers muttered into the phone.

The doors to his private office opened and a man stood trembling in the hallway, flanked by a pair of Lumen agents in their immaculate black suits.

"Come in professor, I've been waiting for you," Chambers announced.

The portly gentleman swallowed hard and crossed the threshold. He was dressed in dark trousers, a tweed jacket and a bow tie. In his hands, he carried a small parcel decorated with ornate carvings. Although the package couldn't have weighed more than a few ounces, the professor appeared burdened by the strange gift in his possession.

"Is that what I hope it is?" Chambers enquired sweetly.

The professor removed a napkin from his pocket and wiped the cold sweat from his face.

"I'm sorry it took so long, sir. The excavations were a nightmare. We lost many men..."

"Yet here you are, alive and well," Chambers interrupted. "Did you find it or not?"

"Yes sir," he stammered.

"Well don't be a tease, bring it here," said the Lumen VP, who was seated behind an imposing desk.

The professor approached with trepidation and laid the tiny box before Chambers like an offering to a pagan god. Indeed, it had taken the blood of several people to unearth this treasure from the hidden bowels of history. Loyalties were sold, alliances were broken, and lives were lost in the search for this relic.

The Vice-president took the object in his hand and opened it. Glistening in the box was a brass iron ring crowned with jewels and inscriptions. He picked up the trinket and held it up to the light. The Star of David gleamed like an ancient signet poised to empower the man who wore it with authority over the dark realms.

The more Chambers pored over the artifact, the more the

professor got excited. Forgetting himself, he started raving about the discovery like a proud miner having discovered gold...

"As you know, the legends behind this ring have been legion. It's hard to know what's true and what's myth. But it was said that the name of God was engraved on it, and any man who wore the seal could bend the will of Satan himself and command the demon armies of hell. In addition, it would give him control over the four elements of earth, water, wind, and fire. Countless rulers and magicians have sought its power through the ages..."

"And now it's mine to possess," the Lumen warlock declared. "You do realize that if this isn't the real deal, I'm going to have you skinned alive and mounted on my wall?"

The professor gulped. "I assure you, sir, all evidence point to this being the Seal of Solomon. It's the real thing, I'm certain of it," he said, trembling.

Chambers flashed the man a dangerous smile. "Well in that case..."

He slipped the heavy brass ring onto his finger. Immediately, his face contorted like a man drawn into ecstasy. His pupils were enlarged and his skin seemed to be on fire. The heavy drapes in the room fluttered with violence while books, paper, and everything else that wasn't weighed down swirled around the Vice-president in a vortex of mayhem.

The professor was terrified. "Sir! Sir! Is everything all right?" he called out anxiously.

Chambers laughed like a man drunk with power.

"Indeed it is, my friend...Indeed it is!"

The End.

About the Author

Thomas Tan adores classic adventure sitcoms and Sunday morning cartoons. He has written widely for print, radio and television, and has won various awards at Promax World and the New York Festival of Arts. He currently lives in sunny Singapore, surrounded by good food, great friends, and a beautiful princess to love. When he's not chasing gigs as a corporate scribe and television producer, he enjoys building castles in the air, with dragons to slay, demons to vanquish, and maidens to save. League of Angels is his debut novel.

58521668R00259

Made in the USA
Columbia, SC
21 May 2019